Gimme an O!

By Kayla Perrin

GIMME AN O!
TELL ME YOU LOVE ME
SAY YOU NEED ME
IF YOU WANT ME

Gimme an O!

Kayla Perrin

An Imprint of HarperCollins*Publishers*

For Harris Katleman—
thanks so much for all your L.A. help!
You rock!

And, of course, for my brother—
without your football knowledge,
I couldn't have written about Anthony Beals.

Kayla

HarperCollins books may be purchased for education, business, or sales promotional use. For information please write: Special Markets Department, HarperCollins Publishers Inc., 10 East 53rd Street, New York, NY 10022.

FIRST EDITION

Designed by Elizabeth M. Glover

Library of Congress Cataloging-in-Publication Data

Perrin, Kayla.
Gimme an O! / by Kayla Perrin.—1st ed.
p. cm.
ISBN 0-06-058709-1
1. Sex therapists—Fiction. 2. Football players—Fiction. 3. Quarterbacks (Football)—Fiction. 4. Los Angeles (Calif.)—Fiction. I. Title.

PR9199.3.P434G56 2005
813'.54—dc22

2004017090

05 06 07 08 09 WBC/RRD 10 9 8 7 6 5 4 3 2 1

One

HOW TO DRIVE YOUR WOMAN CRAZY WITH PASSION!

TEN SUREFIRE STEPS TO KEEP HER SATISFIED ALL NIGHT LONG

Lecia Calhoun cringed as she read the heading of the chapter that the radio host expected her to discuss—in full, juicy detail, no doubt—during her scheduled interview. An interview that was to take place in—she glanced at her watch—eight minutes and counting. And not just with any radio host, but with Depraved Dave, arguably one of Los Angeles' most foul-mouthed, irreverent talk show hosts. Loud and obnoxious, he was the antithesis of the feminist, the kind of man's man who commanded attention in the worst possible way. A chauvinist pig who believed that women had been put on Earth to serve men in general and him in particular. She wouldn't put it past him to roll off a woman and belch right after orgasm, or even to belch as he was coming. He was that kind of guy. A month ago at Spago Beverly Hills she had seen him stuff a tip down the hostess's blouse—groping the startled woman for a good few seconds—and he was at the restaurant with his wife.

She could only imagine how he would handle her now.

Knowing this was going to be her worst nightmare, Lecia again glanced at the open book. The words *How to Drive Your Woman Crazy with Passion!* danced on the page, mocking her. Oh, yeah—she could imagine the fun Depraved Dave would have at her expense. After all, she had written the words.

A part of her had held out hope that Depraved Dave wouldn't earmark this chapter, because . . . well, because one could entertain fantasies, couldn't they? Fantasies were a normal, healthy part of life. It was part of what she preached in this very book, which now felt like a cement block in her hands.

In reality, she was hoping that the universe would spare her this with Depraved Dave, simply because she had already discussed this very chapter with 99.9 percent of the hosts and reporters who had talked to her. It was the very last chapter in the book, but the one the media were interested in. The one that read like a tabloid sex column, a marked departure from the other chapters. The one that was thrown in half as a joke, but her editor had loved it nonetheless.

Given that she had discussed this chapter so many times, she knew she should be prepared for any question. But she had not yet discussed it with Depraved Dave, whose middle name was Shocking. He poked fun even at the holiest of topics. She had once listened to his show in open-mouthed horror as he challenged nuns to "get laid" so they would know exactly what they had given up.

Oh, God. How was she going to handle him?

Slinking down in the worn leather chair, Lecia lifted her face to Angela, the publicist who had accompanied her from her publishing house. Angela was a tall, pretty blonde who could easily have been a model if she'd decided to pursue that career. She was smiling and chatting with Joe Balfour, the producer of *Get Real with Dave*.

"Um, excuse me. Angela. . . ."

Angela glanced down at her. Lecia realized she must have worn a petrified expression on her face, because Angela's eyes narrowed with concern. "What's the matter? You need to use the bathroom?"

"Not exactly." *And thanks for saying that in front of Joe!* "I, uh, need to speak with you for a moment." She paused. "Privately."

Joe's eyes flitted between both women. "No problem. I need to get some water anyway. I'll be back in a couple of minutes to bring you in for the show."

Even though Lecia had heard the man speak already, Joe's voice was still a shock to her. A shock because it told a lie. Deep and husky, it said he was at least six feet of well-muscled man. In reality, he was five-foot-four—max—and if he had any rippling muscles, they were camouflaged by layers of fat. Yet Joe had an easy smile and a confident glint in his eyes that said he thought he was as sexy as the Denzel Washingtons and Brad Pitts of the world.

Lecia forgot about Joe the moment he left the room. She was on her feet in a flash, holding her book open for Angela to see. "Chapter Thirteen," she said, aware that her voice was higher than usual. "Depraved Dave wants me to discuss *Chapter Thirteen*. You assured me we'd discuss something else!"

"I tried," Angela said. "I told Joe you'd been interviewed about that chapter several times already, that I thought it'd be a more interesting slant to concentrate on another aspect of the book. Last I heard from him, he said Dave was more interested in you and your background. But what can I say?" She shrugged. "It's Dave's show. What he says goes."

"I can't do this," Lecia protested. "Not *this* chapter. Not with Depraved Dave."

Angela took a swig of her bottled water, but Lecia didn't miss the smirk before the plastic had hit her lips. "It'll be fine."

"And when he chews me to pieces before his male chauvinist audience?"

"He won't be able to chew you to pieces. Everything you say in the book is fact. Especially Chapter Thirteen. If you ask me, it's high time men get it."

"Like that's gonna happen with his audience."

"Lecia?"

"Yeah?"

"Calm down. Honestly, there's no need to panic. You know your stuff, and when you're through with Depraved Dave, he'll know it, too."

"I'm not too sure about that."

"Stop stressing about it. No one's gonna remember what you said anyway. They'll tune in for one reason only—the topic. Sex sells. Men are as intrigued by the female orgasm as women are. Which is exactly why your book is hot."

Lecia drew in a sharp breath, willing herself to relax. Angela was right about sex selling. Did it ever. Her sister said the same thing when she'd first broached the topic of perhaps writing a book for women about sexuality and orgasm, considering that so many of the women she'd met in her medical practice had trouble achieving one. Not only had Tyanna encouraged her to write the book, she'd challenged her to do it. And not because of the money potential—anyone with a brain knew most writers didn't make squat—but because her sister knew that writing was what she had always wanted to do.

From the few fiction-writing courses Lecia had taken, she knew that the first rule was to write what you knew about. She knew the female anatomy. As an obstetrician-gynecologist, she knew it inside out. Then, as a sex therapist, she learned a thing or two about female orgasms. In fact, after dealing with more clients than she could count who'd either never experienced orgasm or had trouble experiencing it, she had veered off the fiction-writing path and toyed with the idea of nonfiction. It was her sister's challenge that gave her the final push that led to *The Big O*—a lighthearted but factual look at women's orgasms and how to achieve them.

Lecia was proud of the book, even if her parents blushed when reading it. And with its surprising success, she would never be able to put herself in the category of the writer who didn't make decent money. She was loving every minute of her accomplishment, even the crazy interviews. Her only concern was that with the focus of the interviews being on the so-called cheesiest part of her book, people might forget that she was actually a medical professional. A doctor and not a hack. Chapter Thirteen screamed hack.

Then again, maybe she was simply obsessing because Depraved Dave scared her to death. She wouldn't have agreed to the interview if Angela hadn't begged and pleaded with her to do it.

Lecia frowned, then said to Angela, "Maybe you could suggest to Joe that we discuss the first chapter. Myths about the female anatomy."

"Honestly, Lecia. It's not like you haven't done this before."

"No, no. You're right." It was high time she resigned herself to her fate, she told herself. "It's no big deal," she added. Digging into her shoulder bag, she withdrew her inhaler, and holding it like a lifeline, she shook it, exhaled then inhaled while pressing two spurts of the medicine into her mouth.

"Oh, God. You're really not okay."

"I'm fine," Lecia said when she released her breath. "My asthma acts up a few times a day. This is simply one of those times."

"You're sure?"

"Yes, I'm sure." She ran her fingers through her short tresses. "How's my hair?"

"This is radio."

"Right," Lecia conceded. But she still didn't feel better.

"What's the worst that could happen even if Depraved Dave chews you up, as you say? People love controversy, especially in this town. They'll buy the book for that reason alone. If men in production offices or on film sets are standing around the water cooler dissing your work, that's fabulous."

Fabulous? "Um . . ."

"The more they talk about you, the quicker you'll become a household name. And that translates into more sales."

Lecia's lips twisted as she gave Angela's words thought. Maybe the energetic publicist was right. "I didn't think about it that way."

"Listen, if I'd written this book, I'd be riding the sex wave until the orgasm died. And laughing all the way to the bank. Because the way sales are going, this is a multiple orgasm."

Lecia managed a genuine smile at Angela's sexual puns. And they were right on the mark. The book was making her a pretty penny. "You're right, Angela. I'm forgetting the bigger picture."

"Exactly. What's half an hour with Depraved Dave in the grand scheme of things?" Angela looked beyond Lecia. "Joe."

Lecia whipped her head around. Joe stood with both hands shoved in the front pockets of his khaki pants. Perhaps to make his bulge look bigger? "Ready, Dr. Love?"

"Ready as I'll ever be."

"Let's head inside the studio and meet Dave Brooks."

"This is WXJY, All Talk Radio, and you're listening to *Get Real with Dave*. This is your host, Depraved Dave, and for the next two hours, I'm yours, baby. If you're listening to me for the first time, congratulations! You've finally crossed over to the other side, and no, you didn't have to die to do it. Now, you're probably wondering why they call me Depraved. I dunno. Maybe it's because I like to call it as I see it. I don't tiptoe around issues. Maybe that's not politically correct, but hey, at least I don't make small talk with people I can't stand. So, if you've got a problem with me, you can exercise your constitutional rights and switch the dial. You know what—forget I said that. What you ought to do is expand your horizons. Listen to my show and maybe you'll learn something.

"All right. On to today's show. Do I have a treat for you. You may have already heard of her, and if your woman's now getting off—and I'm not talking about off the telephone—you probably have this lady to thank."

Lecia winced.

"Who am I talking about?" Depraved Dave panted like he was in the throes of passion. "Why, I'm talking about Dr. Love. Author of the runaway bestseller, *The Big O*. And I have to tell you, this woman is hot. She's like Halle Berry, only better. Dr. Love, it's a pleasure to have you in my studio today."

Lecia steeled her shoulders and forced a smile. "It's a pleasure to be here."

"Good. Now let's get to the nitty gritty. To the nuts and bolts, if you know what I mean. Because we have a lot to talk about. Your book." He held it up high, as though he were presenting an item to a courtroom. "*The Big O*," he all but shouted. "And no, I'm not talking about Cheerios, guys. I'm talking about orgasms. Female orgasms, to be exact. When I learned about this book, my first thought was, why isn't there a book like this for guys? But I know why. Because guys don't need help when it comes to orgasms. We know how to do it. We don't get all emotional and weepy and mentally shut down. We know how to have a good time."

As Lecia watched Depraved Dave emote with his hands, spittle flying from his mouth as he spoke fervently into the mike, her stomach sank. He didn't seem at all interested in talking to her. He wanted to preach his own opinions.

What am I doing here?

"No offense, Doc," he said, finally facing her. "A certain ex-girlfriend of mine—who shall remain nameless—should have had a copy of this book when we were together." He laughed, his voice hoarse from years of nicotine abuse. "Okay, about your book. You tell women how to get themselves off?"

It couldn't have sounded more crude. Which made her hate to have to admit, "Well, to a certain extent, yes."

"I could talk about your credentials, but I don't want to bore anyone to tears. Besides, anyone who looks as good as you must know her stuff when it comes to orgasms. So let's get right to the book. I decided to skip all the crap at the beginning and go right for the juice. Chapter Thirteen." He held the book open and read. " 'How to make your woman scream with passion.' And before any of you guys out there think I want to discuss this because I need pointers, let's not get stupid. Because I make all my women scream. Even that certain ex-girlfriend of mine, who had issues up the wazoo. But there are some guys out there who don't know the first thing about pleasing their women, which is why I'm assuming you wrote this chapter."

This was going to be bad. Very bad. Lecia hoped the thirty

minutes wouldn't feel like thirty years. "Actually . . ." She cleared her throat. "As you can see, that's the last chapter of the book. And the story behind my motivation for it is kind of funny. I received one of those 'enlarge your penis' e-mails—you know, that annoying spam everyone gets—and the subject said something like, 'Lecia, make your woman scream.' After I rolled my eyes and deleted the message, I thought, why not put something like this in the book? Not that exactly, but something as . . . I don't know. Shocking? The kind of thing that would get people talking. So I did. But while the chapter title is a bit outrageous, it's actually a serious—"

"Right, right," Depraved Dave said, cutting her off. "Let's get to the juice. The creamy center," he added in an exaggerated tone. "The stuff everyone in America has tuned in to hear about. Point one. *Talk to her*. Okay, Doc. What exactly do you mean by that? Role-playing? Pretending, for example, that your wife is a French tramp? Or a school girl who's begging to get laid?"

The guy sounded like an advertisement for a porn network. Lecia wanted to smack him. "If role-playing works, yes," she began slowly, "but I was referring to romantic—"

"Point two. *Butter her up*." Dave chuckled. "I love this one already. They've got body butter in all sorts of flavors. The wife says she loves the taste, not that I'm not sweet enough already."

The image of anyone getting down and dirty with Depraved Dave was enough to make Lecia want to puke. He was tall, but that was all he had going for him. He had long, stringy blond hair, way too pale skin for a guy who lived in the Golden State, and a body undefined by any muscles but undoubtedly defined by a beer gut. That and coffee-stained teeth. In other words, he was the kind of guy who attracted women only because of his fame and his net worth. They certainly weren't attracted to him for his charm.

"I guess this isn't a family show," Lecia joked, knowing full well that Dave's show was often X-rated. "Actually, what I meant was butter her up with words, not—"

"Body butter's the way to go. But I guarantee you, no woman needs any of that extra crap when she's with me. With what I've got, women never complain about being satisfied."

Women. She didn't put it past him to screw around on his wife. In fact, she was certain that he did. Why was the beautiful brunette still with this pig?

Lecia said, "I'm sure you know, Dave, that size isn't everything. That's a male misconception."

"You find me a woman who's happy with three inches."

"Is that why your exes left you?" Lecia couldn't help asking, the syrupy smile on her face making a lie of her concerned tone.

Sound effects of a jeering crowd filled the airwaves. "Hey, I may be a white guy, but I'm hung like a horse. Fourteen inches. And I don't mind proving it to you."

"Men and their toys," Lecia *tsked*. "I didn't think we were talking about strap-ons."

There was a moment of dead air as Depraved Dave stared at her in shock. Then he grinned and said, "I like you. Let's take some calls. The phone lines are lighting up like a Christmas display."

Lecia felt victorious. She'd won the battle with Depraved Dave. It was yet to be seen if she would win the war.

Two

Anthony Beals shot to his feet, slammed his hands down on his lawyer's desk and bellowed, "What do you mean there's nothing I can do?"

"Sit down, please."

"I don't want to sit. Not until you tell me how my wife can get away with this."

Keith Alabaster sighed, as if to say he'd explained this a million times already and didn't want to do so again. "Your prenuptial agreement is explicit. It says that if you cheat, she gets five million."

"But I didn't cheat on her!"

"Calm down, Anthony."

Anthony stood to his full six-foot-three-inch height. "Calm down? You tell me my wife is about to take a good chunk of my cash, and you expect me to calm down?"

Keith simply stared at him. "This is a . . . *tricky* situation. If this was simply he said she said, I'd say we fight it in court. But with this whole situation being very public, I'm not comfortable leaving it up to a court of law. I think it's wise to meet with Ginger and discuss an offer."

"No way." Anthony planted both hands on his hips and began to pace.

"Anthony," Keith said firmly. When Anthony looked his way, Keith continued. "With everything that's happened in the media, I wouldn't trust this case to a judge."

"But I didn't cheat on her."

"The world thinks you did."

Damn the media and the way they manipulated the facts. "I wasn't charged with anything."

"No, but—"

"But you're telling me that doesn't matter?"

"It should matter, yes. But who're we kidding? With television and the Internet replaying only the sordid details of any given case, people are convicted in the court of public opinion. The truth gets lost, assuming it mattered in the first place."

In this case, once those damn pictures of him had circulated, the media had touted the image of the womanizing ball player, which was a stereotype if ever there was one. He was far from a womanizer. Sure, when he'd been single, he had his share of good times. His share of women. But he had changed as he'd grown older. Matured. Even before he got married he stopped hanging out with the boys every night, chasing a piece of ass. He'd stopped that crap in college, long before he started playing pro ball. And he had most definitely sworn off all other women once he'd said "I do."

"Let me set up a meeting with Ginger's attorney to discuss some type of settlement."

"Making an offer will be the same as admitting guilt," Anthony protested.

"It's a moot point. The question is, do you want to lose five million in addition to half of everything you own? Let's meet with Ginger and her lawyer. I'll get her to settle for a million."

"A million bucks? We've barely been married for five months."

"I won't start the negotiations there. If she says yes at $250,000, great. If not . . ." Keith ended his statement with a lame shrug.

Gritting his teeth, Anthony crossed the carpet to the floor-to-ceiling windows and stared outside. Stared, but didn't see a thing other than the blur of buildings in downtown Los Angeles.

He couldn't believe this was happening to him. His life had taken a turn for the worse and everything was spiraling out of control. A cruel twist of fate had him meeting that hooker on West Hollywood, and as pathetic as it sounded every time he heard the story on the news, he *hadn't* known the woman was a prostitute. He had truly believed her to be a woman in trouble. A woman in trouble who had flagged him down for some help. By the time he got a clue that she wasn't down on her luck that cool May evening, the time bomb on his life had been about to explode. Literally. Just as he had been ready to head back to his car, several sudden camera flashes blinded him.

The woman shrieked and ran off, and so did the photographers.

Anthony had stood there in shock.

No one was more proud than he of his success—except, perhaps, his mama. He'd led the Oakland Raiders to the playoffs this past season with an incredible 3,008 yards passing and 351 passes completed. His best game had been against the Miami Dolphins, when he completed twenty-five of thirty passes for 333 yards. He also rushed for sixty yards for a touchdown that game. Since being traded to the Raiders the year before he'd set them on fire. Voted the league's MVP, he had achieved fame not only in the Bay Area, where he played, but in L.A., where he chose to live, and wherever he traveled. Never in his wildest dreams, however, would he have thought himself popular enough to have the paparazzi trailing him.

The camera flashes had been startling, but he'd written the whole thing off as some overzealous photographer or even a fan hoping to get a candid shot of him. Until the next morning when Ginger plopped the *Daily Blab* onto his stomach while he lay in bed. He had popped open an eye, seen her tearstained face, and quickly gotten up. His stomach bottomed out when he saw the front page. A large color photo showed him turning, a stunned look on his face, while he stood beside a dark-skinned woman who wore far too much makeup and wild hair to *not* be a prostitute. Of course, he had been turning to head back to his car, and because it was so dark, he hadn't noticed all the makeup on the woman's face right away.

He had gone on to tell Ginger that, but she wasn't interested in anything he had to say. At least not until she had settled down after a good hour or so of crying. He finally had the chance to talk then. But after listening to his truthful although admittedly lame-sounding explanation, she threw every piece of his clothing onto the lawn of their Beverly Hills home, then started smashing the glassware in the kitchen. There was only one thing he could do to make anything better—leave the house. At least until Ginger had cooled down.

He'd moved into the presidential suite at the Raffles L'Ermitage Beverly Hills. Equally as elegant as the Regent Beverly Wilshire, Raffles L'Ermitage had far fewer rooms, which meant he would have more privacy. More than anything, he had wanted to keep a low profile until he and Ginger smoothed things over.

That was two weeks ago, and he still hadn't been back to

the house. No, that wasn't true. He had gone back, only to be dragged off the property by the police. Another embarrassing photo of him appeared in the papers the following day.

Ginger had gotten a restraining order against him. She wouldn't take his calls. She wouldn't leave a message for him. The only thing she wanted to do was end the marriage and get what she said had been promised to her in the prenuptial agreement. That much Anthony knew because of his wife's lawyer's correspondence with his lawyer.

One thing had become clear. She hadn't turned out to be the stand-by-your-man kind of woman he'd initially thought her to be. Not the through-good-times-and-through-bad wife he'd expected.

He could hear his mother's words: *Child, why are you marrying this girl? How well do you even know her?*

"You knew Dad two years before you married him," Anthony had replied, watching his mother's face crumble at his words. "I'm only trying to say—"

"I know what you're saying. And believe me, I don't want the same for you that I've had. You're a good son. A decent man. You deserve a decent woman."

"Ginger *is* a decent woman."

"Then why haven't you met her kinfolk?"

"She's had a rough past," was all Anthony had said. He hadn't felt it was right to discuss the deeply personal things Ginger had told him in confidence.

"Something's not right, son. I feel it."

He had ignored his mother's warning. After all, it only made sense that she was wary when it came to marriage. Her husband had cheated on her like it was a sport, and she'd been miserable. That was bound to make anyone distrustful.

"Anthony."

At the sound of his lawyer's voice, Anthony snapped back into the present. He dragged a hand over his face. "Sorry, Keith. What did you say?"

"I said, do you want me to schedule the meeting with you or without you? I know we have the restraining order to consider, but I think I can persuade Ginger to revoke that."

Anthony could hardly believe this conversation was actually taking place. "This is a nightmare, Keith."

"It happens every day."

"Great. So I should just get over it?"

"Sorry," Keith said, standing up. "This is L.A. I tend to forget that *some* marriages do last a lifetime."

"That's what I was hoping for me and Ginger."

"I know. But it doesn't look like that's gonna happen. She's already served you with divorce papers."

"You don't have to remind me."

"Sorry," Keith said again.

"No, I'm the one who's sorry. You're only doing your job. It's this situation that's frustrating me." He had sworn that when he walked down the aisle, his marriage would last forever. The last thing he'd wanted was to follow his father's disgusting path. His father had been married six times. Divorced six times. He'd had countless lovers, almost from the moment the bastard married his mother. And his poor mother—she had cried herself to sleep for years. In the beginning, Anthony hadn't understood why, but on more than one occasion he had left his bedroom to crawl into her bed and wrap his little arms around her when he had heard her sobbing. Later, he understood the reason for his mother's tears. The day she had finally told his father to leave, Anthony had vowed he would never hurt a woman the way his father had hurt his mother.

To his lawyer, Anthony said, "I always swore I'd get married and stay married."

"That's what I said the first time I got married. Doesn't always happen that way."

Anthony inhaled and exhaled slowly. "I still don't get it. She barely even spoke to me, then she's serving me papers?" How could Ginger have turned on him this way? "You know whose fault this is?" he went on, wagging a finger as the answer came to him. "That Dr. Love woman. The last time I tried to speak with Ginger, she told me that Dr. Love advised her to put me in the past and move on with her life."

Keith's face paled. "What do you mean, you tried to talk to Ginger? When?"

"Two days ago."

"For God's sake. Do you want her calling the cops again? You barely escaped a trespassing charge two weeks ago."

"It's my house."

"Yeah, but she's got a restraining order."

"Don't remind me."

"Someone needs to remind you. This situation is bad enough. You don't need a stalking charge on top of everything else. You want to spend time in jail?"

"No, of course not."

"Then let this go. I know you love her, but you've got to cut your losses and move on. Before you're really sorry."

Cut his losses, as if they were talking about a bad stock or something. But he knew Keith was right. Things could potentially get much worse. "Fine. Set up a meeting."

"Given what you just told me, I doubt she'll okay a meeting with you there, so it might have to be on the phone. But I'll do my best. I'd like everyone to meet face-to-face if at all possible." Keith groaned softly. "But please, no more calls to Ginger. Let me handle this."

"All right," Anthony agreed grudgingly.

"I'll call you as soon as I have the details."

Anthony left his lawyer's office in a foul mood and was still fuming when his cell phone rang a couple hours later. "Yeah?" he practically barked as he answered it.

"T?"

T was the nickname that those in Anthony's inner circle called him. "Yeah, this is T."

"Hey, T, it's me. Ben." Anthony heard a soft chuckle, as if Ben were relieved. "You're finally answering your phone."

Shit. He was in no mood to talk to his agent. "Ben, can we chat later? This is a bad time."

"I'll make this quick. What do you say I swing by your hotel at two o'clock to pick you up? We can grab a quick bite—"

"Pick me up? For what?"

There was a pause, then, "What do you mean, 'For what?' The *Tonight Show*. Your guest appearance today. Remember?"

"Aw, shit." He hadn't remembered. It had been that kind of day. "I'm sorry, Ben. A lot's going on." He glanced at the Lincoln Navigator's digital clock. It was three minutes after twelve. "It totally slipped my mind."

"That's okay. We still have plenty of time. As long as we're at the NBC studios by four—"

"I don't know, Ben." Anthony looked out at the waves. He'd driven to Huntington Beach hoping to clear his head, but all he had for his efforts was a migraine. "I'm not feeling up for it. It's early, though. I bet if you call them now, they can find a replacement for me."

"A replacement?" Ben sounded truly perplexed. "Oh, I get

it. You're joking, right?" The older man chortled as if to make his point a reality.

"Naw, man. I'm serious. I'm having a very bad day. I saw my lawyer this morning and things went right down the toilet. He suggested I offer Ginger some type of settlement rather than go to court. It'd be one thing if I'd had sex with that prostitute, but I swear to God I didn't. But no one gives a damn about the truth, and I just wanna—"

"Wait, wait," Ben said quickly. "I hear what you're saying, believe me I do. And I know you feel like crap right now. But T, life goes on. I don't say that to be crude, but it's the truth. Ginger's moving on, and trying to clean you out in the process. In the meantime, you've already lost one endorsement. I don't want you losing any more. The world needs to see you as the good guy again. That's why I set this appearance up. We talked about this, remember?"

"Yeah, I remember. But I'm in no mood to smile all evening for a national audience."

"It won't be *all* evening."

"Even half an hour is more than I can handle."

"Whoa. Okay, now I know you must have forgotten our conversation. This whole issue with Ginger is exactly why you *have* to go."

Anthony knew Ben had worked his butt off to get him this appearance, after he had rejected Ben's suggestion to smear Ginger in the media. Ben had figured if they made Ginger look bad—with real or imagined dirt—then he would come out of the entire mess smelling a whole lot better. Anthony refused, but agreed to do the talk show circuit to prove that he was still the decent guy people had come to know and love. But he wasn't in the mood to play smiley-face on television tonight. He needed to speak with Ginger.

"Have you been listening to me?" Anthony asked.

A horn blared. "Son of a bitch!"

"Yo, Ben. Maybe you ought to call me back. When you're off the road."

"No, I'm not calling you back. Are you at the hotel? I can swing by and pick you up for lunch."

"I'm not hungry."

"You need to do this interview, T. If for no other reason than to prove to the world that you're not some type of pervert. This isn't just about you and Ginger. This is about your career. The Raiders love you, but for how long? If they think you're a liability, you can kiss your career good-bye. Then there's your charitable work. Who will want you at their events? It doesn't matter if anything is proven in the eyes of the law; all that matters is the appearance of impropriety."

"You sound like my lawyer."

"Things are iffy now, but they don't have to be. They can turn in your favor. So far, you've hidden behind your lawyer and haven't come out and made a statement. The world needs to hear from you. Not about what happened that night, but about the Anthony Beals they know and love. Especially if you want to win this battle with Ginger in court."

"I'm hoping I won't have to go to court."

"Forget court for now." Ben's voice held a note of exasperation. "You need some good press. Go on the show. Do the interview. Relax and be cool. Project the image of the successful quarterback that you are."

"And what if it backfires?"

"We're talking about the *Tonight Show*. How can it backfire? Be funny, be smart, and people will love you."

Anthony hedged. He had to admit, the idea was sounding better by the minute. "You really think so?"

"Of course I do. You've got natural charm. People want to believe you, but they can only do that once you stop hiding. So go on the show and promote yourself. Be a walking infomercial for Anthony Beals. Keep the topic focused on what you're good at—your game. Your Big Brother stuff."

Anthony hated that he had to do this. He'd had a good name, and it had been smeared. No doubt everything looked much worse because his own wife refused to believe him.

Maybe his appearance on the *Tonight Show* would get through to Ginger.

"You really think I ought to do this?" Anthony asked.

"Hell, yeah. Make the most of this opportunity. But whatever you do, don't mention a word about what happened on May twenty-third. Not *one* word."

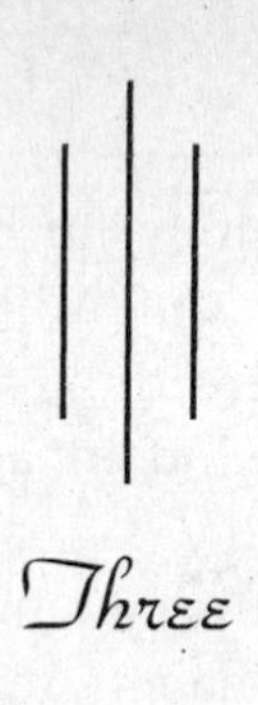

Three

"It was a cold evening, Jay, and when I saw the woman beckoning to me, I stopped. Hell, I had to stop—she practically jumped in front of my SUV. I barely avoided hitting her as I slammed on the brakes. Then she's motioning to me to roll down my window. So I did. I figured, who'd be so desperate as to get a passing motorist's attention? One who needed a few bucks, that's who. Or maybe a ride home. But as I roll down the window, she's looking around like she's scared or something, so I got out of my car to see how I could help her." Anthony turned toward the audience. "Maybe it sounds crazy, but I didn't know better. I'm not from here. I'm from small-town Tennessee." Anthony chuckled lightly to poke fun at his own ignorance. "In small-town Tennessee, people help those in need."

"That's very noble of you."

"This is my first year with the Raiders, and the first time I've lived in L.A. I guess I was so naive, I didn't even realize that part of Hollywood was famous for . . . well, you know."

Jay's expression was sincere as he said, "You seem like a nice enough guy. And I know Raiders fans love you. And since the Raiders played here for a while, I'd say you have quite a few fans right here in L.A."

Cheers and whistles pierced the air.

Anthony held up a hand in appreciation. "Thank you, y'all."

"You also give back to the community."

"That's right. I think I have a responsibility to do so. Athletes are high profile. People look up to us. Kids look up to us. For that reason, I think it's especially important to be a positive role model. I make appearances at various events for children, fund-raise for good causes, but my main gig is being a Big Brother."

"I'm impressed," Jay told him, no hint of humor in his voice.

This is working, Anthony thought, barely suppressing a smile. And it was much to his surprise. Earlier, he had dreaded doing the show, expecting people to snicker and jeer as he walked onto the stage. He knew how fickle the public was when it came to celebrities. One minute they loved you, but one wrong move and they turned on you. He had been so wary of coming out on stage that he'd chugged back a couple shots of vodka to loosen himself up. The alcohol had worked wonders.

"Now, one more personal question," Jay said. "If you don't mind."

Anthony knew he'd already opened the can of worms about what had happened that night. And public sentiment seemed to be going his way. What did he have to lose?

"Sure, Jay."

"I've been following your love life in the tabloids."

"Oh, great," Anthony replied without mirth.

"I know you and your wife aren't living together right now.

But like I said before, you seem like a nice guy. One who can be trusted."

"Thank you."

"I'm wondering," Jay went on, "is there any chance you two might reconcile?"

"I love my wife, Jay. We love each other. But the media intrusion has been too much for her to handle. She's laying low for a while. We're both taking a break, but I have full confidence that when this dies down, we'll work things out."

There was more applause. Anthony gave his best smile, hoping to hell that Ginger was watching.

"If my next guest isn't a household name yet, she will be soon. She's a sex therapist who's giving Dr. Ruth a run for her money. Her first book, *The Big O,* has been on the *New York Times* bestseller list for twelve weeks. Please join me in welcoming Dr. Lecia Calhoun, aka Dr. Love."

Cheers and whistles erupted as Lecia made her way onto the stage. She remembered to smile, although her face actually ached from all the practicing she'd done. She faced the bright lights and waved, praying that she wouldn't fall flat on her face. Angela had insisted she wear a sexier outfit than her normal conservative attire, which was why she now wore a V-neck black Armani dress with a provocative slit up the side. Her Gucci slingbacks had a higher heel than her usual shoes, and it took all the skill she possessed to actually walk in them.

The cheers continued, and the moment felt surreal. Especially when Jay Leno met her onstage, leaned forward and gave her a peck on the cheek. She resisted the urge to pinch herself to confirm that this moment was true.

"Welcome, welcome," Jay said as she took a seat on the sofa beside his desk.

Jay's previous guest had moved over, and in her nervousness, Lecia barely took note of him. "Thank you, Jay," she said, crossing one leg over the other, the slit in her dress exposing a good portion of her thigh. Should she switch legs? she wondered, feeling a moment of horror. Her parents would be watching the show in Florida, and she didn't want to embarrass them.

She also knew that her sister Tyanna was in the audience, and that she would have told her, "Forget Mom and Dad. Live your life for you."

"You're looking very *happy,*" Jay said. "*Satisfied.*"

Lecia laughed airily, knowing exactly what Jay was implying. "I am," she said in reply. To her ears, she didn't sound nervous at all. She allowed for a dramatic pause so the audience and Jay would let their thoughts travel to the gutter. Then she said, "As you pointed out, my book has been on the *New York Times* list for twelve weeks, so yeah, I'm pretty happy."

"Everywhere I go, I'm hearing, 'Dr. Love.' How did that get started? Is that a name you picked out for yourself?"

Lecia's heart was beating so fast, she almost didn't know if she would be able to speak. But she found her voice. "Pick for myself, are you kidding? That's a name the media gave me when the book came out, and it's stuck."

"So tell me." Jay lifted the book and held it up for the camera. The silhouette of a woman covered by a satin sheet was barely discernable beneath the title, a subtle hint that the book was geared for women. "*The Big O: Getting Everything You Want and More.* What made you decide to write a book about women's . . . Well, why *The Big O*?"

Lecia drew in a shaky breath. She hadn't tripped on the

stage, the audience seemed to love her, and Jay was being as nice as could be. Yet she doubted she would get over her jitters.

"I started off in medicine," she explained, as she had on other talk shows. "I was an OB/GYN."

"Okay."

"In my practice, not only did I deal with women having babies, but a large number of them confided in me about their sexual frustration."

"Was this surprising?"

"Oh, absolutely, yes. I expected some concerns, but the kind of things I could treat medically. You know, like pain during—" She stopped short, and instead used a hand gesture to try to convey "sex."

"Sex," Jay said frankly.

Lecia's face flamed. "Yes."

"My wife complains about that all the time," Jay said in a jovial tone, then adjusted his tie in a boasting gesture.

"Really? Well, you should tell her to come see me."

There were cheers, and Jay laughed. Settling back, he said, "All right, back to our serious discussion. You found that women were sexually frustrated. How many, if you had to break it down percentagewise?"

"Probably seventy-five percent."

Jay's eyes widened. "Seventy-five percent were sexually frustrated?"

Lecia nodded. "And I'm talking about women who were involved in relationships, some pregnant when I was dealing with them."

"Really?"

"Really."

"Okay, so you realized women were frustrated and needed

some help. How did you jump from that point to writing this book? Because I always wonder how one goes about shifting gears like that. You're a doctor, then a writer."

"I've been a closet writer all my life."

"A closet writer, then you came out."

"Uh-huh. I was scribbling stories from the time I was a kid. But I never thought I could ever make it as a writer. So I followed my parents' path and went into medicine. But I still had the writing bug. I'd always thought I would write fiction, but I couldn't get past the first two chapters of any story I started. I finally decided, why not nonfiction? I had the expertise."

"I can't dispute that. I read the book and found it quite . . . *interesting.*"

"Did you, now?"

When the audience cat-called, Jay faced them with a dumbfounded expression. "Yes," he said firmly. "I did. I didn't see a disclaimer that said the book was *only* for women."

"Actually, I think the more men who read it, the better off women will be."

Hoots and howls of agreement.

"Exactly, as my wife can attest to." Jay paused at another round of cheers. "Anyway, back to the book. You take a therapist approach."

"I've always been the type of doctor who likes to talk to my patients, counsel them. I'd also studied psychotherapy. Anyway, I finally decided that with so many women sexually unsatisfied, perhaps I should consider going into sex therapy. So I switched gears, got my therapy accreditation, then began counseling patients on sexuality. I set up my practice primarily for women, by the way, since I'd dealt with women as a physician. If I thought women were unsatisfied while I was an

OB/GYN, did I ever get an earful as a therapist. That's when I made the decision to do what I'd originally considered: write a book on the subject. And that's how *The Big O* came to be."

"And with its runaway success, I think it's safe to say that there are a lot of men out there who are pretty surprised."

Women whistled their agreement.

"*I* was pretty surprised. Not to say there aren't satisfied women out there, but there are a heck of a lot who aren't."

"Why do you think that is?"

"First of all, men and women still have trouble communicating. Beyond the superficial, anyway. To complicate things, speaking about intimate matters is always a hard thing to do without hurting someone's feelings. Add egos to the mix and it's damn near impossible. Now, I can't say this is the case for everyone, but based on my experience, women are much more concerned with sparing their partner's feelings. So, if anyone ends up dissatisfied, it tends to be the woman. And men—God love 'em, but they're not always the best listeners."

Jay half shrugged, half nodded. "I can see that."

"So, I don't know." Lecia turned and looked out at the audience. "I guess the book has been helping."

There were exuberant female cheers.

"I've heard this book is so successful that women are now hosting 'Big O' parties—where they get together to candidly discuss their sexuality issues."

Lecia blushed. "Yes, I'd heard that."

"Did you ever imagine you'd affect the women of America this way?"

"No, I didn't."

"Well, I think it's just amazing."

There was a round of applause. Lecia smiled graciously.

"You're Dr. Love," Jay said when the applause died down. "You've written a successful book. You must be happily involved with someone."

Lecia shook her head. "Actually, not right now, no."

"Ah, it figures."

Lecia swung her head to the right. She'd seen Anthony Beals when she came onstage, and for all she knew, had shaken hands with him, but was too nervous to pay him any attention. Now she saw that he was one fine-looking brother.

He looked sharp in a black blazer and white shirt that was open at the collar. His wide shoulders carried the blazer to perfection. He had flawless dark skin, well-defined cheekbones, and a neatly trimmed goatee that framed sexy full lips. If only he would smile. He also had piercing brown eyes. Or were they only piercing because he was glaring at her?

The realization made her heart skip a beat. He truly was glaring.

She knew of the infamous Anthony Beals. Had heard about his escapades on the news. She had even talked to his wife when the desperate woman approached her outside a bar one evening.

A shiver of worry slid down her spine. He didn't know that she'd talked with his wife, did he? Oh, Lord. Maybe he did. Why else would he be looking at her with such . . . contempt?

Lecia wasn't about to ask. She decided it was best to ignore him and continue her interview with Jay.

But then Jay looked at Anthony Beals and asked, "What are you saying? That a therapist has to be in a relationship in order to give advice?"

"You want the truth?" Anthony asked.

"Sure," Jay replied nonchalantly.

Oh, God, Lecia thought.

"I think a stable relationship would be a good start, yeah," Anthony replied.

There was some snickering in the audience.

Lecia felt anger rising in her chest. She bit back the urge to make a snide comment because that would accomplish nothing. Instead she said, "I'm a trained physician and a trained therapist. I think that qualifies me to do the job I do."

"Maybe on paper, yeah. But if you ask me, real life experience is more important. Especially when you're telling people to leave their husbands."

Later, Lecia would realize that Anthony's comment had been bait, and that she'd taken it as easily as a toddler takes candy. "I don't advise people to leave their spouses," she replied.

"Really? You don't remember telling my wife to leave me?"

There was a chill to Anthony's voice as he spoke, and the audience picked up on it. The tension changed, becoming taut, like a too-tight violin string. You could hear a pin drop in the studio.

"Is that true? You're his wife's therapist?" Jay was grinning, no doubt expecting her to deny Anthony's claim. Either that or he thought it was a hilarious coincidence.

"I'm *not* her therapist."

"Oh come on," Anthony said. "You're gonna deny you told her to leave me?"

"Your wife is not my patient," Lecia insisted.

"But you spoke to her, didn't you?" Anthony's eyes challenged her to deny the truth. "Told her I was a pervert and said she should end our marriage as quickly as possible."

A collective "Ooh" spread across the studio audience.

"This, ladies and gentlemen, is an impromptu segment of 'Battle of the Sexes,'" Jay announced, then laughed.

If only it were a laughing matter, Lecia thought. For her it was anything but.

Facing Anthony, she steeled her jaw. "I meet a lot of people when I'm out, and many of them ask for bits of advice. It's all very casual, not in the least professional—"

"Casual?"

Anthony's stunned tone silenced Lecia. She thought he was going to tear a piece off her hide, but he merely shook his head before leaning back in his seat. Thank God, she thought, only to be horrified an instant later when he leaned forward again.

"You think telling my wife I'm a pervert is *casual* advice?"

"If I met her, I don't even remember her," Lecia lied. Because she remembered the woman, all right. Remembered how she had begged her for a moment of her time outside a Beverly Hills bar, almost on the verge of hysteria. Lecia had agreed to talk to her, although she'd had her reservations, given the woman's agitated state. In the end she'd written off the woman's hysteria as desperation over a critical situation in her marriage. "And I wouldn't have said . . . what you said she said."

"According to her, you did. In fact, she made sure to tell me a number of times that you'd called me a pervert, so I knew exactly why she was ending our marriage."

"I did not call you a pervert." Lecia knew she should stop there. She *wanted* to stop. But somehow her mouth opened and she heard herself saying, "Deeply troubled, perhaps, but not a pervert."

"Ha!" Anthony sounded victorious as he aimed a finger at her. "So you do remember!"

Lord, she should have kept her big mouth shut. But she was a Gemini, and hard-pressed to back down from an argument. And hell, she was only human. How was she to remain dignified and stiff-lipped with the likes of Anthony Beals egging her on?

Lecia acknowledged to herself that she shouldn't have commented on Anthony's character at all with his wife. With her patients, she remained impartial, even when they confided the strangest of fantasies. But Ginger hadn't been a patient, so she'd spoken to her woman-to-woman. Given everything Ginger had told her about her superstar athlete husband in the span of five minutes, she couldn't help but give the woman her honest opinion.

And maybe, just maybe, her attitude toward Anthony had been soured even before she met his wife. Infidelity was a personal sore spot for her. Especially with men who felt it was their inherent right. Men like her ex-husband.

"Serious bit of advice," Anthony said. "Think twice before you mess with people's lives. Because I'd still be with my wife right now if it weren't for you."

Lecia grinned sweetly as she said, "No, you'd still be with your wife if you'd kept your pants zipped up. That's another area I cover in my book—women who find intimacy too difficult because they can't trust their partners."

"Whoa, wait a second." Anthony looked genuinely offended. "You don't know me. Where do you get off saying that?"

"I know a lame story when I hear one. Small-town Tennessee boy. Please."

There was another hum of perverse excitement throughout the audience. Lecia met Anthony's hard stare before turning away. She picked at an imaginary piece of lint on her dress.

"You think you have my number?"

Shut up. Don't say a word. . . . "I know I do."

Anthony shook his head in disbelief. "I hope you're happy." There was venom beneath his words. "Because not only did she leave me, she's gonna take me to the cleaners. All thanks to your advice."

"That is not my problem," Lecia countered.

"Down, folks," Jay Leno said. He made the sound of a cat meowing as he extended a clawlike hand in the air. "Any more of that and I'll have to see if we can find a pair of boxing gloves." He paused briefly. "Or I can send you to the Springer show, two doors down."

Breathe, Lecia told herself. She felt her lungs constricting, and wished she had her inhaler.

"Oh, that won't be necessary," Lecia said, laughing. She sounded like someone had put a gun to her head and screamed, "Laugh!"

In her peripheral vision she saw a man standing near a camera whirling a finger in the air.

Jay said, "I wish we had more time."

"Me, too," Lecia lied. She pasted a smile on her face, though her heart beat out of control. It was all she could do to pretend this situation wasn't the worst she'd ever experienced.

Looking into one of the cameras, Jay said, "The book is called *The Big O: Getting Everything You Want and More.* You can pick it up at your nearest bookstore. We'll be right back with our musical guest, Forgotten Promise."

Kevin Eubanks and the *Tonight Show* band began playing. Kevin wore that permanent and ever annoying smile of his. Or maybe she only found it annoying because this interview had turned into a certified disaster.

Leno leaned forward and said, "I didn't realize you two knew each other."

"I apologize, Jay," Lecia said.

"No, don't apologize. This is great. You're not taking yourselves too seriously. My viewers love that."

Lecia snuck a glance to her right. Anthony looked like he was barely containing a keg full of anger.

Anthony said, "Maybe I should get out of here."

"No, no." Jay held out a hand to keep him at bay.

"Then maybe I should," Lecia said.

"Neither of you has to go anywhere. I'm telling you, this was great."

"Great?" Lecia asked, horrified. "You *will* cut that before tonight's broadcast, right? The last thing I need—"

"The audience loved it," Jay said, dismissing her protest. "Hey, wait a second—"

Lecia looked up to see Anthony Beals give Jay a wave as he exited stage left.

Four

Lecia had been silent on the drive to her sister's place, but as soon as she crossed the threshold into the Baldwin Hills home, she kicked off her shoes and said, "Oh . . . my . . . God."

"I see you have your voice back," Tyanna commented wryly.

Lecia darted into the living room. She plopped her body down onto Tyanna's sofa, throwing an arm across her forehead. "Tell me that didn't just happen," Lecia said. "Tell me I wasn't just humiliated on a taping of the *Tonight Show*."

"It wasn't as bad as you thought."

"No," she whined. "It was worse."

"Speaking as someone who was at the taping, I think the audience found it funny."

Lecia lifted her head and met her sister's gaze. "Funny? You are joking, right? I thought that guy was going to . . . going to pummel me or something. And I think he would have, if the cameras weren't rolling. According to his wife, he's got an explosive temper."

"I don't believe that."

Lecia whimpered as she dropped her head back. "I think I'd have preferred a pummeling to national disgrace."

"Relax," Tyanna told her. "It really wasn't that bad."

Easy for her sister to say. She was the one who had lived a life full of drama. The latest had occurred a couple years earlier, when Tyanna's boyfriend had been working undercover to find his brother's killer. The guy behind the murder had kidnapped Tyanna and would have killed her if the police hadn't shot him dead first. Tyanna had gone on to marry the boyfriend, and Sheldon was now Lecia's brother-in-law. He and Tyanna had moved to Los Angeles to pursue Tyanna's new career as a fitness video star.

"You want some tea?" Tyanna called from the kitchen.

"No."

"Coffee?"

"No."

"Juice?"

"No. I don't want anything."

Tyanna waltzed back into the living, her arms crossed over her chest. "You're not gonna sulk all evening, are you?"

"Yeah, I think I will, thanks."

Shaking her head, Tyanna sank onto the leather sofa beside her sister. "Come on, sis. Don't let this ruin your day. If anything, Anthony Beals is the one who's gonna look bad when the show airs tonight, not you."

Lecia sat up, a sigh escaping her. "I should have kept my mouth shut. Why didn't I keep my mouth shut? No woman will trust me to ever give her advice again. My career is over."

"That's not true. Mark my words. You'll be more popular than ever."

"That's what Angela said," Lecia said glumly. "But how can

anyone have faith in a therapist who . . . who goes on national television and acts like a three-year-old? And then there's Mom and Dad." Lecia groaned.

"Oh, don't worry about Mom and Dad. You thought they'd have heart failure when you gave up practicing medicine to be a sex therapist, then again when you decided to write a book about sex. They survived."

Yeah, they had. But just barely, Lecia was sure. "They'll be horrified by this."

"Think of it this way: if you had to verbally spar with anyone on national television, you couldn't have picked a better person. That Anthony Beals is a definite hottie."

Lecia gaped at her sister. "Like that matters."

Tyanna raised her eyebrows suggestively. "So you noticed. You wouldn't act so offended if you hadn't."

"I did not!" But despite her words, Lecia felt a flutter of nerves deep in her belly. She *had* noticed. However inappropriate it was.

"Of course, he's married."

"Not for long." At Tyanna's suspicious gaze, Lecia added, "And it's no wonder. Talk about a walking powder keg."

"It's called passion." Tyanna smirked. "You have to admit, there's nothing sexier than a passionate man."

Lecia scowled at her sister. "I forgot, you're still honeymooning. No wonder your judgment is lost in your libido."

Ignoring her, Tyanna asked, "Did you believe his story about not knowing that woman was a hooker?"

"The last thing I'm concerned about is his story. Do you think they'll cut that piece from the show?"

"I don't know. But I imagine they will if they think it's bad enough."

"It *was* bad enough."

"Then you have nothing to worry about." But Tyanna sounded as if she was just saying that to make her feel better.

"I still can't believe Angela," Lecia went on. "She wouldn't stop saying that negative publicity is still great publicity, how I'll sell a gazillion more books."

"She's right. Even the people who e-mail me to whine that my fitness video is lacking are helping to spread the word. I'm not gonna complain."

"It's my reputation I'm worried about."

"The truth is, even if it is controversial, people will forget about the incident by the end of the week."

"That's not making me feel any better."

"All right." Tyanna held up both hands as she stood. "I was trying to help, but I'll keep my mouth shut. I'll let you sit here and mope."

"No. No, wait. There is something I need. Anything extra strength for this headache would be great."

"I'll see what I can find," Tyanna said sweetly.

When her sister was out of the room, Lecia buried her face in both hands. She had begged Angela to get the *Tonight Show* to cut that piece from tonight's show, and Angela had promised that she would. But she wasn't sure she could believe her. Angela was a publicist, after all, and one who thought only of the bottom line. Lecia had no doubt the woman would have her mud wrestle for a national audience if it would sell more books.

"Here you go."

Lecia looked up to see Tyanna, a glass of water extended in one hand and two small pills in another. Lecia accepted the pills. She popped them into her mouth and dry-swallowed them.

"God, how do you do that?" Tyanna asked.

"Practice." Years of it, actually. Medical school had been a very stressful time. So had the years married to Allen. Especially after she learned of his numerous affairs.

"Now I could use some scotch," Lecia declared.

"Come on. You're making things much worse than they already are."

"You don't mind if I stay here until they air the show?" Lecia asked.

"No, of course not."

"Good. Because I have a feeling I'm going to need the support."

Ben slammed the *Los Angeles Times* down on the desktop. The headline, REALITY BITES: SEX THERAPIST AND FOOTBALL STAR CLASH ON NATIONAL TV, jumped out at Anthony.

"Damn it, T. I told you not to talk about that night. Did I or did I not tell you not to talk about it? I knew it would be bad news, yet you ignored my explicit instructions."

"Do you need to walk around like that?" Anthony asked from the seat across his agent's desk. "I've had a headache since last night."

"A headache is the least of your problems."

"I didn't want to do the show, remember? But you kept forcing the issue."

Ben moved away from the desk, pacing, then stopped to face him. "I told you to talk about *you*, not that tramp, and certainly not your marriage. You remember that conversation, don't you?"

Anthony merely shrugged. He was used to much more shocking press than this, and he figured there was no point getting upset over what he couldn't change. Hell, he might as well slug back a beer and celebrate the misery of his life.

"I thought for sure they'd pull it from the show," he said.

"Pull it?" Ben laughed mirthlessly. "This is Hollywood, T, where the lives of the rich and famous are more scandalous than what we see on the big screen. People *love* this stuff."

"Sorry."

"I didn't want to deal with this, not when you're a free agent. I was hoping for bigger bucks out of the Raiders this year, but who knows now? They may just want to cut their losses."

"What was I supposed to do? I didn't think that hack who calls herself a therapist was going to be there."

"Look at the picture, T." Ben strode to the desk and jammed a finger on the paper. "The woman looks terrified. You've thrown an interception, and Ginger has taken it all the way into the end zone."

Anthony studied the color photo plastered on the front page. The good doctor *did* look terrified. "Shit."

"I'm working on damage control, some sort of spin we can give this, but I have to say, I'm not sure I can undo this mess."

"The woman all but ruined my marriage. It was all I could do to sit there and listen to her go on and on about how qualified she is. I had to say *something*."

"Do me a favor, T."

"What?"

"Shut up and listen."

Anthony raised an eyebrow. He had taken his chances by signing with an independent sports agent, rather than a large, established agency. He had admired Ben's spunk, his passion. So far, his agent had done good by him, and he hadn't once regretted his decision. But he didn't appreciate being spoken to this way.

"I say that with much love, of course," Ben added.

"Of course," Anthony said, a subtle warning in his voice.

Ben smiled sheepishly. "You know I want what's best for you."

"And ultimately you." Anthony held no illusions that Ben had warm and fuzzy feelings for him. This was about business. The bottom line was how marketable a commodity he was. Right now he was still hot, and, he thought, Ben would do well to remember that.

"I was out of line, sorry," Ben said. His tanned face had turned beet red.

"What do you want me to do?" Anthony asked him. This time his tone was soft, conciliatory. If nothing else, he respected Ben's opinion and his advice. In addition to Ben being his agent, Anthony considered him a friend.

"I think it's best that you lay low. Don't answer the phone unless you see my number. And forget ordering room service. I'll bring you what you need."

"And?" Anthony asked, because he knew there was more.

"And pray. Pray that Ginger hasn't seen any of this."

Five

Sighing with contentment, Ginger rolled away from the strong, warm body and onto her other side. As her elbow jammed against something lumpy, she stirred, sensing that something was wrong. It took half a second for her to realize that the something lumpy was part of the mattress, which instantly made her remember where she was.

Her eyes popped open. Jerking her head up, she glanced at the glowing red digital numbers on the bedside clock.

"Holy shit!" Ginger was up in a flash, throwing the thin sheet off her body and scrambling from the bed.

"What is it, babe?"

"The time," she answered, as she reached for the lamp switch. The bulb blew as she flicked it on. She dashed to the curtains instead and yanked them open, only to realize a moment later that anyone passing the motel window could see her naked form.

"Shit," she repeated. "This place is hardly better than a roach motel." She turned on the light near the door, then went back to the bed. As she sat on the edge, she searched the worn carpet for her underwear among the strewn clothes.

She felt Bo's fingers stroke her butt. "Come on back to bed."

"Bo!" Finding her underwear, she bent to snag it, then whirled around to glare at him. "It's minutes to ten."

"Yeah. You know I love to get my groove on in the morning."

She shimmied into her panties. "I have to go see the lawyer, remember?"

"Oh. Well, maybe a quickie?"

Ginger rolled her eyes. She and Bo had already made love four times, which was why she was late getting up this morning, even if she was extremely satisfied. "You want this plan to work, don't you?"

"It is working. That punk's out of your life."

Ginger slipped her form-fitting lycra top over her head. She didn't bother with her bra. Her cosmetically enhanced breasts didn't need a bra, anyway. Besides, she had a lot more leverage with men when she wasn't wearing one, and given how late she was, she had a feeling she would need leverage when she met with the lawyer.

Ginger forced her voluptuous body into her low-rider jeans. "Tony may be out of my life, but you're forgetting the biggest issue. The money. I don't have it yet." She enunciated the last five words. "This game ain't over till it's over, and I'm supposed to be meeting with my lawyer in—" She groaned as she glanced at the clock. "Three minutes."

Bo sat up. "All right. Gimme a minute."

She may have been late, but Ginger couldn't help pausing to gape at Bo. "Whoa—wait a minute. You're not coming with me."

"I figured I'd come along for the ride."

"No! What would people say if they saw the despondent

wife of Anthony Beals leaving some run-down motel room with another guy?"

It was a rhetorical question, and Bo didn't respond. Instead he frowned and reached for the remote. He flicked the television on and began whizzing through channels. Ginger headed across the room to the small counter and tiny sink outside the bathroom.

She turned on the faucet and splashed lukewarm water over her face. Towel-drying her face, she headed back toward Bo. She was tossing the towel on the bed when she caught a glimpse of her husband's face on the television.

"Bo, stop. Go back."

Bo looked up at her with confusion.

"The TV." She waved a hand frantically. "Go back."

Bo began flicking backward, but too quickly.

"Not so fast, Bo."

He stopped on a commercial for Zack Mulroney, some hack of a lawyer speaking about personal injury lawsuits. "This guy?" Bo asked, a confused expression on his face.

"No, not that. Go back again. There!"

It *was* Anthony. His picture was transposed on the screen behind some blond anchorwoman's head.

". . . last night. Apparently, Anthony Beals had a bone to pick with the infamous sex therapist and author of the popular new book, *The Big O*."

As a clip from the *Tonight Show* ran, Ginger watched the screen, her smile growing wider.

"Oh, this is good," she said. She erupted in a fit of laughter at Jay's line about the *Jerry Springer* show. "This is *perfect*."

"With this latest fiasco, people can't help but speculate if Anthony Beals will be joining the ranks of other Athletes Behaving Badly."

The camera moved to a male newscaster, and he started talking about a high-speed chase on Interstate 5.

Ginger jumped onto Bo's lap and planted kisses all over his face. "Ooh, baby. Do you believe it? I can't believe it. What a stroke of *luck*! And thank God, I now have a reason for being late. I can say I caught the news and wanted to know what was going on with my husband. How I was distressed by his behavior."

"Cool. So we can have a quickie?" Bo cupped one of her breasts.

Ginger climbed off Bo's lap. She ignored the question. "Tony's proving to the world that he's an ass. Any judge will have to rule in my favor."

She snatched up her purse and hustled to the door. Bo called out to her, "Hey, babe. Where's my kiss?"

"Sorry." Spinning around, she rushed back to Bo. She gave him a soft kiss on the lips.

"I hate when you run off like this."

The tenderness in Bo's voice got to her. She loved this man. They'd spent too much time apart already.

All the more reason to head to her lawyer and get this situation resolved once and for all.

Ginger stroked Bo's hard abdomen, an abdomen she had first come to appreciate in the backseat of his '83 Cadillac during her senior year in high school. They had been through so much together.

"I hate running out on you, too. But I'm doing this for us. The sooner this is all over, the sooner we can get together again."

"Am I still your boo?" Bo asked.

"You'll always be my boo." She gave him another kiss, a deeper one.

"When will I see you?" he asked as they pulled apart.

"When it's safe."

"Tonight?" His voice held a hopeful note.

"I don't know. I'll call you as soon as I can. I at least have to make an appearance at the house so those nosy neighbors don't get suspicious."

" 'Kay, babe." But Bo didn't sound all right.

"Don't worry, Boo. It'll all be fine. More than fine. Just remember why we started this. Keep your eyes on the prize."

Bo swatted her ass as she got off his lap. A tingling sensation spread through her. You'd think with the amount of times they'd had sex over the years, she wouldn't feel any sparks when he touched her. But she did. She always did. Which was why, even though she had been with other guys, she knew that Bo Baxter would always be the One.

He had stood by her through more than one money-making scheme, including the big disaster, which had led to her marrying Anthony Beals. Meeting Anthony Beals had been a stroke of luck; marrying him, an act of pure genius. Bo hadn't been happy about it, but she had convinced him that Anthony was their meal ticket.

"I love you," Bo said.

"I love you, too," Ginger replied. Then she slipped out the hotel door and closed it behind her.

Sliding on her sunglasses, she glanced in all directions to make sure no one was around before heading toward her late model Mercedes. She was so happy, she almost wanted to scream out loud. Lord, but Tony was an idiot. She couldn't have picked a better target. By the end of the day, she would be well on her way to ensuring that she and Bo would never have to go back to the ghetto. From here on in it would be Easy Street. And she damn well deserved it.

The only cloud in her silver lining was that she'd have to pay off that slimy loan shark, Pavel.

She told herself not to think about that as she opened her car door. Thinking about Pavel only made her remember the one time she had strayed from Bo, and how things had gone so horribly wrong.

But how could she not think about it? Freddie Monahue was the reason for the current mess she was in. He had promised her happily-ever-after with tons of dollar signs. But the man had been a sweet-talking con artist, and she was still paying the price for her stupidity.

Ginger sighed as she started her Mercedes, thinking of how gullible she had been. Freddie had convinced her she would become a multimillionaire with an investment in a dot-com company. It had seemed too good to be true, and wouldn't you know it—it was?

As she started out of the parking lot, she reminded herself that it would all be okay now. She was about to make things right again. She had to—her very life depended on it.

Because she and Bo owed Pavel half a million dollars, and he wanted his money in the worst possible way. She'd kept him at bay with sex over the past year, but not even that was working anymore. He was getting impatient, which was not a good thing.

Thank God this would all be over soon.

Ginger rubbed her eyes with the heel of her hand as she drove, hoping to make them good and red. She needed to look like a basket case when she got to her lawyer's office. She was the distraught wife, distraught over her husband's infidelity, and she simply wanted to move on. If there was any talk of reconciliation, she'd bawl her head off—whatever it took to be convincing in her grief.

One way or another, she would make this work for her. She would get her divorce from Anthony on the grounds of adultery. And with that declaration would come five million smackeroos.

The ticket to solving all the problems in her life.

Six

"I slept with him." Liz Stewart—blond, big-busted, and beautiful—spoke with unmistakable remorse. She was Hollywood's newest obsession, a sexy "girl next door" type who was fast making a huge name for herself, practically overnight.

"And how do you feel about that?" Lecia asked.

"I feel awful." She covered her face in shame. "Absolutely awful. I mean, I *knew* he was married, and *I'm* married. I told myself to ignore his flirtation. 'Whatever you do, don't sleep with him,' I told myself. But suddenly I was in his trailer going over the script, and the next thing I know, I was undoing his pants. . . ."

Lecia didn't speak. She observed Liz, trying to read her true emotions.

Liz sniffled. "Now he won't even talk to me. The whole cast is looking at me suspiciously. I'm sure they know, and they think I'm a dirty slut who seduced a world-famous director. Before I know it, rumors will be flying that I slept my way to the top. Which is absolutely *not* true. Oh, God. What have I done?"

Liz seemed truly remorseful. But then, she always did. In the two months that Lecia had been seeing her, Liz had had seven affairs.

"So you're concerned about your role on this film?" Lecia asked. "Your reputation."

"No," she answered quickly. Then, "Well, yes, but that's not the most important thing. The worst part is that I've betrayed my husband once again. And every time I cheat on Rod, I feel like I lose a part of myself."

"The last time you were here, we talked about the triggers for this behavior," Lecia said calmly. As a therapist, it was her job to remain impartial, no matter what her patients told her. "You said you were going to work on recognizing the triggers so you could avoid behavior you considered unhealthy."

"I know. And I shouldn't have gone back to Hunter's trailer when he said he wanted to go over my lines, because there was something about the way he said it. I *knew* it was trouble. But I went anyway. I needed . . ."

"What?" Lecia asked when Liz paused. "What did you need?"

"The thrill, I guess. This stupid quest of mine to achieve orgasm is always getting me into trouble."

Lecia jotted down Liz's comment. "And did you achieve orgasm?"

"Man, did I ever," Liz replied, her voice brimming with what sounded like pride. Then it cracked. "But then I felt like a dirty whore. Which I'm not. I'm just a woman with some problems, you know? Everyone's got problems."

"Was this time any different than the other times? Once you went home, I mean?" Liz had always been intimate with her husband after having an affair.

"No. When I went home, I told Rod that I'd had another episode. We took a shower together, and then we had sex."

Lecia didn't know whether Rod was a rare, supportive husband or a spineless fool. Liz had admittedly cheated on him at least ten times in their fourteen-month marriage.

"And?"

"And I couldn't come with him." She started to softly sob. "I love my husband. Why is this happening to me?"

"One of the things I've noticed, Liz, is that you almost use your affairs as foreplay. You like the excitement of being with someone new, perhaps even the risk factor is a turn on. But you always go home and make love to your husband."

"Yes."

"Do you want your marriage to work?"

"Of course I do. I can't stand hurting my husband this way."

"The first step in changing negative behavior is to acknowledge that behavior."

"I know. That's why I'm here."

"Obviously, sex outside of your marriage is not good behavior for many reasons, not the least of which is the risk factor of picking up diseases. But each time you have sex with another man, you're betraying the intimacy of your own marriage. Now, if this is some kind of kinky sex game you and your husband play, that's one thing."

"It isn't."

"What is it that you want?"

"Hot, mind-blowing sex with my husband."

"And why do you think you're not having that? Is your husband willing?"

"Oh, yes."

"And you're willing?"

"I *want* to be willing."

"Why do you say that? That you *want* to be willing?"

"I guess because I only seem to be turned on after I've cheated on him."

Lecia paused, made some more notes. "Some couples get into a pattern with their lovemaking, a routine so to speak. This can be a big turn off, because there's no spontaneity. But it's also a problem that can be easily resolved. Have you explored toys with Rod, different settings for lovemaking?"

"With my lovers, yes."

"Why not your husband?"

"I don't know." Liz looked away. "Rod did suggest trying sex toys, but once he did, it turned me off. I don't know why. When I suggested using sex toys to my lovers, I was always very turned on."

"*You* suggested them?"

"Always. With my lovers, I call the shots. I don't know . . . it's like I'm playing out a part in a movie, the role of a temptress. I feel . . . I feel powerful."

Bingo. So this *was* about control. Lecia had wondered as much, based on everything the woman had told her during their previous sessions.

But control was only the surface of the problem. Beneath it, Lecia was certain there were myriad issues dealing with sexual abuse. Liz had admitted to a scandalous number of sex partners during college, and the kind of dangerous behavior sexual abuse survivors were famous for. Once, Liz had left a party with three strange men and ended up in a hotel room having sex with all of them. According to her, it had been the quest for the mighty orgasm. Lecia knew otherwise.

But if Liz had been abused, she had either repressed the memories or deliberately not told her about them.

"Liz, I think we're really beginning to scratch the surface here. You're seeing me for a sex addiction, but the problem in all likelihood has nothing to do with sex. You need to find the reason behind the addiction." Lecia paused. "There's a new therapy I'd like to try, if you're willing."

"Of course."

"It's called EMDR—Eye Movement Desensitization and Reprocessing. It's a process that helps clarify what you may be thinking, feeling. But it is a slow process. In other words, there's no quick fix. But if you're serious about changing your behavior, you need to get to the bottom of what's behind it, and I think this can help."

"I understand."

Lecia would say nothing of her suspicions to Liz. If the woman had been sexually abused, she would have to discover that on her own, through treatment. There were stories of patients uncovering repressed memories through the guidance of therapists, only to realize later those memories had practically been implanted. Families had been torn apart by such painful accusations.

Lecia concentrated on what Liz was cognizant of. "In the meantime, you need to encourage open discussion with your husband about how your behavior has hurt him. This may serve as a sort of wake-up call for you. I'm hesitant to suggest couples counseling yet, because you need to work on yourself first."

Liz dabbed at her eyes with a tissue. "Okay."

Lecia glanced at the clock. She was a couple minutes over her time. She rose. "I'll see you next week, Liz. Same time."

"Thank you, Dr. Calhoun." She stood as well. "By the way, I saw you on the *Tonight Show*. I was like, you go girl."

"Thanks."

Lecia sensed that Liz wanted to say more, but she didn't. And Lecia was glad. She had spent half the night trying to put Anthony Beals out of her mind, and hadn't succeeded. She didn't need anyone else reminding her of him and what had been an incredibly embarrassing episode.

"Next week," Lecia said.

"Yes, next week."

Alexander Brody eyed Ginger with an uncompromising gaze. "Maybe you didn't hear me correctly. I said a *million* dollars."

Ginger met the look with one that was equally unwavering. "With all due respect, I heard you the first time. And I'm more than a bit confused. Why do you think I'd want to settle for a million?"

The lawyer exhaled his frustration. "Quite frankly, I think a million is a great deal."

"For my husband, yes, because *five* is what we agreed upon," Ginger pointed out. "It's written in black and white in a contract that's binding. If he cheats, I get five million dollars. He more than cheated on me. He humiliated me with some lowlife prostitute."

"The allegations of infidelity are unsubstantiated," the lawyer pointed out.

"He did it."

"No one can be sure." Brody shrugged. "Who knows—maybe things did happen as your husband said. Maybe he didn't know that woman was a prostitute."

Ginger snorted her contempt. "He knew. And he was willing to pay for sex because he's a pig. Who knows how many other women he's been with?"

"Accusations are one thing. But it's my job—the court's

job—to deal with fact. And without any proof of infidelity, your prenuptial agreement can't be enforced."

"But—"

"In light of that, I think the offer of one million dollars is very generous. You were only married for five months."

Ginger summoned her tears, hoping they would do the trick. "What's that supposed to mean?" she sobbed. "That he hasn't ripped my heart to shreds?"

The lawyer was unimpressed by her display of melodrama. "It means that you should consider yourself lucky. A million dollars will go a long way to helping you start your new life."

"It's not enough," she hissed through clenched teeth.

"Enough for what?"

Shit. She knew she shouldn't have spoken that aloud. But whose side was this lawyer on, anyway? What kind of high-powered lawyer to the stars was he? She snatched a tissue from the jerk's desk and dabbed at her eyes before speaking. "Enough for . . . for my emotional pain and suffering."

"It'll buy you a good shrink."

Ginger sucked in a shocked breath.

"Sorry." Brody held up a hand. "That was out of line. I've made my position clear. I think you should take the offer."

"It's not what we agreed upon."

"When you told me your husband had been unfaithful, I thought you had proof. That's why—"

"A judge may believe me."

"Sure. That's possible, however unlikely. Even still, it could take several months before it's decided in court."

Ginger clutched her Louis Vuitton Murakami handbag. Certainly this wouldn't be the last one she would ever buy. "But I . . . I've already become accustomed to a certain lifestyle. How can he get away with such a small offer?"

The lawyer sighed wearily. "Perhaps you want to reconsider your petition for divorce. After all, your husband seems willing to work things out."

"No. That's out of the question." It wasn't part of the plan. She needed a divorce from Anthony as soon as possible. "I, uh—I'll never be able to trust him again." She sniffled.

"Fine." Brody's smile was as fake as they came. "Shall I call your husband's lawyer and tell him we have a deal?"

What was wrong with this man? Was he deaf *and* unambitious? "Mr. Brody, I've already made myself clear. I hired you to make sure that I get what was promised to me in the prenuptial."

He pushed his chair back and stood. "Then I'm sorry, Mrs. Beals. I cannot in good faith continue to handle your case."

"You're kidding, right?"

"No, I'm not."

Ginger got to her feet. "B-But—what do you mean?"

"We have nothing else to discuss."

"You're—You can't do this. You can't just drop me. You work for me."

"With all due respect, Mrs. Beals, I quit. If you refuse to accept my advice, there's nothing more I can do. I won't waste your time or mine fighting for something that will never be. Another lawyer might, but I won't."

"I don't believe this." She needed Alexander Brody. He was one of the best divorce lawyers in Los Angeles.

As Brody rounded the desk he glanced at the ornate wall clock in a less than subtle hint that her time was up. "I'm more than happy to continue on as your attorney if you're willing to accept the deal your husband's lawyer has presented."

"I won't be bullied into selling myself short."

"Then I wish you luck. And good day."

Seven

After a hectic morning schedule, Lecia needed to get out of the office. She had been keeping a low profile, even from the rest of the staff, all because she felt embarrassed about last night's appearance on the *Tonight Show.* Instead of passing through the main office to head out, she had slipped out the back door and across the street for her lunch break. No one had noticed.

Now, sitting at a table in Nora's Café, she sipped a strong black coffee as she reviewed the latest issue of *The Journal of Sex Education and Therapy*, a publication of the American Association of Sex Educators, Counselors, and Therapists. She wore a large straw hat and sunglasses, a feeble attempt to disguise her appearance.

Most people at this shop knew who she was—regardless of any disguise—but thankfully, they left her alone. With her newfound fame, she not only enjoyed a semblance of normalcy in her life, she craved it. Part of normal was being able to sit down in a coffee shop and enjoy a coffee and a pastry. She was able to do that at Nora's Café.

Sensing someone behind her, she turned. Lawrence, the proprietor of the shop, smiled down at her.

"Afternoon, Lecia."

"Good afternoon," she replied. Lawrence couldn't see her and not say hi. He was like that with all his customers. He treated them like friends.

"I missed you this morning."

"I was running late. I didn't have time to come in for my morning coffee."

"At least you're here now. Like I always say, you bring a piece of the sunshine in with you."

Lecia simply smiled.

"What're you reading?"

"Oh . . ." Lecia closed the journal and covered it with her arm. She had been reading an enlightening article about new perspectives on sexual pain disorders, but she didn't feel like sharing that information. "Just boring medical stuff."

Lawrence held the coffeepot high. "Need a refill?"

She held a hand over the opening of her cup. "I've had two cups already, thanks."

Lawrence nodded, and should have been on his way, but he lingered over her, as Lecia knew he would. She glanced at her magazine, then back up at him.

He said, "I saw you on TV. Heard you on the radio, too."

"Did you, now?"

"Yeah, and you looked great. But then, you always do."

"You're too kind."

"I have to say, I was a bit surprised with what happened on the *Tonight Show.* That football player attacking you the way he did. But I thought you handled him real well."

"I tried," Lecia said simply. *As though she hadn't replayed every second of the confrontation over and over in her mind!* She wished she could put Anthony and the whole event behind her. But that wasn't easy to do, not with the television stations replaying the juicier clips.

The one thing she'd noticed while watching the show at her sister's place, was how adamant Anthony Beals had been. How *passionate*, her sister had said. He hadn't flinched when he told his version of what had happened the night he was alleged to have propositioned a prostitute, and, in fact, nothing about him made her think he was lying. She'd had preconceived ideas about him, all implanted by the media story and his wife's description of a man who enjoyed perverted sex, strip clubs, and hookers.

"Lecia?"

Her eyes flew upward. "Oh, sorry. I . . . What were you saying?"

"I said that I thought you put Depraved Dave in his place."

Lecia rolled her eyes, remembering the radio interview. "That was crazy. I won't ever be doing that show again."

"What about other interviews? Any more lined up?"

"Not in the near future, thank God." She'd had a crazy few weeks with the book's tenth printing and was ready for a rest.

"So you'll be around?" Lawrence asked, his tone unmistakably hopeful.

"Well . . . I'll be around, yes, but I'm busy with work." Lecia didn't want to give Lawrence any type of opening to ask her out. Because she knew he wanted to.

"Maybe," he began slowly, "maybe sometime we can get together outside of my shop. Perhaps dinner?"

Lecia knew all about Lawrence. At sixty-three, he had lost the love of his life, Nora, four years ago. He had once been a high-powered executive, but a heart attack at the age of fifty-one had made him realize that life was too short to spend working ninety hours a week, only to keel over before you'd had a chance to enjoy it. After that, he and his wife—the parents of four sons who lived in the Northeast, where they had been born and raised—decided to retire in the Golden State. After a year, they decided to open up a small coffee shop, a homey kind of place where the owners knew everyone by name. It had been an instant success.

Lecia had first started coming there when she began working in Los Angeles, just over two months ago. And she'd known that Lawrence had taken a liking to her since that time.

"I'm honestly so busy," she told him. "I really can't say yes."

"Oh. I see."

She didn't want to hurt the man's feelings. "But if my schedule changes, I'll let you know. I'd enjoy a friendly dinner."

Lawrence nodded his understanding. "I'll let you get back to whatever you're reading."

She tucked the magazine under her arm and stood. "Actually, I'd better be off. I wouldn't mind a fresh cup of coffee to go."

"Large?"

"Medium this time. I don't want to be too wired this afternoon."

"Sure thing."

Lecia followed Lawrence up to the front of the shop. She opened her wallet, but as he turned to hand her the to-go cup, he closed his hand over hers and pushed the wallet downward.

"You know all refills are free."

Lecia didn't bother to argue. She grinned, nodded her appreciation, then headed to the door.

* * *

On the short drive from Nora's Café back to the office, the sky had gone from bright and sunny to overcast, promising rain. Lecia took her umbrella out of the backseat of her Lexus before making her way to the clinic's back door.

The Merkowitz Wellness Center had started out as a three-room building, but had been expanded over the years to house offices for six therapists. Sharon Merkowitz, a psychotherapist, had built the clinic twenty years ago as a single therapist operation. Now, four full-time therapists worked out of the offices, while part-time therapists shared the other two.

Two and a half months ago Lecia had joined the Merkowitz Wellness Center as a part-time therapist. Sharon had been ecstatic to have her, as the previous sex therapist had left to start his own practice. Between all the counselors, they covered every aspect of mental health, sexual health, and spiritual well-being.

Located on Wilshire Boulevard, the center was close to many film studios and busier than it had ever been. Several film executives had appointments during the day. Lecia had acquired regular patients almost from the moment the word went out that she had joined the clinic.

Between the clinic, her own website clinic, and her writing, she barely had any time to herself.

There was no one in the hallway when Lecia entered the building, and she quickly slipped into her office. As she dumped her purse in her desk drawer, she decided it was time to stop hiding. If nothing else, she needed to retrieve her mail.

When she reached the front desk, Samantha, the receptionist, grinned up at her widely. Sam was an attractive, robust woman of African-American and Mexican descent. Now in her mid-forties, she had been with the clinic from the moment it first opened its doors.

"Dr. Calhoun," she said. "You're finally coming up for air."

"Yes." Lecia smiled sheepishly. "It's been a busy morning."

Sam gave her a knowing look, but Lecia didn't mind. If there was one thing she could rely on here, it was that the staff would respect her privacy.

"Saw you on the *Tonight Show,*" Sam said. "I thought you were great."

"Thanks." Lecia supposed there was no avoiding the topic, which was to be expected, especially in this office.

The phone rang. As Sam answered it, Lecia turned to her mail slot. There was a ton of it. She had no doubt much of it was fan mail. Even though she hadn't listed an address for mail in her book, people had tracked her down to this office.

"That was *another* woman interested in an appointment with you," Sam said, spinning around in her swivel chair to face her. "The phone's been ringing off the hook, by the way. More potential clients."

Lecia knew that if she took on many more clients, she would have to increase her time at the office from three days a week to five. Sharon had already told her she would be more than happy to have her on a full-time schedule, but she wasn't ready for that yet. Yes, therapy was unlike obstetrics, where she had been on call during the middle of the night. But she wanted more time to work on her second book. She hadn't decided yet what it would be, but she and her editor were tossing around the idea of a book based on actual clinical experience, something for which she would have to get permission from interested clients. She liked the idea, but wasn't sold on it. For the time being, she was still in *The Big O* mode, and more than happy to continue promoting that book.

"I've input all the messages in the computer, and I'll send you the attachment via e-mail."

"Thanks." Lecia had her phone set up to bump people directly to voice mail this morning, something she did when she was in the middle of a session. Sometimes, people called back to speak directly with the receptionist, feeling that was a better way to get through to her.

"Oh, and your publicist called twice already. Said she keeps getting bumped to your voice mail, and that she couldn't reach you on your cell phone."

"Oops. Must have forgotten to turn on the ringer." In reality, she had deliberately left it off. She wasn't interested in chatting with Angela right now. Knowing Angela, she was calling with an idea on how to maximize yesterday's negative publicity.

Lecia was mid-pivot when Sam spoke again. "And a reporter from the *L.A. Times* called. He'd like you to get back to him."

As if! The last thing Lecia needed was any more rope with which to strangle herself.

Eight

"Ginger didn't want to settle," Keith said.

Anthony gripped the receiver with all the strength in his fist. "Son of a bitch."

"I have no clue why," Keith went on. Anthony could envision the man shaking his head. "She can't possibly expect to get more than what we offered."

"Apparently she does." Anthony couldn't believe that his wife wanted to slug it out in court. Unless . . . "Maybe she doesn't want to end the marriage."

"Oh, she wants out. Her lawyer said that she explicitly stated she's not interested in any talk about reconciliation. She wants to move on with her life."

Why was Ginger doing this? "If she wants out of our marriage, I want her to tell me that face-to-face. She needs to talk to me. Can't you force a meeting?"

"Ginger said she doesn't want to see you. That there's nothing to discuss."

How could she totally dismiss him without even sitting down to talk about what had happened? Before they'd gotten married, she had always listened to what he had to say, even when he was discussing football plays she didn't understand. Whenever they had a disagreement, they talked things out at length. She was always patient and peaceful. So what had happened to the woman?

Ginger had explicitly told him she wanted to be married once, and had presented herself as the type never to bail on him. Hell, she had nursed a paraplegic mother from the time she was only fourteen, until her mother's death a couple years ago. A woman who would do that certainly wouldn't up and leave a guy based on one problem. Anthony didn't understand the change in her.

"Try again," he told Keith.

Keith sighed wearily. "Can I ask what you hope to accomplish?"

"I want to save my marriage."

"You know my—"

"I do, but I'm telling you to try again. My mama always said that anything worth having doesn't come easy."

"All right." Keith's tone sounded defeated. "I'll see what I can do."

"Maybe I should have shown him my boobs."

Bo stopped kissing Ginger's inner thigh and looked up at her. "What'd you just say?"

Damn her big mouth. She would have to do a better job of keeping her private thoughts private. "Nothin'. I didn't say nothin'."

Bo frowned. Clearly he didn't believe her. But he lowered his lips back to her leg again.

He rained gentle kisses along her skin, and Ginger wished she could let herself be seduced. But she was upset with the way things had gone today. She was back at square one, and she needed a new game plan.

Bo's lips moved higher. Ginger lay back, sighing softly. But seconds later she abruptly sat up. "What an asshole lawyer. I mean, who does he think he is, quitting on me?"

"Ah, hell." Bo rolled onto his back in frustration.

"Sorry, Boo." Ginger sat up and reached for his arm. "I just . . . I can't stop thinking. I've got a headache over this whole thing."

"Time was, I could help you get over a headache."

"Not this time. All the lawyers I've called can't see me for at least a couple weeks. I don't have that kind of time. *We* don't."

"Why don't you try that guy we've been seeing on all those commercials? Don't he say if your case is urgent, he'll see you right away?"

Ginger stopped moping to look Bo in the eye. "What guy?"

"You know. We seen him at least ten times tonight alone. Jeff or Bob. Something like that."

"You mean Zack Mulroney?"

"Yeah. That's the guy."

Ginger rolled her eyes. "He's an ambulance chaser."

"A what?"

"Doesn't he deal with personal injury?"

"I don't know." Bo shrugged as he sat up. "Seems to me he's the kind of guy who dabbles in a bit of everything. It wouldn't hurt to call."

Zack Mulroney. He was sleazy, that was obvious. Ambitious—certainly. He was . . .

Ginger leapt onto Bo, pinning him on the bed with her legs astride him. "Bo, you are the *smartest*!"

"Really?" He eyed her suspiciously.

"Really. You're right. That guy'll see dollar signs and do exactly what I need him to do. Boo, I love you so much."

Ginger smothered his mouth with a kiss. Suddenly, her headache was gone.

Anthony spent the next two days on edge. Waiting for word from his lawyer was driving him nuts. He had been keeping a low profile, fielding calls from reporters about the incident on the *Tonight Show.* The way these people were keeping after him, it was obvious they needed to get a life.

Low profile or not, he had gone to Cal State each day for a run and to throw the football. Kahari Brown, his best friend off the field and key receiver on the field, always went with him. But even Kahari had noticed his slump over the past two days.

"Dawg, maybe you need to rest your arm," he'd said after Anthony had nearly taken off a female jogger's head. Today, he had skipped the ball throwing and stuck to racing Kahari around the track.

Anthony was a runner—he had first toyed with the idea of a career in track before making the move to football—but Kahari had beat him by a country mile when Anthony tripped over his own feet and landed on a knee. His ego was hurt more than anything else, but he had been walking with a slight limp ever since.

He simply didn't feel like himself.

He was preoccupied with thoughts of Ginger, yes, but the moment when he'd stumbled over his feet, he'd actually been thinking about Dr. Lecia Calhoun. A dozen times he had contemplated making a few inquiries about where he could reach her. A dozen times he had decided against it.

Calling her would be a bad idea. In the clip they kept replaying from the *Tonight Show*, she looked afraid of him. Could she actually have believed he was going to hurt her? And if she did, who knew how she would react if she heard him on the other end of her line? Yet that was exactly why he wanted to reach out to her. Maybe it was a moot point, but he wanted her to know that she had no need to fear him. Not then, not ever.

Now, back at the hotel, he wondered what harm there would be to try and get through to Dr. Love. Freshly showered, he was sitting on the sofa, wearing a plush terry-cloth robe. He had his right leg extended and resting on the coffee table, a bag of ice plopped on his injured knee.

He glanced at the phone. All he had to do was pick it up and call Ben. His agent would be able to track the sex doctor down.

"Forget the doctor," he said aloud. "All you're trying to do is pass the time, waiting on Keith to call with some word about Ginger."

But he found himself reaching for the receiver. And before he knew it, he was dialing Ben's number.

Ben's voice mail came on. "Ben, it's T. I need you to do me a favor. Find out how I can get in touch with Dr. Love. A phone number to her office would be great, or even the office address. Get back to me."

Screw the right thing. He wanted to talk to Dr. Love, and soon.

Ginger blew her nose into the soggy tissue, then began sobbing loudly once again.

Zack Mulroney passed her another Kleenex. Ginger paused to look up at him through her tears. "Thank you," she said. "So, will you take my case?"

"Of course," Zack told her, gently patting her back.

Thank God for her acting experience, she thought. Though she had a feeling Zack wasn't as hard-nosed as her old lawyer and would have been willing to take her case with a lot less tears. There was something to be said for B-list lawyers. Or C-, or D-list. Whatever Zack was. Just like there was something to be said for B-list actors. They tried harder, were hungrier for that big break.

Thinking of B-list actors made her remember the message Sha-Shana Dane had left on her cell phone this morning. Lord, but wasn't Sha-Shana becoming a big thorn in her side? She would just have to keep putting her off—until she had the money in hand.

"So you think I won't have a problem collecting the five million?"

"Your pre-nup is explicit. If your husband cheats, you get five million dollars. He cheated."

"Finally, someone who understands."

"Of course I understand. I'm glad you chose to trust me with this case. Believe me, I'll give it the attention it deserves."

Of that, Ginger had no doubt. She was probably the most affluent wife Zack Mulroney had come across in his career. It didn't matter to her, as long as he could get the job done.

She sniffled, then said, "I won't have to go to court, will I? The other lawyer I spoke with said something to that effect. But I got the feeling he just wasn't as conscientious as you are, ya know? That he wanted to milk me for every last dime . . ."

"Well . . ."

"Oh, no."

Zack held up a hand. "Hear me out. I have every confidence it won't come to that. But there's a chance, if your husband refuses to negotiate, that yes, you could have to go to court to prove your allegation of infidelity."

"But his picture was plastered on every paper with that—that whore!"

"Calm down, Mrs. Beals. I said that was a worst-case scenario. If I get your husband to admit to his infidelity—"

"But he's denying it!" Ginger sobbed harder. This time, Zack handed her the entire Kleenex box.

"Where is this woman?"

"The prostitute, you mean?"

"Yes."

Ginger didn't answer right away. She dabbed at her eyes, her nose. "I don't know," she lied. She didn't want to bring Sha-Shana any further into this, but she would if she had to. Just like she'd go to court and cry a river if that would help.

Zack bit his bottom lip. "That's too bad."

"But I'm sure I can find her," Ginger quickly said. "Through the police, I mean. Or an investigator."

Zack lowered himself onto his haunches beside Ginger, who sat on the pleather chair opposite his desk. The fabric was a plastic leather imitation. "I think if this woman comes forward, we could present her to your husband's lawyer in a meeting. It would be a damn good argument for settling. At the very least, it would be in your husband's best interest to settle, unless he wants even more bad press."

"I would think so, yes. But he can be very stubborn. He's . . . spiteful. He doesn't want to see me get a penny. After everything I did for him."

"How long was the marriage?"

Ginger swallowed. She knew this was the sticking point. "Five months. But to me, it was like five years. I gave him everything I had."

Zack stood to his full height, which couldn't have been more than five feet seven inches tall. "Look, if he doesn't want to pay, we'll just play hardball. If we can find this woman, I'll make sure she talks to anyone who will listen." Zack shrugged, as if to say, What more could I do? "Depraved Dave will be only too happy to give her air time. And all the tabloids will eat this up. Your husband will be paying you just to make her shut up."

That's exactly what Ginger was counting on.

"Thank you, Zack. I could tell from the first moment I saw you that you were the kind of man who would understand."

As he sat behind his desk, his eyes suddenly narrowed on her. Ginger's heart slammed against her chest. "What?" she asked, alarmed.

"I don't know." He continued to scrutinize her. "You look familiar to me. Could we have met somewhere before?"

"I—I—" Ginger stammered. "I'm sure you've seen me on the news, in the papers. After this story broke—"

"Of course," Zack said. The answer satisfied him.

Ginger pulled her purse strap off the back of the chair. The way she saw it, the sooner she got out of there, the better.

"Not so fast," Zack said. He leaned forward in his pleather chair. "One more thing to discuss."

Ginger swallowed. "Oh?"

"My fee. Twenty-five percent."

"Twenty-five!"

"Ten thousand when you agree for me to represent you, the rest once the deal is worked out."

"But twenty-five percent—that's more than a million bucks!" And from the look of the wood-paneled walls and dollar store ornaments on his desk, it didn't look like Zack had ever seen that kind of money in his life.

"Fifteen, then," he quickly said. "But that's as low as I'll go. I have things to consider—like extra safety precautions. You say your husband has a violent temper. I don't want him coming after me."

She had already promised Sha-Shana fifty grand. Another fifteen was a huge chunk of her change.

But fifteen percent of five million was a helluva lot better than fifteen percent of nothing.

"All right," she told him. "But I pay you when I get paid. My money's tied up, so I can't afford the ten grand right now."

Zack frowned ever so slightly but finally said, "Okay."

"Hopefully this will be resolved sooner rather than later, and neither of us will have to wait on the money."

"Don't worry. You'll see the money very soon. I'm certain of that."

Nine

Hours later, Anthony had fielded calls from reporter after reporter, and was wary about answering his phone. But when it rang late in the afternoon, he snatched up the receiver nonetheless. "Yo."

"Anthony, hi. It's Keith Alabaster."

His lawyer. Thank God. Hopefully, he had some good news. "Hey, Keith. What's the word?"

"I have some news. Ginger's switched lawyers."

"What?"

"It's true. Her first one dropped her. He finally returned my call this morning to explain what's going on. He said he didn't feel Ginger was being reasonable regarding the settlement and he wasn't the lawyer for her."

"She no longer has legal representation?"

"No, she's got a new lawyer. I heard from him just minutes ago. You'll never believe who. That slimy character, Zack Mulroney."

"Wait a minute—that guy you see all over the TV?"

"That's the one."

"I thought he did personal injury."

"He's the kind of lawyer who bends to your specifications."

"Great. So what do you think this means?"

"That she knows she doesn't have a good case. She's pulling out all the stops."

"And?"

"Now we wait and see. Her new lawyer said he wants a meeting as soon as possible. Tomorrow's good for me, so we're going to get together and go over the case."

"Just you and him?"

"Yeah. I'll see if I can't convince him that Ginger'll lose everything if she decides to see this case taken to court."

"Whoa—what about setting up a meeting with all of us?"

"I'm going to suggest that once we've gone over the facts. We'll see what happens."

"All right. Thanks, man."

"Hang in there. We'll get this resolved one way or another."

If the gods were on his side, Anthony thought, Ginger would see reason. And by this time next week he would be moving back into his house, getting his life back on track with the woman who had sworn to love him for better or for worse.

So much for wishful thinking.

It was clear that Ginger wasn't about to see reason any time soon, and even more clear that his life as he had known it would not soon return to normal.

"Sorry to be the bearer of bad news, bro."

Anthony stared up at Kahari with a dumbfounded expression. "What is her game? I mean, she won't talk to me, wants me to pay her five million, and now she goes and does this?"

Anthony's gaze went to the tabloid, the *Daily Blab*. Though as far as he was concerned, it should have been called the

"Daily Rag," considering the pathetic lengths their writers went to verify any truth to their alleged stories.

Ginger's picture took up the bottom right of the front cover, below the grainy picture of an alien from another of the rag's Pulitzer prize-winning stories. His wife's eyes were red and swollen in a photo that did her beauty no justice. The caption below read, HORNY BALL PLAYER'S WIFE LIVES IN CONSTANT FEAR.

Anthony wanted to rip the paper to shreds, but that wouldn't give him any true satisfaction. He needed to see the extent of this paper's story, so, with reluctance, he flipped it to page five.

"Wow. A whole full color page." There were pictures of him and Ginger during happier times, then a picture of him and the prostitute. In the court of public opinion, pictures like this would lead to him being stoned in the town square.

> Ginger Beals, wife of famed football star Anthony Beals, said today that she lives in fear of her husband's temper. Since their very public breakup, Ginger claims that Anthony has made several attempts to get in touch with her, despite a restraining order.

Anthony tossed the paper onto the lounge chair beside him. He couldn't stomach any more of this.

He had gone to Kahari's place to work on some details of the youth center the two planned to open, but now he was in no mood for that. God only knew if he ever would be, with this nightmarish Ginger situation hanging over his head. If she succeeded in getting five million out of him, he would be short that much for the center.

"Maybe she's on drugs," Anthony suggested lamely. As far as he knew, Ginger didn't touch the stuff. He'd never even seen her drink more than one glass of wine. But what did he really know about her?

"Stranger things have happened."

"Not to me." For the life of him, Anthony couldn't understand what was wrong with his wife. Afraid of him? Since when? Why the hell would she tell the media this? Unless she was trying to smear him in the papers in hopes that he would pay her the money she wanted.

Never in a million years would he have expected this to be his fate, not after promising before God, family, and friends that he would love Ginger forever. So what if they hadn't had the explosive kind of love most people had when they married? His parents had had that kind of love. Then his father went on to have it with five more wives.

He'd had it once, too, in college. His relationship with Claudette had ended in disaster. Anthony had learned from watching his parents that the explosive kind of love was overrated. Now he knew that a person needed someone with whom they were compatible, someone who would respect them. A person you could talk to and never feel angry enough to argue with. Arguments led to places he didn't want to go.

Which is exactly what pissed him off about what Ginger had told this rag. She knew how much he detested fighting, that his own father had beaten a couple of his wives and landed in jail.

Was that what worried her? That he was more like his father than he knew?

Truth be told, it was his secret fear. Which is why he knew that a stable, friendship-based marriage was the way to go for him.

"Has LaTonya heard from Ginger?" Anthony asked Kahari.

LaTonya was Kahari's sister. She and Ginger weren't close friends, but they talked at least once a week.

Kahari shook his head. "If she has, she hasn't told me. Which I'm sure she would."

"Will you ask her?"

"Sure."

"Let me know. Better yet, tell LaTonya that if she speaks to Ginger, to tell her to call me. Or maybe I ought to give LaTonya a list of questions to ask her, 'cause I sure as hell can't figure the woman out." Anthony watched Kahari take a long pull off his beer. "And don't say 'I told you so.' "

"Hey." Kahari held up both hands. "I didn't say a thing."

"But you were thinking it."

"All I'm thinking is that I'd like to know what Ginger's game is, too."

Anthony bit down on his bottom lip as he stared out at the waterfall structure in Kahari's pool. He missed his home. Not being able to return was a son of a bitch.

"Maybe what I should be doing is talking to Dr. Love. She talked to Ginger. She's probably the best one to give me an idea of where my wife's head is at."

"I thought they only spoke in passing."

"Passing or not, she had to have formed an opinion of Ginger."

Kahari shrugged. "What are you gonna do—call her up?"

Anthony stood, an idea taking shape in his mind. "I'm gonna use your computer."

He went inside, and Kahari followed him. He didn't break stride until he reached the large office adjacent to the living room.

"What are you doing?" Kahari asked.

"Searching the web for Dr. Love. I think she said something to Jay Leno about having an online clinic."

Kahari watched silently as Anthony punched in his search options. "Bingo," Anthony said. "This is her site."

On the homepage of Dr. Lecia Calhoun's site, there was a color picture of her. She wore a smart business suit, a very different look than the sexy one she'd sported on the *Tonight Show.* He liked the sexier look, but not for obvious reasons. This business suit made her seem more uptight. More reserved. Not at all the woman full of spunk whom he had dealt with on national television.

"Let me see." Anthony scrolled down the page. "Contact info. Okay, good." He clicked on an e-mail icon. The e-mail address popped up, and he jotted it down on a notepad beside the mouse. Then he logged onto his personal e-mail account, to send her a message.

He was about to write something when he looked over his shoulder at Kahari. "Bro, do you need to hang all over me?"

Kahari eyed him skeptically. "Oh, I see. You want to write Dr. Love for some personal advice."

"I just want a moment to think in peace. You understand."

Kahari smirked. "Yeah, I know. It's the same way you are when you're thinking about your plays. I'll be outside. Holla when you're ready."

Anthony nodded his appreciation. Then he thought about exactly what he would write to Dr. Love.

Ten

Lecia's heart rammed against her chest when she read the simple e-mail from Anthony Beals. Her first instinct was to reach for the delete key. Her finger hovered over the key, but she couldn't bring herself to press it.

Instead, she found herself rereading the message.

Dr. Love, this is Anthony Beals. Please don't delete this e-mail. I'm sorry about what happened on the *Tonight Show*. It seems that you and the rest of the world think I'm some perverted monster, but believe me, I'm not. I'm really hoping that you'll agree to meet me for a coffee so I can offer you an apology in person.

Anthony

Instead of her heart rate calming, it continued to accelerate and was now beating overtime.

It was the shock, of course. The last thing she had expected to receive was an e-mail from Anthony Beals, much less one in which he offered an apology.

Oh, damn. What to do? It was a surprise that she was even

contemplating the situation. Her brain told her that talking to Anthony Beals was not advisable. Yet the earnestness with which he'd written had touched her.

She pulled her hand back, deciding to leave the message in her inbox. She would sit on it and decide the best thing to do later.

Damn it all to hell.

There was no point in cursing his bad luck any longer. He had done plenty of that and it hadn't changed a thing. At this point, the situation was laughable.

In a twisted, not really funny sense, of course.

He supposed he had gotten what he asked for. He'd begged Keith to set up a meeting with Ginger, despite his lawyer's better judgment, and Ginger had finally agreed. But it had been a disaster.

He could still hear Ginger's outrageous sobs as she and her scam artist lawyer left Keith's office. To anyone within hearing distance, the woman seemed terrified of him. He was thankful that at least there were no media people hanging around, although he wouldn't bet his life on that.

"We tried," Keith had said once Ginger was gone. "Now will you let me handle this my way?"

"Sure," Anthony replied, his voice void of emotion. He was still reeling from the fact that Ginger had actually cowered as she sat across the table from him, as if she expected him to lunge over it and give her a good ass-whooping.

Either she really believed that—though he could see no reason for her to think he would ever lay a finger on her—or she was acting for Keith's benefit. If his own lawyer believed him capable of violence, that rationale went, then maybe Keith would encourage him to give her what she wanted.

That was Anthony's best guess to explain her bizarre behavior.

What he needed to do was find a way to talk to her alone, without an audience. Although after today's disastrous meeting, he wouldn't be surprised if she didn't want to speak to him again.

There was no way he could call her up without her saying he was harassing her. And he certainly couldn't go to her door. *His* door.

Anthony laughed out loud as he slammed a hand on the steering wheel of his Navigator.

"Shit," he mumbled. Then he started the engine. He'd be damned if he was going to be coerced into giving Ginger five million dollars, even just to shut her up.

He needed help. Someone who could talk to his wife on his behalf.

Someone like . . . Dr. Love.

His spirits lifted. He'd already e-mailed her to apologize. Now he thought about what she might say to Ginger, who was into all those therapy gurus, like Dr. Phil and Dr. Love. No doubt that was why Ginger had spoken to Dr. Love in the first place. Surely if Dr. Love attempted to talk to her, she would listen.

And as far as he was concerned, the good doctor owed him. She was the one who had put the final nail in the coffin of his marriage. It was only fair that she extract it.

Oh, yeah. This was a beauty of a plan. If Dr. Love told Ginger that she should give her husband a second chance, Ginger would seriously consider the doctor's advice.

Dr. Love still hadn't replied to the e-mail he'd sent last week. He wouldn't bother trying to reach her that way again. And she could easily avoid his phone call.

No, he had to see her in person. And thanks to Ben, he knew exactly where to find her.

It was time for Plan B.

Perhaps Plan B could have waited a few days, but when Kahari's phone call woke him up bright and early the next morning, he knew he didn't have the luxury of time. "Yo, T," Kahari said. "Turn on the radio."

"What?" Anthony asked, barely able to figure out if he was dreaming or not.

"Ginger's on Depraved Dave's show, and dawg, it ain't pretty."

That got his attention. Anthony threw off the covers and swung his legs off the bed. "What station is it?"

"It's 90.5, WXJY."

"I'll call you back."

Anthony replaced the receiver and rushed out of the bedroom and to the living room, where he turned on the stereo and searched for the station.

". . . did you expect?" That was Depraved Dave's voice. "I mean, sports figures—I don't know one of them that's ever faithful. Not even with a woman as hot as you."

"He always told me he was different, and I believed him."

"And I've got some swampland in Florida for sale. Wanna buy it?"

"I know now how stupid I was," Ginger said. She sounded defensive. "You live and you learn."

"So you've gotten over him. You're moving on."

"Trying, yes."

"Are you seeing someone else?"

"No. I'm still grieving the loss of my marriage."

Grieving, my ass, Anthony thought.

"The problem is," Ginger went on, "Anthony has been completely irrational. I guess he didn't expect me to kick him out. Now he says he wants to work things out. . . ."

"But?"

"But I think he's lost his mind. He's harassing me. Calling and leaving horrible messages. He says that if he can't have me, no one can."

"He said that?"

"Well, not in so many words . . ."

"Liar!" Anthony shouted.

"And have you gone to the police?" Depraved Dave asked.

"I've got a restraining order, yes."

"Son of a—" Dave stopped short. "If there's one thing I disagree with," he began emphatically, "it's violence against women. If your wife wants out of the marriage, let her go."

"That's all I want," Ginger said. "To be able to get my divorce, and what I'm due based on our prenuptial."

If he could, Anthony didn't know whether he'd have Ginger committed to an asylum or smack her senseless. He knew the latter would give him a hell of a lot more satisfaction—if he were the type to ever touch a woman. But he never would, no matter how far a woman pushed him.

"Ginger, I thank you for taking time out to talk with us today."

"I thank you for having me."

"And, buddy—yeah, I'm talking to you, Mr. MVP, Mr. Raiders star—let this beautiful woman go. You messed up. Deal with it."

"Screw you," Anthony said to the radio. Then he shut it off.

Seconds later he was in the bedroom reaching for his jeans. He had originally figured Plan B would wait a few days, but now he knew it couldn't.

If he was going to get through to Ginger, he had to act now.

And Lord only knew he needed to get through to Ginger. It would be one thing if he had cheated on her, or had even tried to cheat on her. But he hadn't, yet he was being crucified in the media.

He needed this remedied. Fast. The sooner he and Ginger publicly reconciled, the sooner he would regain credibility and get on with his life.

Fully dressed, an Oakland Raiders cap on his head, he headed downstairs. His walk was purposeful, the kind that told people not to get in his way.

It was time to pay a visit to the notorious Dr. Love.

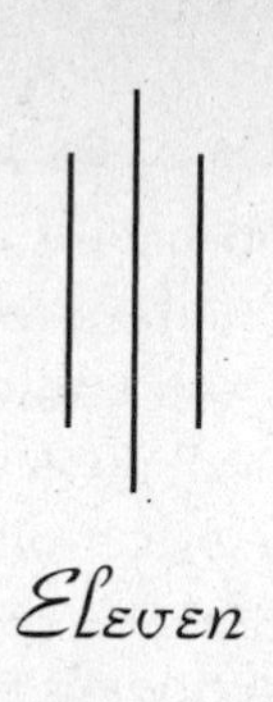

Eleven

Sha-Shana Dane had done a lot of performances in her life, most of which would make her mother roll over in her grave, but at least she'd been paid for those gigs. Now, she was beginning to wonder if she'd get paid for her best performance yet.

"You better answer the phone, Ginger," she said as she held her cell phone to her ear. She had called twice already and hung up both times when the voice mail picked up. But she wouldn't stop calling until Ginger answered.

On the third ring, Ginger answered. "Hello?"

"Finally, girl."

"Mia?"

"*No*. It's Sha-Shana."

"Oh. Sha-Shana, can you call me later?"

"Don't tell me to call you later. You've put me off every time I've called you. And you damn well know we need to talk."

"I know. I'm not avoiding you, I swear. Just trying to work things out on my end."

"I heard you on Depraved Dave's show."

"It's been a busy morning. Now I have to call my lawyer."

"You and your husband have split, just like you wanted. That was the deal. Now you need to pay me."

"Come on, Sha-Shana. You know that's what I'm trying to do. That's why I've got to call my lawyer."

"If you're giving me the brush-off—"

"The brush-off?"

Ginger said it as though it wasn't even an option. But Sha-Shana knew better. The woman lied like it was a sport.

"You know I wouldn't do you like that," Ginger continued. "All of this is taking a bit longer than I thought it would. Look, are you at home?"

Sha-Shana made a fist. She breathed in slowly to curb her anger. "No."

"Then I'll call your cell."

"I'll give you an hour. Otherwise, I'm sure your husband would be very interested in hearing what I have to say."

"You'll hear from me."

"I'd better."

Anthony wore the baseball cap far over his forehead as he sat behind the wheel of his Navigator. He had been parked outside of the Merkowitz Wellness Center for a good hour and fifteen minutes. The windows were tinted, so he wasn't concerned about being spotted.

He was getting restless, and his right leg was starting to fall asleep, but he was determined to see the doctor today. The question was, how should he approach her? Go into the office and demand to see her? Or wait, as he was doing, for her to make an appearance?

He thrummed his fingers against the steering wheel as he contemplated what to do. After several minutes, he ruled out going into the office. The last thing he needed was another confrontation, or the appearance of one. He'd had enough negative media attention to last a lifetime.

He gripped the steering wheel and groaned. He'd been waiting forever, but he'd just have to be patient. Hopefully, Dr. Love would make an appearance soon.

Lecia was striding down the street in front of the clinic when she felt the strong hand on her arm.

As her mouth fell open in shock, she heard, "Come this way." Before her brain could work fast enough for her to form a scream or a protest, she was at the door to a Lincoln Navigator. Gold in color, it looked to be top of the line.

"Get in."

She had visions of being whisked into a car and never heard from again. Her brain kicked into action. "I know kung fu."

"So do I." He reached for the door. "Get in."

Lecia knew that voice. As she looked up at her kidnapper, her eyes narrowed. "Anthony?"

Even though he was wearing dark glasses, she could see the smile in his eyes. "Yeah."

"Oh my God." Lecia's head whipped around in all directions. With his brawny body blocking her escape, she wasn't sure how she'd get away.

"For God's sake, stop looking around for help like you're scared to death I'm going to hurt you. I'm here to take you for coffee, like I promised in the e-mail I sent you."

"I didn't say yes to your offer."

"But you didn't say no. I just want half an hour of your time."

"I have nothing to say to you."

"That's fine. Because I plan on doing the talking."

"Don't do this."

"What? Take you out for coffee?"

"Don't . . . don't stalk me."

"Stalk?" Anthony balked. "Oh, you probably heard my wife on Depraved Dave's show. Actually, that's why I want to talk to you."

"I don't want to talk to you."

"Name your price. I'll pay for your time."

"I don't want your money."

"Come on. Let me buy you a coffee." When Lecia didn't move, Anthony leaned closer and said, "You have a cell phone, right?"

Lecia felt an unexpected shiver of excitement as his warm breath fanned her ear. You'd think he'd suggested using the phone as a sex toy. "Yes."

"Good. So if you feel scared you can call the cops."

She merely stared at him.

"I'm trying to prove to you that I'm not planning to hurt you. I just want you to hear me out. Half an hour, tops. Then you can go on your merry way."

Her brain screamed *No!* but her mouth apparently had a mind of its own. Because she found herself saying, "Fine. Half an hour. But that's it."

Lecia watched the scenery change from office buildings to the trendy shops of Beverly Hills with a sinking sense of dread. Anthony wasn't stopping. She had the feeling the word "sucker" was tattooed on her forehead.

But she didn't say anything, not even when Anthony turned from Santa Monica Boulevard onto Beverly Drive. Finally, when he crossed Sunset continuing to Benedict Canyon Drive, she couldn't keep quiet a moment longer. "Um," she began as they passed house after house. "You said we were going to have coffee."

"We are."

"You already passed about half a dozen Starbucks." Lecia craned her neck over her shoulder as they drove past large trees and wide gates that no doubt led to enormous houses. "And why do I have the feeling we won't be finding any in this neighborhood?"

"I'm taking you to a very special place."

"Oh." More dread.

"I hope you like Jamaican Blue Mountain coffee."

"Where are we going to have it? Jamaica?"

Anthony actually chuckled, a soft, warm sound. "Naw. I just figured it was best that we have some privacy. Especially with what's been going on with me in the media recently. I don't want you to feel uncomfortable."

"Uncomfortable? You're taking me to God only knows where and you think that'll make me feel comfortable?" She dug her phone out of her purse.

"Whoa, whoa, whoa. Put that away."

"Give me one good reason why I should." She recognized where they were heading: Beverly Park, an exclusive Beverly Hills neighborhood where some of the richest people lived.

"Geez, if you want Starbucks that badly—"

"You think this is funny?"

"No."

"I have to get back to the office."

"You will. How much time do you have?"

"Half an hour." Though the truth was, she had planned on

taking a two-hour lunch to catch up on reading. "Which leaves you about ten minutes."

"Okay—when do you absolutely have to be back?"

"This is insane."

"You might want to stay a while."

Lecia sighed her frustration. "About another hour and a half," she grudgingly admitted. "But I'd planned on eating something."

"No problem."

Anthony pulled up to the security gate leading to the community of Beverly Park. Lecia tuned him out as he spoke to the guard.

This truly *was* insane, even if she was the teeniest bit intrigued to see where the great Anthony Beals lived. Assuming he was taking her to his house.

Don't start liking this, she told herself. *Who cares how much money he's got?* He was too sexy for his own good, and the sooner she got this over with, the sooner she'd get back to her office and away from him.

"Are we cool?" Anthony asked as he drove through the gate.

"As a cucumber." Lecia dropped her phone back into her purse. "But the clock's ticking. I have a patient at two-fifteen who desperately needs me. She has a particular . . . Let's just say it's important that I'm back for that appointment."

Anthony raised a curious eyebrow but didn't say anything. He drove a short while longer, until he came to a private residence outlined by shrubs and a salmon-colored brick wall. He stuck his hand through the open window and pressed a card against a sensor box. The gates slowly pulled apart.

"Oh my," Lecia couldn't help saying as the impressive house came into view. She knew a little about architecture, and this had an Old World design. It was probably an Italian-style villa, or Portuguese.

"Can I ask where we are?" Lecia asked.

"Kahari Brown's."

Lecia gave him a dumbfounded look. "Am I supposed to know him?"

"You don't know Kahari Brown? Plays wide receiver."

"Nope."

"I thought you were a California girl."

"Florida girl. Miami. Well, I grew up in Fort Lauderdale."

"Oooh, the Dolphins."

"Actually, I don't watch football. I had to watch it with my ex but never got into it. Sorry."

"Well, you'll like Kahari."

It struck Lecia that they were being entirely too casual for what, in effect, was a kidnapping. And if kidnapping was too strong a word, this was hardly a social call.

Even if she'd just been taken to Paradise.

They drove past a parkette, complete with large palm trees and an exquisite lawn, before pulling up to the front of the house. The paved driveway could easily hold thirty cars. Anthony parked beside a white Bentley, popped the locks, then opened his door to get out. Lecia was surprised to see him round the corner to her as she was climbing out of the Navigator. He offered her a hand, but she got down on her own and stepped to the side.

Anthony started to walk, and Lecia followed him. Her eyes swept over his broad back, clad in a form-fitting T-shirt. There was no doubt, Anthony Beals was one sexy man.

She wrenched her gaze away from him and took in the magnificent view of the house. Pale brown in color, it had at least a dozen archways. The arch above the door had to be a good fifty feet, behind which large windows from the second floor displayed fancy curtain swags. Her family had money, but she had never set foot on such an opulent estate.

"I don't want to gawk. Okay, I'm gawking. How big is this place? Fifteen thousand square feet?"

"Twenty."

Lecia's mouth fell open. She surveyed the ornate light fixtures outside the door while Anthony pressed the doorbell. The theme song from *Monday Night Football* sounded.

Of course, Lecia thought, rolling her eyes. Kahari Brown was probably the type of ball player into the bling bling—large gold chains, gaudy gold and diamond rings. How could he not be, with an estate this size?

The door opened. A man whose chest looked as big as a Mac truck greeted them both with a warm smile. He wore khaki shorts and a T-shirt, but no jewelry, except for one class-type ring.

"Yo, T."

Anthony stepped into the massive foyer. It rivaled some of the hotel foyers Lecia had seen. Twin staircases led to a large landing overlooking the lower level. The banister was most likely cherry wood, the steps and floor marble. A gigantic crystal chandelier hung above their heads. Lecia wouldn't have been surprised if the metal was platinum. Straight ahead, past the area beneath the landing, was what appeared to be a living room.

"'Sup, dawg," Anthony said.

The two men greeted each other with a chest-knocking hug.

"So this is Dr. Love." Kahari's eyes roamed lazily over her.

Lecia stopped gawking to face him. "That's me."

"Pleasure to meet you."

Kahari Brown seemed polite enough. Not at all like a cocky star athlete. "Thanks."

"Thanks for letting us come by," Anthony said. "We'll just head on to the kitchen." He turned to Lecia. "Unless you prefer to sit outside?"

"Wherever we'll get this done ASAP."

"You'll like the view outside."

Although this situation was hardly ideal, Lecia couldn't help looking around the massive house with wide-eyed wonder. It wasn't a house; it was a palace. The walls were stark white, but the furnishings were dark colors. She continued to gawk as she absentmindedly followed Anthony. This place was so big that two people could live here and never see each other.

The kitchen boasted a large metal fridge, black marble floors, black granite counters, and white cupboards.

Lecia supposed there was a first for everything, and seeing an actual café-style sitting area in the kitchen complete with leather sofas was a first for her. Surrounded with an alcove that had a coffeemaker, cappuccino machine, and bar, it was like this kitchen had its own Starbucks. The only thing missing was the menu display showing prices for calorie-ridden specialty coffees.

She would have been more than content to sit and have a coffee there—until she caught sight of the backyard. Wow—she had been kidnapped and taken to heaven. In immediate viewing range was a large pea-shaped pool with a cascading waterfall. Surrounded by lush foliage, Lecia couldn't help feeling that she had stepped out of L.A. and onto a Caribbean island. Several lounge chairs lined the pool's perimeter. In the distance behind the pool, she could see the hillside and other houses across the valley.

Clearly, the wide receiver liked to entertain.

Women?

"So, where will it be?"

Lecia spun around. Her heart slammed in her chest when she saw Anthony standing so near to her. He truly was one fine-looking brother. Tall—at least six feet two. Smooth, dark skin. Strong arms. And for the first time, she realized that a T-shirt could be sexy as hell—as long as it was on the right man.

Startled by the turn of her thoughts, she turned, hugging her torso. What was wrong with her? This was a man who had come unglued, to her detriment, on national TV.

"Dr. Love?"

"Please, call me Lecia." Dr. Love sounded silly on his lips.

"As long as you call me Tony. Or T."

"All right."

"So, would you rather sit inside or outside?"

"Outside's fine," she said.

"Coffee or coladas?" That was Kahari speaking from behind them. "And what theme do you want—Caribbean or Mediterranean?"

"I'll let the lady decide."

"Caribbean or Mediterranean?" Lecia looked at both Kahari and Anthony. "I don't get it."

"Music," Kahari explained.

"Oh."

"I like to call my backyard my home away from home." Kahari strolled to a wall between two floor-to-ceiling windows that showcased the impressive backyard. Pressing the heel of his hand on one section, the marble popped open. It was a secret compartment, and within it was a compact stereo. "With the touch of a button I can have whatever music I'd like in the backyard. So, what do you feel like?"

"Caribbean," Lecia told him, shrugging.

Moments later the upbeat sounds of instrumental reggae came to life. The sound was so crisp and clear, Lecia could easily picture a steel band outside playing on the deck.

"And could you grab a sandwich for Lecia?" Anthony asked. "She hasn't had any lunch."

"You don't have to—"

"It's no problem," Kahari told her. "Turkey okay?"

She did need to eat something, and she realized she probably wouldn't have time to go somewhere else for food. "Turkey's fine, thanks. Mustard, no mayo."

"Coming right up."

As Kahari headed toward the fridge, Anthony opened the sliding patio door and extended a hand, motioning for Lecia to pass him.

She paused briefly, then walked over the threshold and into the backyard. As she scanned the vast property, she realized the word "backyard" was hardly adequate. The pool was as large as some hotel pools, and besides the lounge chairs, there was a tiki bar and an area with at least five round tables and umbrellas. Behind that, a massive deck boasted two barbecues and a giant-size hot tub.

This *was* an entertainment complex. The only thing missing was the attractive bartender tossing bottles into the air and catching them before pouring shots of liquor into huge glasses.

Instead, Anthony made his way behind the bar. "I make a mean chocolate banana drink, which you can have with banana liqueur or without any alcohol. Or perhaps you would prefer a banana daiquiri?"

Just thirty minutes ago she had been planning on a large coffee with milk and sugar, and now she had a host of exotic drinks to choose from. This was entirely too surreal.

"I'd be happy with coffee."

"I can make a coffee smoothie."

"Whatever's got caffeine."

"Make yourself comfortable."

Lecia made her way to one of the tables with the straw umbrellas. No sooner had she sat than Kahari appeared. "Oh, my," Lecia said. "This is huge." The turkey sandwich was on thick whole wheat bread, bursting with lettuce and tomatoes. "You didn't have to go to this trouble."

"No trouble at all."

Maybe this place was the equivalent of the playboy mansion, but for women. Because here she had two men serving her.

A girl could get used to this, she thought, a wicked image of barely clad men hanging around the place making her chuckle to herself.

"Enjoy," Kahari said simply. Then he quietly walked away and back into the house, leaving Lecia alone outside with Anthony.

Her fantasy died as a warning bell sounded in her brain.

I can't be alone with this man.

As she watched Anthony pour the blended drink into a large, curvy glass, she pushed her chair back and stood.

This was bad. Very bad.

She had to get out of here.

Twelve

Anthony saw Lecia practically jump out of her chair, and wondered what the heck was going on. He stared at her until she met his eyes. Either some bug had spooked her, or . . . or she was planning on taking off. Damn, she couldn't do that before he talked to her.

"Going somewhere?" he asked nonchalantly.

"Um . . . uh, Kahari's leaving?" Lecia asked.

"Yeah." Anthony came around the bar holding the coffee smoothie and a vodka tonic. "He's giving us privacy."

At Lecia's alarmed look, Anthony added, "We're gonna talk, remember?"

"Is he married?"

"Kahari? Naw." Anthony paused. "Why—you interested?"

"No. No, of course not. I'm just . . . making conversation. Since I'm . . . here." She sat back down, looking glum.

Anthony could see that something had changed. She sounded on edge, but he decided not to ask her about it. He'd keep the conversation casual, and hopefully that would calm her. "Kahari was engaged, though," he told her as he placed her drink before her. "It didn't work out."

"Let me guess—he found greener pastures?"

"Damn, girl. What do you think—all men are commitment-phobic players? His ex was the one who left him."

Her nonchalant shrug made a blast of fury hit him in the face. He wanted to shake some sense into her, prove to her that not all men were dogs.

He wanted to kiss her.

No, no, no. He did *not* want to kiss her. Well, maybe he did—but only to make a point. The point that . . . that . . .

Screw the point. Instead, he reached for his own mixed drink and took a sip.

After a moment he said, "When you're worth as much as Kahari is, you have to be careful whom you date. And believe it or not, Kahari's looking for love. Not fling after fling with bimbo after bimbo."

"I guess I shouldn't ask, but I can't help it. How much did this place cost?"

"A little over twenty million."

Lecia mouthed the figure, stunned at Kahari's wealth. "Wow."

"With his Nike endorsement, he's worth over five times that much."

"Now I feel stupid for not knowing who he is."

"He's a decent guy. I knew him before he ever dreamed of owning anything like this."

"Oh?"

"We went to Notre Dame together, so it's cool we're playing together now. And I can tell you, no one deserves this success like Kahari does. He grew up in a really rough area of Fort Worth, and I'm glad he got a good break."

Lecia wondered what kind of fool woman would have left a

guy like Kahari, considering so many gold diggers would have been more than happy to sink their claws into him.

"How's the sandwich?"

"It's really good. You can have half of it." Lecia pushed the plate toward him, offering him the second half.

"Thanks."

Lecia slipped out of her light blazer, and her silk camisole strained against her breasts. The bite of turkey sandwich got caught in Anthony's throat. There was no doubt about it—the good doctor was hot. Her breasts were normal-sized, soft and feminine.

He was distracted by her mouth as she placed it around the straw and tasted the drink. This woman had some seriously sexy lips. He hadn't noticed them on the *Tonight Show* because he had been more focused on getting his point across. The point that he was angry with her for meddling in his marriage. But now he wasn't thinking about anger or anything that had to do with Ginger. How could he, when those lips looked so soft and sweet—

He stopped his ridiculous thoughts abruptly and took another sip of his vodka and tonic. "You like the drink?" he asked her.

"Yes," she replied coolly. "It's delicious."

She said that with all the enthusiasm of a woman about to be beheaded. Anthony said, "Look, I know this is weird for you. I understand why you're wary."

"You said you wanted to talk."

"I do. And the first thing I want to do is offer you an apology about that night on Leno's show. I lost my cool, and I shouldn't have."

"Apology accepted."

Anthony blew out a deep breath, and Lecia knew he was

steeling himself for something else. She was wondering what the something else could be when he said, "My wife looks up to you. You're her idol."

"I'm sure you're being much too kind."

"You are, trust me. Which brings me to my issue. I don't know what she said about me when the two of you talked, but I know your opinion of me had to be tainted because of the media story. I'm not holding that against you," Anthony quickly went on when Lecia opened her mouth to speak. "I mean, it's to be expected, right? My concern is my wife. I guess this whole situation has affected her more than I thought it would, because she's done a total one eighty. Her attitude, her behavior. She's not herself. She won't even talk to me."

"And you want me to give you some advice?" Lecia asked.

"You could give me all the advice in the world and I don't think it would help. What I need you to do is talk to my wife."

"Anthony—"

"Tony."

"Whatever. I don't see how talking to your wife—"

"Like I said, she idolizes you. If you tell her that before she rushes to divorce court, she ought to at least talk to me, I'm sure she'll listen."

"Surely you can tell her that yourself."

"I've tried. She won't give me the time of day. She never did, not from the moment the story broke about me supposedly propositioning a prostitute."

"She must have her reasons."

"Yeah—the fact that the media was making me out to be some type of freak. I ought to sue the people from the *Daily Blab*. They ran a supposed interview with the prostitute, and she told them all sorts of crap about what the two of us did together. Of course, she wouldn't even give her name. No one

else has found this woman. I really doubt the *Daily Blab* found her, either. That story was a complete fabrication by a staff writer."

"I don't doubt it," Lecia said, surprising herself with how easily she was voicing her support of him. But everyone knew that the *Daily Blab*'s stories were sometimes so off the wall, there was no way they could be true. "I mean, they reported that the two of us were having a secret affair and you got angry with me on the *Tonight Show* because I pretended not to know you."

"For real?"

"Oh, yeah."

"I didn't see that one." He blew out a ragged breath. "So now you know what I'm dealing with. What Ginger must be dealing with. She's probably thinking that she married a freak, all based on this media bullshit. What I'm hoping is that you'll call her—"

"Me?"

"I've just told you she won't give me the time of day. That's why I need you to call her on my behalf. Tell her that you've spoken with me, that I want to do couples counseling and you've agreed to be our therapist. I'm sure she'll agree."

"I'm a sex therapist."

"I don't think Ginger's gonna care, not as long as we deal with you."

"I understand your frustration, but I can't get involved."

Anthony paused, then said, "You owe me."

"Oh? How do you figure that?"

"While I'm sorry for what happened between us with a national audience watching, I stand by what I said. It was your advice that made her decide to leave me."

The way Lecia saw it, she had merely confirmed for the

woman what she wanted to do. But there was no point in telling Anthony that. She had a feeling he wouldn't believe her.

Although based on the exterior package and his enormous success, it was hard to imagine any woman leaving the great Anthony Beals. It was just as hard to picture him propositioning a hooker when he could have any woman for free.

"Anthony—"

"Tony."

"Tony," she echoed, exasperated. "I . . . I can't do this. Even if I wanted to, I don't have time."

"I need you to make the time."

"Excuse me?"

"It'll probably only take one session. If you simply tell her to give me a chance—"

"It's not my place to tell her that."

Anthony took another bite of the sandwich as he contemplated what to say next. He needed Dr. Love to do this. It was the only way to get through to Ginger.

Something made him lean forward and reach for both her hands. "I need you to make it your place. I've got a lot at stake here, most importantly, my marriage."

Meeting his gaze, Lecia slowly ran her tongue along her upper lip. Anthony's eyes narrowed. What was she doing? Coming onto him?

A flush rose to his cheeks—one that she would thankfully never see because of his complexion. He quickly released her hands. "Lecia—"

"Your mouth," she said. "You've got mustard on your lips."

Anthony stared at her for a good beat and a half before realizing what she was saying. He jerked backward and quickly grabbed a napkin.

So much for misreading intentions.

"Why don't you call your wife and tell her exactly what you've told me?" Lecia said. "You sound sincere. And determined to work things out. I know you said you've already tried, but why not try again? Or better yet, go see her. Let her see for herself how sin—"

"I can't get within one hundred feet of her."

Lecia's face dropped. "What are you saying?"

"It's just temporary."

"A restraining order?"

"Which won't be an issue if she *agrees* to see me. So what do you say? Will you call her and arrange a session?"

Lecia suddenly had a vision of her two favorite newscasters broadcasting breaking news. *Today, in a bizarre series of events, overnight success Dr. Love was coerced into helping former football star Anthony Beals kill his wife. . . .*

"Lecia, what are you thinking?"

She got up. He didn't want to know what she was thinking. "If you want to get your wife back, you're gonna have to do it on your own."

Anthony rose to meet her. "You won't help me?"

"I want no part of this." Lecia turned and headed back to the house.

"Lecia. Come on."

"This is a very bad idea. Restraining order?" She spoke without turning. "I can't get involved in this. God only knows what you really have planned for your wife."

"What's that supposed to mean?"

Lecia opened the sliding door and her low heels clicked against the kitchen floor. She would have continued on to the front door and out of this place except she remembered that she didn't have her car here.

"It means . . ." The last thing she wanted to do was enrage this man without a means of escape. Even though he didn't at all seem dangerous. But Ginger had painted him out to be practically psychopathic. The woman really had conveyed a lot about him in five minutes. "It means . . ."

"You're afraid of me."

"Of course not." She laughed mirthlessly.

"Then why are you clutching your purse like that?"

"Um, where's Kahari?"

"Forget Kahari."

"He didn't leave the house, did he? I want to thank him for the sandwich. It really was deli—"

Lecia stopped short, flinching when she felt Anthony's hand on her arm. "See," he said. "You *are* afraid of me. Damn."

"No . . . I'm just . . ." *Don't let him see your fear!* ". . . ready to leave."

"I don't believe you. And that hurts, Lecia, after I poured my heart out to you. But if you really think I'm some type of monster, at least have the guts to turn around, look me in the eye, and tell me so to my face."

Thirteen

Lecia turned around. Her eyes met Anthony's. She fully intended to tell him that yes, he scared the hell out of her. But when she saw the honesty in his gaze, she knew the words would be a lie.

Not entirely a lie. He *did* scare her. But not because she thought he'd murder her and dump her body in the Pacific. She was afraid that if he touched her, if he tried to kiss her, she would be utterly powerless to stop him.

There was something entirely too sexy about Anthony Beals, something wickedly dangerous. He had an intensity that she could only imagine was explosive in the bedroom.

Anthony looked at her curiously. "Why are you looking at me like that?"

"You're married."

His expression changed to confusion. "What— You think . . . you think I'm trying to come onto you?"

Oh, darn. She hadn't meant to say that. It was supposed to be a mental note as to why she needed to stay away from him.

But she didn't get to say another word, and neither did Anthony, because a woman's high-pitched squeal made them both jump apart.

Lecia turned her head toward the scream. A drop-dead gorgeous woman scurried toward her, arms flailing with excitement.

"As I live and breathe. Dr. Love!"

The woman had a southern accent. Maybe from somewhere in Texas?

Lecia actually braced herself for the woman's hug, considering she was coming at her like a speeding train.

"Oh my God. It's really you. Dr. Love, I am *such* a big fan!"

For her twiglike size, the woman had a surprisingly strong grip. With much effort, Lecia wormed her way free. Taking a few steps backward, she forced a smile. "Hello."

"I can't believe it." The woman fanned a hand in front of her mouth. "I just hugged Dr. Love."

Lecia continued to smile politely. What else could she do? She was a regular person, and having people treat her like some major star was going to take a lot of getting used to.

"I take it you read my book," she said for lack of anything else to say.

"Cover to cover, at least ten times."

"Wow."

"That book was a lifesaver. Especially that chapter on how women have to give themselves love first if they ever want to receive it. How that will open you up to experiencing true sexual intimacy."

Knowing how that must sound, Lecia glanced Anthony's way. She was suddenly embarrassed. As she feared, Anthony was giving her an odd look. She explained, "It's a chapter about self-esteem, body image. I tell women to mentally throw their baggage in the garbage if they want to find true sexual fulfillment."

"I didn't realize until I read your words what I was doing." The woman lowered her voice and said, "Sometimes I didn't even want to get naked, because I was afraid the cheesecake I'd eaten the day before was showing on my thighs. But you got me over that."

"Well. I'm glad I could help. What's your name?"

"Oh, God. How stupid could I be? LaTonya. LaTonya Brown."

"Brown?"

"I'm Kahari's sister."

"Ah. Nice to meet you, LaTonya."

"I hope you don't mind me asking, but will you sign my book for me?"

"No problem."

"My friends are gonna *die*."

Barely suppressing another squeal, LaTonya whirled around and ran out of the kitchen.

"I thought for sure you were some kind of diva," Anthony said. "But you're not. You're real."

"I'm just a person making a living. Same as you."

"I understand. It was never about the fame for me. Football's been in my blood since I was a kid."

"There's nothing better, is there?" Lecia said, grinning up at him. "Making a living doing what you love?"

"Nope. Except having someone to share it with."

Lecia narrowed her eyes in speculation. Was Anthony saying this simply for her benefit, or was he, as his words implied, a romantic?

It seemed the air in the kitchen had suddenly grown thick

and difficult to inhale. Lecia felt her airways constricting, and she turned, strolling toward the café area. As she did, she reached inside her purse for her inhaler.

Hoping that Anthony wasn't watching, she inserted the inhaler into her mouth and squeezed. She held the breath in her lungs until she couldn't hold it anymore, then exhaled.

She nearly choked when she felt the large hand on her back. She hadn't expected it.

"Hey, you okay?"

She nodded. "Yeah."

"You just took some type of inhaler."

"Uh-huh. For asthma."

"And you're sure you're fine?"

For a moment Lecia didn't want to move. Except perhaps to edge even closer to him. She faced him now, standing tall. "Yes, I'm fine."

"Good. 'Cause I don't need you dying on me."

His words soured what had actually been a nice moment. At least what she had thought had been a nice moment. It was clear that Anthony had only one interest in her—to help him get his wife back.

That shouldn't have bothered her, but it did.

LaTonya was back in a flash, clutching her copy of *The Big O* as if it was gold. As Lecia took the book, LaTonya said, "My friends and I were thinking of starting a women's night. A time when we can frankly discuss everything about women's issues—our bodies, love, sex. All that. I hear others have been having them, and we think it's such a great idea."

"I think it is, too. And if my book has gotten women talking frankly about love and sexuality, then it was well worth the effort to write it."

Lecia scribbled a personal note to LaTonya, then passed the

book and pen back to her. As Kahari strolled into the room, Lecia glanced up at Anthony. "Are you ready?"

"Yeah."

"Again, it was wonderful meeting you, LaTonya. I'm glad the book's been helpful. Kahari, thanks for your hospitality. The sandwich was great."

"No problem. You're welcome here anytime."

"I'll call you later," Anthony told Kahari. "We still have to discuss business."

"Sure thing."

Then Anthony once again placed his hand on the small of Lecia's back as he led her out of the house.

"I have news, Ginger."

Thank God, it was her lawyer. And not a moment too soon, as she was meeting with the loan shark later today. She had put off Pavel time and time again, but she didn't know how much longer he would give her before he demanded payment or finally killed her.

Ginger covered the mouthpiece of her cell phone and said to Bo, "It's my lawyer. He has news."

"Who're you talking to?" Zack asked.

"Oh. Um, no one. Actually, I'm at a friend's place. Tell me," Ginger went on. "When will I have the five million?"

"Uh, that's what I wanted to talk to you about."

Ginger's stomach plummeted. But she refused to even consider defeat. "It won't be this week?" she asked hopefully.

"No."

"When? Next week?"

"Not exactly."

The sinking sensation intensified. "Then when?"

"Maybe never?" Zack's tone was questioning, as if he was guessing a trivial pursuit answer.

Ginger paused a beat, then said, "This is some kind of joke, right? I mean, you all but promised me you could resolve this case for me."

"I can. And I do have an offer. Just not what we'd hoped for. Your husband's lawyer said one million."

"*One*? That's the same he offered me the last time."

"I'm sure I can get him to raise it." Zack now spoke with a confidence his voice had lacked before. "The starting offer is always low."

"Then call me back when you have something we can talk about." Zack didn't answer, and Ginger had to wonder if he had heard her. "Zack? Are you still there?"

"Yeah."

"You heard what I said?"

"Yeah, but I'm thinking. I guess I just . . . well, it seems . . ."

"What?"

"This whole thing could be tied up in court for years. Unless you're willing to settle. My guess is they might come up to a million five, maybe two. And if they do—"

"Turn it down."

"What?"

"I said turn it down. I've seen my husband give tons of money to lots of causes. He can damn well give to his wife."

Ginger wasn't sure, but it sounded like the lawyer whimpered. "Ginger," he said. "I strongly advise—"

"I'm not interested in what you advise. You work for me. You do what I say."

"I'm just saying—"

"Call me when you have news I want to hear."

Then Ginger hung up. But there was no satisfaction in it.

Fourteen

"Wait a minute." Tyanna stopped searching through the row of Gucci jeans to face her sister with a wide-eyed stare. "You were out with Anthony Beals—the same guy you said you didn't ever want to see again, much less be in the same room with?"

Lecia had decided to tell her sister about it while shopping on Rodeo Drive. In the posh designer stores, she figured Tyanna would keep her natural curiosity and excitement under control—so as not to draw attention to them. But when had Tyanna ever cared about attention? Her baby sister had a flair for the dramatic. And this story was drama with a capital D.

"Tyanna," Lecia whispered. She glanced around, but no one was within immediate hearing distance. "Let's not talk for the whole world to hear."

"Sorry," Tyanna spoke in a quieter tone. "But you drop a bomb on me like that . . . how do you expect me to react? After the *Tonight Show,* I didn't think you'd be spending any more time with Mr. Beals."

"I don't think you heard me correctly. I said the man showed up at my workplace and all but kidnapped me."

"Did you call the police?"

"I . . . I almost had to."

Now Tyanna frowned. "Almost? If you felt threatened, why wouldn't you call the police? Hell, you have Sheldon's cell number. You know he would have come to your rescue with as many members of L.A.'s finest as necessary."

Lecia sighed her exasperation. "I didn't say I needed rescuing. Let me finish my story."

"Okay." Tyanna continued perusing jeans.

"He claimed he wanted to take me for a coffee, to talk. In the e-mail he'd sent, he said he wanted to apologize. I figured if he had shown up at my workplace to say he was sorry, the least I could do was hear him out."

"Uh-huh."

"I was worried at first. But it's not like he tried to gag me and force me into the car. And he told me I could use my cell to call the police if I truly felt threatened. Which I almost did when he took me into an exclusive Beverly Hills neighborhood. I guess that sounds weird. The problem was, he was taking me fairly far from the office, and I knew we wouldn't find a Starbucks in that neighborhood. Turns out, he took me to some football player's place. Kahari Brown."

"Kahari Brown!" Tyanna couldn't hold in her excitement. "Get *out*!"

"So you know who he is."

"Of course I know who he is! Sheldon's gonna die when he finds out you met him. Is he nice?"

Lecia should have known that Kahari was a huge star, simply because of his house. "Actually, he seems very nice. Grounded, too, despite the fact that he's got this enormous mansion. Maybe one day you'll see it. He said I was welcome anytime."

"Oh my God." Tyanna practically danced on the spot. "I guess you and Mr. Beals kissed and made up."

"These jeans would look good on you," Lecia said, holding up a pair of faded denims with slightly flared bottoms. "You should try them on."

"Forget the jeans." Tyanna took the pair from her and put it back on the rack. "Tell me what else happened."

Lecia told her sister the rest of the story, complete with Anthony's request that he help her get his wife back. "I have to admit, my view of him has changed, although I don't know why he's bothering with any effort to win his wife back. That's a lost cause, as far as I'm concerned."

"I don't know, sis. Going off on an adventure with L.A.'s newest bad boy? You're becoming almost as reckless as me." She laughed.

"Maybe it's this town. People move here and suddenly their lives are embroiled in scandal."

"Uh-huh," Tyanna said, as if she knew better.

Lecia ignored her sister and took a pair of jeans off the rack. When she lived in South Florida, she'd gone to the shops of Bal Harbour only once with Tyanna. But since moving to California, she and Tyanna had become frequent shoppers at the designer stores. It wasn't so much about buying the expensive stuff they could both now easily afford. It was about time to bond as sisters—something they hadn't done much in Florida since they'd both led very different lives. Shopping together gave them a lot of time to talk.

"Have you heard from Mom and Dad?" Tyanna asked.

"Yes," Lecia replied, rolling her eyes. "Dad didn't have much to say about the *Tonight Show* in particular, but he kept telling me to 'stay grounded.' Guess he thinks I've changed—for the worse."

"Oh, don't worry about him."

That was easy for Tyanna to say. Dubbed the "wild child" of the family, she had always played by her own rules. Lecia supposed the youngest child could get away with that. As the oldest, she could not. Her parents had put pressure on her to be like them, and that's exactly what she did, following in their footsteps and becoming a doctor.

She'd also married the man they'd wanted her to, and that had been the biggest mistake of her life. And because of their hopes for her, she had put her dream of writing on the back burner.

She finally felt in control, though. Even her parents had to respect her success. And ever since she'd begun living life on her own terms, Lecia had found a new respect for her sister.

"What I want to know," Tyanna said, "is are you gonna see him again?"

"I didn't say Dad and I weren't talking."

"I'm not talking about Dad, silly. I'm talking about Anthony Beals. Are you gonna see him again?"

"Of course not." But despite her words, Lecia's stomach fluttered. "I told him I'm not interested in helping him get his wife back. I can't even imagine getting involved."

"But that doesn't mean you can't see him again."

"Why would I?"

Tyanna shook her head. "Oh, boy. It's been that long that you don't remember why a single woman might want to see a man like Mr. Beals?"

Lecia scowled at her sister. "I don't want any of these jeans. You want to look at shoes with me?"

"Okay, sis. We won't go there."

"Good." Lecia led the way to the vast selection of shoes.

"Oh, and I have to tell you, Lecia, those shoes I bought the last time—Sheldon took one look at me in them and bam! We forgot all about heading out for dinner and stayed home for dessert."

Lecia leveled a lopsided grin in her sister's direction. If there was one couple that didn't need any help in the sex department, it was her sister and Sheldon. The two were lovebirds who were very open with their affection. They could barely keep their hands off each other. It was nice to see.

"I'm happy for you," Lecia said.

"You can have it, too."

"The shoes?"

"No, great sex. Though the shoes will probably help."

"We're not going there, remember?"

"I can't help it. How long has it been?"

"Wow. Look at this pair." Lecia grabbed the first pair of sandals she saw. She didn't care that the several feet of straps were totally not her style.

"I think if you had sex, you'd be less uptight."

Lecia wagged the shoe at her sister as she spun around to face her. "Spare me the sex talk. I don't even have a man."

"You don't necessarily need one."

"Oh yes I do. I'm not into casual sex."

Tyanna sighed sadly.

"Please, spare me the pity," Lecia told her. "I'm not dying."

"But you're not really living, either."

"One can live very well without sex."

Tyanna made a face to say that was debatable. "I did for a year, and it was the worst damn year of my life."

"That's because you were in love with Sheldon and he had left you without an explanation. Sure, he'd been on the run to save his life, but you never stopped loving him even when you thought he had abandoned you. So when he came back into your life—"

"I thought we were talking about you."

"Okay, I admit. Sex might be nice."

At Tyanna's smirk, Lecia glanced over her shoulder. To her horror, she saw one of the sales associates standing behind her.

"Maybe I could come back," he suggested.

"Yes, please." Lecia groaned as he walked away.

"He was kind of cute, sis."

"And probably just as horny as the other guys I've dated. Come on, Tyanna. You more than anyone know the kind of men I've met since I've been out here. Men who think that because I'm a sex therapist, I'm some sort of porn queen. Every one of my last five dates ended horribly, because every guy expected me to take him home in the first half hour."

Tyanna shrugged. "I guess that's the L.A. way."

"It's not my way."

"I'll ask Sheldon if—"

"No, don't ask Sheldon anything. I'm not interested in being set up."

"Not every guy is Allen."

"I know that. I do." Just the mention of her ex-husband's name was enough to give her a headache. "But the last thing on my mind is a relationship. I'm so busy with my work. And even if I was interested in finding someone, the truth is, all the good ones are married."

"All right, all right. I can tell I'm not gonna win this argument. Let me change the subject."

"Yes, please."

"Wendy and I will be filming a new video."

Now this was something she could sink her teeth into, Lecia thought. "Great."

"This one will be abs. After that, we'll do legs."

"I still can't believe how well things are going for you. And me. One minute we were in Florida. Now here we both are in Los Angeles, living our dreams in a way we never thought possible."

"I know. I love it here. I miss Mom and Dad, though. But mostly I miss Charlene and Michelle."

Charlene was the middle sister in their family of three daughters. Michelle was Charlene's only daughter. Charlene had suffered a huge loss when her husband was killed in a car accident while she'd been pregnant.

"I miss them, too. I spoke with Charlene a couple nights ago, and I think I convinced her to head out here at the end of the summer. I hope she comes. I miss our niece."

"That girl is getting so big. Time flies. Which is another reason we need to find someone for you to settle down with. If you're ever going to have a family."

"Me? You're the one who has been married for a year and a half. When are you going to start making babies?"

"When we stop honeymooning," Tyanna replied, winking as she laughed.

Lecia linked arms with her. "You buying anything?"

"Nope."

"Then come on. Let's go get something to eat."

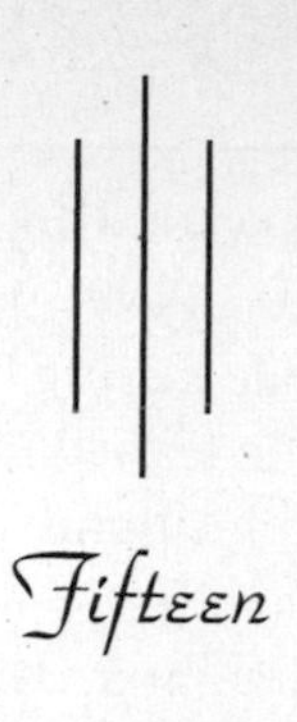

Fifteen

Ginger spotted Pavel's mop of dirty blond hair the moment she and Bo entered The Farm of Beverly Hills. The restaurant's warm and charming atmosphere was the height of irony—considering she expected the exact opposite in attitude from the lowlife loan shark.

He had his head buried in a book, so although he faced in their direction, he didn't notice them. Her stomach fluttering with nerves, she contemplated turning around and leaving. She didn't have news that Pavel would want to hear, and she could only imagine how he was going to react.

Ginger wrapped her fingers around Bo's thick wrist. "Bo, I don't know—"

Pavel looked up then. Seeing them, he smiled.

Shit. Too late.

He stood, adjusted his suit jacket, then beckoned Ginger and Bo over like he was a longtime friend looking forward to an early dinner. In reality, he was the loan shark who would surely tell them that if they didn't pay up the money they owed, they would pay the consequences.

Very dire ones.

Her hand gripping Bo's wrist, Ginger headed toward Pavel's table. Arms outstretched, Pavel walked toward her and wrapped her in a hug while kissing both of her cheeks. When he finished with Ginger, he leaned toward Bo, but Bo stepped back and offered the man his hand, not his face.

Pavel smiled. "Sit, sit."

Like a lamb to the slaughter, Ginger thought as she sat down.

"Good news, I'm hoping," Pavel said, getting right down to business.

"I'm well, Pavel. Thanks for asking."

Pavel chuckled softly. "Oh, Ginger. You are so funny. But yes, I am happy to see that you are okay. If you are not okay, how do I get my money?"

He laughed again, and Ginger joined in, her own laughter sounding completely sarcastic. All the laughter faded and died when the waiter appeared moments later.

"Ah, let us talk business after we eat. Order whatever you like. Chicken, steak. It's on me."

"You go ahead," Ginger told him. She glanced at Bo. He was perusing the menu. He didn't look like he had a care in the world.

That pissed her off. He could at least say *something* to Pavel, try to make nice with the guy so he wouldn't blow their heads off in the alley behind the restaurant.

"I will have the Farm Steak, medium rare," Pavel said. "No garlic mashed potatoes. No broccolini. Nothing with starch. In fact, make it two steaks on one very big plate. That is it. Okay? No, wait. Give me white wine. A nice Chardonnay. This one," he said, pointing to the wine list. "From France. Let us have a bottle."

The waiter nodded, jotting down the items. Then he turned

to Ginger and Bo. Bo said, "I'll have a steak, too. But I want mine with the potatoes."

Ginger kicked Bo beneath the table. The last thing she wanted to do was sit through a meal with Pavel. It would feel too much like her last supper. She wanted to explain that she needed an extension on the time to repay the loan and get out of there. She had already made him wait a year, paying him instead with sex on demand, but Pavel wouldn't be satisfied with her body forever.

"Watch your leg, babe," Bo said, clearly not getting the point.

Ginger resigned herself to her fate. "I'll have the Classic Caesar Salad with chicken. No, wait. Make that the Ginger Poached Salmon Salad," she decided. It was the more expensive option. If Pavel was going to kill her, she at least shouldn't be a cheap date. "And sparkling water."

When the waiter left, Ginger asked Pavel, "Two steaks?"

"Ah, yes." He lifted a book off the chair beside him and showed it to them. "The Atkins diet is very good. All the protein you want. All the fat you want. But no carbohydrates. Bo, I think you should not eat the potatoes."

Bo shrugged nonchalantly.

Ginger forced a smile. "Your latest diet?" What was it with the man and his diets, anyway? He looked in amazing shape. There was no doubt he'd be able to chase her down and bludgeon her to death.

"Yes. So far, I think is good. But, I think I will be bad and have a Farm Brownie Sundae."

Ginger nodded as her gaze wandered around the elegant restaurant. If this was going to be her last supper, at least it was a decent place.

Perhaps she *should* have a steak.

"Ah, I am excited," Pavel said. "I saw Dr. Love walk by this table. I waved at her, and she waved back."

"Dr. Love is here?" Ginger asked. God, she hoped the woman didn't see her here with Bo. Not that it really mattered. The doctor surely wouldn't remember her. It's not like she'd been an actual patient.

"Maybe she is gone now. I don't know. But she is sexy black woman. Like you."

"Gee, thanks."

Pavel folded his hands on the table. "I cannot wait anymore," he said, as though he was a child anxious to learn about a surprise. "Tell me—you have the money?"

Ginger glanced at Bo. He gave her a blank look, letting her know he didn't know what to say.

It didn't matter. She was the one best to deal with Pavel, anyway. He appreciated her feminine charms, and she had used them to her advantage several times already.

"Pavel—"

"No no no. I do not like the way you say that. I think you are going to say that you do not have my money."

God help her. Ginger kept a half grin plastered on her face. "It's just going to take a bit longer than I expected."

"But this is what you say every time."

"Pavel, I know you've been so patient. Believe me, I wish I had better news. I had to change lawyers. The new one is much better, and he's working to get the divorce settled much more quickly—"

Ginger stopped talking when she noticed that the bread roll in Pavel's hand had been crushed to smithereens. He hadn't been eating it, just playing with it like it was a test of his resistance to carbohydrates.

"I do not like . . . how you say—being played like a fool."

"Played for a fool," Bo supplied.

Ginger cut her eyes at Bo. She loved him, but God only knew why sometimes.

"Yes. Played for a fool."

"Pavel, you know that's not the case. If we were playing you for a fool, we'd already be long gone by now." She patted his hands. They were cold. "We wouldn't come out to have a very nice dinner with you."

He eyed her, as if trying to determine whether he could believe her. "Maybe."

"Come on. You know ours is a special situation. Freddie Monahue scammed us. We would have had the money to you ages ago—oodles of it—if the dot-com company we'd invested in had been legit. We got ripped off, and that's the only reason we haven't been able to pay you back. I feel real bad about that, you know I do. That's why I agreed to double your money for the inconvenience."

Pavel nodded. Ginger leaned back in her chair and relaxed. Thank God he wasn't going to press the issue.

"I think it is fair, for my *inconvenience*, I will need more than one million dollars. I will need another two hundred thousand."

"Two hundred thousand!" Ginger shrieked, then immediately hunched into her shoulders when she saw half the patrons staring at her.

"Yes. It is fair."

"It's highway robbery."

Pavel narrowed his eyes. "What is this? Highway what?"

"It's an expression," Bo replied. "You know, like 'played for a fool.' But listen, I think we've been more than fair. You only gave us half a mil to start with."

"Of my very hard-earned money."

Hard-earned money, her ass, Ginger thought. But she said, "The point Bo is trying to make is that we were being more than fair in offering to double your investment. Nothing's changed. The money's still coming, just as soon as the lawyers—"

"One point two million. Not a penny less."

"Christ," Ginger muttered.

"Such bad language." Pavel reached across the table and patted her cheek. "But I like you. You know, in my country, you are ebony beauty."

"Yes, I know." He'd told her that a million times. For all the good it had done her. He was more determined than anyone she'd ever met. He had even tracked her down to Los Angeles after she'd fled her home in New Orleans, hoping to escape him.

"But I still need my money. Nothing personal. You understand."

She did. She had sold her soul to a devil, and now she had to pay the price. There was no getting around it. The longer she took to pay him, the more outrageous the fee would be.

Her cell phone rang, thank the Lord. "Excuse me for a moment?"

"Of course," Pavel said.

Ginger was relieved as she got up from the table and walked toward the front door. She answered the phone when she was out of earshot. "Hello?"

"Yo, Ginger."

Oh, God. She should have let it ring. "Sha-Shana."

"I know. You've been too busy to get back to me. So just tell me—do you have the rest of my money?"

Hell, she should have read her horoscope before leaving the

house today. Maybe it would have told her to avoid all business associates. She replied, "It's gonna take a bit longer than I thought it would."

"Wow. How'd I know you would say that? Thanks for nothing. I think I'll go to the hotel where your husband is staying—"

"No!" Ginger lowered her voice when she noticed the maitre d's look of reproof. "Sha-Shana, how long have you known me? Ever since I left Kansas City and moved to New Orleans. You damn well know I'm good for the money. As soon as I get it, which I'm working like hell to do. But I'm not about to settle for a lousy million."

"A million?"

"You know all about the loan shark. He's supposed to get a million, so I need more than that. But don't worry. I think Anthony's gonna bend soon."

"Girl, if you're getting that kind of cash, then I can't settle for fifty grand."

"Come on, Sha-Shana!" Ginger headed for the restaurant door and stepped outside. "Five minutes of work. Fifty grand is plenty."

"A hundred, or I'll go to your husband."

Fuck. "Fine," Ginger lied. She had no intention of giving this bitch more than what they'd agreed upon. *If* she gave her anything more than the five grand she'd already paid her as a down payment. "But I really do have to go. I'm in a meeting with that loan shark right now."

"You better not be trying to screw me."

"Of course not. But I have to play this smart. Otherwise I'll never end up with the money."

"That's not what I want to hear."

"Don't worry," Ginger told her. "Everything's on track. I'm sure it won't take more than a few weeks to finalize the deal. Then we'll both be on Easy Street, just like we planned."

Ginger ended the call and turned her cell phone off. With the way her luck was going, Dr. Love would probably try to extort her, too.

Back at the table, she slumped into her chair. Pavel was devouring one of his two steaks with all the finesse of a pig at a trough. She had to admit, all that red meat smelled divine. She wished she had ordered one.

Pavel paused to ask, "Your lawyer?"

"No."

"Ah, too bad. Go ahead. Eat."

Was that a threat?

Ginger looked at her salad. She didn't feel like eating. Her stomach was in knots.

Because she knew that if she didn't come up with the money, and soon, she was as good as dead.

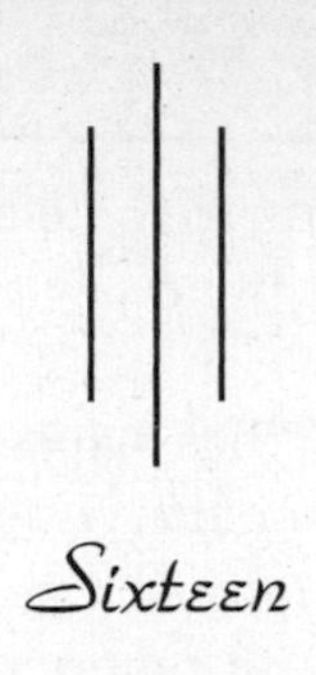

Sixteen

Anthony wasn't in the mood to chat with anyone tonight, which is why he'd put a Do Not Disturb instruction on his hotel phone. So when it rang shortly after eleven P.M., he eyed it with suspicion.

Then he quickly dashed across the suite and snatched up the living room phone. He'd had one exception to the Do Not Disturb, and that was to put through any calls from Ginger Beals.

Anthony brought the phone to his ear and tentatively said, "Hello?"

"Hi, Tony."

That wasn't Ginger. It was . . . "LaTonya?"

"Yeah. Let me pass you on to my brother."

Anthony wondered why Kahari was calling. And why he'd put his sister up to saying she was Ginger.

"Hey, T."

"Kahari, what's up?"

"Man, you better turn on the TV."

"Why?"

"Just flick it on. Any of the news stations. They're talking about Ginger."

Anthony reached for the remote and turned the television on. He channel-surfed until he saw a picture of Ginger on the Channel 2 news.

". . . don't know what has happened to her. Friends say they're worried she may be the victim of foul play."

A big, husky guy Anthony had never seen before filled the screen as he spoke into the reporter's microphone. "The last thing she told me was that she was going to meet her husband. I warned her not to, because he's so out of control, but she went anyway. I haven't seen her since."

"Aw, *shit*!" Anthony exclaimed.

"Where are you?" Kahari asked.

"I'm at the hotel, dawg. You just called me."

"My bad. What I meant is, where were you earlier?"

"Here. I've been here most of the day. I did go out around ten this morning for a run. Drove to Cal State. Got a Big Mac at the drive-through." The reason for Kahari's question suddenly dawned on Anthony. "Oh, shit. Some guy just said Ginger was supposed to be meeting me today?"

"And she hasn't been seen since."

"But I haven't seen Ginger. The last time I saw her was— Oh, man."

"The time you showed up at your place and she called the cops."

"No, when we met at my lawyer's office. And she acted like she was afraid I'd beat the crap out of her." And since that time, Ginger had told any tabloid or talk show hack who would listen that he had harassed her, threatened her. "I've been staying away from her. So why is this guy on TV saying I was supposed to meet with her earlier?"

"Did she call you at all? Try to make plans to hook up?"

"No. I haven't even heard a peep from her. She made it

clear that the only time she wants to hear from me is when I'm ready to pay her five million dollars."

"Maybe it's nothing to worry about," Kahari suggested. "Her friends could simply be worried about her."

"Ginger isn't in touch for a day and they're worried?" This didn't sit right with Anthony. "Besides, that guy specifically said that I was supposed to be meeting with Ginger earlier. And that's a lie. Unless Ginger planned on calling me but didn't get around to it."

"That could be it. Hey, don't worry about it. She's probably off at some spa somewhere."

"I sure as hell hope so." Because he couldn't imagine his current situation getting any worse than it already was.

But it did get worse.

By the next morning, Anthony had eighteen cell phone messages. His lawyer and his agent had called, as well as many of his friends. They were all concerned about Ginger's disappearance.

"We're not treating this as a crime . . . yet," a police officer told a reporter as Anthony had his eyes glued to the television. "But we are concerned about Mrs. Beals and are paying close attention to this case."

Anthony had tried Ginger's phone at least two dozen times since last night's newscast. Two dozen times it had rung until her voice mail picked up. He had even called from his hotel room and the hotel lobby so Ginger wouldn't recognize the phone number. It hadn't changed the outcome. She still hadn't answered.

Anthony couldn't help wondering if something bad *had* happened to her.

He flicked off the television and finally returned his

lawyer's calls. When Keith answered, Anthony said, "Keith, it's me."

"Anthony. Thank God. Do you have any idea where Ginger is?"

"No. Tell me this isn't really true. Tell me she's not missing. Tell me the police are overreacting."

"I don't know, but I can tell you that I've already heard from them. They want to talk to you, ask you some questions."

Panic made his stomach twist in knots. "I had nothing to do with this."

"According to Ginger's friends, she was heading to see you the last time anyone saw her."

"That's a lie. Ginger and I have not talked since the time I saw her in your office."

"You haven't gone by the house?"

"No! Well, not since the restraining order." Even as Anthony spoke, he knew how bad that sounded. The cops would think him guilty even before they talked to him. "Hell, what am I gonna do?"

"Look, don't panic. I'm sure you have an alibi for yesterday. So when you talk to the police, you'll easily be able to clear yourself off any potential list of suspects."

"Suspects? You think it's that serious?"

"The spouse always has to be ruled out as suspect. It's standard procedure, especially since you two are separated."

"Yo, Keith. Give it to me straight—are you trying to tell me that the cops think I actually hurt my wife?"

"I suggest you don't talk about Ginger being hurt when they question you. Just say you have no idea where she is."

"But I don't!"

"I know. You don't have to convince me."

Anthony had to wonder.

"Listen, the detective I spoke to is named Hernandez. He'd like us to schedule an appointment as soon as possible. So, when can we head to the police station?"

Visions of OJ swam through Anthony's mind. Hell, no. He couldn't deal with this. To Keith, he said, "I'll, um, call you back."

"When?"

"There's something I've gotta do."

"Where are you going?"

"Out."

"Anthony—"

Anthony hung up. Then he rested both hands on the end table and breathed in and out in rapid succession.

Ginger was *not* missing. People were overreacting, but God only knew why.

It was like Kahari had said. Ginger was probably off at some spa somewhere, taking some time to think.

An image of a quivering Ginger in his lawyer's office zapped into his mind. He remembered her words on Depraved Dave's show.

He had to find her, talk to her.

But he needed help. Someone to approach Ginger once he found her so she didn't freak out.

He needed Dr. Love. She hadn't exactly agreed to talk to Ginger on his behalf, but she hadn't disagreed, either. It didn't matter. She was the woman for the job.

And the job needed to be done now. If Ginger was lying low, only Dr. Love could get him out of this mess.

He had to see the good doctor, and the sooner the better.

Anthony scooped up his car keys and fled the hotel room.

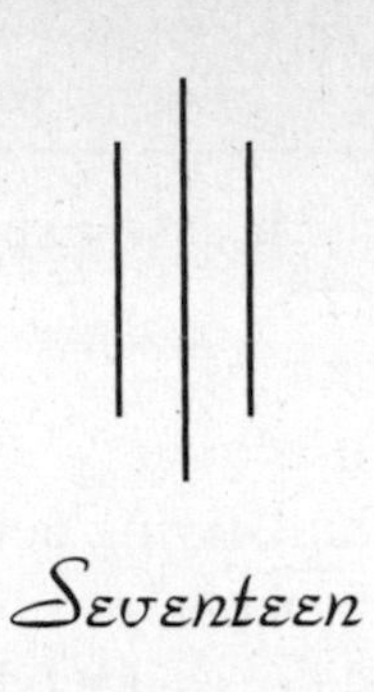

Seventeen

"I went to confession immediately afterward."

"But you had sex with your husband."

"Yes, I know. But . . ."

As her client's face grew a bright shade of red, Lecia studied the older woman. This was her third time seeing Gertrude Kennedy, but the first time the woman had had the courage to share her thoughts about sex and why she thought it was "dirty." Before today, Gertrude had simply told her that she had problems with intimacy and it was ruining her relationship. From what Lecia had learned today, the woman's biggest problem with sex was enjoying it.

"You have to understand, I was raised a good Catholic girl. I told you that. The way my mother went on and on about sex, I thought it was a horrible thing, an evil thing. I grew up believing it was for my husband's pleasure, and of course to make babies. When I first made love to my husband, I wondered what my mother had been talking about. Sex wasn't horrible. But then I remembered that she said it was also evil, that it wasn't a woman's place to like it. Whenever I think of my mother, I know she would be ashamed that I'm still having sex at my age, much less experiencing new . . . new *things*."

"Your mother's dead?"

"Going on twelve years."

Lecia nodded. "You think trying new things is bad?"

"I guess it depends on what you try. I'm not supposed to like anything dirty. But I do. God forgive me, I do."

"Do you believe that what two people do in a committed relationship is dirty? Not an expression of love?"

"It depends on what you do. And how much you enjoy it," Gertrude added, grinning from ear to ear.

Lecia raised an eyebrow. "Oh?"

"Please understand, I started off doing this stuff for my husband," Gertrude explained, as though Lecia was judging her. "Because it turned him on. Now, it turns me on."

"So you're both enjoying it."

"Oh, yes."

"Why do you think that is bad?"

"I can see in my husband's face that he's disappointed with me. Oh, I know he enjoys himself, but he doesn't really expect me to have fun doing it."

So far, the woman hadn't explicitly said what "it" was. Given the woman's age—mid-fifties—it could be anything from oral sex to swinging. She had grown up in a different generation, and being a churchgoing woman had only made things more complicated.

"Has your husband explicitly told you he's disappointed in you?"

"Oh, no. Harry would never tell me that. He tells me that he loves me."

"And you believe him?"

"Yes."

"Gertrude, you're really feeling guilt where there's no cause."

"I know that rationally—but how do I get over it?"

Lecia didn't anticipate many sessions with this woman. She leaned forward across her desk. "One thing I've never bought into is the view that sex is more for men's enjoyment than it is for women's. Nor that sex is strictly for procreation. You need to allow yourself to enjoy whatever it is you're doing. Are you hurting anyone?"

"No."

"Hurting yourself?"

"God, no."

"Then what exactly is the problem? That you enjoy it?"

"When you say it like that, it doesn't really make sense."

"I have a great book I can recommend for you and your husband to read. It's about love and intimacy. I think it will be a great help to you." And just maybe that should be her next book, she thought. Too many women she met had the view that if they enjoyed certain sexual acts, they were whores. Of course, it was fine and dandy for men to do whatever they wanted sexually and not be branded.

"Does it have a chapter on . . ." The woman blushed. ". . . on . . ."

"On?" Lecia prompted.

"On dressing up?"

"What kind of dressing up—cross dressing?"

"Good Lord in heaven, no." Gertrude's hand flew to her heart. "Dressing up like . . . like a schoolgirl. You know, the way that Britney Spears did once in a video. That's where my husband got the idea."

Lecia bit back a chuckle. It was almost sweet, this old-fashioned woman feeling guilty for some innocent role-playing. Especially in this town.

"Gertrude—" Lecia stopped talking when she heard some sort of commotion outside her office. There were at least two sets of voices.

"—not go in there." That was Sam's voice.

"Get out of my way." That voice was deeper, and clearly belonged to a man.

"Sir!"

"Gertrude, will you excuse me a—"

The door flew open, startling Lecia. But she was even more shocked when she saw Anthony Beals standing there.

"Lecia, I need to speak with you. Right away."

Lecia's brain scrambled to make sense of the situation. Anthony was barging in here to see her? What on earth for?

She had the sudden image of a hero at the end of a movie when he tracked down the heroine to proclaim his undying love for her.

"Anthony, I'm in the middle of a session."

"I tried to get him to leave," Sam said.

"It's okay, Sam. I'll take care of this."

Sam scowled at Anthony before she disappeared. Anthony watched her walk away, then said, "This is urgent. It's about Ginger."

Lecia wanted to throw her notepad at him. Not Ginger again. And God was she ever way off base with that ridiculous movie thought. "Then it's definitely going to have to wait."

"No can do, Dr. Love."

"Excuse me?"

Anthony looked at Gertrude. "Ma'am, I'm sorry to do this."

Lecia glanced at her patient. Gertrude's eyes were volleying back and forth between the two of them. "Gertrude," Lecia said, "I'll be back in a moment, okay?"

"Oh, no." Gertrude got up. "I don't mind finishing early. You take care of this man." As Gertrude hustled past Lecia, she winked at her. "You've just given me an idea for Harry."

Good grief. If the woman only knew.

"This had better be good," Lecia told Anthony once Gertrude closed the door behind her.

"It is. I need you to come with me. Now."

"Anthony, you can't just barge into my office—"

"I'll explain everything when we're in the car."

"The car? Oh, no—" But Lecia stopped short when Anthony strode toward her desk. A moment later he lifted her purse off the back of her chair. "Hey!"

"I'm not robbing you, so don't freak out. But I really do need you to come with me. I'll bring you back as soon as I can."

"And if I say no?"

"I'll drape you over my shoulder if I have to."

"A modern day Tarzan. How sweet. Please put my purse down."

Anthony started toward her, and Lecia's heart leapt to her throat. "Oh, God. What are you doing?"

"I just really . . . I really need you."

There was a vulnerable edge to Anthony's voice, one she couldn't quite ignore. "This feels like . . . a nightmare. A recurring one."

"All the more reason for you to help me as soon as you can."

"You won't leave me alone, will you? Not until you win your wife back?"

Anthony merely shrugged.

Lecia sighed. "Lucky for you my next appointment canceled."

Anthony's face exploded in a grin. "I appreciate this, Lecia. Really I do."

Lecia walked up to him and plucked her purse from his hand. "You had damn well better."

When Anthony was driving on Wilshire Boulevard, Lecia faced him and said, "You know, if this is a ploy to spend time with me, there was a better way than this."

Anthony's eyes nearly popped out of his head. "That's what you think this is about?"

"Actually, that was a joke. You know, ha ha. I guess a bad attempt at one. I know you want your wife back."

Anthony didn't say a word, and Lecia lay her head back against the headrest. When Anthony turned left onto Beverly Drive, she asked, "Where are we going this time?"

"My place."

"I really would have appreciated you setting something up with me. We could have made arrangements for me to meet—"

"I guess you haven't heard the news."

Anthony met her eyes briefly before looking back at the road.

Lecia asked him, "What news?"

"People are saying that Ginger's missing."

"Missing as in no one can find her?"

"That's right."

"But you . . . I thought you wanted me to talk to her. You must think she's at your place. I'm confused."

"I'm hoping she's there."

"What aren't you telling me?"

"I just want to get to my place, and if Ginger's there—"

"Wait a second. Are you even supposed to go to the house? Didn't you say she has a restraining order against you?"

"Right now, that's a moot point."

"Is winning your wife back worth landing in jail?"

"Why don't you try calling?" Anthony suggested, ignoring her question. "She doesn't know your number. She might pick up."

"My God. You have no clue what you're doing. Do you hear yourself? Anthony—"

"Tony."

"Tony," Lecia repeated, exasperated. "You're sounding . . . insane. I know that sounds harsh, but I have to call it as I see it. If you have to go to these lengths to get your wife even to speak to you—"

"It's about more than that. I think she's playing some kind of game with me, and I don't know why. The big issue is seeing whether she's at the house. Then we can go from there."

Lecia bit her tongue and stared out the window. They were on Coldwater Canyon Avenue now. As they traveled the winding road she couldn't help thinking that this truly *was* a recurring nightmare. Perhaps Anthony would show up at her workplace once a week, force her into his car, and take her to swanky Beverly Hills mansions each time—over and over again until he finally got his wife back. How much more of this could she stand? She had to help him get his wife back, and as soon as possible.

Why did that thought not sit well with her?

"I think this is a bad idea," she suddenly said. "If your wife is avoiding you, then showing up on her doorstep is bound to make her feel cornered."

"Yeah, you should give her a call. See if she picks up."

Lecia sighed. "I think it would be better if I called her in the morning. In fact, we can do all of this in the morning. I'm not in the office tomorrow."

"And if I wait until tomorrow, I won't find you, will I?"

"Of course you will."

"No, because you think I'm a nut. You said that only moments ago."

"I'm not going to tell you where I live, if that's what you're asking. But we can meet somewhere. And I'll even give you my cell number."

Anthony gave her a saccharine-sweet smile. "I wasn't born yesterday."

"You can call it now if you like. It's my voice on the message."

"Let's get real. I know you don't want to spend any more time with me now, much less tomorrow. So I say you grin and bear it and we get this over with today. I told you before, Ginger's a big fan. She'll be thrilled to hear your voice."

"You have serious control issues," Lecia said, glaring at Anthony.

"I just want my life back. I don't want to wait another day."

For some reason Lecia couldn't fathom, Anthony's words stung her. But why should they? She knew what she was to him, simply a tool for him to win back his wife's affections.

All the more reason to call the woman now, get it over and done with, as he'd suggested. Then she could look forward to a future without Anthony Beals constantly barging into her life.

"What's the number?" she asked.

Anthony recited the number, and Lecia punched it into her cell phone.

The phone rang and rang as they drove past the gated

mansions along Mulholland Drive. Lecia ended the call. "No answer."

Anthony nodded his understanding, but Lecia watched his face change. His jawline tightened, growing tenser. She was no psychic, but something else had to be going on here.

Lecia didn't ask. The best thing she could do was keep out of the Bealses' marriage. At the house, she would be as brief as possible and hope that Ginger didn't make this difficult for her. Then she would call a cab and leave Anthony and his wife to talk.

As Anthony's Navigator started to slow, Lecia perked up. So he actually lived on the ritzy Mulholland Drive. Her eyes took in every detail. Leafy tree branches hung over a stone wall. Where the wall ended, a gate began. Anthony pulled up to it, and moments later they were rolling forward onto the property.

Large pines and oak trees helped obscure the view of the house from the main road, but once they were past the gate, it came into view. And what a house it was. It wasn't as large as Kahari's, but it was certainly impressive. Probably around eight or nine thousand square feet, she thought. Enough to hold a few families.

The stately white mansion could easily have been located in the South. Two stories, it was complete with four large columns on either side of the front door. Two shorter columns stood on each side of the house, holding up two sizable balconies.

Lecia couldn't stop staring. The red interlocked driveway was extensive, wrapping around a water fountain. Pristine lawns started at the edges of the driveway and went on for several yards, leading to the backyard. An array of potted flowers hung from the window ledge on the right, where there were also two white wrought-iron chairs and a table. It was the only homey touch.

"Ginger's Mercedes isn't here. Unless she parked it in the garage."

"You don't think she's here?"

"I won't know until I check." Anthony opened his car door and climbed out.

"I'll wait here."

"I'd rather you come inside with me," Anthony said. "I need you as a witness."

Lecia's eyes widened at that statement. "A witness?"

"That I didn't come here to hurt her," Anthony explained. "'Cause Lord knows, with the negative press I've gotten, I need witnesses for everything I do these days."

"Tony, is this going to get you arrested?"

"I'm hoping this will do the opposite."

"You're speaking in riddles."

"Just come with me to the door. Please," he added when Lecia didn't move.

She heaved a weary sigh and hopped down from the SUV. God help her, she hoped she hadn't gotten herself into a mess she couldn't get out of.

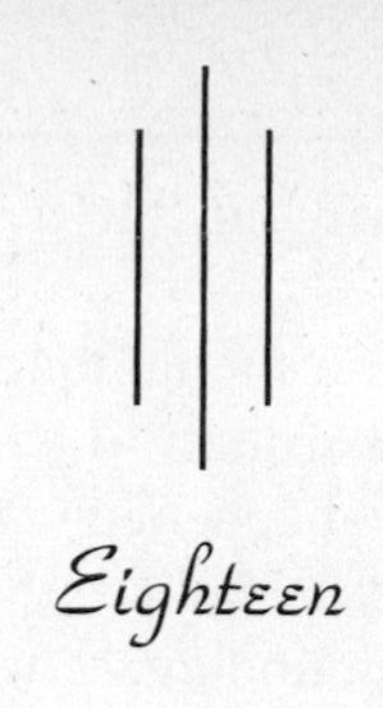

Eighteen

Anthony decided to use his key to gain access to the house. What was the point in ringing the doorbell? If Ginger was inside, that would just give her the opportunity to take off before he had a chance to talk to her.

The door unlocked, Anthony swung it open—then felt as though he'd been tackled from behind. He swallowed a shaky breath as his gaze swept the foyer. A pile of broken glass littered the foot of the stairs beneath the landing, as did a dozen white roses and baby's breath. The vase and flowers from the foyer table had clearly been knocked to the ground.

But while that was disturbing, it wasn't the worst thing. Ginger's Louis Vuitton handbag—the one she never left home without—lay on the tiled floor, its contents strewn across the vast area.

"Aw, hell."

Anthony rushed toward the handbag. He dropped to his knees and scooped it up, but he spotted her wallet about ten feet away before he even opened the purse. It was the wallet he wanted to see. Two seconds later he had it in his hands. Opening it, he found it full of her credit cards. Ginger wouldn't leave home without her credit cards. "Damn, this isn't good."

"Tony, I don't think you should touch anything."

He whipped his head around to look up at Lecia. "I can't believe it. Something *has* happened to her."

"Then we need to call the police."

Anthony's head was pounding. "The police?"

"Yes, the police. Who else do you call in a situation like this?"

"I can't call the police," Anthony told her, rising. "Look at this place. If they come over here, what do you think they're gonna say? They'll take one look around and label me suspect number one."

"I came here with you. I know this is how you found the place."

"Yeah, but I could have stashed Ginger's body before I brought you over here."

"Don't . . . don't even joke about that."

"Who's joking? It's a compelling reason why I can't call the police. I'm also Ginger's husband."

"You think that automatically makes you a suspect?"

"Ginger told friends that she was meeting me yesterday morning, and she hasn't been seen since. She's told half the media in Southern California that she's afraid of me—which is a lie. She damn well knows I'd never hurt her."

"My God." Lecia's eyes filled with horror. "I can't believe you came here."

"I had to come here. I had to find out if it was true. If she was really missing." He needed to think. Needed to figure out what to do. Realistically, he knew the cops had to be called. And he'd have to go through rigorous questioning.

What was wrong with him? He was actually moaning

about a few questions when he needed to find out what happened to his wife.

"Maybe you're right and I ought to just call the police," he said after a moment. "Like you said, you came here with me. You saw how I found this place. I can only hope they believe me. Because I swear, I haven't seen Ginger in ages, much less yesterday morning."

Lecia's expression grew pensive. Anthony eyed her with interest. "What is it? You know something?"

"When did you say she went missing?"

"Yesterday morning. At least that's what some big, burly dude said on the news last night. Said no one had seen her since she was supposed to meet me early yesterday."

"Well, I know that's not true."

"Thanks, Doc. It's good to know you believe me."

"I do believe you—but not for the reason you think. I saw Ginger yesterday. Well after the morning. Probably around four-fifteen, four-thirty."

"What?"

"I saw her at a restaurant in Beverly Hills. When you mentioned a big guy, that triggered my memory."

"You saw Ginger?"

"Yeah, and she was with a couple of men. A white guy, and a big black guy."

"Wait a minute," Anthony said. "I saw a burly black guy on the news talking about Ginger, saying he was a friend of hers. He said Ginger told him she was meeting with me the morning she disappeared. Was this guy you saw bald?"

"He was."

"Damn," Anthony cursed. "And you saw Ginger at four-thirty?"

"Around then. I went out for dinner with my sister, so I'm

sure about the time. In fact, I'd wanted to go to Johnny Rockets, but my sister made reservations at The Farm of Beverly Hills. Otherwise I wouldn't have seen her."

"Two guys," Anthony said, more to himself. He clenched a fist.

"I'm guessing you don't know the guy you saw on the news," Lecia said.

"I didn't even know Ginger had any male friends in L.A. She never told me about any of them."

"None?"

"No. She said she moved here and found the men too aggressive so really didn't date. Said all they were interested in were her . . . her breasts."

"You get 'em enhanced, you've got to expect guys to look."

Anthony shrugged, and Lecia was happy enough to let the subject drop. "Does the timeline help you out?" she asked.

"I'm trying to make sense of it."

"All right, I'll let you think."

"So if you saw her late afternoon, that means . . ." Anthony paused, his thoughts trailing. From what he could tell—although he hadn't done an extensive search of the house—there were no signs of forced entry. But that didn't mean that a friend or lover couldn't have entered the house with Ginger and then attacked her. "Either she went missing after her dinner at that restaurant, or . . ." He barely wanted to voice what was going through his mind. "Or this is all a setup?"

Lecia shrugged. "You know Ginger better than I do."

That was the problem. He was beginning to wonder if he knew her at all. Based on the smear campaign she'd executed against him in the media, he had to wonder if faking a kidnapping was beyond her.

Would she have been cunning enough to stage this scene, knowing how this could affect his life?

"What are you thinking?" Lecia asked him.

"I don't know what I'm thinking. No, I'm thinking that I need to go through her things. Get a clue as to where she may have gone."

"You're pretty much ruling out an abduction, then?"

"Right now, a lot of things don't make much sense. Maybe if I go through her things, I'll get a better understanding of what's going on. Who knows? Maybe there'll be a receipt for a plane ticket to Hawaii. Or something else. I don't know."

Lecia crossed her arms over her chest. "All right. So you don't need me. If it's easier, I can call a cab—"

"No, I'm gonna need you."

"But Ginger's not here."

"I still need your help."

Lecia hesitated before speaking. "Quite frankly, I don't feel comfortable standing around in what could be the middle of a crime scene."

"You're a doctor," Anthony quickly replied. "If I find something suspicious, you can tell me what it means."

A look of total disbelief crossed Lecia's face. "Something like what?"

"Something like . . . like what if her shoes are in some sort of bizarre order or something."

"*What?*"

"I don't know," Anthony hedged, knowing that sounded like a crock of shit. "Aren't therapists able to figure out weird things? Look at a scene and tell if someone is crazy?"

Lecia gave him a deadpan look. "Ah. I hear you."

"Good. So you understand."

"Oh, yeah. I understand. And guess what I just figured

out?" she asked, her voice filling with excitement. "You're a crack head."

Anthony reeled backward as if he'd been slapped. Her insult hurt. "I don't do drugs. My body is my temple."

"Your body may be your temple, but your brain is messed up. Tony, you sound like a complete nut. I'm not a cop. I'm not a crime scene investigator. I can't help you in any way except to tell you to call the police and report what you've seen."

"You don't date much with that razor-sharp tongue of yours, do you?"

"Oh, now we're making this about me?"

"Just help me go through Ginger's stuff." The truth was, he didn't want Lecia leaving him yet, even if her tongue was liable to scar him. "Forget all that bullshit I said. I just want you here with me."

Lecia's expression softened. There was a flash of confusion in her eyes, then something else Anthony couldn't quite read.

"Okay," she all but whispered. "Where do you want me to start?"

The first thing Lecia saw when she walked past the French doors with beveled glass into the master bedroom suite was the four-poster bed. It was in the middle of a room so large, it even had a lounge area. The suite was beautiful, as was the rest of the house. But it was lacking something.

Heart?

Yes, that was it. The house was large, filled with expensive things, but it didn't have a homey feeling. You'd never know anyone lived here, much less a married couple.

Lecia ventured farther into the large space. There were his and her bathrooms at either end of the room, and beside both were double doors that stood open, revealing enormous walk-in closets—the first sign that anyone lived here. The one closest to the main door was unmistakably Anthony's—filled with suits, shirts, jerseys. It was large, but from first glance, Ginger's was at least twice the size. Filled to capacity with designer outfits and shoes, Ginger's closet could easily have been another bedroom.

"Wow, that's a big closet," Lecia said, for lack of anything better to say. "Your wife could open a shop."

"Ginger complains that it's not big enough."

"You've got to be kidding me."

"Nope."

Lecia gaped at Anthony. Every item of clothes she owned fit in a closet a fraction the size. "To each her own, I guess. At first glance, can you tell if anything's missing?"

"I haven't a clue."

"Have you ever been through Ginger's stuff?"

"Never, so I'd have no way of knowing if anything *was* missing."

"There's a lot of crap in here. *Designer* crap, mind you," she added, giving Anthony a syrupy grin. "Ginger quite obviously has expensive taste."

"Yeah, she does. But this is Beverly Hills." Anthony shrugged as if to say, What could one expect?

"All right, what do you want me to look for?" Lecia asked.

"Phone records. Receipts. Anything. If there are boxes, go through them. Jacket and pants' pockets, too. Anywhere she might have a scrap of paper."

Lecia's gaze swept over the massive closet. Lord, this was going to be one huge task. At least she didn't have to go back to the office. Her next appointment had canceled, and she had booked an afternoon online counseling session. "This could take a while."

"I know. And I appreciate you helping me do this."

Lecia met Anthony's gaze. "Do you think she's really hurt?"

"I hope to hell not. I don't want to lose her to divorce as it is. I can't imagine losing her to anything else."

Lecia understood firsthand the pain of divorce. How it ripped a hole in your heart so big, you never knew if it could ever be filled.

"For your sake, I hope she's okay, and that you two work things out." The words sounded sincere, but saying them made her feel a little odd. Like there was a small part of her that didn't agree.

"Yeah, so do I."

Lecia planted her hands on her hips and started for the closet. She stopped before she reached it, turning to say, "By the way, I'm supposed to be doing an online counseling session in a little over an hour."

"No problem. You can do it here."

"Do my session here?"

"Why not? I've got high-speed Internet. I'm assuming you only have to go to your website and sign on with a password, right?"

"Well, yeah."

"Then sure. Do it here."

It was a feasible suggestion. So why did the reality of doing her session here make her feel a twinge of unease?

Because the last thing she wanted to do was counsel women about their sexuality with Anthony standing over her shoulder.

"Let's just hope we find what you're looking for before that," Lecia finally said.

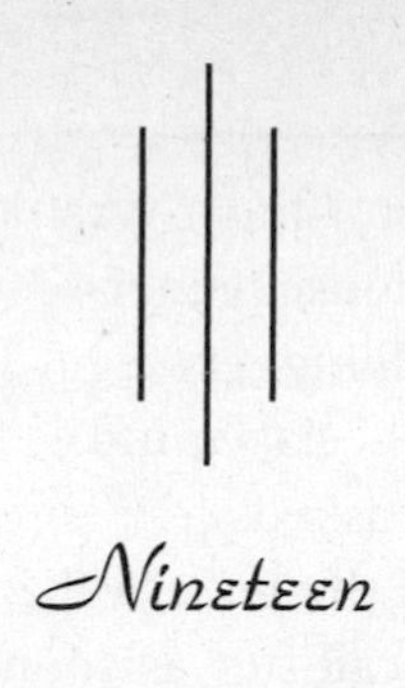

Nineteen

After a tedious forty-five minutes, Lecia dropped the umpteenth shoe box at her side and crawled over to the closet door. She peeked her head out. Anthony sat on the edge of his bed, a pile of letters and papers in his hands.

He saw her and asked, "Have you gone through all the boxes?"

"I wish. I've never known anyone to have so much stuff." Lecia slowly adjusted herself so she was sitting on her butt. "Can you pass me my purse, please?"

Anthony lifted Lecia's purse from one corner of the bed and tossed it to her. It was such a good throw, the purse actually landed in her palms.

"Thanks," she said, then dug the Ventolin out of her purse and inhaled two puffs.

"You okay?"

Lecia held her breath for as long as she could before speaking. "Just because I take my inhaler doesn't mean I'm dying. Certain things trigger it, like dust. But I take a puff, and in moments I'm fine."

"Sorry about the dust. Ginger wasn't exactly a homemaker. And I don't think the housekeeper—"

Anthony stopped talking. His eyes lit up at the same time the thought came into Lecia's mind.

"Housekeeper?" she asked.

Anthony jumped off the bed. "What's the matter with me? Why didn't I think to call her as soon as I came in? Claudia should have been working yesterday, the same day Ginger supposedly went missing. She's gotta be able to give me information."

Anthony's excitement was contagious. Lecia scurried over to him and stood behind his massive back as he punched in a number.

"Hey, Claudia. This is Anthony Beals . . . I'm okay, thanks. Listen, I have a question. You were here yesterday, right? . . . What time did you leave? . . . Really? . . . Oh. Well, okay. Thanks . . . No, nothing's wrong . . . Tomorrow? Um, I'm not sure. You know what—why don't you take the rest of the week off. Actually, I'll call you when I need you, okay? . . . Great."

"Well?" Lecia asked the moment Anthony replaced the receiver.

"My housekeeper came in for work yesterday, but Ginger sent her home early. Ginger apparently told her I'd be stopping by and that we'd want privacy."

"Oh, no."

"I wish to hell I knew what was going on." Anthony dragged a hand across the back of his neck. He stared in the direction of the bay window for several seconds before sinking onto the softness of the mattress.

Lecia watched him, an unusual feeling taking root. She wanted to do something to make him feel better, but the only thing she could think of was to wrap her arms around him. Yet that would be entirely inappropriate.

Anthony turned toward her. "I totally forgot. You need to use the computer, right?"

Lecia half nodded, half shrugged. "Maybe I'll just sign on and let people know that today's session will be canceled." She hated to do it, but she didn't want to take a break from going through Ginger's things until they were finished. And the plot was thickening. She wanted to know what was going on with Ginger as much as Anthony did. "You know what? Forget it. People will figure out pretty quickly that I'm not showing up." She groaned, slapping a cheek. "I can't believe I just said that. I'm never one to shirk my responsibilities."

"I don't have a problem with you using my computer."

Lecia waved a dismissive hand. "It's fine, really. Sometimes I do an actual online counseling session if people can't make it into the office to see me, or if people want to talk to me from across the country. It's always a tricky situation, though, because without seeing a patient, it's hard to ascertain exactly what's wrong. Today's session was simply going to be an informal chat, where people could sign on and ask questions. I'll e-mail the moderator and tell her that something has come up and I can't do the session."

"You're sure?"

"Uh-huh. It's not a big deal."

Anthony got to his feet. His knees cracked as he did. Lecia watched him walk away, noting his firm butt and strong legs. Her breath actually snagged in her throat.

She wrenched her gaze away. She was lusting after another woman's husband.

Lecia followed Anthony out of the bedroom and down the hall. He opened the last door on the right and entered. It was bright, filled with natural sunlight. She couldn't help thinking, *what a great place it would be to write.*

"It's already on," Anthony said, gesturing to a state-of-the-art computer that stood on a desk along the side wall. "Do your thing."

"I'll only be a couple minutes."

She went to her website, then signed in to access her e-mail. She was in the middle of typing a message to her moderator when she heard, "So, what kinds of questions do people ask you? How to masturbate?"

Spinning around in the swivel chair, Lecia gaped at him. "Tell me you didn't just say that."

A playful grin danced on his delicious-looking lips. "I'm curious."

"Go away."

"No, really. I'm curious."

"Oh, I'll bet. I've met plenty of guys like you. Curious in a perverted way." Most of the men she met didn't understand that sex therapy was serious business. They wanted to know the titillating details of her work, as if it might turn them on. Worse, practically all the men she had dated expected her to put out after the first date, and thought because she was a sex therapist that gave them the right to talk dirty to her at every opportunity. It disappointed her that Anthony seemed to be cut from the same cloth.

"Why is that perverted?"

Lecia finished typing her simple message, then sent it to the moderator. She logged off her website and got out of the chair. "I'm finished," she announced.

"Don't you think it's natural to be curious about certain things?" Anthony went on. "You drive along the highway and see an accident. It may be morbid, but you stop to take a look."

"I don't."

"You're the exception to the rule, then."

"I guess I am."

It seemed that Anthony was content to stay in the office and chat, so Lecia left the room. He quickly caught up with her, his proximity filling her senses. He wore no cologne, yet his unique, alluring scent called out to her in the most primitive way. She could easily imagine him wrapping her in his big arms, imagine her teeth nipping at his jaw—

"Doc, what's with the look?"

Lecia shook her head, hoping to toss the disturbing images from her mind. She had to snap out of whatever spell she was under. She was *not* attracted to Anthony Beals. But she knew all about scent, how it could drive a person wild.

If only she had a cold . . .

"Doc?"

"Um." *Get a hold of yourself!* "I was thinking . . . why don't you just call Ginger's family?"

Anthony paused in his bedroom doorway. "If I knew how to reach her family, believe me, I already would have called them."

Lecia let what he'd said sink in for a full five seconds. Then she said, "I thought you hadn't called them because you figured she wouldn't go there. But you're saying—"

"I'm saying I have no clue where they are."

Lecia could hardly believe her ears. "I thought you said this woman was your wife."

"Very funny."

"How well do you know her?"

"Well enough."

"Well enough that you don't know where her family is? You at least have to know who they are, right? What state they live in."

"Ginger wasn't in touch with her family."

"You know *nothing* about them?"

Anthony shook his head.

"Oh my God."

"Her mother was the only one she was close to," he explained, "and after she died, she pretty much cut off ties with the rest of them. She has a sister somewhere she doesn't talk to. New Orleans, I think. An alcoholic father. From what she told me, I can't say I blame her."

"I don't believe this. How on earth do you expect to track her down?"

Anthony paused, scratched his goatee. "Luck?"

"You are—"

"Crazy. You've already told me. But wherever Ginger is, I need to find her. I know it won't be easy."

"Impossible is more like it."

"I figure there's got to be a name stuffed in a pocket, a phone number. Something that will give me an idea of where she lived before she came to L.A."

Anthony returned to the bed and the pile of papers he had retrieved from Ginger's drawer. So far, they were all receipts for the marathon amount of shopping she had done in the short time they were married. He picked them up again, although he didn't expect to find any clue in that pile. The truth was, he didn't want to see the look of disillusionment on Lecia's face.

He had explained his marrying Ginger to his family, and he didn't feel like doing it again. His mother hadn't approved, calling their wedding hasty. But she had attended the ceremony out of respect for him. Anthony had hoped that at least one member from Ginger's family would attend, but none had.

"Did Ginger ever speak to her family on the phone?"

Anthony turned to face Lecia again. Clearly, she wasn't going to let the matter drop. Not that he could blame her. She was a therapist, trying to make sense of what now seemed a not so sound marriage.

If he'd had to do it over again, he wouldn't have married Ginger so quickly. But at the time, he thought he knew her. Or rather, he liked what he'd gotten to know. Liked it enough to believe it could be the foundation for a lasting marriage.

Ginger had been easy to talk to, and surprisingly positive, considering the crap she'd been through in her life. She hadn't been like the other women he'd dated—women who were totally into themselves and into his money. Nor did she seem brainless, like the females his father preferred. Ginger had been . . . well, she had seemed more like his mother, even with the enhanced Barbie doll body. A stand-by-your-man type of girl who was sweet and homey and simply wanted a good man.

"Ginger didn't talk to her family," he said. "And if she ever called them without my knowing, I'd be very surprised. She told me she had a very bad childhood. Her father was an alcoholic who'd abused her mother so badly, he left her a paraplegic. The bastard then bailed on Ginger's mother, taking her younger brother with him. Ginger took care of her mother until she died. Like I said, she also mentioned a sister. Apparently much older. Got away from the family and the abusive father before he paralyzed the mother. She married some rich doctor someplace but never helped them out."

"That sounds like a story line from *All Our Days.*"

"Tragic shit, I know."

"No, I mean that really sounds like a story line from *All Our Days*. About a year and a half ago. The girl's name was Linda, the brother's name was Chad. The older sister who married the doctor was Emily, if memory serves me correctly."

Anthony had a sinking feeling in his gut. "You're trying to mess with me, right?"

"I swear to God." Lécia made a sign of the cross over her heart. "I got hooked on the show when I was writing my book. During my lunch break, I'd watch it."

"Are you saying Ginger . . . that she made up that stuff about her family?"

"All I know is that exact scenario you just mentioned took place on a soap opera over a year ago. If Ginger's family truly went through that, then what can I say? Stranger things have happened, I guess. But right now—"

"Hell, no." Anthony slapped a fist against his palm. "If that bitch played me—"

"Tony, calm down."

"Why?" he challenged. "Because you're afraid I'm gonna lose control? Turn into the monster that Ginger's been painting me out to be?"

Lecia didn't like the anger in his words, but she heard the utter pain beneath them. Everything he'd believed was turning out to be a lie.

She replied, "You need to calm down because anger won't solve anything."

"Thanks, Doc, but I didn't ask for any psychobabble."

"Excuse me for offering an opinion," Lecia retorted.

"I'm sorry." Anthony drew in a deep breath and released it slowly. "I thought I knew her. I thought what we had . . . Ah, what the hell does it matter?"

The exasperation in his voice—the defeat—touched her deep in her soul. Lecia knew what it was to discover that the person you loved wasn't the person you thought them to be. It was one of the worst blows someone could ever be dealt.

"I'm sorry, Tony."

"Yeah. Whatever."

"I wish there was something more I could do." Some people threw words like that out without meaning them, but Lecia was sincere. Clearly, Anthony cared for his wife. She knew that in Hollywood people often married for recreation, but she got the sense that Anthony hadn't. For him, marriage was about commitment. Ginger, however, hadn't struck Lecia as the type who cared much about sticking to her word once she'd promised "I do." She couldn't stake her career on it, but it was the vibe the woman had given her in those brief minutes outside the bar.

"I just need to find her," Anthony said. "And she's got a helluva lot of explaining to do."

"You didn't find any cell phone bills?" Lecia asked. Surely there had to be *something*.

"Naw." Anthony paused. "But . . ."

He turned with lightning speed and started to walk out of the room. Lecia hustled to keep up behind him. "But what?"

"But maybe, just maybe, something new came in the mail. Claudia always piles the stack in the office. And Ginger wasn't only lazy when it came to housework. Sometimes she'd leave the mail sitting there for a week."

Lecia's stomach fluttered with nervous energy. Maybe she was insane, but she was taken up in this drama.

"Oh, baby," Anthony said after sifting through the mail. His face lit up like a Christmas tree.

Lecia's heart pounded. "You found something?"

He spun around, facing her. "There is a God." He held up a number ten envelope. "This, Dr. Love, is Ginger's cell phone bill."

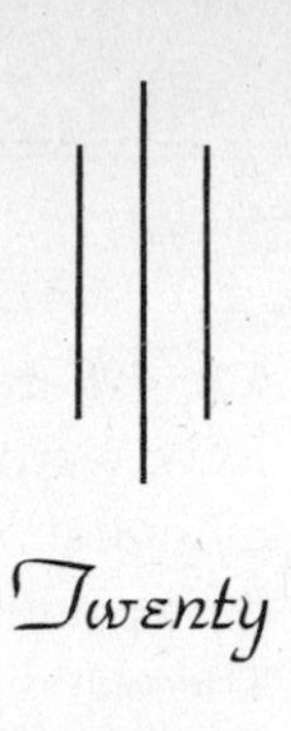

Twenty

Ginger's cell phone bill. Anthony held it up like it was a check for ten million dollars. Lecia's own heart beat in rapid succession.

"Now what?" she asked. Her voice brimmed with excitement. "You want to make some calls?"

"You're damn right I'm gonna make some calls." Anthony slapped the envelope against his palm. "Except that wherever Ginger is, I don't want her to know I'm coming."

"But if you're able to track her down, you'll at least know that she's all right."

"Then what? She takes off, telling the media that I tracked her down and stalked her? Right now I'd bet my life that she's all right. But that doesn't make a bit of difference, not if she still pretends she's scared of me. No, I need to find her. Talk to her. That's the whole reason I got you involved, remember? This will all be pointless if I don't get to talk to her."

Lecia couldn't see how it would be pointless if he figured out his wife was alive and well, off somewhere of her own free will. That would have to make a difference to the police. But she bit her tongue.

"There is something," he said.

"What?"

"It'll be in my records somewhere." He started toward the large filing cabinet. "When we were planning the wedding, I insisted that Ginger send an invitation to her family. She gave me an address to give to the wedding planner, which is why New Orleans rings a bell. The wedding planner gave me back all that info, and I put it in my files."

Lecia folded her arms over her chest as Anthony opened the top drawer and began flipping through the hanging folders. "An address will be perfect."

Anthony withdrew one of the hanging files and started sifting through its contents. "Now you'll really think I'm a crack head, since I didn't remember this before."

"I was kidding about the crack head bit."

"Here we go," Anthony said, sounding proud. "This is the address."

Lecia couldn't hold back a wide-mouthed grin. "After all our searching, you actually have an address."

"And all the people she's called in the last month."

"Do you think she would have gone to her sister's place? You said they weren't close."

"If her story wasn't entirely fiction, I'm thinking that would be the best place for her to go. Because I'd never expect it."

Anthony was thinking about how he would get to New Orleans when his cell phone rang. He dug it out of his back pocket and said, "T here."

"Anthony, Keith."

"Hey, Keith. What's up?"

"I've heard from the detective again. Says you haven't called him to arrange a time to turn yourself in."

"Turn myself in?"

"Wrong choice of words, sorry," Keith quickly said. "I mean turn yourself in for questioning."

Was Keith telling the truth? Anthony wondered. His own lawyer shouldn't try to railroad him. But then, his own wife shouldn't try to set him up.

And even if Keith was advising him to the best of his abilities, this detective could easily be lying, assuring Keith that they only wanted to question him, when in reality they could be planning to slap cuffs on him.

"I've been busy," Anthony said.

"The guy's pretty anxious to speak to you. And, quite frankly, I think the sooner you go in and rule yourself out as a suspect, the better."

Anthony wondered if he should tell his lawyer what he'd learned about Ginger. He didn't want to make a decision without weighing the pros and cons. And he knew, regardless, that the best thing would be to find Ginger and return her to Beverly Hills so the whole world would know he hadn't done anything to hurt her.

"I will," Anthony told Keith.

"When?"

"Soon. But look, I'm in the middle of something. I'm gonna have to call you back."

"That's what you said earlier." Keith sounded wary.

"I know. Stay by the phone." Then Anthony ended the call and turned off his cell phone.

"What?" Lecia asked.

"Come on."

"Where are we going?"

"I'm getting a bad feeling." And if there was one thing his mama had always instilled in him, it was to trust his gut.

Too bad he hadn't had any premonition that something was wrong before he married Ginger.

Anthony strode down the winding staircase and toward the front door with Lecia close at his heels. He had his hand on the doorknob when she said, "Wait. My purse."

Anthony couldn't explain it, but he felt a sick, nervous energy. He had felt it often during the two years he'd played for the Buffalo Bills, standing on the sidelines, knowing his team was going to lose, and wishing the coach would put him on the field to prove what he could do.

As he watched Lecia hustle up the stairs, he wondered if there was anything he was forgetting. He had his keys in his back pocket. His wallet. He could use some more cash, though.

Before Lecia returned, he took the steps two at a time and all but ran into his office. He pulled aside the painting of Martin Luther King, Jr., behind which was a safe. He was in the middle of punching in the combination when he heard Lecia's shoes clicking against the marble as she descended the stairs.

"I'm in the office," he called out to her. "I won't be long."

"Where's your bathroom?"

"The door right at the top of the stairs."

Lecia didn't say anything else, and Anthony went back to the business at hand. He popped open the safe and stared at the piles of money. Thank God Ginger didn't have access to this cash. And not because he hadn't trusted his wife, but because this was emergency money that even he didn't want to touch unless necessary. Now, he was dipping into the secret stash because of the nagging feeling in his gut.

The one that told him he wouldn't have time to go to the bank.

* * *

Minutes later, as they were driving, Anthony slapped his palm against the steering wheel and cursed.

"What's the matter?" Lecia asked him.

He glanced in the rearview mirror. "Do you think that cop was slowing down?"

"What cop?"

"The one who just drove past us."

"I didn't even see him." Lecia turned in her seat, looking behind her. "He's not there now."

"Because he disappeared around a curve," Anthony said. "Something's not right," he mumbled, as though speaking to himself.

"You think he was heading out here to arrest you?" Lecia asked, her tone full of doubt.

"Who knows?"

Anthony thrummed his fingers on the steering wheel. The expression on his face said he was thinking hard about what to do.

"Honestly, Tony, I don't think it will be as bad as you expect if you turn yourself in."

"What's with all this turn myself in talk?"

"Sorry. I only said that because you said that before, but that's not what I meant to say. Okay, I'm rambling."

"You don't think I hurt Ginger, do you?"

"No," Lecia responded, impassioned. "You know I don't."

"What are you doing for the rest of the day?"

"Other than work from home?"

He faced her. "You don't have to meet anyone, do you?"

"No."

"Good."

"Good?"

"Yeah."

"Good why?"

"Because."

"I think I'd rather be talking to a brick wall."

"I'd rather not be talking. I'm trying to think."

Lecia waited a whole two seconds before asking, "Do you want me to make some calls?"

"No."

"Where are we going?" she asked, surprised to hear the question from her lips. She should have asked him if he was taking her back to her office. He had what he needed—Ginger's cell phone record and an address where he could possibly find her. He didn't need her anymore.

"I said I'm trying to think."

Lecia stared out the window. It had been a stressful enough day, and she thought she should tell him to let her out so she could catch a cab and go on her merry way. It was a great idea—yet she couldn't voice the words.

After several minutes Anthony said, "Naw, I can't do that."

Lecia stared at him, waiting for him to realize that he hadn't completed his thought. When he didn't, she asked, "Can't do what?"

"Head to my hotel."

"I thought you were staying with Kahari."

"Naw. He's got enough room, but I didn't want to impose. Besides, when I left my house, I hadn't figured I'd be gone more than a night or two."

"Why can't you head to your hotel?" Lecia asked, getting back to his comment.

"The cops have got to know that's where I'm staying."

So he still didn't want to talk to them. "You can't avoid them forever."

"Wanna bet?"

Anthony hit the brakes and made an abrupt U-turn. Lecia gripped the door handle as her heart leapt to her throat.

"What are you doing?"

"I have to find Ginger. I sure as hell won't be able to find her if I stay here and deal with police bullshit."

"Tony . . ." Lecia said warily.

He picked up speed as he headed toward 101.

"Tony, please tell me where you're going."

"New Orleans," he answered simply.

"Now?" Lecia cried.

"I have no other choice. It's time to pay a visit to Ginger's sister, and hope to hell that I find Ginger there."

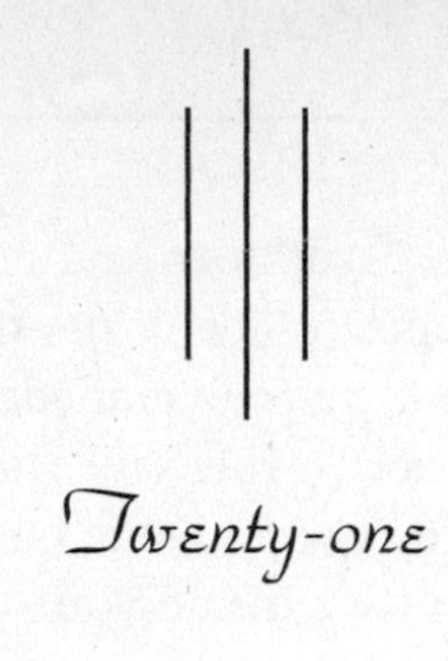

Twenty-one

"Oh, no no no no." Lecia shook her head vehemently. "You can pull off at the next exit and drop me off, thank you very much."

Anthony glanced her way, held her gaze. "Come on, Doc. You're not gonna leave me to do this on my own?"

"I never wanted to be involved in the first place, remember?"

"You think I wanted any of this?" he asked. "Hell, no. But this is the way things are, and I have to deal with it."

"That's right. *You* have to deal with it. I don't."

Anthony was silent a moment, then he said, "If I head to New Orleans on my own, the cops will think I took off. As long as you're with me, you can verify that I was truly trying to find my wife."

"I'll do that now. If we head to the police station together—"

"No way."

"Anthony, you're only going to make things worse."

"You know the cops will slap a pair of cuffs on me if I show up there. Especially if they're on the way to the house, which I have a feeling they are."

"You see *one* patrol car—"

"That's another one," Anthony said as another police car passed them on the opposite side of the road. This time there was no doubt that the cop inside craned his neck to see who was in Anthony's vehicle. "You saw that, right?" Anthony asked. "You saw that cop checking me out."

"Not that anyone can see inside your vehicle. The tint's so dark."

Lecia groaned loudly when she saw they were heading toward the Hollywood Freeway. After that it would be Interstate 10, at which point she was certain he wouldn't turn back.

"It's not too late to turn around," she told him.

Anthony glanced her way and said, "I can't risk having my ass thrown in jail before I find Ginger."

"You'd rather be a fleeing felon?"

Lecia's words only solidified his position. "See—you're referring to me as a felon."

"I'm only trying to say—"

"If you're calling me a felon, what do you think the police will say?" He paused, let his words sink in. "I have to do this. My life will only be normal again once I find Ginger."

"That's what you're hoping, but what if you're wrong?"

"There's only one way to find out."

Lecia grunted her frustration.

"Wouldn't you do the same thing, in my shoes?" he asked her.

"Maybe. But I wouldn't drag anyone else into my mess."

"You're forgetting this mess started when you told my wife to leave me."

"It did not!"

"Okay, maybe not. But if you hadn't told her I was a pervert, I'm sure we'd have worked everything out by now."

"Sure, blame me."

"This isn't about blame. This is about . . . solving a mystery."

"Won't you please drop me along the highway? I can call for someone to pick me up."

Lecia's voice was soft, shaky even, and Anthony felt like a sack of shit. He was tempted to pull over right there and do what she asked. He wanted her with him, but he wanted her to *want* to be with him.

"It's just that . . ." His voice trailed off. "I'll still need you when I find Ginger. And, um, I'll need you to give me advice along the way." Why didn't he want to let her out of his car? "I just . . . need you." He spoke honestly, not exactly sure what had gotten into him. He certainly didn't need a kidnapping charge on top of everything else. "Will you please just stick it out with me?"

Lecia shook her head slowly as she stared at him with a frown. "Anthony Beals, this has got to be the lamest, most spontaneous, ill-thought-out plan . . ."

A grin broke out on his face. "So, we're on?"

". . . ridiculous waste of time . . ."

He extended a fist for her to knock with her own.

"Not to mention that I have a million and one things to do."

"I love it when you talk dirty."

Lecia smacked his hand. "You are—"

"Crazy. I know." He shrugged. "That's why I need a therapist with me on this trip. Can you imagine me on my own?"

Lecia glared at him, but there was a hint of a smirk beneath her scowl. Warmth tingled across Anthony's chest.

"We have to go to New Orleans and head straight back. Okay? Because I wasn't kidding when I said I have a million things to do."

"No problem. I'm gonna head to this address, see if Ginger's there, and if she's not, I'll turn right around."

Lecia mumbled something Anthony couldn't quite understand.

"What was that?" he asked.

"You don't want to know."

He glanced to the left so she wouldn't see that his lips were fighting a smile. Then he reached for the stereo, turned it on, and found Hot 92 Jamz.

"That okay?" he asked her.

"As long as I still have my ear drums when this road trip is over."

The good doctor and that tongue. He wondered how she put it to use when she wasn't arguing with a guy.

Say, when she was kissing one.

Where the hell did that thought come from? Anthony asked himself. Especially at a time like this, when he was on the road to find his wife. He shouldn't be thinking any wayward thoughts about Dr. Love.

But he was a guy. Guys thought these kinds of things even when they didn't want to. It was ingrained in their genes from the time they hit puberty. Before that, really. Thinking them didn't make him like his father.

"What's with that look?" Lecia demanded, her tone accusatory.

Whoa, did this woman have radar or what? "What look?"

"That one. The one that says you're getting some perverse pleasure out of this."

Anthony held up a hand. "Come on, Doc. We're barely into our trip. Can you at least wait a few minutes before you bust my balls?"

She sneered at him, then looked away.

"If you want me to change the station—"

"Don't talk to me. I don't want to hear your voice for at least six hours."

"Whatever you say, Doc."

"I just told you not to talk."

Anthony held up a hand in surrender, letting her know he'd gotten the point. Then he suppressed a smile as he headed toward Interstate 10, the road he would take all the way to the Big Easy.

Twenty-two

"Good God, this is one hot place." Anthony dragged the now damp handkerchief across his forehead, but still sweat oozed from his pores.

Lecia pulled her silk camisole away from her skin. She blew down her shirt in a useless attempt to cool herself. "And to think, people talk about Florida being a killer in the summer. Dry heat my ass."

They were currently in Hottest Spot in the World, Arizona, standing outside of their vehicle. They had stopped at some nowhere gas station because they needed to fill up and get some refreshments, but after being cooped up for so long, they had opted to walk around first and stretch their legs. Barely five minutes later the heat was almost unbearable.

"It's at least one hundred degrees in the shade," Anthony commented, clearly still miserable.

"We should probably just hit the road as quickly as possible." Lecia didn't care if her butt went numb back in the car. Right about now the air-conditioned Navigator was far more preferable to this heat. "You want me to get the refreshments while you gas up?"

"Yeah, sure."

"What do you want? Juice? Soda? Water?"

"All of the above. We may as well stock up."

She didn't bother to again suggest that they fly to New Orleans. Anthony had nixed that idea the first time. He was concerned that if any type of law enforcement were looking for him, they'd be able to track him down from flight information.

Which meant they were resigned to a wretched thirty-hour drive. So far, they'd driven for four hours. They had a very long way to go.

Pushing that troubling thought from her mind, Lecia headed into the store, which from the outside looked like little more than a shack. Inside, however, the place had clearly been renovated. The tile floors sparkled. Bright halogen lights illuminated the entire store. Every rack looked brand spanking new, as did the fridges filled with juice and other cold beverages.

The interior put her mind at ease. She had a phobia of public rest rooms, but if they were as clean as the rest of the place, she didn't think the experience would be in the least traumatic.

Sure enough, the rest room was not only clean, it smelled faintly of citrus. Lecia relieved herself quickly, washed her hands, then headed back into the store.

Anthony had said to pick up a variety of cold drinks, so she grabbed a six-pack of soda and two large bottles of water, then brought them to the counter. The guy who'd been sitting behind the register stood when he saw her coming. No older than twenty-one, he was as thin as a rake, wore a black AC DC T-shirt, and sported a dark brown mullet. If his name wasn't Billy Bob, then her name wasn't Lecia Calhoun.

Lecia dumped the armful of items and headed back to the

fridge for juice. She chose an orange-banana combo as well as raspberry-lime. This would be more than enough to last them before they had to stop for gas again.

Maybe it was seeing all the bars of chocolates and bags of chips that triggered her hunger, but her stomach rumbled. Pausing on her way back to the counter, she nabbed a large bag of potato chips and two packages of Twinkies.

So much for healthly eating, she thought. She was sure the junk food would add five pounds to her thighs the moment she inhaled it, but hey, a girl had to splurge every now and then.

"That everything?" Billy Bob asked. One of his two front teeth was half rotted.

"Uh, yeah." She smiled sheepishly. Then nearly burst into laughter when she saw that his name tag actually read BILLY BOB.

The door chimes sounded and both Lecia and Billy Bob looked in that direction. Anthony flashed an easy smile as he strolled inside.

Lecia turned back to Billy Bob to settle the bill, but the young man wasn't looking at her. He stared at Anthony, a sparkle in his eyes and an open-mouthed grin on his face.

"I know who you are," he said in an excited drawl.

Lecia saw the look of panic flash on Anthony's face. They'd heard no news to the effect that the police were looking for him, but it was entirely possible. If word had reached this remote spot . . .

"You—You're that famous actor. Eddie Murphy!"

Anthony looked too stunned to speak. Almost as if he wasn't sure whether Billy Bob was pulling his leg.

"Oh my God," Billy Bob went on. "I can't believe you're here."

There was no doubt about it, Billy Bob wasn't pulling Anthony's leg. He truly thought that Anthony was Eddie Murphy. Lecia didn't know whether to be relieved or roll her eyes at how this kid could be so blind. The only resemblance Anthony had to Eddie Murphy was that they were both black.

"Shucks," Anthony said. He even snapped a finger. "I didn't think anyone would recognize me out here."

"Are you kidding?" Billy Bob's eyes nearly popped out of his head. "Man, I'd recognize you anywhere. I love your movies."

Lecia fought to suppress a chuckle. She hadn't expected Anthony to go along with Billy Bob's mistake, but now that he had, she thought the joke was priceless.

"You do?"

"'Course I do!"

"So you're a big fan, huh?" Anthony probed.

"Oh, yeah. I loved you in that movie with Robert DeNiro. The one where you played a cop."

"You mean *Showtime*."

"Yeah, that's the one. Man, you were funnier'n shit." Billy Bob threw a hand over his mouth. "Oops."

Anthony waved a hand. "Aw, don't worry about it," he said, chuckling softly. Then, "Where are your rest rooms?"

"Straight back."

Anthony turned to start off, but he caught sight of all the stuff Lecia had on the counter. "You sure that's enough?" he asked, his tone playfully sarcastic.

"It's going to be a long trip."

He shrugged, then started for the back of the store.

Billy Bob's gaze followed him until he was out of sight. "Oh, man. I can't believe this. Eddie Murphy in *my* store. Where're you two heading?"

"Um . . ." What should she say? "Well, it's private. As I'm sure you can understand. Not that we can't trust you to keep quiet, but it's the only way to make sure no one will bother us. Some people—not you, of course—like to sell that kind of info to tabloids."

"I'd never do that," Billy Bob said, signing a cross over his heart. "But I sure do understand where you're comin' from. Sometimes I read those stories, and I feel so bad for y'all famous folks."

"I'm glad you understand," Lecia said.

"Um, maybe . . . you think I could get his autograph, though?"

"I'm sure he'd be happy to do that for you," Lecia told him, smiling sweetly.

And Anthony did just that, much to Billy Bob's absolute thrill. At least he didn't have a camera to snap the fraudulent moment. Though he would probably save the store's video surveillance tape, if he could.

"Okay, babe," Anthony said, placing his hand on the small of Lecia's back. "We've got to roll."

Lecia's body tingled at Anthony's touch, which meant, she told herself, that she had to be completely insane. Because obviously he was only touching her for Billy Bob's benefit. It *wasn't* supposed to feel so damn good.

He didn't let go of her until they were outside the store. "Did you believe that guy?" he asked, laughing. "Eddie Murphy? Gimme a break."

"It's gotta be the goatee."

Anthony rolled his eyes playfully, saying he knew better.

He unlocked the doors and helped Lecia pile all the stuff in the Navigator. "All this junk food's gonna make you hyper," he told her.

"The place wasn't exactly overflowing with healthy choices. Besides, I'm hungry."

"Me, too." He pulled his shirt away from his chest. "And sweaty. Damn, I wish I had a change of clothes."

"I saw a rack of stuff in the store."

"I didn't."

"It was at the back, near one of the fridges. We could at least get another T-shirt or something."

"I guess you're right. We still have a ways to go."

"All the more reason to get on a plane and get there as soon as possible."

Anthony leveled a lopsided grin in her direction. "Nice try, but you know why we can't do that."

"It was worth a shot."

Billy Bob's eyes lit up when they entered the store again, but he left them to their shopping in peace.

The clothing section—if you could call it that—should have had a sign over the top of it that read, "Tacky." Because that's exactly what the selection was. Most of it looked like it had been salvaged from a bin at a dollar store, or even pilfered from a Good Will donation drop box.

"I don't want to wear any of this," Lecia complained. But she also didn't want to stay in the camisole that was sticking to her body like a second skin. With the heat, she had shed her blazer once they stepped outside the car, but that had left her feeling quite naked. One of these cotton T-shirts would be much more comfortable all around.

The shirt in the best condition was one that read, TRY A VIRGIN in bold letters and beneath that caption, *U.S. Virgin Islands.*

Anthony groaned pitifully as he skimmed the rack. "Man, we stopped at the wrong place."

"Better than being recognized at some bigger service station," Lecia whispered. "By someone who can actually discern faces."

"Guess this will have to do." Anthony lifted a tropical print shirt. "If only they had the matching straw hat."

"They do."

Anthony's gaze flew to Lecia's. "You're kidding me, right?"

She giggled. "Yeah, I am. But they've got some cute floppy hats." She picked one up from a second rack and dangled it before him. "Bend down." Anthony did, and she placed the hat on his head. But he didn't straighten right away. Instead, his eyes met hers. Held. A frisson of heat traveled through Lecia's veins.

She swallowed. Was she mistaken, or was Anthony looking at her like . . . like he wanted to kiss her?

Looking down, she stepped backward. She tried to keep the emotion out of her voice as she said, "Now people will mistake you for Gilligan."

"I think you need one, too. The sun's hot." Anthony picked up a pale blue hat and planted it on her head. His finger skimmed her cheek as he pulled his hand away. "Ooh, that's cute, Doc."

Lecia inhaled a slow breath as she tried to figure out if Anthony was flirting with her. But she wasn't able to give it much thought because Billy Bob's voice intruded on the moment.

"Y'all need some help?"

Lecia whirled around and found Billy Bob right behind her. "No. No, we're fine."

"I've got some more T-shirts in the back," Billy Bob went on.

"No. This should do it. For me, at least. What about you, *Eddie*?"

"I'm cool."

At the cash register, Billy Bob punched in all the items. Then he announced, "Thirty-four seventy-seven."

Anthony handed him a fifty and told him to keep the change. Billy Bob actually squealed in delight. "Aw, man. Thanks."

"No problem."

"If you're driving back this way," Billy Bob said, "be sure to stop by."

Anthony raised a hand in a good-bye as he and Lecia left the store.

Twenty-three

Anthony had been driving for about five minutes when Lecia reached into the plastic bags filled with the stuff they'd bought. Then she announced, "Don't look."

Anthony immediately glanced her way. "Don't what?"

She took out the T-shirt and placed it on her lap. "Don't look at me."

Lecia grasped the bottom edge of her camisole, and Anthony narrowed his eyes in her direction. "Yo, Doc. What are you doing?"

"Changing."

Anthony forced his gaze back to the road, then swerved to the right when he realized he'd moved out of his lane.

"Pay attention," Lecia told him. "To the road."

Easy for her to say. Although he stared ahead, he couldn't resist a quick glance to the right. He caught a flash of a lacy white bra and the curve of her breasts just before the T-shirt covered her skin.

A quick flash, yet his mouth watered. Suddenly irritated with himself, he jerked his gaze back to the highway. What the hell was wrong with him?

It didn't help matters when Lecia drew the seat belt across her body. The shirt tightened over her breasts.

Again Anthony looked away. But not without feeling the tickling of an arousal. Not enough to give him a hard-on, but enough to give him pause.

Ginger was a throw-it-in-your-face type when it came to sexuality. In the bedroom, she was voracious. When she went out, her style was skimpy and provocative. She liked men to check her out, no matter how much she would deny that fact.

But that wasn't what had drawn Anthony to her. In fact, she hadn't been that way when he'd first met her, but she changed practically the day after they'd gotten married. "I don't want you tempted to look at anyone else," she told him. He'd figured she was insecure that she might lose her star-athlete husband to temptation, and he didn't entirely blame her. Lots of men in his position strayed from their wives simply because they could.

But despite Ginger's obvious sex appeal, she hadn't stirred him on quite the same level as Lecia had just done. And Lecia had done it unintentionally.

The heat must be getting to him, he thought.

And maybe, just maybe, he was a little intrigued about the good doctor because of her job. Hell, she talked sex for a living. That would turn any hot-blooded guy on.

Wouldn't it?

"New Orleans is a long way off," Lecia said. "What's the plan for tonight?"

"Ah, yeah. Tonight." He hadn't really thought about it, but it suddenly dawned on him that they'd have to stop somewhere and sleep. "I guess we'll stop when I get tired of driving and then start off in the morning."

Lecia nodded, then asked, "At a hotel?"

"Of course." He leveled a lopsided grin in her direction. "I kidnap in style. I wouldn't have you camping out in my car."

"That remains to be seen. You may take me to the Roach Motel."

"You in the Roach Motel? Never. You're the kind of girl who makes a guy want to splurge."

Lecia had a light, easy laugh. The kind that emanated warmth from her body straight to another person's.

Anthony said, "You seem okay with all this now."

She faced him. "Hmm?"

"Five hours ago you weren't too happy. In fact, you looked mad enough to kill someone."

"I know. But . . ." She shrugged. "Life's an adventure, right? Sometimes, you just have to roll with it. This is kind of sad to say, but in a way, taking off like this was just what I needed. To get away. Because my life has been one crazy string of promotional events and I'm *really* getting tired of that. I need a break."

"You need to call anybody—let them know where you are?"

"Are you fishing?" Lecia asked, a laugh in her voice.

"Fishing for what? Oh, to see if you have a man? No, I wasn't. But . . . do you?"

"I'm free, single, and disengaged."

Anthony simply nodded. At least he wasn't keeping her from some jealous lover who might want to blow his head off. He hadn't even thought of that when he'd hit the road. "What I was really asking is if you've got to call someone at the office to let them know you won't be there."

"I'm not in the office tomorrow."

"Then I picked a good day to do this."

"Don't push your luck."

"Whatever your reasons, thanks for sticking with me."

"I know you didn't do anything to your wife. That's the main reason I'm here."

"It means a lot to hear you say that."

Lecia pulled down the passenger seat visor and checked herself out in the mirror. She ran her fingers through her short hair, ruffling the already messy coif. Frowning, she pushed the visor back up. "That's a lost cause."

"Your hair looks great. You look great."

Her lips twisted in an expression that said she didn't believe him.

"I swear. You've got that Halle Berry thing happening, which is *hot.*"

"Oh, yeah. Like anyone could ever compare me to Halle."

"You've got to know you're hot."

"Let's change the subject."

Shock of all shocks, Lecia looked embarrassed. A hint of pink even touched her honey brown cheeks. She didn't know how attractive she was, and it made him like her that much more. Clearly, Dr. Love was down to earth. Real.

"I was thinking," Lecia began, "that I could call the numbers from Ginger's cell phone bill. Pretend to be an old friend looking for her."

"An old friend?"

"I don't know. I can always say I'm calling from Publisher's Clearing House," she said with a wry grin. "That might get her to come to the line."

"You go, Tuppence."

Lecia's eyes narrowed. "What did you say?"

He shook his head briefly. "Nothing."

"Did you call me Tuppence?"

"Yeah. It's from—"

"I know what it's from," Lecia said, cutting him off. "But I have to admit, I'm surprised you do."

Anthony took his eyes off the road to face her for a couple beats. "You a Christie fan?"

"Totally," Lecia replied, as if anyone who met her should know that off the bat. "You, too?"

"Agatha Christie's my girl."

Lecia continued to eye him skeptically. Could it be that this man, a superstar jock, was indeed an Agatha Christie fan? "So I should call you Tommy."

"Tommy and Tuppence. Two of the best amateur detectives in fiction. I loved *Partners in Crime.*"

Lecia gaped at him. "Wow. You're not kidding."

"Of course, no one beats Poirot. What?" he asked when she wouldn't stop staring at him. "You don't believe me."

"I believe you. I'm just . . . surprised."

"I've read every one of Agatha's books at least twice. I even have one on the backseat."

Lecia glanced behind her.

"It's in that black bag with my CDs."

Not sure whether she believed him, Lecia reached for the bag and brought it forward onto her lap. "May I?"

"Be my guest."

She pulled out a well-read copy of *Death on the Nile.* "Well, I'll be damned. I've never met another soul who's as crazy about Agatha as I am."

"You just met him." The light in Anthony's eyes spoke volumes. "What's your favorite title?"

"Hmm. I'd have to say *A Pocket Full of Rye.*"

"Ooh, gotta love Miss Marple."

"What about you?"

"I really loved *Curtain,* Poirot's last case. But I've got to go with *The Murder of Roger Ackroyd."*

"Definitely my second favorite. Well, tied with *Murder, She Said."*

"You're cool," Anthony said, grinning at her. "I dig you."

Lecia thumbed through the paperback, then placed the book on her lap with a contended sigh.

"I have the hardcovers in a special place in my house," he said. "No one touches those. But I carry around the paperbacks to actually read. You fly from city to city to play an opposing team, there's no better way to pass the time than with a Christie title."

Lecia tried to imagine Anthony sprawled out in first class, tuning out his teammates as he devoured an Agatha Christie novel. She couldn't quite picture it. "What about Ginger? Is she a Christie fan?"

Anthony shook his head. "She doesn't read."

"Not at all?"

"Nope. Says it's too hard to stay interested in a story. She'd rather watch a movie."

"That's the problem with people these days. They've forgotten how wonderful books are. And you can take them with you anywhere." She held the book up. "Like a long road trip."

When Anthony didn't make any type of comment, Lecia studied his profile. His happy expression had morphed into something darker. Had she said something wrong?

"Tony, what's wrong?"

"I'm just thinking about Ginger. Wondering how we ended up together when we're so obviously different."

"Opposites attract, as they say."

"Yeah, but . . ." His voice trailed off.

"But what?"

"Nothing."

Lecia waited, hoping he would complete his thought. When he didn't, she said, "You're not going to tell me?"

"You're a shrink. And I don't need a shrink."

"Is that what you think—that I'm trying to psychoanalyze you?"

"Are you?"

"Hey, you brought up your differences, I didn't."

"So you won't mind if we drop it."

"Fine," she told him.

Several seconds passed. Anthony didn't look her way, but he could see that she'd turned and was staring through the passenger window. There wasn't much to see on this stretch of highway except cacti and tumbleweed.

It seemed like ages passed before she spoke. "Can I ask something else?"

"I've already had enough people grill me about why I married Ginger."

"That wasn't what I was going to say, but . . . it's obviously a touchy subject for you."

"Meaning I *should* talk about it?"

"It might help."

"When I'm ready for your input, I'll let you know."

He realized his tone was sarcastic, though he hadn't meant it to be. It was just that he didn't want to talk about his relationship with Ginger. Especially not with a shrink.

He felt stupid enough with the way things had turned out for him. Not only did he live in Beverly Hills, it seemed he fit right in, and in a way he didn't want to. So many stars married and divorced like it was strictly for entertainment, and while that had never been his plan, it appeared to have become his life.

And fine, things happened. People split. That was a part of life. What nagged at him was that he should be hurting over Ginger's leaving because he loved her. Instead his biggest concern was that she'd take him to the cleaners. Granted, he'd known her less than a year, but still, what did that say about him?

You're more like your dead-beat father than you ever thought.

Anthony's hands tightened on the steering wheel as his thoughts ventured to his father. He barely talked to him these days. They kept in touch at birthdays and Christmas, but that was pretty much it. He did the same with his half siblings, of which there were plenty in the state of Tennessee. The moment he'd gotten a great contract, most of them came out of the woodwork, looking for handouts. In the beginning he hadn't known how to say no. He'd also figured it was some sort of familial duty to spread the wealth. That had turned out to be a disaster, because no matter how much he gave, it never seemed enough for them.

His father had known better than to ask him for a dime. The man had barely been in his life. There'd been at least eight years when they hadn't spoken at all.

The years when he had grown into a man, under the guidance of his mother.

In fact, it was his mother who had encouraged him to reach out to his father. Reluctantly, he had, and they'd salvaged some sort of relationship, but it certainly wasn't a father-son one. Anthony knew he didn't need that, not at this stage of the game. He was a grown man, taking care of himself, making his own way, and doing a damn good job of it.

He still wondered what had possessed his father to call him after the story about him and that prostitute had broken. A sense of newfound kinship? His father's words still pissed him off.

"I know there are things that happened between your mother and me that you didn't understand when you were a kid, but it seems that now you do. Because now you're a man."

"Pops, I didn't do anything with that woman."

"Whatever happened, just know that you have my support. I'm sorry you're going through this. And don't worry about Ginger. If she's a decent woman, she'll forgive you."

It wasn't that his father's words weren't true—if Ginger had trusted him the way a wife should trust her husband, she would have heard him out. What peeved him was his father's implied jab at his mother. That if *she* had been a decent woman, she would have stood by and watched him have affair after affair.

She practically had. It was Anthony who'd sat his mother down one day and told her that he would kill his father if she didn't kick his ass out. He hadn't been able to deal with her tears night after night. It had broken his heart to know what kind of pain his father was causing her with his philandering ways.

The way he saw it, neither he nor his mother had needed his lowlife father. He'd barely been there for them anyway, with all the partying and screwing around he had done. Anthony had vowed to take care of his mother when his father left for good, and he had kept his word. Even now.

Being dumped hadn't even given his father pause. The bastard had gone on to marry one of his mistresses before the ink on the divorce papers had dried.

"I'm nothing like him."

"Nothing like who?"

Anthony whipped his head in Lecia's direction. Shit, he'd spoken aloud.

"Nothing like—" Lecia's voice broke off as a look of horror flashed on her face. She screamed, "Watch out!"

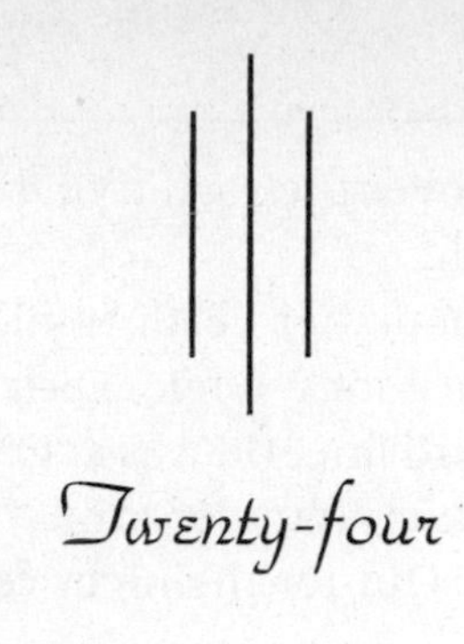

Twenty-four

His heart lurching into his throat, Anthony snapped his gaze back to the road before him. He saw the flash of an object and yanked the steering wheel to the left. The Navigator screamed as it careened onto the shoulder, spitting up dry earth and rocks.

He eased his foot off the brake to steer the vehicle back into the lane. Only when he was fully back on the asphalt did he allow himself to breathe.

Then he glanced at Lecia.

She withered under his gaze.

"Are you crazy?" he asked, unable to keep his voice calm.

"I'm sorry. I—I didn't want you to hit it."

"I thought I was about to run smack into someone's bumper. But no, you scream your head off for a freakin' armadillo?"

"I . . ." Words were inadequate. "I saw it. I got scared. I'm sorry."

Anthony blew out a ragged breath. If he was feeling anything like she was, Lecia knew that his heart was beating out of control.

"Leave the driving to me," he said after a long moment.

"You can't swerve all over the road trying to avoid critters. It's liable to get you killed."

Chagrined, Lecia shook her head. "I said I'm sorry."

They drove in silence for a while. Lecia stared at Anthony. His jaw was set in a hard line. He was angry. She couldn't fault him, but she wanted him to understand.

"I was twenty-one. Out for the night celebrating my birthday, actually."

Anthony glanced at her, the flash of anger in his eyes replaced by curiosity.

"I was nearly home. Rounding a corner. I didn't even see it until it was too late. Then there was a thud. And this awful scream."

"What'd you hit?"

"A dog. A cocker spaniel. I raced out of my car, but it was too late. It was dead."

When Lecia's voice trembled, Anthony's insides tightened. "Ah, geez. Shit, don't cry."

"I'm okay." She blew out a few quick breaths. "It's just that . . . well, ever since I killed that dog, I have a horrible paranoia about hitting any animal."

Anthony reached for her hand. He squeezed it. "I'm sorry that happened to you. And I shouldn't have yelled."

She gave him a soft smile of appreciation. It occurred to him that a person could appear bright, sophisticated, and totally together, yet still be affected by something that had happened in his or her past.

She pulled her purse onto her lap. "I'm okay," she said as she withdrew her inhaler. "My chest is just starting to feel a little tight. Emotions can sometimes trigger an attack." Moments later she was puffing on her inhaler.

Anthony watched her. He realized she was holding her breath. She released a gush of air.

"How often do you take that?" he asked.

"Usually once a day. Sometimes more, if the weather's really bad. If it's too hot out to breathe properly."

"So me taking you to the desert hasn't helped matters."

"The L.A. smog doesn't help. But I take a puff and life goes on." Lecia stuffed her inhaler back in her purse. She placed it at the floor by her feet and picked up one of the plain white plastic bags. "You want chips? A Twinkie?"

"You bought some cola, right? I could use the caffeine."

Lecia withdrew a soda and passed it to him. She opened a water for herself, then pulled out one of the packages of Twinkies. Her eyes fluttered shut as she took a bite.

"You've got a thing for Twinkies, huh?"

Lecia's eyes widened in horror as she swallowed, and Anthony realized immediately what she must be thinking. That he was alluding to the Twinkies' phallic shape.

"Get your mind out of the gutter," she told him.

"*Me?* You're the one with your mind in the gutter. That's not what I meant."

"Yeah, right."

"I swear," he said. Although now, thanks to her, his thoughts had quickly turned primal. What was Dr. Love like in bed? he wondered. To look at her, she appeared conservative. Even uptight, sometimes. But did she completely let loose in the bedroom and get her freak on? After all, she *was* a sex therapist.

So was Dr. Ruth, and Anthony couldn't picture her getting laid.

But Lecia . . . He watched her lick cream from the Twinkie and damn if his groin didn't start to tighten.

You'd think he hadn't had sex in a year, rather than a month.

He needed a distraction. He needed to talk about Ginger. "So, Doc. What you said to me on the *Tonight Show,* was that true? Did Ginger call me a pervert?"

Lecia took a long swig of her water. Long enough that Anthony had to wonder if she wanted to answer the question. But she finally said, "Maybe we should just find Ginger first."

"Why? What does that mean?"

"It means . . . to say the least, the two of you have a lot of talking to do."

"But what's your take on this? Because I was thinking, maybe she had some kind of breakdown. I don't know. The pressure of everything got to her and she just couldn't take it."

"That doesn't explain the lies about her family."

Lecia's words gave Anthony pause. "You don't know that she was lying."

She held up both hands in a sign of surrender. "You're right. Forget I said that."

Anthony did just that, staring ahead at the road. He could see the orange sun along the horizon in his rearview mirror. *Think about the sunset,* he told himself. *Think about how great it looks from Beverly Hills.*

He turned, forgetting the sunset and instead concentrating on Lecia. "No, I don't want to forget it. You don't think Ginger had a breakdown?"

"I think her behavior is very suspicious."

"What did she say about me?"

"We didn't speak for long. Only a few minutes."

"Come on. Just tell me."

Lecia sighed, resigning herself to the fate of answering Anthony's question. "Since you must know, she didn't speak too kindly about you. At first, I thought it was because she was hurt by what you'd done."

"What the media said I did."

"Right."

"And then?"

"Well, I've been thinking about it since." Since she had met Anthony and found him entirely credible. There was a clean, down-home quality to him, and it made it impossible for her to imagine him propositioning a hooker. "I really wonder why a woman who's supposed to love you wouldn't even hear you out. And then, of course, you're saying that she's smearing you in the media."

"That's why I'm wondering if she's having some kind of meltdown."

What Lecia thought was that Ginger was a lot smarter than Anthony was giving her credit for being. She was a woman with an agenda, and she was working her butt off to get what she wanted. Maybe she saw his supposed infidelity as an easy way out of the marriage and she was hoping to take it, along with a ton of cash. Maybe she had met someone else. Or maybe she was just as flaky as many of the other people in Hollywood, and her marriage vows hadn't meant anything to her.

Regardless, the way Ginger had described her husband to Lecia in those minutes outside the bar still didn't sit well with her, now that she knew Anthony to be so very different.

"What are you thinking, Doc?"

She knew he didn't want to know what she was really thinking. "I'm thinking that you and Ginger will need some serious counseling, should she decide she wants to save the marriage."

"*Should* she decide? I'm counting on you to make her see the light."

"I'll do what I can," she said, "but I can't work miracles."

"I hope to God she's at this address in New Orleans. We really need to damn well talk. For better, for worse. That's what she promised, and that's what I expect. I'd never turn my back on her without hearing her out."

Sighing deeply, Lecia leaned back in her seat. Turning her gaze to the desert landscape, she tuned Anthony out. She wasn't interested in hearing him go on and on about his precious wife.

They were an oddball couple if she ever saw one. Ginger came off as an airhead who was full of herself. There was nothing real about her, not her long fingernails or her huge fake breasts. But Anthony . . . despite his obvious star status and his wealth, he didn't come across as pompous or fake at all. He could have any woman he wanted, yet he was driving halfway across the country in hopes of saving a marriage that appeared one-sided.

But who was she to judge why certain people got together? Maybe Ginger offered Anthony intellectual stimulation that he couldn't live without.

Yeah, right. The woman doesn't even like to read.

"You sleeping?"

Anthony's deep voice startled her, like a splash of cold water in the face. A splash that reminded her it was her job to remain objective, never to judge. "No, I'm not sleeping."

"Then can I ask you a question?"

"Fire away."

"It's about you."

"Oh." Lecia considered that as she opened her bottle of water. "Okay."

"I'm kinda curious. You said you're not dating."

"Right." Lecia brought the water bottle to her mouth.

"So tell me, Dr. Love—how is it that you've written this successful book about women's orgasms, yet you're not getting laid?"

Twenty-five

The sip she'd taken went down the wrong way and Lecia started coughing. Loud, hacking coughs.

Anthony slapped her back. Once. Twice. Still she kept coughing.

"Shit," he muttered.

As Lecia felt the car slowing, she did her best to regain control. Swallowing two giant breaths, she felt the crisis passing. "I'm all right," she told him. Lord, but this was embarrassing! "You don't have to stop."

Anthony's eyes flitted between the road and her. She saw genuine concern in his expression. "You're sure?" he asked.

Lecia tapped on her chest as she inhaled another deep breath. "Yes, I'm sure. I just feel . . . stupid." She didn't know why, but the man had her on edge, acting like a klutz.

Anthony didn't say anything, just continued to drive, and Lecia was hugely relieved. Apparently he had forgotten the question he'd asked her. Which was a good thing, since she didn't want to discuss her sex life with him.

But moments later he glanced at her and said, "So?"

Oh, no. "So what?" Lecia asked, playing dumb.

"You've written this book about sex and orgasms. You're doing interviews all over the place, spreading your vast knowledge with the world. Yet when you head home, you hang with your cat?"

"Oh, God. The cat!" In the frenzy of everything that was going on, she had forgotten all about Moaner. She quickly dug her cell phone out of her purse.

"I was kidding about the cat."

"You might have been kidding, but she exists."

"You've got a cat?"

"Well, kind of. No, I do. Yeah, I do."

"I guess if football falls through, I can always get a job working for the Psychic Network."

"She's a stray. Came up to my door one day and I fed her. Now, she keeps coming back. I haven't let her in the house, though."

"Yet."

Lecia's lips curled in a smile as she thought of the orange tabby. "Yeah, yet." Her face grew serious. "I don't want her to get attached to me. Maybe her owners are simply out of town."

"Sounds like she's already attached. And you, too."

"Someone's got to take care of the poor thing."

Lecia turned away from him and entered a number on her cell phone. Anthony watched her, wondering whom she was calling.

"Hey, Sheldon," she said.

Sheldon?

"It's me, Lecia . . . Yeah, I'm cool. You? . . . Great. My sister there?" She paused several seconds. "Oh, that was today? All right, can you do me a favor? Please tell her to head to my place and pour some food in the bowl outside for Moaner . . .

Yeah, she knows where it is. In fact, if you can ask her to head back in the morning to do it again . . . Well, I'm . . ." She paused to glance at Anthony. "It's work-related. Came up suddenly . . . Yeah, I know. Thanks, Sheldon. I owe you big-time."

The moment she hung up, Anthony said, "You named the cat Moaner?"

"Uh-huh."

"A sex therapist with a cat named Moaner. If that doesn't take the cake."

"Well, that's how she got my attention. By moaning all the time. I'd be sleeping, and I'd hear this cat outside my window."

Anthony found himself wondering if Lecia was a moaner or a screamer. Or the type to leave scars on a guy's back when he was doing her. Beneath that prim and proper image, was she wild and untamed?

Ginger was wild. More than wild. Like a nympho, really, the way she was always horny for sex. It was strange, and most guys wouldn't give it a second thought if their wives screwed like porn stars, but Anthony had never felt connected to Ginger during sex. He always had the feeling that any guy would do with her, that there was nothing special about him.

The lack of a true connection between them was one of the signs early on that made him wonder how well their marriage would fare. But then he'd reminded himself that he hadn't married Ginger for passion. He had married her because he'd wanted a friend and *not* passion, a woman who would stick by him as they built a solid future together.

Thinking about Ginger was giving him a headache. He turned to Lecia. "So, tell me. Why are you a celibate sex therapist?"

"Because men can't be trusted."

"Ouch." He reached for his soda and took a swig. "You really believe that?"

"I know it."

"I know there's a story behind that comment. Who was he?"

"My ex-husband," Lecia answered easily.

"He cheated on you."

"Several times."

"Ouch."

"Oh, it hurt. But I'm over it."

"If that's true, why aren't you dating?"

"How can I date?" Lecia answered quickly. "I'm much too busy with work."

Anthony cut his eyes at her. "The truth."

"That is the truth."

"Come on, Doc. You psychoanalyze people. I know you can do better than that."

"All right." Lecia slapped her hands against her thighs. "The truth is . . . I've lost my mojo."

"No shit."

"Not that you have to tell anyone. I'm sure the media would have a field day with that bit of info."

"Who would I tell? The *Daily Blab*?"

"Things you don't want people to know have a way of leaking once you're in the limelight. And I'd really like to keep my private life private."

"Hey, you're preaching to the choir. But all the same, don't you miss not having a man in your life?"

"Not really."

"Because you've lost your mojo?"

"Exactly. I know most people don't understand. My sister certainly doesn't."

"Why—how long's it been?"

"Oh, very long."

"Like what? Three months?"

Lecia threw her head back and roared with laughter.

"Longer?" Anthony asked. "Six months?"

"Try three years."

"Three years?"

"I haven't keeled over yet."

"Wow." Anthony shook his head slowly, as if pitying her. "There are plenty of guys out there who will help you get your mojo back."

"Oh, I've met them, believe me. At book signings and other events. The losers who think that because I wrote a book about women's sexuality I'm a slut."

"I can't see anyone thinking you're a slut."

"No, but you can see uptight bitch, can't you?"

Anthony frowned as he looked across the front seat at her. "Is that what you think I see when I look at you?"

"Don't you?"

He shook his head. "Not at all. I see beautiful. Smart. Witty. Sexy."

Lecia's face flamed. Surprisingly, it was difficult to hear Anthony compliment her in this way. Because while she would never tell him, he was the first man in a long time that she had started to feel any stirrings of attraction for.

It was clearly the circumstance, she thought—being alone together, their body scents mingling in the confined space of his car. Logically, she knew that, which was why she was doing her damnedest to push these ridiculous feelings out of her head.

"Maybe I can hook you up with Kahari."

Lecia felt a stab of disappointment at Anthony's suggestion. Kahari was attractive. Available. Rich beyond her wildest imagination. But he wasn't Anthony.

She said, "I'm so not into dating right now."

"Ah, I get it. This is the twenty-first century. A woman can please herself."

"Argh!" Lecia punched his arm. "I can't believe you just said that to me."

"Why not? You're Dr. Love."

"Oh, stop that Dr. Love business. I'm Lecia. A woman with feelings, a woman with—"

"Needs."

She lowered her eyes, then slowly raised them to meet his again. "Maybe."

Her voice was so soft, yet it hit Anthony like a ton of bricks. And like the flick of a switch, something changed between them. Maybe it was the honesty that had shimmered in her voice, but Anthony felt the strongest urge to reach out to her. He wanted to stroke her face, run his fingers along the column of her neck. He wanted to flick his tongue along her skin and see if she tasted as sweet as she smelled.

He wanted to help her get her mojo back.

"I think I'm tired of talking," Lecia said. "I'm gonna close my eyes, okay?"

"Yeah, sure," Anthony replied, his throat suddenly dry. "You do that."

Lecia opened her eyes when she realized the Navigator had stopped. Looking to the left, she saw that she was alone.

She sat up straight and peered through the windshield. In front of her was a small road in what appeared to be the middle of nowhere, based on the fact that there was zero traffic.

Unbuckling her seat belt, she turned to look through the back window. The dark tint obstructed her view, but she could see some sort of flashing light and make out the shape of a building.

They were at a hotel, she realized. No, given its small size, it had to be a motel.

Lecia opened her door and got out. She gave her body a good stretch, yawning as she did. The night air was warm and smelled faintly of jasmine.

With its neat and tidy outside appearance, the place certainly couldn't be called a Roach Motel. In orange neon lights, it boasted a name Lecia had never heard of. It was probably a family-run operation, and hopefully as well maintained on the inside as it was on the outside.

As she slowly made her way toward the front door, Anthony exited the office. She met him en route to her.

"It's small, clean," he said. "And they didn't care about a credit card once I offered them cash."

"Where are we?" Lecia asked.

"Just east of El Paso."

They had stopped for burgers around ten P.M., before reaching the Texas border. Once they started driving again, Lecia had drifted off to sleep.

"What time is it?"

"About one-fifteen."

"One-fifteen!"

"Because of the time zone difference."

"That's right." She yawned again.

"You have everything you need out of the car?" he asked.

"My purse is still in there."

"Give me a second."

Anthony trotted back toward the Navigator, and Lecia was

tempted to follow him. She didn't want to be standing out there alone. Not that she had anything to worry about, she realized. It was very quiet here. Peaceful.

Lecia yawned again as Anthony reached her. "I know, it's late," he said, placing a hand on her back.

They were quiet as he guided her to the first floor room. Only when Anthony opened the door did Lecia realize he hadn't offered her her own key.

"We're . . . sharing a room?"

"I figured it was easier this way. Besides, it's only for a few hours."

Her heart thumped hard in her chest.

"Lecia?"

Anthony's voice prompted her to step into the room. Well, if he didn't have a problem sharing the room, why should she? They were both adults. They both knew the deal. They were here together to get some sleep.

Lecia glanced around. She was expecting the worst, but aside from being small, the room was very clean. Even the burgundy-colored carpet was nice and thick and appeared to be brand new.

There were two double beds, which could be a problem for Anthony, given that he was tall. But they weren't moving in. He could survive.

"You go ahead and use the bathroom first," Anthony told her.

Now, alarm bells sounded in Lecia's head. She had the clothes on her back, a camisole and blazer in the car, and nothing else. No fresh clothes. No clean underwear.

"Oh, gosh. I don't have anything. No toiletries. No nothing."

Anthony lifted his shirt and pulled out two little packages

from the waist of his jeans. "I picked these up at the front desk. Toothbrushes and toothpaste."

"But what about clean clothes? I can't wear these again tomorrow."

"We'll worry about that in the morning."

"Right," Lecia said softly. But she wondered how Anthony could be so nonchalant about everything. As far as she knew, he didn't have a change of clothes, either. And what on earth was she supposed to sleep in? The nude?

"Lecia?" he prompted.

"Right, right," she said. "The bathroom. I'm going." Exhaling a sigh, she headed in that direction.

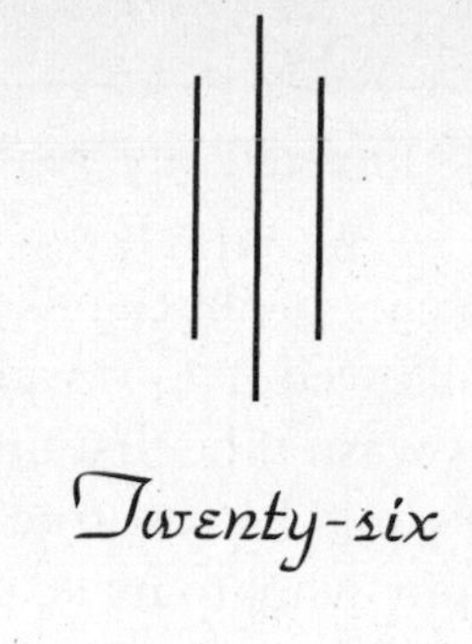

Twenty-six

Lecia thought she would have been sleeping by the time Anthony came out of the bathroom, but she wasn't. She was suddenly too wired to nod off. Today had been long and tiring—too long and tiring—and she wanted to talk to him about the option of flying out of El Paso to New Orleans. Even if it would only take another day to drive there, they would still have to drive back the way they had come, meaning two more grueling days of travel after they had reached their destination.

The bathroom door squeaked as it opened. Lecia looked in that direction, then zapped her head around with lightning speed when she saw that Anthony wore only a towel wrapped around his waist.

"Oh, gosh," she said. "Sorry. Tell me when you're decent."

"You don't think I'm decent?"

His voice was deep, velvety smooth, making her stomach flutter. "Not like that you're not, no."

"Ouch."

"I didn't mean . . ." He was more than decent. Which was

exactly the problem. "Just tell me when you've put your clothes on."

"Not interested in seeing me buck naked?"

More fluttering, followed by a warming sensation all through her body. This wasn't the first time Anthony had said something to her that could be construed as . . . well, as sexual. And she didn't know what to make of it.

For one thing, the guy was married. Her whole reason for being with him was to help him get his wife back. So, clearly he couldn't mean anything by his words. It was that simple. It was late, they were both tired, and he was simply being silly to lighten their stress level.

So why did that summation make her stomach churn with disappointment?

Because she was sick in the head, she thought. Weren't most therapists? It was a laughing joke she had heard, more than she cared to, that people who became therapists did so because they needed help themselves.

"You can turn around," he told her.

She did. Then, "Oh, God." She covered her face with both hands.

"What's wrong with you?"

"I thought you were getting dressed. Putting some clothes on."

"I did."

"Barely."

"I'm sure you've seen a guy in briefs before."

"That's not the point."

"Will you take your hands off your face? I can barely hear you. Aren't you a sex therapist? Given what you do, seeing me in briefs has got to be tame by comparison."

She opened her hands a crack so she could speak. "Hey. What's that supposed to mean?"

"Sex . . . therapist."

The meaning of Anthony's words washed over her like a giant wave. "You think I sleep with my patients."

"Isn't that what sex therapists do?"

"Oh, God!"

"You don't?"

"No!" Now she dropped both hands to gape at him. "I can't believe you believe that." She spoke with more gusto than necessary, but she wanted to drive the point home. She most certainly did not want Anthony thinking she slept with men as a profession.

He shrugged nonchalantly. "My bad. That's what I thought you guys did."

"I told you how long it's been since . . . you know. And professionally I'm not a surrogate. Surrogates have sex with their patients. Therapists *talk*."

"Oh." He paused, let that sink in. "You know, I like that a lot better."

"Like what?"

"That you don't have sex with your patients."

"Really, now?"

"Yeah. Having sex with your patients is pretty freakin' weird."

"I never even considered that when I decided to go into sex therapy. It wasn't for me. My interest has always been in getting people to dig beneath the surface of a problem so they can finally solve it."

Anthony pulled back the covers as if to get into bed, then apparently thought better of it and wandered toward the door. Lecia gave in to temptation and watched him. Lord, but he was one hunk of a man. Every muscle in his body was honed to perfection. The man was sexy as hell.

He secured the dead bolt and chain lock. As he turned, Lecia threw her hands over her face again.

"You're gonna give me a complex."

"I'm sorry. This just seems . . . wrong. You're married."

"We have separate beds."

This wasn't working. She was protesting way too much, which would only make Anthony think she wanted him.

"You're right. I'm being silly. We're both adults. No need to be embarrassed."

She reached for the lamp on the night table, then remembered her purse. She always had it nearby in case she needed to take a puff of Ventolin in the middle of the night.

Looking around the room, she saw her purse on the small table near the door.

Damn!

"You're not getting the light?" Anthony asked.

"Well, um. Yeah, of course." It would be totally asinine to turn off the light and feel her way across the room, all to avoid Anthony seeing her in her very short shirt. She had waited until he disappeared into the bathroom to disrobe, and thought she was home free.

"It's late," he prompted.

"I just need to get my purse." With her words, she crawled out of bed and pulled her TRY A VIRGIN shirt down as far on her thighs as it would go. It achieved the same effect as a wet T-shirt, perfectly outlining her breasts.

She released the shirt when she realized she was giving Anthony an eyeful.

You're being absurd, she told herself.

As she snatched up her purse, she was certain she gave Anthony a good view of her thighs, if not her ass. She all but ran back to the bed and escaped under the covers.

"Good night," Anthony said.

Lecia turned the lamp off. " 'Night."

Something was wrong.

Lecia's eyes popped open, the memory of where she was and why she was there zapping into her brain. She immediately glanced to the left.

The bed beside her was empty.

She pushed herself up onto her elbows, listening.

She heard nothing. Where was Anthony?

Her eyes went to the clock. Ten-nineteen in the morning. Wow, she'd slept longer than she thought. Of course, it had taken her quite some time to fall asleep, because every time Anthony tossed or turned, she wondered if he was going to get out of his bed and slip into hers.

It was ridiculous, of course, but for some reason, she had lost her senses around this man.

Lecia threw off the covers and got out of bed. She wandered to the window and looked outside. Panic seized her when she didn't see the Navigator.

She spun around. Surely Anthony wouldn't have left her here in the middle of God only knew where. So where the hell was he?

"Getting breakfast?" she thought aloud. Or gassing up. But he would be back. She was sure of it.

Deciding this would be the perfect time to shower, Lecia hustled to the bathroom.

* * *

Lecia exited the bathroom with the flimsy towel wrapped around her body and stopped dead in her tracks. "Tony," she rasped.

From the bed where he sat, he held up a large bag. "Clean clothes," he said. "I found a Wal-Mart not too far from here."

Her shoulders drooped with relief. "Oh, thank you!"

"I didn't know what you wanted to eat for breakfast, so I figured we could stop somewhere."

"Sure." Lecia held the towel in place with one hand and took the bag from him with the other. Whirling around on her heel, she headed back into the bathroom.

"I didn't know what you'd want. So I picked up a few choices."

Lecia's relief over the idea of fresh clothes soon fizzled when she saw what was inside the bag. A floral miniskirt, a body-hugging *short* black dress, and a form-fitting white lycra top. There was also a pair of low-rider jeans and three pairs of black thongs.

"They didn't have any regular underwear?" she called out.

"There are three thongs in there."

"I don't—" She shut up.

"I thought every woman wore a thong these days."

"I prefer sensible underwear," she replied. "But this will do." At least everything was clean.

She went into the bathroom with the clothes, put on a thong panty, then slipped into the jeans. They were too big and hung off her hips. She could never wear these, not without a safety pin.

That left . . . either the dress or the skirt.

She opted for the skirt. It barely covered the top of her thighs. The white top hugged her like a second skin.

As she checked out her reflection in the bathroom mirror, she groaned. This was so not her style. What was Anthony thinking?

But there was nothing she could do about it, not unless they headed back to Wal-Mart. Surely she could survive until they reached New Orleans, where she could buy some decent clothes.

She strolled out of the bathroom. Anthony's eyes instantly perked up. He whistled. "Doc, you look hot."

"I don't usually dress like this," she said glumly. She wasn't sure she'd ever get used to the thong lining the crack of her butt, but kept that thought to herself.

"Then you should. It's very flattering."

"You really think so? I don't look like a tart?"

"No, you look cute. Sexy."

Lecia wandered to the large mirror in the middle of the room. Through the reflection, she could see Anthony checking her out. Suddenly, the outfit didn't look tartish or sleazy. It looked flirty and feminine.

Noticing that Anthony had already changed, she asked, "You ready to head out?"

"Uh-huh. Aren't you?"

"Well, not quite. I thought I'd put on some makeup. I want to look civilized."

"You look great."

"Thanks. But all the same . . ."

"No problem. I'll settle the bill and be right back."

Lecia's eyes lingered over Anthony's body as he left the room. He had a commanding presence, one that mesmerized her. He had the kind of arms that would make a woman feel safe and secure. And a body that . . .

She closed her eyes, trying not to think about his body. But instead she saw a clearer image of it, clad only in the briefs he had worn the night before. He had an impressive physique. Strong legs, washboard stomach. Ooh, man. What would it be like to ride him?

Her vagina tingled, startling her. Oh, boy. Was she actually getting her mojo back?

Talk about *completely* bad timing!

Lecia applied eyeliner and lipstick before there was a knock on the door. She hustled to answer it.

Anthony grinned down at her as she opened the door. "You know what else I have?" he asked, stepping into the room.

Lecia followed him, her eyes narrowing with suspicion. "What?"

He dangled a small plastic bag as he walked backward.

"What is that?" Lecia asked anxiously.

"A surprise."

Lecia marched toward him. "I don't do surprises." She reached for the bag, but he pulled his hand back. Losing her balance, her body lurched forward, tipping onto his.

Anthony fell backward on the bed, making a sharp moaning sound as he did. One of his strong hands snarled around Lecia's waist as she landed on his chest.

She was too startled to say anything. She simply looked down at him. He looked up at her. For several seconds neither said a word. Only the sounds of their ragged breathing could be heard.

Lecia jerked when she felt the light, feathery touch on the back of her thigh.

"No, don't get up." Anthony's arm tightened around her.

Her eyes widened in confusion. "No?"

"No." His voice had lowered several octaves. "This feels good. Just like this."

Her heart rammed against her rib cage. This couldn't be happening. But it was. She was perched on top of Anthony Beals, wearing a wisp of a skirt and a thong beneath that. Not nearly enough clothes to save her from herself.

Her brain registered the sounds from the television. A newscaster was talking about rain in the Midwest. It dawned on Lecia that it was strangely intimate to be lying on a man who had a growing erection with ambience from the Weather Channel. Intimate because the moment was comfortable, like they had lain like this a million times and didn't need soft music or other mood enhancers.

Anthony raised his head, buried it in the groove of her neck. Lecia bit down on her lip as a wave of exciting sensations washed over her.

"I swear, I don't know what it is about the way you smell. . . ."

Her eyelids fluttered shut. Lord help her, they hadn't even kissed, but she wanted to get naked with this man.

"Look at me," he whispered.

Lecia opened her eyes. Anthony's gaze was filled with heat and longing—everything she was feeling.

Then, tangling his fingers in her hair, Anthony pulled her head down and kissed her.

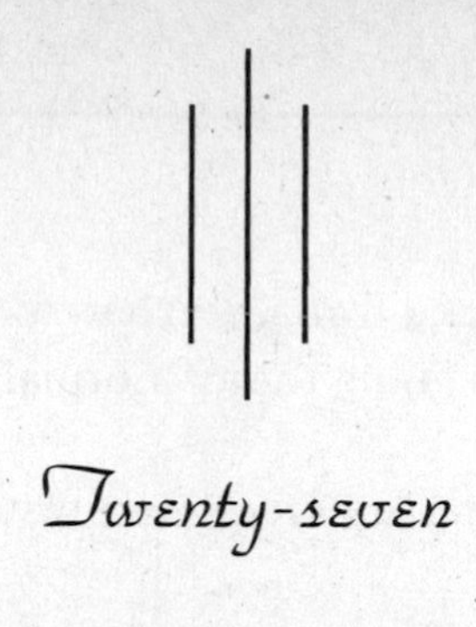

Twenty-seven

The kiss went on. And on.

And on.

Anthony nibbled, sucked. His tongue delved.

Lecia opened her mouth to receive more of him. Her tongue mingled with his, hot and desperate.

Only when she physically needed to take a breath to save her life did she tear her lips from his.

"Wow," he said.

A simple word, but it packed a lot of punch. No one had ever said "Wow" after kissing her.

"Those lips . . . I knew they'd be sweet."

Lecia bent a leg at the knee, swaying it a little as she gazed into his eyes. "You just kissed me."

"That's for damn sure."

A beat passed. "Why?"

"Because you had a neon sign over your head flashing 'Kiss me.' "

Lecia buried her face in his wonderfully strong chest and laughed. Laughed because his words were probably true.

"I guess I want to feel . . ."

"Me?" she supplied.

He chuckled, low and throaty. "That, too." His finger tickled her thigh. "But I was going to say 'normal.' "

"Oh?"

"Like we met under different circumstances. I picked you up at a bar—"

"A bar?"

"Okay, you picked me up at . . . at a sex therapists' convention. You were looking for new patients."

"I don't sleep with my patients."

"You make an exception for me." Looking very much like he wanted to kiss her again, he added, "That's how we end up here. At least, that's what I'd like to pretend. Rather than face the truth that I'm on a wild goose chase to find a wife who doesn't want to be with me."

His words sobered her. This was about Ginger. A rebound thing.

Then he trailed a hand under her skirt, to a spot on her butt that a sensible panty would have covered, and she was suddenly losing her head again.

"Oooh." Lecia blew out a slow breath against Anthony's shoulder.

"Oooh good or oooh bad?"

"Oooh maybe I should get up now."

She squirmed a little, and he released her. Although she didn't want to, she pushed herself off him. Once on her feet, she adjusted her clothes.

Anthony stared at her but didn't say anything. Still, his gaze made her uneasy. His eyes said he wanted her naked body writhing beneath him, and Lecia had to admit she wanted that, too.

"Um," she began, remembering the bag, "what's the surprise?"

Anthony's eyes lit up, and Lecia's heart rate quadrupled. "A book on tape. *Murder on the Orient Express.*"

"You're kidding! You found it at Wal-Mart?"

"No. There was a little used bookstore on the way there." Anthony stood. "Ready for some food?"

Oh, she was ready for some food, all right. Just not the kind he was referring to.

They gathered up their belongings and went outside. Minutes later Anthony was maneuvering the Navigator out of the parking lot, and Lecia sat back, inhaling slow, calming breaths. But instead of helping, her body temperature continued to rise. She wasn't sure she could stay this close to Anthony for another thirteen or so hours without completely losing her mind.

Or jumping his bones.

With this skirt and this thong, it would be so easy to slide onto his lap . . .

Lord help her, they needed to get to New Orleans as quickly as possible.

"You know," Lecia said. "I was thinking."

He faced her. "Thinking what?"

"That we should head back to El Paso and catch a flight to New Orleans."

"Lecia—"

"No, hear me out. There's heavy rain in east Texas, but that's not the main consideration. If the police were looking for you, I think we'd know by now. But we saw nothing on the local news. Nothing on CNN."

"Yeah, but we've already come all this way."

"Which means we have that much farther to drive back.

Even if I don't go into the office tomorrow, I'll need to be back in good form on Monday morning."

"It's only Thursday."

"Yeah, but we won't be able to look for Ginger until tomorrow if we get in late tonight. Another reason to consider flying."

Anthony bit down on his bottom lip. "I don't know."

"You can't only consider yourself in this."

"I know that." He paused. "I guess I'd feel better if I checked my voice mail first. If I'm in some kind of trouble for taking off, my lawyer will have left me a message."

Anthony picked up his phone, which was between them, on the console. He'd pushed the speed limit and made pretty good time getting to El Paso, but knew it would be a long drive ahead. If it were only him, he wouldn't worry about it. But he had to be fair to Lecia.

He punched in the code to check his messages. The automated voice told him that he had five new ones.

He had planned to listen to them all—until he heard the first one. He disconnected, then slammed a hand on the steering wheel. "No, not this."

"Oh, my God," Lecia said in a horrified whisper. "It's Ginger, isn't it? They've found her. She's dead."

Ever since he was a young boy, Pavel had dreamed of coming to America. Every movie, every television show, reinforced his belief that it was a land of opportunity. In America, he knew he would not have to struggle to survive as he had struggled every day in Russia.

Since his move here six years ago, he had learned that he was right. There were many jobs to do in this country, many ways to make a buck. There was the fast way and the slow way.

He had chosen the fast way. Why work your way to the top when you could start there? Control your own destiny? There were more risks this way, of course, but greater reward.

And, unfortunately, greater headaches.

Ginger was giving him a very bad headache. If she wasn't dead, then surely he would have to kill her.

Pavel sipped ice water through a straw as he walked across the hotel's carpeted floor. News reports were saying that she was missing under suspicious circumstances. It was possible. But it was also possible that this was a trick. The little bitch liked to play games.

He had come to L.A. only to get his money, and he was already staying longer than he'd planned. But he liked this place. There was always sunshine, and the women were beautiful. Maybe he would stay. After all, there were many girls who came here to become stars. He could find many women here for his side business—porno films.

He would decide that later—after he found Ginger. So far, he could not reach her by phone. He had left her many messages, but she was not calling back.

He considered himself a patient man, an understanding one, even, but even he had his limits. Ginger was fast pushing him to his.

Strolling back across the room, he sat on the bed. The whore he had picked up last night was still sleeping. I will miss screwing Ginger, he thought, sighing softly. But he would enjoy his $1.2 million more.

Pulling open the drawer, he fingered his gun. The serial number on the nine-millimeter had been destroyed. Even if it could be traced, it would never be traced back to him.

Ginger was beautiful. He didn't want to hurt her. But he would.

Using his cell phone, he called her again. When he got her voice mail, he said, "Ginger, Ginger. Why you won't call me back? Surely you know you cannot hide from me." He paused, carefully considering his next words. "I like you, Ginger. You know that. That's why I gave you—what you say—some slack. But now, I wonder are you trying to put the wool over my face? I am running out of patience."

He closed the drawer and climbed back into bed with his whore, but his thoughts were still on Ginger.

Lecia held her breath as she looked at Anthony. They'd driven all this way, only for this news.

"No," Anthony replied, shaking his head. "It's not Ginger. It's the kid I'm a Big Brother to."

Relief washed over her in waves. "That's right. You're a Big Brother. Is something wrong?"

"Yeah. Donovan's in trouble."

"What kind of trouble?"

"I'm not sure. But he sounded pretty upset in the message he left. I'm gonna have to call him."

"Of course."

Anthony turned into a McDonald's lot and parked the car. Then he dialed Donovan's home number.

"Hey, Little D," he said when the kid answered the phone. "What's up, man?"

"T?"

"Yeah, it's me. What's going on?"

"It's my mama. She got arrested last night."

"Arrested? Why?"

"I dunno. She was probably sellin' again, even though she promised me she wouldn't. I was almost home when I saw the cops draggin' her outta the house. I didn't want 'em to take me away, so I hid in the bushes. I thought she'd be back by now, but she's not."

Damn. Donovan didn't need this. His mother had already spent time behind bars for a narcotics offense. When was she going to learn? She had two kids who needed her: Donovan's older brother, who had already taken to the streets, and Donovan. Anthony was hoping to make a difference in his life, to save him from the life his brother had chosen.

"You've been home alone, Little D?"

"Yeah." His voice trembled.

"Okay, I know you're scared, but it's gonna be okay. You said you have a cousin in Long Beach?"

"Uh-huh."

"Have you called her?"

"No."

"You have to call her."

"I dunno—"

"You've got no other choice. Can you get to her place?"

"I ain't got no money."

Anthony thrummed his fingers on his leg. "I'll get some to you. As long as you promise to go to your cousin's."

"She doesn't want me there. She hates me."

"She doesn't hate you," Anthony assured him. Though the sad truth was, he couldn't say that for sure. Donovan Wright was an eleven-year-old with a hard edge because of the circumstances of his life. He'd been raised practically with no discipline, something Anthony had realized when he first met him at a fund-raiser for an inner city kids day camp program. Kids like him could be hard enough for their parents to handle, much less an extended member of the family.

"Listen, if you want me to call her for you, I will."

"I want you, T. Where are you?"

"I'd be there for you if I could, but I'm on the road, taking care of some business. I'm not sure when I'll be back."

"I'm scared," Donovan said.

Those two words broke Anthony's heart. More than ever, he wished he were back in L.A. so he could head to Donovan's place and be there for him. The kid didn't have a father, and Anthony had vowed to be the man to look out for him. But there was no way he could do that now.

"Little D, can you get to the youth center?"

"Uh-huh."

"Go there. I'm gonna call someone to pick you up once you get there. Kahari Brown. You met him once at the center, remember?"

" 'Course I remember."

"Good. Kahari will come get you and take you to your cousin's place. I'll be back as soon as I can, okay?"

"Okay."

"Hang tight till then, Little D."

"Okay," he said again.

When Anthony hung up, Lecia asked, "Problems?"

"Yeah. The kid's mother's gotten herself arrested. Damn, I wish I was back in L.A."

"If you want to head back—"

"It won't help. Donovan needs me now."

"Kahari's going to meet him?"

"He'll have to."

Anthony punched in another number, and Lecia knew he was calling his friend. When Kahari picked up, he filled him in on what was happening.

"Is everything going to work out?" Lecia asked when he hung up.

"Yeah. Kahari'll take care of it."

"Sounds like he's a good friend."

"He is." Anthony started the car. "You wanna go through the drive-through or go inside?"

"Whatever you want."

Anthony drove the car around to the drive-through entrance and inched it forward behind two others in line for the pickup window. They were about to have breakfast together, and Lecia hoped it would be a pleasant experience, but given the firm set of Anthony's jaw, he was clearly still upset about his conversation with Donovan.

"Try not to worry about Donovan," Lecia said. "I'm sure that's not easy, but you've got Kahari—"

"Try not to worry?"

His incredulous tone surprised her. "I'm just saying, we're already out here. You've done all you can. I'm sure everything's going to be okay."

"Is that your professional opinion, Doc? Because from where I sit, it seems like *nothing* is okay."

Lecia turned away from him. She'd been trying to help, but for her effort she'd practically been slapped in the face.

"I can't deal with this," Anthony went on. "I don't recognize my life anymore. I need to be in L.A., not out on the road in the middle of nowhere. I need Ginger to forgive me and get over this whole mess so I can get on with my life."

Lecia nodded solemnly. "I see." More than she wanted to. Much to her surprise, it hurt her to hear Anthony say that he wanted to save his marriage after admitting he believed his wife no longer wanted to be with him.

But why should it hurt her? He wasn't her man. And the kiss . . . Well, that kiss had been meaningless.

At least to him.

"I guess you're right," Anthony said after a moment. "We'd better fly. I don't know what I was thinking."

He drove up to the pickup window, settled the bill, and accepted the order. Lecia dug into her egg sandwich, but she was no longer hungry.

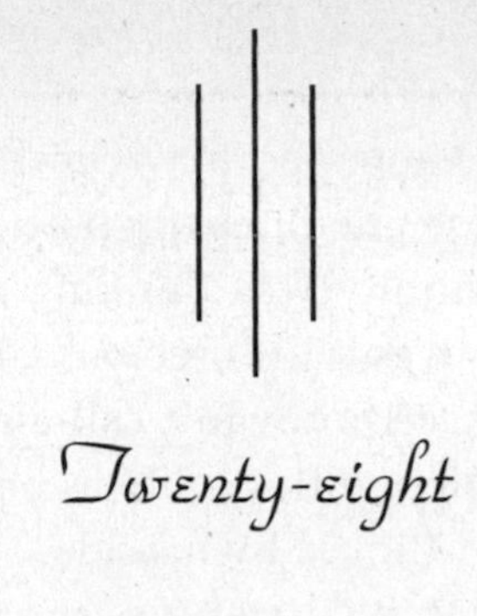

Twenty-eight

"I hate to say it, but I told you so."

Replacing the receiver, Anthony shrugged nonchalantly in response to Lecia's comment. They were at the airport hoping to find a flight to New Orleans, but instead of going up to the various counters to check availability, they had both called a few airlines from a pay phone. As Lecia had suspected, there were no direct flights to New Orleans from El Paso.

"Let's run down our options," Lecia suggested. "America West has the earliest flight, but we'll have to backtrack to Phoenix before we head on to New Orleans?"

"Right."

"Didn't I tell you? When we were driving through Phoenix, I said we ought to take a flight out of there. I knew we'd get something direct. And it'd be a much shorter drive back to L.A."

"I blew it, okay?"

There was definitely tension between them now. They hadn't spoken much on the way to the airport in El Paso, but Anthony had popped in the book on tape. As much of an Agatha Christie fan as Lecia was, she hadn't paid attention to the story. What had happened between her and Anthony in the motel room still weighed heavily on her mind.

Was that what Anthony was thinking about, too, why he seemed so serious, or was it his precious Ginger? He'd been in a foul mood ever since Donovan's call and his proclamation that he wanted to get on with his life as he'd known it.

A life that included Ginger by his side.

Reminding herself that Ginger was the reason for this trip, Lecia looked down at her scribbled notes. "American and Southwest also have connections, through Houston, and even though there's a layover, we'd get in a little quicker with either of those as opposed to America West. Really, it's just a toss-up, because either way we won't get into New Orleans until the evening."

"We could have driven."

"But then we'd have to drive back," Lecia pointed out. "What do you want to do?"

"I'd rather fly something with first class," Anthony replied. "Let's go with American."

"Fine with me. That's who I fly with mostly, anyway."

"You want to call in the reservation?"

"We'd still have to go to the counter. May as well head up there and get the tickets."

The line was about a mile long, and by the time Lecia and Anthony got through, they were lucky to get the last two seats in first class.

They had worn their hats and dark sunglasses since entering the airport, hoping that no one would recognize them. No such luck. Three guys had approached Anthony for autographs; four women had approached her. They both obliged, then went to the waiting area at their gate as quickly as possible. Now, with forty minutes before boarding, they sat near the floor-to-ceiling windows, their backs to passing traffic.

Anthony wasn't saying much, and Lecia didn't know what to say to him. That she thought he was an idiot if he expected his wife to take him back? Somehow she knew that wouldn't go over well.

"Are you ever going to speak to me again?" she asked.

He stared straight ahead. "Yeah, of course."

Lecia tapped a finger on her leg, waiting to see if he'd say more. When he didn't, she did. "Will you tell me why you're upset with me?"

"I'm not upset."

"Then why are you acting different?"

"I'm not acting different."

So this was going to be like pulling teeth. "If this is about what happened earlier—"

"Please, Doc—don't psychoanalyze me. The last thing I need is a shrink."

Lecia's breath caught in her throat at his words. They stung. She was a therapist, yes, but did he think that all she did in her spare time was walk around grilling everyone about their feelings? She wanted to know what was on his mind only because she cared.

But she said, "Fine. You want to shut down, that's your choice."

"Christ," he mumbled. "We're not even married, yet we're arguing like we've been together for years."

Lecia turned in her seat to face him. "I am *not* arguing. I'm *trying* to have a discussion."

Anthony stared ahead, stone-faced.

"Is this how you always are? Impossible to talk to?"

He faced her. "I hate fighting, okay? It drives me nuts."

"Why do you think I'm fighting with you? I'm merely trying to—"

Anthony tuned her out as memories of his parents' arguments recurred to him. His head was already pounding with thoughts of the nightmare that had become his life, which was only making Lecia's grilling him harder to bear. Groaning, he leaned forward. If there was one thing he hated, it was fighting. Fighting only made everything worse. And it drained him.

"I can't believe you're dismissing me like this," he heard Lecia say from behind him.

Anthony sat up straight. "Fine. I'm an ass. Let's just drop this whole thing." He had to spend at least the next couple days with her, and he didn't want the constant bickering.

"I didn't say you were an ass. Anthony. Look at me."

Anthony was raising his eyes to meet hers when a high-pitched, giddy laugh sounded behind them. Lecia's gaze flitted over her shoulder, then back to him. But when the laugh turned into a loud sob, both Lecia and Anthony glanced over, to see what was going on.

A group of men and women, all wearing purple shirts, were milling about only a few feet away. Some wore grins so wide, it seemed they were either high on alcohol or drugs, or were high on life. But the guy who had Anthony's attention was the one holding his face in his hands, practically sobbing like a baby.

The crying made him think that someone had died, but if that was the case, why were others laughing like idiots? Despite their varying ages and mixed races, they had to be part of the same group, traveling together for some reason.

Anthony counted eight of them. They settled in, some sitting on chairs, others sitting on the floor. The four on the floor sat in a circle and held hands.

"What is this?" Lecia asked.

"Hell if I know."

"Maybe a church group," Lecia suggested.

As one of the younger women got up from her seat and jiggled on the spot, Lecia checked out the writing on her shirt. It read, LOVE TO FLY, but the woman wasn't close enough for Lecia to read the smaller subtext. Though she was practically dancing on the spot, there was a nervous edge to her. A senior citizen was offering comfort to a man who was quite possibly her husband. A man in his thirties had his eyes closed and was doing a series of breathing exercises.

"It's going to be okay," a middle-aged, robust white woman said. "We'll get through this."

Shrugging, Lecia turned away, to again face the view of the airfield. She wanted to continue her conversation with Anthony, but now hardly seemed the time. Especially not with "Breathe, Amy, breathe" sounding behind her.

She had hoped for some quiet on the plane, but to her chagrin, the purple-shirted group filled up most of the seats in first class. Only when she and Anthony were seated did she get a good look at one of the shirts. Beneath LOVE TO FLY, she read, *School of No Fear.*

"School of No Fear?" she said to Anthony. He shook his head, his expression as clueless as she felt, then settled against the window.

She didn't say anything else to him until the plane was taxiing down the runway. "Anthony—"

"My mother calls me Anthony when she's upset with me. Please call me Tony. Or better yet, call me T."

"T," Lecia said, trying the name on her tongue. She preferred Tony. "I'd like to resolve things."

"I feel a little stressed, is all," Anthony replied. Now, there was no angry edge to his voice. "I've got a lot on my mind."

"About what happened at the hotel—"

"Oh, God. I can't do this!"

Lecia and Anthony both jerked their heads to the left at the outcry. The same white-haired gentleman who had been sobbing before looked like he was about to face a firing squad.

The black woman seated directly in front of him twisted around in her seat to talk to him. "Remember what we learned in class? Ascending just feels weird, but it will—" Horror-stricken, she closed her eyes and gripped the edges of her seat.

"It will pass," a young blond guy with multiple ear piercings said from the seat behind the sobbing man. "Hang in there, Luther."

Lecia met Anthony's gaze. She wanted to talk about what had happened between them, but he cracked a smile. "School of No Fear," he whispered, his voice saying he finally understood. "This is a friggin' class trip."

Lecia started to laugh. She couldn't do anything else.

In Houston, they lost the purple-shirted clan. The flight with them had been beyond interesting. Through turbulence, Lecia and Anthony had endured the group's audible panic attacks, then cheers of relief when the turbulence passed. The descent had been the worst part, with most of the group whimpering and praying for the last ten minutes of the flight. Once the plane landed, there was a deafening round of applause.

At least this group had forced her and Anthony to relax, given them a reason to smile.

"I need to use the bathroom," Lecia told Anthony as they walked toward their connecting gate.

"I'll wait for you."

"You'd better."

His warm smile lifted her heart. As she disappeared into the rest room, she was relieved that things between them were back to normal.

Whatever normal was.

There was a lineup, and as Lecia hugged the wall, she kept her gaze on the floor. She was aware that she must look like an idiot, wearing dark glasses in a rest room, but from experience she knew this was the worst place to be recognized. Once, in a restaurant bathroom in Beverly Hills, a woman had asked her advice about using a dildo for the first time. The question was shocking, but she'd been trapped in the line and ultimately had to answer the woman's question.

When you were a public persona, people expected more from you because they felt that they knew you personally. It often led to them crossing the line in terms of boundaries.

Thankfully, no one recognized her here, and minutes later she made her way back out to Anthony. His cell phone in hand, he still looked relaxed.

She fell into step with him as he started to walk. "You checked messages?"

"Yeah. Kahari brought Donovan to Long Beach, so that's a relief."

"I'm glad that's worked out," Lecia said. "And I meant to say, I really admire your being a Big Brother. So many athletes talk about giving back, but it's all for show. But you—you're the real deal."

"I try," he said simply.

"Some of our youth are going through such troublesome

times. The lure of the streets, one-parent families. I always say it would make such a difference in a kid's life if their role models gave back in some positive way, because they sure aren't getting what they need from music videos. Athletes have so much power. It's all fine and dandy to do Nike and Reebok commercials, but what about something to actually reach the kids, inspire them to believe in their dreams? You're doing a great thing."

"I wish there'd been something like that where I lived when I was a kid," Anthony said. "I would have loved a big brother. My pops was hardly around."

"No?"

"Naw."

The plot thickened. Lecia had already sensed deep pain in him. Was it because of his father?

"And no," he quickly added, "I don't want to talk about it."

Lecia mimed running a zipper along her lips.

"I did have some other messages. My lawyer called. Said the police are concerned that I haven't come in."

"Are you gonna call him back?"

"Not until after we get to New Orleans. My agent also called, also expressed concern." He shrugged. "But I'm not gonna worry about anything now. Nothing's gonna change until I locate Ginger. And according to Kahari, there's been no news about her."

"There will be," Lecia said. She touched his arm softly. "I'm sure of it."

Twenty-nine

It seemed they'd been traveling for a week by the time they arrived in New Orleans. Though Lecia had slept during most of the flight from Houston, she still didn't feel rested.

The last two days had been a roller coaster of emotions, and Lecia was physically and mentally drained. But thankfully, this whole ordeal would be over soon. Before long, Anthony and Ginger would be reunited and discussing their marriage. Not that the reality of it sat particularly well with her, but what business was it of hers? Her whole reason for being here was to help Anthony get his wife back, no matter how futile she thought the effort. She would facilitate a reconciliation in whatever way she could, then most likely catch a plane back to Los Angeles.

She glanced at Anthony, whose eyes were steadfast on the road ahead of them as he drove the rental car. Then her gaze wandered to the tree-lined streets of New Orleans. She tried to concentrate on the spectacular view of the large, gnarled branches covered with moss, but she couldn't. Despite having known that her time with Anthony would be short, she was regretting the fact that she would be leaving him soon.

God, but she was a moron. She had to be. Why else would she feel sad over leaving another woman's husband? Especially when she hadn't wanted to be with him in the first place?

Except she knew that somewhere along the line that had changed, though she wasn't sure exactly when. Perhaps around the time she found herself draped all over him on that motel bed?

Her stomach fluttered with the memory. Then disappointment gripped her as she remembered how she had pulled away. She suddenly wished that she'd let the moment continue and seen where it would lead.

Oh, it was foolish, she knew. A foolish thought born out of their crazy adventure together. Still, she couldn't help feeling that not giving into her passion was something she would always regret.

Anthony made a series of turns, and Lecia paid attention to the view. They had now passed the old mansions in the garden district and were traveling in a more industrial area.

"This can't be right," Anthony muttered.

"Where are we going?"

He passed her the slip of paper with the address. Lecia looked at the street sign. They were on the right street.

"Maybe 1922 is behind us," she said.

"I didn't see it. But I'll head back that way if I have to. No, wait. That's 1886. And that plaza is 1892," he added, pointing so Lecia could see. "We're going the right way."

Lecia's lips pulled in a frown. The numbers were right, yes, but this certainly didn't look like the right way. Unless Ginger's sister lived on top of a store. Which was a distinct possibility, because Lecia didn't for one minute believe that she was married to a doctor.

Anthony slowed the rental car to a crawl. Then slapped a palm against the steering wheel as he stared at the building.

"Damn," he cursed, and Lecia felt his pain. After all this driving, after how far they'd come, the building before them wasn't a house or an apartment. It was a Mail Boxes Etcetera.

"A mail box? She sent her sister's wedding invitation to a friggin' *mail box?*"

Anthony had turned off the ignition, and Lecia listened as he let out a long string of expletives, wincing at some of the cruder ones.

"I can't believe this."

"Tony, I'm sorry. I don't know what else to say."

His eyes flew to hers. "This is a nightmare. What else is there to say? I came all this way hoping to find my wife, only to find out I don't know her at all."

Lecia placed a hand on Anthony's arm, but he pulled it away, instead dragging both hands over his short-cropped hair.

He faced her after several minutes of obvious agony. "So that story she told me, the one about the paraplegic mother, alcoholic father—that *was* from a soap opera."

"I was hoping it wasn't."

"She didn't just lie to me, she played me." The woman he thought he'd be able to trust forever had sold him prime Florida swampland. "God, I've been such a fool."

"You couldn't know."

"Easy for you to say. You didn't marry Ginger."

Lecia didn't respond, just looked down, and Anthony knew that she thought him the world's biggest idiot. How could she not? He *knew* he was.

In his mind, he replayed all the objections his mother had

voiced to his marrying Ginger. Why hadn't he listened to her? Because Ginger had portrayed herself as the epitome of loyalty, especially with that story of how she'd never abandoned her ailing mother. And he'd wanted someone who was loyal above all else when it came to building a future. He hadn't cared about passion. Many a good marriage had been built on mutual respect.

Ginger hadn't hounded him the way some groupies did. In fact, when he'd met her at the restaurant where she worked, she sounded down to earth. According to her, it was her mother's dream that she pursue an acting career, which was why, she told him, she'd moved to L.A. The sad twist was that her mother had died before she would ever see her succeed.

Anthony chuckled mirthlessly. What a load of bull. Thanks to some soap opera, he had been conned big-time. The real Ginger wasn't a loyal, doting daughter. She was some bitch who had set out to ruin his life.

"All right. This was a dead end," Lecia said. "But there's got to be another lead. We still have Ginger's cell phone bill. I say we start calling the numbers."

Anthony met her gaze, slowly shaking his head with disbelief. Here he was, wallowing in misery, and Lecia was offering him a light, a way out of this mess. "I forgot all about Ginger's cell phone bill."

"That's because you're upset right now. Understandably."

"God, I don't know." This dead end was a wrenching blow. "What's the point?"

"I know this isn't how you are on the field. If your team is down twenty to seven, do you just throw in the towel?"

He shook his head. "No, of course not."

"Then why would you throw in the towel now, about something so much more important? You started this expedition because you wanted to find Ginger—alive—so you could prove to the world that you didn't hurt her."

"I know."

"Remember Agatha Christie's *The Clocks*?"

"Of course."

"There was the dead guy no one could identify. And no one was who they seemed to be."

"Uh-huh?"

"That's got to be what's going on with Ginger. I mean, why bother going to the trouble of giving a fake address for her sister? And not only that, but an elaborate concocted story about her family? She didn't only want to marry you, she wanted you to think she was someone else. The question is, why?"

God, she was right. Anthony didn't know what it meant, but she was right. Something else was up with Ginger. Something he didn't understand.

"I think I ought to call her cell again. See if she answers." He retrieved his phone and punched in Ginger's number. "Who knows? Maybe she decided to go to Palm Springs for the weekend and the media is blowing everything out of proportion."

Lecia started to speak, but Anthony held up a finger to quiet her as he listened to Ginger's cell phone ring. He waited, and Lecia watched him wait. Then Anthony shook his head and disconnected the call.

"No answer," he told her.

"All right, so she's still incommunicado."

"Or missing," Anthony said. "Who knows what kind of trouble she's in? Maybe someone *is* out to get her. It just wasn't me."

"There's so much we don't know. Anything's possible." Lecia paused. "How do you want to go about calling the numbers on her cellular bill? I'd be happy to do it, if you'd rather not have anyone hear your voice."

"You're a doll, Doc."

"Just trying to help," Lecia said, smiling.

"And I appreciate it. But . . ." He glanced at the digital clock. It was minutes after seven o'clock. "We may as well find somewhere to settle first. Then you can make the calls from the hotel room."

Lecia drew in a slow breath, her nerves tingling at the prospect of making the calls. She was nervous, but she was also excited. Never in her wildest dreams would she have believed that she'd be on an adventure with one of the most popular sports figures in America, trying to solve what was becoming a more complicated mystery by the minute. Especially considering how little excitement she'd actually experienced in her thirty-three years.

"You have any idea where you want to stay?" Lecia asked.

"In the heart of N'Awlins, baby. The French Quarter. If this is my last trip before I spend my life in jail, I may as well enjoy it."

Lecia knew she should have been thinking about Anthony's dismal sentiment. Instead, she was thinking of the way he'd called her *baby*. Surprisingly, the simple word made her feel all warm and fuzzy inside, as if he'd intended the word in a literal sense.

When she got back to L.A., maybe *she* would have to book an appointment with a therapist. It was so unlike her to react to a man the way she was reacting to Anthony. Not even Allen had been able to arouse her with one word, or a look, or an accidental touch.

So what was wrong with her now?

The answer came almost immediately, and it was so simple

that it flooded her with relief. When had she spent this much time with a man? Not since she'd dated Marlon-the-Ultimate-Bore in Florida. She could spend hours with Marlon during the course of an evening and not even feel a little buzz in her nether region. It was the reason she'd ended their relationship.

None of the men she'd dated in L.A. had done it for her, either. Lawrence at Nora's Café was the only decent man she conversed with these days, and while she knew he was interested in her, he wasn't her type.

And then there was Anthony. Tall and muscular, he was gorgeous as sin. He exuded raw sexuality even sitting in a car brooding. How could she *not* feel something for him? But it was all based on this unique situation, not on anything real.

"Lecia?"

"Huh?" she said, whipping her head up to face him.

"I said, unless you have any objections. Which I can't help thinking you might, since you got all quiet."

"Objections?"

"To heading to a hotel now."

"Oh. Um, no. I don't." What a lie! She had no clue how she would handle spending another night with him.

"All right, then." Anthony stuck the key in the ignition.

"Wait!" Lecia suddenly cried.

Anthony looked at her. "What is it?"

"I . . . I guess I'm thinking . . . wondering . . . what are we going to do about the sleeping arrangements?"

Anthony's eyebrows shot together in question. "Same as we did last night, why?"

"Well, that's a fine plan, but . . ." *But what?* "But what if people see us together? It'd be one more negative thing in the media where you're concerned. I can see the headline now, 'Football Player Gallivanting While Wife Is Missing. Duh, Do

You Think He Killed Her?' It's probably wise just to get separate rooms."

"You weren't exactly concerned about being seen together when you suggested we fly here."

Shit, good point. "And I was wrong. People *did* recognize us, despite our attempts to obscure our faces."

"If you go in and rent two rooms, you'll just attract attention." Anthony shrugged. "Besides, people have already seen us together. The *Daily Blab* could be writing their feature story about us as we speak."

What a horrible thought. "It's just that the French Quarter is much busier than where we stopped last night, and certainly busier than either of the airports. There's a greater chance of being recognized."

"Have you been there before?"

"No."

"No?" Anthony repeated, his tone relaying his shock. "Well, let me tell you, when it comes to Bourbon Street, people don't see anything except the signs for cheap booze and the barely dressed women."

Which meant she'd stand out like a sore thumb. "I can just imagine."

"You haven't sampled New Orleans until you've had a Hurricane at Pat O'Brien's. That drink will knock you flat on your—"

"Let me guess," Lecia said, pasting a syrupy smile on her face. "You've been here for Mardi Gras."

"Once. And I've been back for football. . . . What? Why are you looking at me like that?"

Lecia *tsk*ed softly as she shook her head. "I can only imagine what those trips were like."

"I'm not gonna lie—"

"Here we go."

"Hold up. Hear me out. Yeah, it can be pretty crazy. Groupies always know where we'll be staying, and let me tell you, they show up in droves."

"And you athletes just can't help yourselves, right?"

"*Some* players."

Lecia looked away, unable to bear the sight of Anthony a moment longer. She was disgusted with herself for even feeling a smidgen of jealousy, but that's exactly what was making her stomach clench. "Are we gonna head off?"

"Not until you look at me."

Like a spoiled child, Lecia stubbornly refused to look his way.

"Lecia . . ."

"God, I'm acting like an idiot," she said after a moment. "Like whatever you or any of your teammates do matters one lick to me."

"You think that when I stay at hotels, I have some hedonistic orgy in my room? Damn, I hate it when you roll your eyes like that, like you think I won't notice."

"I didn't roll my eyes."

"You've been with me for a good forty-eight hours. Have I given you any reason to believe that I can't control myself around a woman?"

"I, Mr. Beals, am not throwing myself at you."

"What do you call flattening me on my back this morning? If I didn't have any self-control, we'd still be in that hotel room, going on round thirty."

Oh, man. What a thought that was. To think she'd missed out on something so spectacular.

No, no, no. You did not *miss out.* "Um, nice try with the revisionist history, but *you* pulled me onto your body."

Anthony laughed. "Oh, I did, did I?"

Lecia wanted to wipe that smirk off his face—with her lips. "You . . . you ball players."

"Exactly, babe." Meaning she couldn't deny his claim. "Not that I minded, because Doc, you are hot."

Lecia opened her mouth to protest, then realized what she'd be objecting to. She managed a very dim-witted "Oh."

"Yeah, I think you're a babe."

Maybe it was where they were, and the fact that she had been living and breathing Anthony Beals for the past two days. But she was suddenly ballsy enough to follow this train of thought through to its logical conclusion.

She said, "You're saying I could tempt you?"

"*Could?* Doc, you already are."

His affirmation sent a zap of heat right to her vagina. But then she remembered what they were talking about, and realized she had just proven her point. "Aha!" she boasted. "There you go. Women tempt you all the time."

"I know it's hard to believe, but not every ball player is a philandering asshole. I'm human. I can't say I haven't been tempted. But when it boils down to it, a piece of ass for one night sure as hell isn't worth me losing my marriage."

It was strange, but her heart said she could believe him. She barely knew him, but there was a ring of honesty to everything he told her. Allen would have flat out lied and said he was never tempted by another woman, and as soon as she was out of the room he'd be screwing a patient.

"What the hell," Anthony said flippantly. "See what happens when a guy tries to be honest?"

"I believe you," Lecia told him. For some reason, it was important for him to know that. "I guess I have my own hang-ups with infidelity. My ex. He believed that if he could get away with it, why not do it."

"I don't get some men. If I had a wife like you to come home to . . ."

Anthony let his statement hang in the air, but he thought about his own words after uttering them. Wasn't that the way life went? The good ones got burned time and time again. They gave their hearts fully, only to have them trampled on.

Lecia was one of the good ones. She wouldn't be here with him if she weren't. And deep in his gut, he knew he could trust her. Unlike the woman who'd sworn to love him forever. He couldn't imagine Lecia lying to him the way Ginger had.

But he *could* imagine her in his home, lying on his bed—

Startled at the direction of his thoughts, Anthony started the car. He didn't know what was wrong with him, but maybe he really ought to see someone when he got back to L.A. Someone he could talk to who would help him sort out his feelings. Because right now his biggest concern should be Ginger, yet he was getting a hard-on thinking of boning Dr. Love.

Anthony tried to keep his thoughts in check as he drove through the New Orleans streets. He suspected Lecia was thinking, too, because she was quiet. The silence seemed to stretch for hours, but it couldn't have been more than twenty minutes before they arrived in the French Quarter. Anthony pulled the car up in front of the Sheraton.

"Here," he said, handing Lecia a handful of hundred dollar bills. "Pay cash."

She looked at the money, then at him. "I'm sure they'll want an imprint of a credit card. They always do at the bigger hotel chains."

"You don't mind using yours, do you? No one expects you to be traveling with me. There'll be no questions."

Lecia shook her head as she got out of the car. "No. I don't mind. But this is a lot of money. You want the presidential suite?"

"A clean room with two beds. Or a king," he added, then wanted to kick himself. The words had escaped, as if they had a mind of their own.

"I'm going to pretend I didn't hear that," Lecia said, and closed the car door.

Anthony watched her walk toward the Sheraton, his stomach sinking with chagrin. *And I'm gonna head straight for the cold shower when I get in that room.*

Thirty

A cold shower was exactly what Anthony needed to give him a fresh perspective on the situation. His head was clear and his libido was no longer raging. With his thoughts of Lecia under control, he'd concentrated on figuring out his wife's motives. And realized that the answer was probably a lot simpler than he'd thought.

A towel wrapped around his waist as he stepped out of the bathroom, he said to Lecia, "Maybe Ginger just needs therapy."

Lecia looked up from her spot on the queen bed closest to the window. "Excuse me?"

"Ginger. I was thinking about everything in the shower, how nothing about her behavior makes sense, and I can't help wondering if she just needs a bit of therapy. If she told me this big lie based on a soap opera, don't you think she's suffering some kind of breakdown? Then she runs her mouth to the media acting like she's afraid of me, which is a total lie. I'm being quick to judge her as a cold, calculating bitch, but maybe she's got some kind of emotional disorder and needs me now more than ever."

Lecia didn't say a thing. She gaped at him as if he had turned bright green.

Then her expression changed. Grew darker. Her eyes narrowed into thin slits as she shook her head.

"Why are you looking at me like that? You're upset?"

"You want the truth?"

"Yeah."

"Then yeah, I'm upset."

A few seconds passed before Anthony asked, "Why?"

She got up and paced to the window, gripping the sill. "You really don't want me to tell you."

"Yeah, I really do," he replied, wondering what was up with her.

"Okay, fine." She spun around. "I'm looking at you wondering if I should smack you or commit you."

"Whoa—"

"Ginger is suffering some sort of mental breakdown? For God's sake, Tony, why are you grasping at straws? Do you want to live in the dark forever with blinders on, while this woman brings you down to the gutter?"

"I was only thinking out loud."

Lecia threw her hands in the air, letting them fall and slap against her thighs. "The way it seems to me—but who am I to judge, right? I only listened to your wife tell me what a sick pervert you were—but it's pretty clear to me that she wants nothing to do with you, so if you're on this cross-country expedition in hopes of getting her back, you're a bigger fool than I ever thought you were." She marched toward him. "That woman doesn't love you, Anthony. You hear me? She doesn't love you. When are you going to get it?"

He swallowed as she stepped to within one inch of him. Her words bothered him, but not as much as they should have. "Are you finished?"

"That about sums it up, yes."

"I don't think it does."

"Oh, please. No more about your precious Ginger."

She whirled on her heel, but Anthony grabbed hold of her arm, whirling her back around so she landed against his chest. Lecia's gaze flew to his, bug-eyed and questioning.

"No more about Ginger," he said softly. "But how about this?"

And then, without warning, he brought his mouth down on hers and kissed her.

Lecia was stunned out of her mind, more so because Anthony had gone from arguing with her about Ginger than because he'd kissed her senseless without batting an eye.

And she was senseless. Because instead of pulling away from him, instead of telling him she wasn't going to be a pawn in his I-want-Ginger-back game, she stretched up on her tiptoes and pressed her body closer to his.

Lord, but he filled her senses. His body was so strong, she wanted to stay in his arms all day. His unique masculine scent was utterly delicious. He knew just how to touch her to make her crazy with desire.

This man was dangerous.

As he deepened the kiss, his tongue tangling with hers, he pressed his fingers along her spine with a gentle yet firm touch. It was the kind of touch that said she was his for the taking.

And, God help her, she was.

"I want you," he rasped, then pulled her bottom lip between his teeth. "Man, I love your lips. Even when you're yelling at me, I love them." He flicked his tongue over hers. "I love the way you taste."

She wanted him, but not on the rebound. And certainly not

as some way for him to get back at his precious Ginger. She had to know this wasn't about that.

She stepped away from him, backing against a wall. "One minute you're talking about Ginger like you can save your marriage, the next you're tonguing me?"

"You don't want to do this?"

"Hell, yes," she found herself saying. "But not if you're going to run back to your wife."

"My marriage is over," Anthony said softly. "Hell, it was never a real marriage in the first place."

That piqued Lecia's interest. "What does that mean?"

"I liked her, respected her. I thought that's all we needed for a happy union. And don't give me that look. You have no idea what it was like watching my father play the marriage game like it was a recreational sport."

"Your father?" So she had been right. "This is about your father?"

"He couldn't even commit to getting out of bed in the morning. I swore I'd never be like him."

"So you weren't in love with Ginger when you married her?" she asked.

"Not the way I should have been. No, not at all, if I'm being honest with myself. There was mutual admiration, and I thought . . . maybe it sounds stupid now, but I really thought *she* loved me. And I figured that if she cared deeply for me, was someone I could rely on, I would never betray her the way my father betrayed my mother over and over again. I trusted her to be someone with whom I would build a future."

Lecia didn't tell Anthony that what he had done, marrying a woman for any reason other than love, was bound to have backfired.

"I'm sure you'd say my actions were foolish, Dr. Love, especially since it all blew up in my face."

"I've made mistakes, too. I have no right to judge anybody."

"Thanks, but after the way you've been trying to get me to talk, I'm sure you have a lot more to say on the subject. And I don't blame you."

"It happened. The point is that you learn from it."

"I know. I need to think about the future." He ran a finger along Lecia's cheek.

She wanted to say something, but only a breathless sigh escaped.

"You think I'm wrong to want you, don't you? I know," he said when she didn't respond. "Believe me, I'm trying to understand it myself. But you know what? I suck at figuring out my feelings, so right about now, I don't want to analyze a damn thing."

Lecia stopped breathing when Anthony curled his fingers around the back of her neck and drew her close. She landed against the strong wall of his chest with a soft thud. And before she could even utter a word of protest or caution, he pressed his lips down on hers.

Hard.

Her brain told her to end the kiss, push him away. Her heart told her to ride this exhilarating wave as long as she could.

Anthony's hands roamed her body with the deliberate slowness of a person running a finger along a priceless antique. And it was the aching slowness that was her undoing.

Because there was tenderness in his touch. Untamed, tear-your-clothes-off passion, she was prepared for. Tenderness, she wasn't.

His touch said that there was something more between them than a trained counselor trying to help out a guy who needed her. Bizarre as it was, she had felt it from the first night they'd met on national television.

There had been a spark even then, an attraction she couldn't deny. It was that spark that had her saying yes to go with him to Kahari's place, then yes to this cross-country trip. All the while, her brain had advised her to be smart, but for once in her life she was following her heart.

And right now, her heart was leading her to the Point of No Return, a place that was dark and dangerous and absolutely breathtaking.

Anthony's hands explored her body. She tentatively ran her fingers down his back. They stopped at the ridge of the towel around his waist. How easy would it be to slip the towel off and take that piece of forbidden fruit?

Her whole life, she had lived cautiously. Followed the rules. Never done a risky thing until she'd taken a stab at writing, something she had always wanted to do but was talked out of doing.

Being with Anthony might not be smart. It might be stupid as hell. But she was allowed at least one reckless act in her life, wasn't she? She couldn't think of a better way to unleash all the tension bottled up inside her.

As if they had a will of their own, her hands moved over Anthony's firm butt, then up again, over his amazing back. She savored each muscular groove. If his back was any indication, she could only imagine how incredible the rest of his body felt. His pecs. Those thighs . . .

Ooh, those thighs between her legs. Would he be merciless with her?

As her arms looped around Anthony's neck, his own hands ventured lower. She loved the feel of his big palms cruising over her body.

He cupped her butt. A slow groan rumbled in his chest and his fingers went lower still, discovering flesh. They tickled her skin as they ventured beneath her skirt, flirting with her naked backside.

He nibbled on her earlobe. "I love this thong."

Who would have thought, but she loved it, too. Loved it because it made her feel sexy and desirable.

Anthony stepped forward, guiding Lecia backward. When her legs hit the bed they buckled, and she couldn't help going down. Anthony covered her body with his much the way she had covered his body with hers twelve hours earlier.

"I want to do this, Tony. I really do. But—"

"No buts. You're free, single, and disengaged. I'm separated and on the road to divorce."

"But you're a man."

"What—you're into women?"

She angled her head and cut her eyes at him. "Not in this lifetime."

"Then why all this bullshit mumbo jumbo?" His lips found her neck. "I thought we were past the protests." He stopped and looked at her. "Unless you're not attracted to me."

"Like that's even possible."

His smile lit his entire face. "That's what I want to hear." He buried his face in her neck once again.

Lecia's eyes fluttered shut. The pleasure was so delicious, she nearly died from it. And he wasn't even touching her where it really mattered.

"But . . ." She inhaled a deep breath and found the strength to speak. "I've been so out of the dating marathon. Not at the back of the pack—out of the race completely."

"Who's talking about dating, Doc?"

The truth was, it had been so long since she'd had sex that

she wasn't sure she'd remember how. Wasn't sure she'd be any good.

"I . . ." Her shoulders dropped fully on the mattress as she couldn't think of any more excuses. She wanted this as much as he apparently did, wanted this as much as she'd ever wanted anything. "I don't want to disappoint you."

"Oh, baby." His voice was incredibly gentle. So were his eyes. "There is absolutely no way you could ever disappoint me."

Lecia's heart thundered in her chest. She wasn't only feeling lust, she was feeling something else—something she didn't expect to feel. Something deeper than just a physical attraction, and that scared the hell out of her.

"But—"

Anthony covered her mouth with his and practically sucked the breath out of her. But damn if it wasn't the best breath-sucking she had ever experienced.

After what seemed like endless kissing and groping, she managed to tear her lips from his and ask, "Do you have a condom?"

"Ah, damn it. No." Anthony sighed.

"We can't . . . we can't do this without a condom. I'm not on the pill." There hadn't been a need—until now.

"No, you're right."

Anthony eased off her. Lecia was instantly cold where she had just been warm.

"I'm sure they sell some downstairs. I could go, but maybe you ought to. You're the one who's dressed."

"Yes. That would make sense." But Lecia was already wondering if she had made a mistake in halting their hot and heavy session. Maybe they wouldn't pick up where they'd left off when she returned.

She snatched up her purse from the floor. She would buy the condoms, but who knew what would happen then?

"And while you're at it, why don't you pick up a new pair of boxers for me, and maybe another T-shirt. Some shorts. Whatever you can find."

This was now turning into a shopping trip. There went her hot, passionate, reckless affair.

So much for ending her celibacy.

Thirty-one

Lecia stepped into the room—and stopped dead in her tracks. A profound feeling of disappointment swept over her.

Anthony wasn't there.

So much for their night of wicked lovemaking. Clearly, he'd had second thoughts. And why not? She had to be as frigid as they came, stopping him at every advance to babble in his ear, completely spoiling the mood.

She emitted a little moan and closed the door. Then two strong arms made their way around her waist. Her heart nearly exploded from fright.

"Tony, you jerk!" She slapped his arm with her free hand.

Laughing, Anthony turned her in his arms. He took the shopping bag from her fingers and dropped it onto the floor. "I missed you."

She would never tire of his bedroom voice. "I bought a bunch of stuff," she told him coyly.

"I don't care what you bought."

"Oh, I think you might. Three packs of condoms. Different sizes. Different shapes." She paused. "Flavors."

"Oh, baby."

He was still wearing the towel. As he held her close, she rested her face against his hard, smooth chest. She wanted to lick it and bite it. She wanted to feel his strapping body pressed against her naked breasts.

Anthony stepped backward, his eyes roaming over her slowly. "Take off your clothes."

From anyone else it might have sounded like a crude demand, but from Anthony it was an invitation to seduction.

She reached for the bottom of her shirt to pull it over her head, but paused. "I'm hot, sweaty."

Anthony pulled her shirt off for her. "Let's get hot and sweaty together. Then take a shower." His eyes locked with hers, he reached for the clasp of her bra behind her back and popped it with ease. Then he reached for her skirt, pulling it down over her hips. Lecia did a little shimmy, and the material fell in a heap at her feet.

"Turn around."

Inhaling a shaky breath, Lecia did just that.

"I swear, you look hot in that thong."

Lecia's entire body tensed with sweet expectation when she felt Anthony lower himself to his knees behind her.

For several agonizing seconds he didn't touch her. "What?" she asked, hardly able to stand it. "Are you checking out my stretch marks?"

She felt a feathery touch, and wasn't sure if it was his mouth or his finger.

"You have one sweet ass. I want to kiss every inch of it."

She was as wet as the Pacific. "You want to kiss my ass?"

"You better believe it." Those were definitely his lips now, kissing her butt once, twice. "I don't know why, but there's something about you that drives me wild."

His tongue was hot against her skin, his teeth playfully

erotic. As he kissed the entire plane of her behind, he slipped a hand between her legs and ran it back and forth over her. Every inch of her throbbed. She wanted to feel his tongue where his hand now roamed.

"Turn around."

Her knees nearly gave way, but she managed to move without falling. She looked down to see Anthony staring up at her. His eyes never moved as he eased her thong aside and lightly touched her nub.

His touch was electric, and Lecia cried out from the pleasure.

"Oh, baby." He planted a kiss on her inner thigh. "You're so wet. I love that."

Lecia couldn't stand any more of his teasing. She dropped to the floor to meet him, wrapping her arms around his neck. She planted her lips on his, moaning into his mouth.

"Your tongue, baby." Anthony's voice was low and seductive. "Give it to me."

Lecia opened her mouth wider.

"That's it." He flicked his tongue over hers, then suckled the tip softly. "Damn, girl. You're making me lose my mind. I want to do very naughty things to you."

Lecia's heart spasmed. "Oh?"

"Hell, yeah."

She wanted to ask what kind of things, but wasn't much of a talker when it came to sex. With Allen, there had been no verbal foreplay. There had been no foreplay, period.

Their lips locked together, Anthony guided them to their feet. Then he pulled her against him with a sense of urgency and gyrated his hips. His penis slipped out of the towel and rubbed against her belly.

"Oh my," Lecia said, her hands stilling on his shoulders.

"What?" Anthony leaned his forehead against hers. "You want me to stop?"

"No. No, I—"

"Then why'd you go still?"

She hesitated, then asked sheepishly, "The truth?" She didn't meet his eyes.

"Tell me."

"Your . . ." Suddenly, her face was flaming. She talked frankly about sex all the time, yet here she was, unable to say "penis."

He pulled his head back to look down at her. "My what?"

In reply, she shimmied slightly against him. "That."

When his eyes grew wide with recognition, Lecia couldn't help giggling. "Your *package*. I don't think I've ever been with anyone so . . ."

"Hung?" he supplied.

"Oh, God." Lecia burst into laughter.

"That *is* what you were trying to say, isn't it?"

"I was thinking of a better way to put it." She covered her face with a hand. "Don't I feel stupid."

"But you look cute." He looped his arms around her waist.

"I do?" she asked, eyeing him skeptically.

"Oh yeah. Especially the way you blush when you're talking about sex with me. Who would have thought—the sex therapist shy about sex?"

"Do you always talk like this?"

"Usually. Unless I'm doing this."

His mouth came down hard on hers. This time his hands explored her body with more urgency. He cupped her butt, squeezed it. His broad hands moved upward and to the front, covering her naked breasts, stroking her nipples.

Lecia sighed into his mouth.

"You like that, huh?"

"Mmm . . ."

"Tell me," he whispered.

"I like it."

"Like what?" He dipped his tongue into her ear.

Lecia's knees buckled, but Anthony held her firmly. "*That.* Your tongue in my ear. God, do I ever. Oooh, and that, too. The way you touch my nipples."

He moved his mouth to her neck and brushed his lips across her skin. "Is that all you want?"

"N-No . . ."

"Tell me what you want."

Lecia was used to telling her patients to go for what they wanted, yet when it came to herself, she had trouble following her own advice. She wanted to tell Anthony exactly how to please her, how to end her celibacy in grand style. But she was pathetically shy.

"Come on, sweetheart," he urged.

"I want you to . . ." She looked up at him, running her tongue along her bottom lip as she met his eyes. "I want you to nibble on one. Put my nipple in your mouth and make me crazy."

Anthony skimmed the mound of her breast. Closing her eyes, Lecia arched her head backward. The anticipation of his mouth closing over her nipple had her body thrumming.

Slowly, he touched every part of her breast—every part except the nipple. It was exquisite torture. "Tony . . . Tony, please . . ."

"I know what you want." He flicked his tongue over her nipple but didn't take it into his mouth.

"Oh, God. Tony, please tell me you're not going to tease me all night."

Anthony looked up at her. There was a mischievous glint in his eyes. Squeezing the soft mound of her breast, he opened his mouth wide. Lecia sucked in a sharp breath as she watched and felt his hot tongue cover her nipple.

She expected him to be wild and frenzied, but again he was surprisingly gentle. Intense in a quiet way that thrilled her like nothing else ever had.

"Tony?" she managed on a ragged breath.

"I know, babe."

"No, you don't know. I need to . . . I have to say something."

Anthony paused. "Uh-oh."

"No, it's not bad." She blew out a shaky breath. "I just want to say . . . I think I've got my mojo back."

Anthony's sexy lips curled in a smile. He slipped a hand between her legs. "Just in time, baby."

Lecia heard a soft thud as Anthony's towel hit the floor, and seconds later he was pulling that wisp of material people called underwear down her legs. He planted a gentle kiss at the apex of her thighs, sending shivers of delight along all the nerve endings in her body.

"I'd better get a condom," he said after a moment.

Lecia watched Anthony's beautiful form as he tore open a box of ribbed condoms. And knew she wouldn't turn back from what she was about to do, not for a million bucks.

If this was foolish, then so be it. She preached sex for a living. It was high time she got some.

Oh, yeah. She was going to enjoy this ride.

Breathing like he'd run a marathon, Anthony slipped his slick body off of Lecia's and rolled onto his back. A long gush of air whooshed out of her lungs. She felt she could stay like this forever, a smile plastered on her face, her body thrumming from the sweet aftermath of yet another orgasm.

Wow oh wow, had she ever gotten laid.

It couldn't be any better than this. Anthony was . . . simply amazing. Were all athletes like him, with never-ending stamina? For over an hour they'd made love without a break. Every time she thought he would climax, he merely slowed, only to pick up speed and bring her back to the brink of another wickedly delicious orgasm.

She was no longer sure how many she'd had. Somewhere in the vicinity of ten or fifteen. A whopping number that was a record for her.

Anthony draped an arm across her waist, and she snuggled her back against him. Her body was a perfect fit.

"I've got to ask," she said, her breathing still irregular. "Are you on Viagra?"

Anthony roared with laughter. "I lived up to *The Big O*, did I?"

"That was 'the Big Multiple O.' "

Anthony turned away from her. Lecia heard the snap of latex and knew he was taking off the condom. He got off the bed, and she watched the way his firm ass moved as he walked to the bathroom. Moments later she heard the toilet flush.

"Did it break?" she asked when he was returning. If it hadn't, it was the best damn rubber ever made, to endure the marathon session they'd had.

"I don't think so," he replied. He ran a finger along her shoulder as he got back into bed with her. "Would it bother you if it did?"

"Meaning?"

"Meaning do you want to have kids?"

Exactly what was he asking her? Surely Anthony didn't want to go from A to Z in the span of one night.

"I'd love to," she told him. "I have one niece, and she's a total gem. But . . . I'm not sure why you're asking."

"I don't know. Ginger didn't want children."

A lump lurched into Lecia's throat. She couldn't swallow it, but managed to speak around it. "You're thinking of Ginger?" She eased up onto her elbows. "You just made love to me and you're thinking of Ginger?"

Anthony groaned. "I didn't mean it like—"

"I know. You were just thinking out loud." Lecia threw the covers off and leapt out of bed. She searched the ground for her shirt and skirt, then slipped both on.

"What are you doing?" Anthony asked, sitting up.

"What does it look like?"

"Don't do this, Lecia. Don't leave."

Anthony got out of bed, and Lecia quickly grabbed her purse. She wasn't wearing any underwear, but if she stopped to put it on, she wouldn't escape the room in time.

She charged for the door.

"Lecia, will you wait a second?"

"Why? You got what you wanted. There's no need to further humiliate me."

Then she swung the door open and ran down the hall.

Thirty-two

Lecia had to give Anthony credit. He was right about the Hurricanes at Pat O'Brien's. They were pretty damn delicious.

And pretty damn potent.

She'd chugged back the first one as if it were Kool-Aid, and halfway through the second one, the room started to spin. Not so much that she couldn't hold her head up, but enough that she was seeing two of the sandy-haired man seated on the bar stool next to her.

"John," she said to him.

"Joe," he told her.

"Joe, sorry." She took another swig of her drink, wincing as she did. "The reality is, you've got to read between the lines if you want to hear what your girlfriend is saying. You not taking the garbage out is not the reason she won't have sex with you. It's an excuse."

"That's why I figured I'd ask you about this, Dr. Love."

"What your girlfriend is trying to tell you is that when you don't take out the garbage, when you don't do any of the housework, your actions say you aren't concerned about her. If you loved her, you would do those things to make her life a little easier. Why make love to you if you aren't concerned about her happiness? At least, that's the way she sees it."

"I do care. Guess I'm just lazy."

"You have to decide what's important to you."

"You're right, Dr. Love. I'll try to be better."

Lecia took another sip of her drink. "And one last piece of advice," she said, on a roll now. "It should be pretty obvious, but I don't think most guys get it. Whatever you do, *don't* bring up your ex the moment you've rolled off your girlfriend when you finish making love. She'll never want to have sex with you again."

"Huh?" Joe's expression registered confusion. "I didn't say I did that."

"No, um, you didn't. It's just . . . a lot of women complain about that, so I thought I'd bring it up. Just a helpful bit of advice."

Lecia faced forward again, rubbing her temples as she did. She was surrounded by men, most of them cordial, a lot of them good-looking, but this wasn't where she wanted to be. She wanted to be back in the hotel room with Anthony, but that wasn't an option.

The man was stuck on Ginger like gum stuck to the bottom of a shoe. What hurt most now was the deep connection she had felt while making love to him. It had seemed so real; how could it have been one-sided? Maybe because Anthony had closed his eyes and pictured her as his estranged wife.

"Dr. Love? If you have a moment, could I ask you a question?"

Turning to her left, Lecia saw a very attractive, dark-skinned brother. He was definitely hot. The kind of man women lost their heads over. So why wasn't she the least bit intrigued?

Because he wasn't Anthony.

Forget Anthony.

Lecia opened her mouth to speak to the man, but before she could say a word, she heard, "What are you doing?"

Damn if her heart didn't flutter. *Anthony.* He'd come for her.

Tamping down on her excitement, she faced her lover coolly. "Oh, so now you're blind?"

Anthony smiled without humor. "I can see that you're sitting here having a drink. What I want to know is why."

"I didn't realize it was a crime."

"Why don't we step outside so we can talk?"

"No." Lecia squeezed her eyes shut as her head swam.

"How many of these have you had to drink?"

When Lecia opened her eyes, she saw two of Anthony's head. "Only two. I think."

"Two? Holy shit. That's way too much." He slid the mammoth-sized drink glass down the bar, out of her reach.

"Hey!"

"Don't do this, Doc. Don't sit here drowning your sorrows in booze. Hear me out. All I said was—"

Lecia threw up a hand, silencing him. "I know what you said. And worse, I know why you said it, even if you don't. I was just a temporary diversion for you. A warm body to substitute the place of your precious Ginger. Because she's the one you really want. It's always been about her."

Anthony glanced around the bar. One guy looked at him and smiled, and Anthony figured him for a fan. But the others . . . eyebrows were raised superciliously, and he sensed some of the onlookers were itching for a fight. Lecia was airing their private business, and making him look like an ass in the process.

"Let's just go," he told her.

"No," she said, poking a finger against his chest. "You go."

She turned her back on him and Anthony gritted his teeth. Damn the woman. Weren't shrinks supposed to be good at listening?

"I'm not going anywhere."

"You heard the lady," the guy next to Lecia said.

"Listen, buddy. This is between me and her. It's got nothing to do with you."

"Oh, yeah? Well, Dr. Love here's a friend, and if she doesn't want you around, then you best be heading off."

Lecia turned to the man. "John, it's okay. I can handle this."

"Joe," the man said.

"You're on a first name basis with this guy?" Anthony asked, wondering just how cozy she'd gotten with the men at this bar.

"John's been a helluva lot nicer to me than you've been. And he would *never* bring up his ex—"

"Okay, that's enough."

"Yes, it is." Lecia swayed ever so slightly as she wagged a finger at him. "Go away."

Anthony stared at her in disbelief, but she met his gaze dead-on. Surely she couldn't be serious. It had to be the alcohol. "We're in this together, remember?"

"Not anymore we're not. You've taken advantage of me for the last time."

It's the alcohol talking, Anthony told himself, surprised at how her words hurt. He placed a hand on her shoulder. "I'm not gonna leave you here."

"Don't touch me."

Both the bartender and Joe glowered at Anthony.

"All right," Anthony said, pulling his hand back. "I'm not touching you. But at least—"

"You know," she began, "I'd wondered why anyone in their right mind would leave a guy like you. But now I know. Just because you're Mr. NFL MVP, you think everyone around you is supposed to do what you want. Well guess what—even the most patient of women get tired of that kind of ego. You need to get over yourself."

"Ouch," the bartender said.

Defiance shone in Lecia's eyes, mixed with victory. Anthony shook his head. Clearly, he couldn't talk to her. Not like this. They'd only end up in a huge blowout, the last thing he wanted.

"You're a big girl," he finally told her. "Do what you want."

Then he turned and walked out of the bar.

The look of pain that passed over Anthony's face was like a dose of cold water. It sobered Lecia considerably.

She watched Anthony retreat from the bar, thinking she'd be happy to see him go. Instead she felt horrible.

She had been such a bitch. Her words had been harsh, aided by these damn Hurricanes. And they had been uncalled for.

What she really wanted to tell him was that she'd been hurt by his comparing her to Ginger, that she had wanted to savor their intimacy after making love for the first time.

"Oh, shit," she muttered. Securing her purse strap over her shoulder, she hopped off the bar stool. The draft of air under her skirt reminded her that she wasn't wearing any panties.

"Tony!" she called, although the buzz of chatter in the bar was so loud, she didn't think he would hear her. "Tony, wait."

Anthony heard Lecia calling him, but he'd be damned if he was going to stop. Her words had stung, but they'd also brought him back down to earth. He had been fooling around, having a good time, when his wife was missing. How had he lost sight of that?

He maneuvered through the crowd of drunken partygoers and out the bar's door. The air was warm and muggy, sticking to him immediately. He would march right back to the hotel and figure out a new plan of action. He would—

"Tony!"

There was a desperate note to Lecia's voice, and this time Anthony stopped. Turning, he saw her trying to pull her arm free from some guy who looked like a linebacker.

Anthony didn't hesitate. He stormed toward them while Lecia struggled to get free. "Get your hands off of me, you pig."

"C'mon, baby," the guy said, still gripping her.

"Yo, buddy." Anthony put a hand on the big guy's shoulder and pushed him backward. The force of it made him loosen his grip on Lecia. "What's your problem, man?"

Muttering under his breath, the guy turned and walked away. He was probably harmless, just drunk. But drunks could quickly turn nasty.

It was exactly the reason he hadn't wanted to leave Lecia here on her own.

Forgetting his bruised ego, he wrapped an arm around her. She cradled against his side. She probably did so as much because of a throbbing head as for any other reason, but still it felt good to know that he could offer her comfort and she could accept it.

They walked in silence through the crowded streets of the French Quarter until a flash nearly blinded them. Lecia gasped. Anthony drew up short.

The guy who took their picture sprinted off, weaving through the throng of people.

"Hey!" Anthony called. "Hey, buddy!"

Releasing Lecia, he started after the guy, but stopped when he heard her say, "Anthony, no. Please, let's just leave. It was probably just a fan."

Was it? "I sure as hell hope so."

He made his way back to Lecia. Before he could reach for her, she leaned in to him, wrapping both arms around his waist.

Anthony had gone in search of her so they could talk. He wanted to tell her that maybe they'd been hasty in falling into bed. But feeling her warmth now, he couldn't quite believe that what had happened between them had been a mistake. Rather, it had felt right. And something about the good doctor had him wishing this road trip would never end.

At least she seemed to have sobered, although tomorrow she might have a killer headache. He'd have to make sure and order room service once they got back to the hotel.

They didn't say anything else as they walked back to the Sheraton. Once in the hotel lobby, Lecia let him go and walked beside him.

"Tony, I'm sorry," she said after a moment. "I shouldn't have said the things I did at the bar. The truth is, I wanted to lash out at you because I was feeling hurt."

Anthony nodded. "I understand. But maybe you're right. Maybe I do expect everything to go the way I want when I want it. I don't know. Maybe that *is* why Ginger didn't want to work things out."

"No," Lecia said softly as they stood outside the elevator. "Your wife has other issues. She had her own reasons for telling you a web of lies. Just as she had her own reasons for not wanting to save the marriage. Everything she's done seems like some part of a calculated plan."

The elevator opened, and two young couples whizzed past

them, giggling. Anthony's stomach tightened as he watched them disappear around the corner. Never once had Ginger clung to him that way. Never once had he missed that kind of intimacy—until now.

His arms yearned to reach for Lecia, to cradle her against his chest not for comfort, but because she belonged there.

She walked onto the elevator, going straight for the corner. He followed her, only he went to the other corner. Only a few feet separated them, but it might as well have been miles.

"I want to make something perfectly clear," he said as the elevator whizzed up. "What happened between us . . . it had nothing to do with Ginger." Lecia didn't speak, so Anthony continued. "In the beginning, yeah, I wanted to reconcile with her. Even though she said she wanted a divorce, I stubbornly pressured her for another chance. But not for the right reasons. The only reason, really. It should have been about love, but it was about money."

The elevator door opened, but Lecia didn't move. She stared at Anthony, her eyes searching his face, but she didn't say a word.

Anthony was tempted to press the stop button. Something about the way she was looking at him made him want to take her right here, on the elevator floor. But instead he stepped forward and caught the door before it closed. They had a room down the hall that offered plenty of privacy.

"You coming?" he asked her.

Silently, she stepped out of the elevator.

"You know, Doc, you're starting to give me a complex. You say you want me to talk, then when I do, you shut down."

"I'm listening."

Moments later Anthony slipped his key in the door and opened it. He let Lecia step inside first. He lingered a moment at the door, taking his time double-locking and bolting it. But he was really buying time, wondering if he should continue to share his feelings or just shut up.

Inside, sitting on the farthest bed, Lecia stared up at him. And Anthony knew right then that he had to make her understand.

"Tonight, when I went to look for you, it was because I cared. Not because I wanted you back to help me search for Ginger. Yes, that's why we're on this trip, but finding Ginger . . . it's not about what you think it is. I realize that now. Days ago, I thought I wanted to save my marriage for the marriage's sake. Now I know that my only motivation was saving it so she won't get the five million she wants. I need that money. Kahari and I are opening a youth center for troubled teens. That's why it matters." Anthony blew out an exasperated breath. "You're not gonna say anything?"

Lecia wasn't sure what to say. She had told herself that she would snap her fingers and turn off her feelings for him, but now, as he spoke so honestly, she felt her heart melting. She *did* care for him, and she wasn't sure there was a damn thing she could do about it.

"Are you hungry?" she finally asked.

Anthony's eyes narrowed. "Hungry? That's all you're gonna say?"

"I'm afraid to say anything else."

He walked across the room and sat down beside her on the bed. "I'm hard," he said softly. "I have no clue why, but I want to make love to you again."

"I'm not wearing any underwear."

His eyebrows shot up. "What?"

She smiled. "In my haste to get away from you, I didn't have time to put any on."

"You went out to the French Quarter without any underwear?"

"Uh-huh. Are you gonna spank me?"

"I should."

The words were soft and fluttered over her. She didn't want to admit it, but she was already wet and ready for him. Never before had she gotten turned on without even a touch or a kiss. What was it about Anthony?

Surely it had to be his scent. It was powerful and called to her on a primal level she couldn't understand.

She stood up and started for the bathroom. "Maybe it's time we get that shower."

Anthony slowly rose. A smile danced in his eyes as he followed her.

Thirty-three

Staring up at the cracked motel ceiling, Ginger bit down hard on her lip, unsure what to do. Pavel's latest message made it clear that he was not going to back down.

She had contemplated never calling him again, but it was obvious that a few news reports hailing her as missing weren't enough to have him saying, "Aw, shucks. Guess there's no point looking for her." Pavel was so determined to get the money she owed him, he'd no doubt seek out her next of kin to collect in the event of her death.

The guy was ruthless. He didn't leave one stone unturned. Once, during sex, he had whispered in her ear that he'd become a ruthless son of a bitch because he had to fend for himself on the streets of Moscow.

That was the kind of character she was dealing with. He had her backed into a corner, doing anything he wanted until she repaid the loan. Bo would blow a gasket if he knew all she'd done, but the way Ginger figured it, she hadn't had much choice.

Mostly, Pavel had wanted sexual favors. But sexual favors had led to her doing something else the man was passionate about—a sex film with him. Leverage, Pavel had called it. Leverage her ass. The man was a pervert, which he'd proven when he'd forced her to install a hidden camera in her own bedroom to tape her every private action.

If there was one lesson Ginger had learned in her life, it was not to trust men. Yet she had trusted Pavel when he said he would return that sex tape to her once he got his money. Now, in his latest phone message, he promised to air the tape for the media if he didn't hear from her right away.

"Son of a bitch," Ginger muttered.

"Hmm, babe?" The king-size bed squeaked as Bo rolled onto his side. He reached for her breast.

"I'm not in the mood right now," Ginger quickly told him, suppressing the urge to roll her eyes. "I'm trying to think."

"Think about what?"

"About what I should do." About how she could permanently get Pavel off her back. "I don't know—maybe I shoulda just had Sha-Shana dress up like a big whore and go to the papers and blab that she was the one Tony had tried to pick up. Surely if she talked, he'd be signing a check for me already."

"I think this is a better idea," Bo told her, stroking her nipple.

"We've got plenty of days to be together when this is done."

Bo tweaked her nipple again, still trying to arouse her. Frustrated, Ginger sat up. "I'm serious, Bo. This Pavel guy is really getting on my last nerve." *I need to get rid of him.* She faced Bo. "How much do you love me?"

"To the moon and back again, babe. You know that."

"Enough that you would do anything for me?"

Bo ran a finger along her leg. "Anything you want. You name it, it's done."

Suddenly turned on, Ginger stretched out on the bed beside Bo, reaching for his penis. "That's exactly what I wanted to hear, Boo. Exactly what I wanted to hear."

The rustling of paper woke Anthony up. Opening his eyes, he glanced to his left. Lecia sat on the bed next to him, her short hair ruffled, an imprint of the sheet streaking across her face. The bedspread covered her lap, and her arm blocked his view of her breast. Had anyone looked as sexy?

"What are you doing?" he asked her.

"Studying Ginger's phone bill. There are a few numbers she called several times. I say we try those first."

Anthony pushed up onto his elbows. "Now?"

"Why not? It's the only way we're possibly going to get a lead as to where Ginger is."

"Maybe we should make love instead."

Lecia's eyes bulged as she gaped at Anthony. "Is that all you think about? Sex?"

"When I'm around a certain sex therapist, yeah."

She flashed him a mock scowl. "We can't stay here forever."

"Why not?" Anthony wrapped an arm around Lecia's waist. "It's a much better option than running off to find Ginger. Let's face it, she probably staged her disappearance to make me look bad in the media so I'll pay her the money she wants."

Lecia peeled his fingers off of her. "Which is exactly why we need to find her."

Anthony frowned as he lay back on the bed. "Now that I think about it, I should have known something was up with Ginger. She always gave me the sweet and innocent act, and I bought it hook, line, and sinker. But I bet any money there's something shady in her past. And not just because she obviously lied to me about her parents, and about having a sister in New Orleans." Anthony waited until Lecia faced him before adding, "She told me she'd only been with two other men sexually, but I'm telling you, she made love like a porn star."

One of Lecia's eyebrows shot up. "Meaning?"

"Meaning, how innocent could she have been?"

"Oh, come on." Lecia scowled at Anthony. "You actually think that because your wife knows how to please you in bed that means she has a scandalous past?"

"Now you're taking up for Ginger?"

"I'm taking up for womankind." She shook her head. "Men. You want your girlfriends or wives to make love like porn stars, yet when they do, you complain. I don't get it."

"I didn't expect you to understand."

"Oh, I understand all right."

He snaked an arm around her waist. "Don't dismiss me as a chauvinist. You're good in bed, but you don't seem like a porn star."

"Gee. I'm flattered."

"You should be. Porn star sex is mechanical, unemotional. You're emotional. I feel a connection with you when we make love."

Lecia pouted. "But I'm only good."

"You could be great," Anthony said, his eyebrows dancing. "I need another sample to determine your true rating."

Lecia swatted his hand away and held up Ginger's bill. "Focus, Tony."

"Oh, I am." His mouth found its way to her ear. "And you're definitely great in bed," he whispered. "No doubt about that."

Lecia giggled softly as she leaned forward, away from Anthony. "There are a couple numbers on Ginger's bill that aren't L.A. numbers, so I'll try those first."

"God, you're one stubborn woman," Anthony muttered.

Lecia used her cell phone to dial the first of the two numbers. On the fourth ring, she was about to hang up. But someone finally answered. "Hello?"

It was a man's voice, and he sounded like he had some kind of accent. "Hi, um." She suppressed a giggle as Anthony's fingers tickled the small of her back. The man didn't give up. "Um, I'm a friend of Ginger Beals. I'm wondering if it's at all possible that you've heard from her in the last couple days?"

"Ah, you are friend of Ginger."

"Yes." Lecia twisted to glare at Anthony. "Have you seen or heard from her?"

"That is question I should ask you."

Lecia frowned. "I don't . . ." Perhaps there was a language barrier, although he spoke English well enough. "Does that mean you don't know where she is?"

"I call Ginger. She does not call me back."

"Oh."

"Please, will you do me favor? You find Ginger, you call me. I am very, very worried for her."

"Sure," Lecia told him. Although she would do no such thing. "Thanks for your time."

"That was weird," she told Anthony once she ended the call. "That guy seemed more interested in getting info from me about Ginger than in giving me answers. Let me call another number. And please, stop groping me."

"All right, fine." Anthony held up both hands in a sign of surrender.

Lecia called the second number she had marked. A woman answered on the second ring.

"Hi," Lecia began. "You don't know me, but I'm a friend of Ginger Beals. We were supposed to go away this weekend, but she hasn't returned any of my calls. I found your number in her files, and I'm just wondering if there's any chance you've heard from her."

"Who is this?"

Lecia paused. "I told you. I'm a friend."

"A friend who can't tell me her name? Bullshit," the woman said. "She put you up to calling me?"

"No, of course not."

Anthony looked at Lecia quizzically. She shrugged as she stared back at him. He gestured for her to pass him the phone.

"This is Anthony," he said. "Ginger's husband. Do you know where my wife is?"

The woman chuckled, the sound full of sarcasm. "Oh, so you're the one callin' me."

"Yeah, that's right. I'm trying to find my wife."

"If I was you, I wouldn't bother."

There was something familiar about the woman's voice, but Anthony couldn't figure out what. Ignoring the thought, he asked, "What's that supposed to mean?"

"Listen, buddy. I don't know you. I ain't got nothin' against you. In fact, I can make all your problems go away."

"My problems?"

"Yeah, I can help you out—for a price."

"Is that what this is about? You want some kind of ransom for my wife?"

"I don't have your wife—wish I did, 'cause I'd whoop that bitch's ass—but I got something better. Info. The info you need to change the game in your favor. For a hundred grand, I think that's a bargain."

"You want a hundred grand!"

"Believe me, you'll thank me."

"Thank you for what? You've been talking in riddles."

"Sugar, you'll have to trust me. I'll tell you where to wire the money—"

"Whoa, wait a second. Trust you? My mama didn't raise me to be no fool. I'm not gonna wire you a penny."

The woman paused, and Anthony wondered if she had hung up. But moments later she said, "No, no. 'Course not. I'll give you a bite. Something to make you see you can trust me. But you'll have to head to Kansas City."

"Missouri?"

"Nope, the Kansas side. That's where Ginger grew up."

Was this woman for real, or was this more bullshit orchestrated by Ginger? "Are you telling me the truth?"

"Trust me—once you head to Kansas, you'll be calling me back. And when you do, I'll give you the key to solving your current marital problems—as long as you give me the cash."

Anthony had come this far. He had nothing to lose. "Where in Kansas City am I going?"

The woman gave him an address. Then she said, "By the way, my name's Sha-Shana. I'll be waiting for your call."

Sha-Shana had a smugness to her voice, the kind that said she wasn't bluffing. For that reason, excitement was building inside Anthony as he disconnected the call.

"What's going on?" Lecia asked.

"Get dressed," he told her. "We're heading to Kansas City."

Thirty-four

En route to the airport, Lecia decided to check her cell messages. The automated voice told her that she had nineteen of them.

"Holy cow," she said.

"What's the matter?" Anthony asked her.

"I've got nineteen messages. I never have that many. I hope everything is okay."

A little anxious, Lecia listened to message after message, and soon realized that there wasn't a family emergency. Dr. Merkowitz had called a few times, but most of the messages were from her sister. Clearly, Tyanna was desperate to reach her. There were also two calls from her father, and he sounded none too pleased.

"I'd better call my sister," Lecia told Anthony as they neared the airport.

Anthony nodded, and Lecia punched in the number to her sister's cell.

Tyanna answered before the first ring ended. "Lecia?" she said.

"Yeah, sis. It's me."

"Thank God! Lecia, what is going on? I've been trying to reach you forever. And Dr. Merkowitz called here for you, wondering where you are. It's not like you to be a no-show for work."

"I know. I'm going to give her a call."

"I've been worried out of my mind. Talk to me."

"Didn't you get my message?"

"Yeah, Sheldon told me you called, but you didn't give him any details. Where are you?"

"Out of town."

"Where?" Tyanna pressed.

"I'm . . . on my way to Kansas."

"Kansas! What'd you do, change your name to Dorothy? Have you forgotten about Moaner?"

"I'm sorry. You'll just have to keep feeding her, okay? I'll probably be back . . . oh, by Monday."

"Monday!" Tyanna shrieked. "Lecia, this is so unlike you. Who are you with?"

Lecia paused, then mumbled, "You don't want to know."

"Oh, Lecia. It's true, isn't it? I was praying it wasn't, but I guess that picture of you plastered on the front page of the *Daily Blab* isn't a fake. And that is no doubt why Dr. Merkowitz called here—"

Lecia's stomach sank. "What picture?"

"The picture of you draped all over Anthony Beals in the French Quarter. I kept telling myself that it couldn't be you, that it was just someone who looks a helluva lot like you."

Shit! How had this happened? A lightbulb went off. The guy with the camera who'd taken their picture—then taken off.

"Lecia, are you really with Anthony Beals?"

Lecia blew out a sigh and glanced at Anthony. He was eyeing her warily.

"Yes."

"Now I know you've lost your mind."

"It's a complicated situation."

"That man's wife is missing, the police want to talk to him, and you're out of town with him?" Tyanna exclaimed. Lecia pulled the phone away from her ear as her sister continued. "I know I told you that you have to live a little, but this is just plain scary. People are speculating the guy's wife is dead!"

When Tyanna stopped talking, Lecia brought the phone back to her ear. "She's not dead," she told her sister confidently. "And if she is, Anthony didn't do it."

"The way the media is painting the picture, it looks like he ran."

"Damn."

"What?" Anthony asked.

"My sister said they're saying you ran."

"Is there a warrant out for my arrest?"

"Is there a warrant out for his arrest?" Lecia asked.

"Not so far. At least not that I've heard."

"But Sheldon can check on that, right?" What good was a police officer brother-in-law if he couldn't do a bit of digging?

"Lecia, do you hear yourself? Whether or not the police are after him is not the issue. I admit I was initially in the guy's corner because there was an obvious spark between you two. But murder—that's a different matter. If he's as innocent as you say, why'd he take off?"

"He didn't take off. He's trying to find his wife."

"You remember O.J., don't you?"

"Don't even compare this to O.J. Come on, sis. You know the kind of person I am. You know you can trust my judgment. I'll tell you all the details when I get back. Hopefully, by then we'll have the answers we need."

Tyanna exhaled loudly. "I can see there's no changing your mind. Just please, be careful."

"I will. I am. Please take care of Moaner for me."

"All right," Tyanna grudgingly agreed.

"I'll call the office next, but if anyone else by any chance tries to reach me, tell them I'm violently ill."

"You know you need to call me over the weekend. You can't leave me worrying."

"Okay. But I've got to go now."

"Love you."

"I love you, too." Ending the call, Lecia dropped her head back against the headrest and moaned.

"What is it?" Anthony asked, his tone saying he knew something was wrong.

"I don't understand how they did it. I mean, we're all the way in New Orleans—"

"What?"

"The *Daily Blab.* According to my sister, we're on the front page."

"Son of a bitch! What are those fools doing, following us?"

"I guess . . . Yes, they must be." How else could this have happened?

"Anyhow my wife has been hurt or killed, there's no way I'll get a fair trial."

"It almost sounds like . . . like someone's out to get you."

"It damn well does sound like that."

Anthony veered suddenly, pulling the car into a convenience store lot and stopping. She looked at him questioningly.

"Do me a favor, Doc. Would you go in and pick up a copy of the *Daily Blab*? Better yet, pick up all the copies."

"All right."

A minute later Lecia hurried back with an armful of newspapers. She plopped them onto the seat, shaking her head as she did.

Anthony snatched up a copy—and his stomach bottomed out. There he was, his face unmistakable beneath his hat, his arm draped around Lecia's waist, her head cradled against his chest. The headline screamed:

FOUL PLAY?
WILL STAR QUARTERBACK BE BENCHED FOR LIFE
FOR THE MURDER OF HIS WIFE?

"Holy shit," he muttered, although what he really wanted to do was punch a hole through the windshield. He reread the headline, growing angrier. "How the hell can these assholes write something like this? I'm gonna sue them. This kind of headline is totally inflammatory. It's libel. For God's sake, Ginger isn't even dead."

Lecia, next to him, with the papers between them, was reading the story. "On page two it *does* say that Ginger isn't confirmed dead—for all the good it does. It also says you're 'gallivanting' with me in the Big Easy." She looked up and groaned in frustration. "If you want to head back home, I'll understand."

"I can't. Not until I find Ginger."

"And what if she's not in Kansas?"

"Then we'll head back to L.A. I can't search every part of the country for her. But at least I'll have given it my best shot."

Lecia reached for his hand and squeezed it. "No one in their right mind can think you did anything to your wife. And if they do, I know the truth, and I'll testify to that. To the fact that you found your home in shambles, how you went above and beyond the call of duty to find Ginger. We'll get through this, Tony. Well . . . you will."

As Anthony stared down at their linked hands, he felt some of his ire ebb away. Lecia never ceased to make him feel better.

She pulled her hand away. "Better dump these papers."

Anthony watched as she got out of the car, went to the garbage bin outside the store, and threw the papers away.

He had the weird feeling that he didn't want this trip to end. He wasn't yet ready to part ways with Dr. Love.

Their flight landed in Kansas City before sundown. As they had in New Orleans, Lecia rented the car while Anthony waited outside. If anyone had recognized them while they'd traveled, they had kept their distance so far. Recognizing them now, after the story, most people would probably have been afraid of him, he thought ruefully.

Lecia pulled the Explorer up to the curb where Anthony waited. She got out and let Anthony slip in behind the wheel. Getting into the passenger seat beside him, she opened the map. "Where to?"

"Let me take a look." He took it from her. "This isn't a very detailed map. I'll stop at a convenience store and ask someone for better directions."

"I'd better be the one to do that. Considering."

"Right. I'm practically a fugitive."

As Anthony drove off, Lecia stared at his profile. She wasn't sure what was running through his mind. "How're you holding up?"

"Kind of anxious. Wondering what I'm gonna say to Ginger if I find her at this address."

Lecia nodded as she settled back in her seat. What could

she say? This situation had to be horrible for him. She remembered how devastated she'd been when she learned the truth about Allen, and she hadn't been implicated in any crime. There was a lot more at stake for Anthony than simply a failed marriage.

They drove for a distance through the streets of Kansas City, until the landscape changed from industrial to low-income housing. Anthony eventually pulled up in front of a one-story white house with a dilapidated porch.

Is this where Ginger grew up? he wondered. Despite his anger over Ginger's betrayal, he couldn't help feeling a stab of sadness for his wife. If this was where she had been raised, it didn't take a rocket scientist to figure out why she'd headed to Los Angeles with bright lights in her eyes.

Anthony turned to Lecia. "I won't be long."

"Whoa, wait a minute. I'm coming with you."

"Maybe it's best—"

"No," Lecia protested. "No, I won't sit in the car."

"If Ginger's in there—"

"That's the whole reason you wanted me along, remember? To talk to Ginger. To—To facilitate conversation between the two of you. So I don't see why—why you'd want me to wait in the car. What good am I going to be in the car?"

"All right," Anthony said, noticing that she wouldn't quite meet his eyes. "We'll both go."

They both got out of the Explorer and walked up the cracked walkway to the small house. At the door, Anthony took a deep breath and glanced down at Lecia. She nodded as she met his eyes.

He knocked, then waited. Several seconds elapsed with no response. But Anthony could hear the sound of a television blaring inside and knew someone was home.

He pounded on the door this time. Then drew up short when it flew open moments later.

A short, dark-skinned woman with curlers in her hair eyed both of them suspiciously. "Yeah?" she all but barked.

"Uh, hi," Anthony said. "I apologize for disturbing you, but I'm wondering . . . wondering if someone I know is staying with you."

"Ain't nobody staying here with me 'cept my son."

She could be lying, he thought. Ginger would tell her to, of course. "Tell Ginger I just want to talk to her. Make sure she's okay."

"I don't know no Ginger."

This couldn't be a dead end. It just couldn't be. "Maybe you know her by another name," Anthony said, thinking out loud. He dug into his back pocket and took out his wallet. "Let me show you a picture."

Recognition flashed in the woman's eyes as she regarded the photograph. Then she placed a hand on her large bosom as she started to laugh.

"What is it?" Anthony demanded. "What's so funny?"

"*Ginger?* That what she callin' herself these days?"

Anthony's heart slammed against his rib cage. "So you *do* know her."

"Oh, I know her all right. But I sure as hell didn't name her anythin' as stupid as Ginger."

"This . . ." Anthony swallowed as he realized that Ginger had indeed grown up there. "This is your daughter?"

"Much as I wish I could disown her the way she did me, yeah, that my daughter."

Thank God. "Is she here?"

"Nope."

"Hey, it's Anthony Beals!" a young boy shouted. He squeezed past the woman, into the doorway.

"Tyrone." She wagged a finger at him. "I told you to clean your room."

"But, Mama, this is Anthony Beals! Man, I watched every game you played."

Anthony smiled. "*Every* game? You don't look old enough."

"I'm nine," he said proudly. "And believe me, I'm yo' biggest fan."

"Tyrone," the woman said impatiently.

"Can I get your autograph?"

"Tyrone!"

"Ma'am, it's okay," Anthony said to the woman. To the boy, he said, "Sure, Tyrone. I'd be happy to give you an autograph."

"Oh my God," Tyrone said. "I gotta get paper!"

The woman rolled her eyes as her son ran off. "That child. At least he doin' better in school than Takesha ever did."

"Takesha?"

"Ginger. Whatever you call her."

The kid came back with a football and a marker. He passed both to Anthony, then watched with mounting excitement as Anthony autographed the ball.

"Thanks so much, Mr. Beals."

"No problem."

"My friends are gonna be *so* excited when I tell 'em you came to my door."

"You go on and clean yo' room now." Tyrone's mother gave him a light shove, but Tyrone hovered behind her, his eyes dancing.

"So," Anthony began, getting back to the situation at hand. "Ginger—I mean Takesha—isn't here?"

"I ain't seen or heard from that chile in at least a year."

Shit. They'd come all this way for nothing. He knew it would be useless, but still he asked, "You have no clue how to reach her?"

"Nuh-uh. Sorry."

Behind her, Tyrone said, "You lookin' for my sister?"

"What you think?" his mother asked. "He just showed up here so he could sign yo' football?"

Clearly, these people didn't know that he was Ginger's husband. And why should they? Ginger had told him that her mother had died years ago, and that was clearly a lie.

"Your sister's an old friend," Anthony said to Tyrone. "I was hoping to get in touch with her again."

"Oh," the kid said nonchalantly. "Then you might wanna try Bo."

"Bo?"

"Yeah, Bo. You don't know Bo?"

Anthony shook his head. "Naw, I don't know Bo. But your sister has a lot of friends. I don't know them all."

"Bo ain't a friend."

"He's not?"

"Nuh-uh. Bo Baxter's her husband."

Thirty-five

Several beats passed as Anthony's brain struggled to make sense of what he'd just heard. "What did you just say?"

"Tyrone, how many times I have to tell you you talk too much? You need to stay out of grown people's business."

Anthony held up a hand and the woman quieted. "Wait," he said to Tyrone. "Are you telling me that Ginger's married?"

"She was," Tyrone answered, as if he hadn't just been scolded.

"Tyrone, let me handle this," his mother told him. Then she faced Anthony and Lecia. "Takesha was married till about eight months ago, when she got a divorce."

"Divorce?" Anthony repeated, dumbfounded.

"Uh-huh. Though I got no clue why. Not that I know why Takesha do anything. She and Bo been together since grade school. Next thing I know, he's on my doorstep, crying like a baby 'cause she left him."

Anthony thought he couldn't be hearing right. "Takesha was married?"

"Uh-huh."

Anthony did his best to rein in his anger. "Where does this Bo guy live? He, um, might know where Takesha is."

"A few blocks over," Tyrone said. "Though no one ain't seen him around in at least a few weeks."

"He a big guy?" Anthony asked. "Bald?"

"Yeah," Tyrone answered. "You know him?"

"I think I met him once," Anthony lied. "Look, can you tell me how to get to his place? If he's heard from Ginger, I really need to talk to him."

Ginger's mother frowned as she stared at Anthony. "You just expect me to tell you where he live?"

Anthony opened his wallet and withdrew two hundred dollars. "I'll make it worth your while."

The woman looked at the money, then back at him. "You wouldn't be looking to hurt Takesha, now?"

"Oh, no." Lecia finally spoke. "He just needs to find her."

The woman's gaze fell on Anthony's wallet and the other bills inside. "I know this ain't all you got."

Anthony took out another three hundred. "Here. Five hundred. But tell me where I can find Bo."

Grinning, the woman took the money, stuffed it into her bra, then gave Anthony an address and directions how to get there.

The trip to Bo's place had been a waste of time. He wasn't there, and neither was anyone else. However, Anthony had been able to peer through a window and see a large wedding picture of Bo and his wife. If he'd had any doubts about whether Ginger had been married before marrying him, he no longer did.

"What now?" Lecia asked when Anthony got behind the wheel.

He gritted his teeth for several seconds before answering.

"Why would she do this?" he asked. "Marry me when she was married to someone else?"

"She was divorced," Lecia clarified.

"Barely," Anthony pointed out. "She only got divorced eight months ago. She turned right around and married me a few months later."

Lecia shrugged. "Maybe her marriage to this Bo guy was a mistake."

"A mistake? They were lifelong sweethearts. That's no mistake."

"Maybe . . . maybe he was abusing her, and she had to leave him?"

"Then why didn't she tell me about it? And why the hell doesn't her family know I'm her husband?"

"I don't know." Lecia could tell Anthony was hurting, and she wished she could make things better for him. "Maybe Ginger simply wanted to put the past behind her?"

"That's bullshit."

"I'm grasping at straws here, Tony, same as you."

Anthony revved the engine harder than was necessary. "I know what you're going to say, but don't bother."

"Huh? I wasn't going to say anything."

"Yes you were. You were going to say that I barely knew the woman, yet I married her. That I must have been out of my mind."

"I wasn't going to say that."

"You were thinking it." He abruptly accelerated, throwing Lecia backward in the seat.

"Anthony, slow down."

"My parents knew each other forever. But still, their marriage failed. I wanted to do everything exactly the opposite to the way my father did it. You have no idea what it's like to live with the kind of absurdity he subjected us to. The instability. To see your mother cry every night because of how much she's hurting."

"I . . . Tony, if you want to talk, pull over."

"Well, it's not fun." He made a sharp right turn. "I swore I'd never be like him. That I'd get married once and stay married."

He had already told her this. "I'm not judging you for marrying Ginger."

"I met her at a restaurant, did I tell you that?" He laughed mirthlessly. "She served me dinner, along with a plate of crap about her life."

"How long did you know her before—"

"Ah, there we go! I knew you'd have to put your two cents in."

"Tony, listen. Did you meet Ginger before she divorced Bo?"

That got Anthony's attention. Thankfully, he finally slowed down. "I don't know. I guess I met her about a year ago."

"Before she divorced Bo."

"I guess so."

"Was she separated?"

"I didn't even know she was married, remember?"

"Right." Lecia shrugged. "Well, maybe she was. I mean, I'm sure she was. She was separated and didn't want to tell you about the husband because you might not have wanted to date her. And once things got hot and heavy—"

"They didn't get hot and heavy."

"What?"

"Not until after we got married."

"You weren't intimate before you got married?"

"That was one of the things I liked about her. She said she didn't want to have sex until we got married because she thought sex clouded the issue. She also didn't believe in long engagements."

"But you said she screwed like—that she seemed very experienced in bed."

"I know, I was stupid. What can I say? I was living in la la land."

"Tony, stop the car."

He glanced at her. "What? Oh, you want to abandon me, too?"

"Just stop the car."

"Fine." Anthony's voice said he was resigned to her betrayal. "Whatever you want."

He slowed down, then turned into a gas station. "The least I could do is drop you at the airport."

"Shut up," Lecia said. Then she grabbed him by the T-shirt, drew him close, and kissed him.

Lecia thought she was dreaming when she heard, "I never slept with her without a condom."

She didn't answer, and Anthony asked, "Are you awake?"

"What did you say?" Lecia sat up, rubbing sleep from eyes, remembering that she was in a motel.

"I said, I never slept with her without a condom."

"Who?"

"Who else? My wife."

Lecia glanced at the clock. It was minutes to eleven P.M. She had drifted off after making love with Anthony. "I'm not exactly sure what you're trying to tell me."

"We were tested for every disease before we got married," Anthony went on. "The condoms were her idea, not mine. Now that I think about it, it seems a bit strange."

"I thought you said she didn't want children."

"She was on the pill."

Lecia shrugged. "I don't know. You think she had a problem with intimacy?"

"I don't know what to think. That's the problem."

"So now you want to talk?"

"No."

"Good. Because I'm tired." Lecia plopped her head back.

"I called my lawyer. Left a message for him to see what he can find out about Ginger Baxter. I told him to call me back as soon as possible, no matter the hour."

"That was smart. Are you coming back to bed?" Lecia snuggled against her pillow. Seconds later she heard the television come on. As Anthony went through channel after channel, Lecia turned onto her side. Every guy she'd ever known hadn't been able to stop and focus on one channel for longer than a few seconds.

"Whoa," Anthony said.

Lecia had drifted off again, but Anthony's voice woke her. And his tone worried her. "What is it?"

Anthony held up a hand to shush her as he turned up the volume on the television.

". . . Ginger Beals. The tape surfaced earlier today, and due to its graphic nature, we can only show you portions of it."

Ginger's face filled the screen. Her head hanging backward over a bed, she was moaning loudly. Then a white man's face entered the frame, and he and Ginger began to kiss. Their rapturous sounds of lovemaking grew louder until the picture snapped off the screen.

"Ginger hasn't been seen in four days, and now her estranged husband is also nowhere to be found. We'll keep you up to date on this very bizarre case."

"Aw, hell no." Anthony slowly rose, shaking his head in disbelief. "Tell me I didn't just see that."

Lecia was too stunned to speak.

"Who the fuck did I marry?"

"Tony . . ."

"Some—Some whore?"

"Tony."

Anthony whirled around and stared at the television. The remote still in his hand, he pressed it with the conviction of a man squeezing off round after round.

"Tony, don't."

He didn't stop channel surfing, and Lecia crawled out of bed and took the remote from his fingers. She turned the television off.

Anthony drew in an angry breath, then began to pace.

"Tony, that was the guy I saw Ginger with that day. I can't be a hundred percent sure, but the hair color's the same, the sharp nose. . . ."

Anthony stared at her as if she had grown another head. "What?"

"The guy at the restaurant. She was there with the bald guy, who probably was Bo, as well as a white guy."

"That was him?"

"I think so. The only reason I paid attention to him is because he was sitting at this table alone, reading a book, while everyone else was yakking away."

"You just said he was there with Ginger and . . . Bo."

"He was alone when I got there. And he made a point of smiling at me. I thought he recognized me, but maybe he's just got a thing for black women?"

Anthony frowned, then started to pace again. "So Ginger, Bo, and this white guy—they all know each other?"

"As far as I could tell."

Anthony was silent as he digested this information. "This is important, don't you think? I mean, it's not a coincidence that you saw them all together and it turns out that Ginger's been sexually involved with them both. Do you think . . . ?"

"Think what?"

"Think that one of them hurt her, maybe the white guy, and he's throwing suspicion to me?"

"That could be it. Or not. Assuming Bo is still in love with Ginger, why go on the news and tell everyone that Ginger had been heading to meet you, and not this other guy? That's the lie that doesn't make sense."

"I have to stop thinking about it. It's gonna drive me nuts. All I know is, my wife is not just a liar, she's a whore, and thank God I wore condoms with her every damn time."

"I think we should—" Lecia stopped as Anthony stormed across the room to the chair where they'd both dumped their clothes. "What are you doing?"

"I've gotta get out of here." He slipped into his jeans.

"You—you're leaving?" Lecia asked, panic rising within her.

"You heard me."

She made her way toward him. "Tony, don't walk away from me. Don't shut me out."

"Why?" Rage clouded his face as he closed the snap on his jeans. "Because I need to *talk* about this? Talking hasn't done a damn thing for me. Talking isn't going to make this go away. I didn't know my own wife. Hell, she's not my wife. She's every man's whore. Didn't I tell you she screwed like a porn star?" Anthony chuckled, a low, hollow sound. "God, I've been such a moron!"

Lecia wanted to reach out and soothe him, but she didn't.

"Do you know how embarrassing this is?" he went on after a moment. "National news? I won't be able to show my face when I get back to L.A." He snatched up his T-shirt. "This is a nightmare."

"Leaving me isn't going to change anything."

"You can't help me now."

"Maybe not, but I can listen."

"What do you want me to say? That I can't wait to find Ginger so I can wrap my hands around her neck?"

"If that's what you need to say."

"I married Ginger—*Takesha*—because I wanted someone who was safe, someone who shared my values. And now I learn that I married a whore. How is talking gonna make any of that better?"

Lecia finally touched him. It was the only thing she knew to do. Telling him she understood would be a lie. She didn't. Allen's betrayal had been devastating, but it had been nothing like this.

"What are you doing?" he asked.

"Touching you." She slipped her arms around his waist. "Holding you."

He pulled away from her. "Don't."

Lecia wrapped her arms around her torso, feeling suddenly cold. "Your wife turns her back on you, then railroads you in the media, yet you barely backed down from trying to save your marriage. I, on the other hand, stick by you through all this crap over the past few days, and you don't even give me the same respect you give Ginger, or Takesha, or whatever her name is?"

"This isn't about you."

"Of course it's not. I'm just the woman you're screwing at the moment. A dime a dozen, right?"

Anthony's eyes narrowed. "What the hell does that mean?"

"Do I even matter one iota to you?" Lecia asked between labored breaths.

"Since when is that the issue?"

"Since now." Suddenly, it mattered. It mattered that she not simply be a roll in the hay for star athlete Anthony Beals. "Answer the damn question."

"Of course you're not a dime a dozen. And I'm not just *screwing* you."

"Then what are we doing?"

Lecia stared at Anthony for what seemed an eternity before he answered the question. Her heart practically stopped; it mattered that much what he would say.

"We're . . . we're . . . I dunno. Enjoying each other."

Disappointment swelled in her chest. Anthony's words, though true, hurt her. But why should they? In reality, they hardly knew each other. So what if they'd talked more in a few days than she and Allen had ever talked in over five years? She was being immature, getting caught up in emotions simply because she and Anthony had been doing what men and women had been doing together since the beginning of time.

Still, she couldn't stand the sight of him right now. She turned away. "I'm sorry. I'm not exactly sure what's come over me, except I'm tired, and as frustrated by all of this as you are."

Lecia climbed under the covers.

"Look, I don't mean to bring you down—"

"Are we heading back to L.A. in the morning?"

The mattress sank as Anthony sat on the bed beside her. "I've done what I can to find Ginger. So yeah, we may as well head home. I can fly to El Paso and drive back, but I figure you'll just catch a flight back to Los Angeles. To make it easier on you."

"Trying to get rid of me," Lecia mumbled.

"What?" Anthony asked.

She closed her eyes tightly as her insides twisted painfully. What did it matter what she said to him now? It wouldn't change the reality that she meant nothing to him.

"Nothing," she lied. "It was nothing."

Thirty-six

With wide-eyed lust, Pavel stared at the apple, peach, and orange—all of which rested on the car seat beside him. His fingers actually jittered, he wanted to reach out and grab the orange so badly.

He squeezed his eyes shut as he pressed the book in his hand against his chest. "South Beach Diet says no fruit for two weeks. No fruit for two weeks," he repeated, gaining strength with the words. Still holding *The South Beach Diet* in one hand, he grabbed the apple and the peach and tossed them onto the backseat.

He was fingering the orange when his cell phone rang. Dropping the fruit, he quickly dug his phone out of his jacket pocket and read the number on the screen.

A smile spread across his face. *Ginger.* Finally, she was calling. So his little plan had worked, and now she was ready to talk.

He answered the phone, saying, "This is Pavel."

"You son of a bitch."

"Ah, Ginger. How nice to hear your voice."

"Why'd you do it? I told you I'd get you your damn money."

"You have been saying this for very long time. I warned you, but you would not listen."

"You can forget about getting a dime of that money," Ginger told him. "You've ruined my reputation. My husband will never settle with me now."

Pavel did not like this. "Ginger, I think you do not understand. How you get money is not my problem. But I not let you play games with me no more. This is why I gave tape to media. Make no mistake—next time, I won't be so nice."

"Fuck you, Pavel."

"The price is now one point seven million."

"Oh, God. Pavel—you can't."

"I can and I did. One point seven million. Next week, two point five million. Now, when can we meet?"

Pavel waited for an answer, until he realized the line was dead. Oh well, he thought, stuffing the phone back in his pocket.

He didn't want to hurt her, but it seemed he would have to. He would kill her, and kill Bo, then dump both of their bodies in the Pacific.

Ginger paced the carpet in the small, moldy motel room. She didn't dare take her shoes off. God only knew what kind of lowlifes had been in this place before her.

"He's not gonna kill you," Bo said.

"He's a loan shark, Bo. One who's fed up with me. So yeah, I think he's gonna kill me."

"You've got how much cash—twenty-five grand? I say we hightail it to Mexico."

"That's not enough to live on indefinitely. Besides, Pavel will find me. I guarantee it."

If only she had access to Anthony's stocks. She needed to

get her hands on enough money to pay Pavel. In their joint account there'd been a measly forty-two thousand, and she hadn't wanted to take it all. Now, since she was supposed to be dead, she couldn't very well access any of that.

She rued the day she had met Freddie Monahue and was taken in by his dot-com scam. He should be the one taking a bullet, not her.

Ginger stopped wearing a hole in the carpet to plant herself on Bo's lap. The thoughts running through her mind scared her, but life wasn't always a bed of roses. Sometimes, one had to do awful things in order to protect oneself.

"Boo." She stroked his chin. "Remember when you said you'd do anything for me?"

"Uh-huh."

"Did you mean that?"

He met her eyes. "You still wanna remarry me?"

Ginger frowned as she stared at him. "Why are you asking that? Of course I do. And we will. Just as soon as this is all over."

"I just figured . . . We haven't talked about us getting married again. And I kind of wanted to tell you—"

"I know. You don't want to stay in L.A. You want to start a new life somewhere else."

"Actually—"

Ginger framed Bo's face with both hands. "Boo, you gotta listen to me. We can talk about all that other stuff later. Right now I have to talk to you about something very important. I need to know that we're on the same page here. That you really meant it when you said you'd do anything for me."

Bo nodded. "You're my girl. Always will be. You know I'd do anything for you."

"That's exactly what I wanted to hear." She smiled as she

lowered her head and nibbled on his ear, one of his very sensitive spots. Then she whispered, "I need you to be a man of your word." She licked the spot beneath the lobe. "I need you to kill Pavel."

Lecia was overwhelmed by a sense of panic. She opened her eyes, Anthony's name on her lips.

He wasn't beside her. She held her breath and listened, but didn't hear sounds of him running the sink or flushing the toilet.

He wasn't in the room.

Had he left her? Oh God, he must have. She'd sensed his despair last night. He had withdrawn, and they hadn't even cuddled, much less made love.

And now here she was, alone.

Biting back the sting of rejection, Lecia scrambled from the bed. Their talk last night about traveling home separately must have prompted him to leave her here, she decided. And yes, there was a lot to be said for her taking a flight directly back to L.A. She had work to catch up on, Moaner to take care of. And she wasn't exactly stranded, since she could catch the shuttle to the airport. But still, for him to leave without saying good-bye . . .

She was shimmying into her panties when the hotel door opened. She stopped short as a wave of relief washed over her.

Anthony's eyes widened in appreciation. "Now that's the kind of welcome a guy can get used to."

Lecia reached for her bra. "Where were you?"

"I went in search of some food. I thought you might be hungry."

"Oh." She suddenly felt foolish.

Anthony moved toward her. "What's the matter?"

She paused, then lied. "Nothing."

"Don't tell me nothing. I saw the look of fear on your face. Did you think I'd taken off? C'mon, Doc. You've gotta know I wouldn't leave you here."

"It's just . . ." Lecia sank onto the bed. "Allen used to do that. Disappear on me. Even after we'd made love. I'd drift asleep, and he'd get up and leave me the moment I was konked out. It got to the point where I panicked when I woke up, fearing he wouldn't be there."

"Where was he?"

"Sometimes he was gone. Out of the house. He'd tell me that the hospital called him in, and I always believed him."

"But he was lying?"

"He had to be lying at least part of the time. I think I knew that. That's why I felt such panic. Other times, he was home but in a different room. Like in the den, reading a book. Or sleeping. It always made me feel so . . . I don't know. Cheap? The one thing I wanted was to lie with my husband until the morning after we made love. Such a small thing, but it would have meant so much. Oh, God. Why am I even going on about that? It hardly matters now." She blew out a flustered breath. "What'd you pick up?"

"Some muffins from the continental breakfast downstairs. But we can get a real breakfast on the road, or at the airport."

"I don't think I can eat much. I feel a bit anxious."

"Worried about heading back to L.A.?"

"Kind of. Worried about how all this will play out."

"I've checked on flights. You have a couple choices, starting around noon—"

"I want to travel back with you."

Anthony's eyebrows rose as he looked at her. "We talked about this last night."

"No—you suggested I fly directly back to L.A. I didn't agree or disagree."

"You want to be stuck on the road with me?"

A week ago she would have thought the idea insane. But now she couldn't imagine it any other way. "Yes. I've come this far with you, I may as well."

"As long as you're okay with that."

"Hey, we have Agatha to listen to on the drive back."

"True," Anthony said, smiling softly.

"But really, this is about seeing this thing through. I promised I'd be there for you, and I meant it."

What she didn't say was the truth that was in her heart—that she didn't want to leave Anthony's side because she wasn't quite ready to get back to her life without him.

When they reached El Paso, Anthony decided to turn his cell phone on. If his lawyer, or his agent, or even the police were trying to reach him, he could explain that he was en route back to L.A. and would speak to the police as soon as he got there. He still held out hope that Ginger would surface before he returned home, if she hadn't already, but he wasn't going to bet money on it. He was preparing for the worst case scenario—that his wife had disappeared and would never be found, and that he would have to endure a long and ugly trial to prove he didn't kill her.

Now that he had realized there was nothing he could do about it, and that he couldn't simply disappear, he'd resigned himself to his fate. A fate that didn't seem quite so bad, not with Lecia by his side.

"What are you thinking?" Lecia asked. It was dark. They had crossed the border into Arizona and were driving west along I 10.

"Something my mama always used to say. Don't spend energy worrying about something you can't control. I can't control what's gonna happen when I get back to L.A., so as much as I could spend the next several hours sweating over my fate, what's the point? I have nothing to hide, so I've just got to have faith that everything will work out."

"It will work out, Tony. Remember, I'm a witness."

"One who can now be linked romantically to me. No one will believe you're impartial."

"You . . . you regret me coming with you." It was a statement, not a question.

"Like I said, I'm not gonna sweat it. What happens, happens."

"That's easy to say."

"I have learned so many disturbing things about the woman I married that I just can't get upset about what might happen next. I'm not even sure I want Ginger to turn up at this point. Lord knows, I have no clue what I'll say to her."

Lecia didn't say anything, and Anthony was glad for that. He wanted to put this whole situation out of his mind before it ate him alive.

"I know it's getting late, but I wasn't planning to stop," he told Lecia minutes later. "Not unless I get tired. We're this close to home, and I'm kind of anxious to get there."

Get there and close one chapter of his life. He wanted to say good riddance to Ginger forever.

Quiet settled over the vehicle, and Anthony slipped a cassette from the audio book into the tape deck. He listened to the story without fail, but as time passed, Lecia drifted to sleep.

It was his ringing cell phone that woke her up in the wee hours of the morning.

"The phone," she said, quickly sitting upright.

"Sorry—I should have turned it back off."

"Are you going to answer it?" Lecia asked, then yawned.

"I should. It could be Kahari, wondering what's going on." He checked his display, but no number registered. He clicked the phone on and pressed it to his ear. "Hello?" There was no answer. "Hello?" he repeated.

"Tony."

Anthony's stomach fluttered at the sound of the soft, female voice. He waited a beat, then said, "Ginger?"

"Yeah. It's me."

He swallowed—hard. Clearly, his wife wasn't dead. But while he was happy about that, he was still angry with her.

Beside him, Lecia's eyes were now wide open, and she seemed fully awake.

"Tony, you there?"

"Ginger, where are you?"

"I'm . . . I'm out of town. Heading back to L.A."

"Really? Where have you been?"

"I . . . needed some time away. Some time to think. About everything. I've been so mixed up."

"Why didn't you tell anyone you were leaving?"

"I don't know. I just . . . didn't think."

At least she was okay. He still wanted to throttle her, but at least she was okay. "Everyone thinks something bad happened to you. And they think I did it."

"I . . . I know. When I spoke with a friend of mine, she told me that it was on the news. Who would have thought, people worrying about little ol' me?"

"When you're the wife of a high profile athlete who disappears without a word, everyone's gonna speculate. Especially when you tell people that you were supposed to be meeting with me on Tuesday morning, then mysteriously disappear after that."

There was a pause, then Ginger said, "Whoever said that was mistaken."

Was she lying? Did it matter? No, not anymore. "It doesn't matter. I'm just glad this can all be straightened out."

"Yes. That's why I . . . why I wanted to talk to you."

Anthony glanced at Lecia. She was still looking at him. She mouthed the words *What's happening?*

"She's okay," he said.

"Who are you talking to?" Ginger asked.

"A friend," he replied. "Look, I'm out of town as well. I was actually hoping to find you."

"Let me get this straight. You think I'm missing, but you're already off with some bitch?"

"You're one to talk. I saw that video of you on the news, the one where you're screwing some guy's brains out."

"That was an old, old video."

At least she wasn't denying it. "You sure about that?"

"Of course I am. Unlike the picture of you and Dr. Love. That was taken what, a day ago?"

"Look, we need to talk. I should be back in L.A. soon."

"Yes, we do need to talk. Clearly, you can't give up your cheating ways. I hope you're finally ready to settle."

God, no. This couldn't be why she was calling. "Settle? Are you out of your mind?"

"Trust me, this hasn't gotten near as ugly as it can."

"Is that a threat?"

"Listen to me, Tony, and listen good. When you get back to L.A., do the right thing."

And then Ginger hung up.

"Son of a—" Anthony tossed the cell phone into the backseat.

"What?" Lecia asked, almost frantic.

"Well," he began, sarcasm dripping from his voice, "she's not dead."

"Where has she been?"

"I thought she was actually calling so we could talk. But you know what that bitch said to me? That she wants *me* to do the right thing and give her the money. I drive around half the country trying to make sure she's okay, and *this* is what she calls about? I swear, if she was here right now—"

"That's all she said?"

"Pretty much. Oh, and she saw that picture of us together. Geez, could this get any worse?"

"She can't use that against us. Given everything she's done."

"Maybe not," Anthony said, "but I was careless. If she couldn't prove infidelity before, she sure as hell can now."

"You two are separated."

"Do you think anyone's gonna care about that fact? They already think I'm some kind of jerk capable of offing my wife." Anthony shook his head. "What the hell's wrong with me? I should have waited before having sex with a friend."

It took Lecia a good couple seconds to realize that Anthony was talking about her. *She* was the friend. The *friend* he should have waited to have sex with.

Disappointment shot through her body like an injection of poison. She had given this man her body, and he was referring to her as a friend?

I'm a lover, you jerk! she wanted to scream, but knew it would be pointless. Once again it was clear that *she* had read more into their situation than was there. To Anthony, she had been a convenient warm body, a distraction from the reality of his life. Forget that she stood by him while his own wife had abandoned him. She had simply been a way for him to relieve tension. While to her . . .

A lump formed in Lecia's throat. Lord help her, but she suddenly felt absurdly emotional. Then again, maybe it wasn't absurd to feel this way. After all, how many men helped you get your mojo back?

He had done that and more. So much more.

Call her crazy, but she was falling for him. He'd thrown her life into a tailspin, yet she was loving every moment of it. The reality of having to go back home, back to life as she'd known it, made her want to scream. She wanted a different life—one that included Anthony.

But what did he want?

She should ask him, she thought. Or at the very least, tell him how she felt. As a therapist, she believed in honesty and forthrightness. Yet the thought of telling Anthony what was in her heart scared her to death.

What if he rejected her?

Drawing in a deep breath, she stared at his profile. Would this man with whom she had spent an incredible few days head back to L.A. and forget all about her?

Tell him, a voice urged.

She opened her mouth. Tried to say the words. But she couldn't. God help her, she couldn't.

With a soft sigh, she laid her head back and closed her eyes. And when Anthony quietly called out her name, she didn't answer, pretending to be asleep.

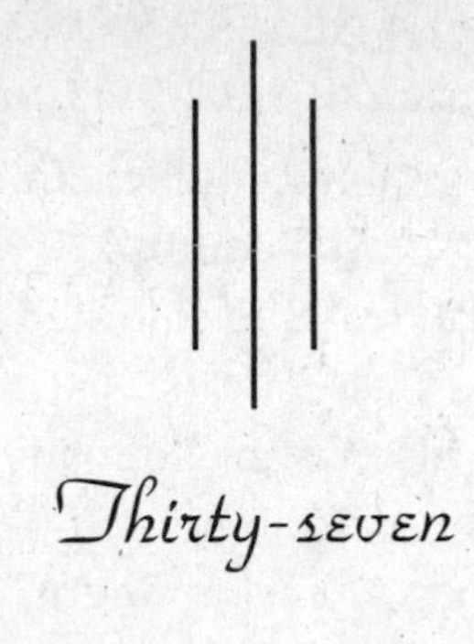

Thirty-seven

When Pavel saw the headlights piercing the darkness, he knew it was Ginger. He quickly ate the last of his Mars bar and downed the glob of chocolate with water. The anticipation of this meeting was what had him breaking his diet, but once he did what he had to do, he knew his stress level would return to normal.

Ginger had called him in the middle of the night, urgently begging him to meet with her. It was why he was here now, on this deserted parking lot near the pier. Perhaps because she was in hiding she wanted to give him his money in darkness and then disappear. He didn't care. As long as the bitch gave him his money.

And if she didn't . . .

The Mercedes pulled up alongside his rented Corvette, and Pavel lowered his hand from the glove compartment. He had been about to take out his gun, but would leave it for now. If she did have his money, he didn't want to scare her.

Pavel got out of his car a moment before Ginger and Bo got out of theirs. He smiled widely at both of them, playing nice.

"Ginger, Ginger." He reached for her and kissed each of her cheeks. "Like usual, you are beautiful."

"Why thank you, Pavel." She sounded happy. "C'mon, Bo. Say hi to Pavel."

Like a dog obeying his master, Bo made his way around the car from the driver's side. "Yo," Bo said.

What a pathetic man, Pavel thought. He would not deal with him, only with Ginger.

"So," Pavel began pleasantly. "You have suitcase with my cash?"

Ginger's smile was clearly forced. "Um . . ."

"Um . . . ?" Pavel echoed.

"Well, um, yes," Ginger went on. "Of course I do. I brought a check."

"A check?"

"But don't worry," she quickly said. "I spoke to my husband not more than an hour ago, and he said he's having the money wired into my account in the morning. You see, he needs me to prove to everyone that I'm not dead, and I won't cooperate unless he wires—"

Pavel held up a hand, silencing her. "A check? Do you take me for fool? And tomorrow is Sunday. No bank open Sunday."

"Then he'll wire the money on Monday. Look, Pavel, don't make this difficult. Please, just take the check. I promise—"

"No more games," Pavel told her. He whirled around then, reaching for his car door. But he collapsed against it when he felt something slam into his back. Once, then twice.

"C'mon, Bo. He's down," Ginger said urgently. "Do it. Shoot him!"

They were going to kill *him*. It was supposed to be the other way around.

"I . . . I can't," Bo said. "You already stabbed him. Let him bleed to death."

Pavel managed to turn around. The moonlight illuminated a small knife in Ginger's hand. Bo held a gun.

"*Shoot him!*" Ginger cried.

Bo pointed the gun toward him, but his hands shook. Pavel knew the man didn't have the guts to pull the trigger.

This was his only chance to escape. He pushed the pain from his mind and opened his car door. He was reaching for his glove compartment when he felt another stab, this time in his butt. The knife tore into him, slicing down his leg.

"Please, no!" he cried. He could not die like this. "Forget money!"

"Oh for God's sake," Ginger said, ignoring him. "Give me the damn gun."

And Pavel knew it was too late.

The next second, everything went black.

Lecia mulled over her cowardice the rest of the night as she and Anthony drove, and realized that no one ever got anywhere being afraid. So when Anthony pulled up in front of her house early that morning, she told herself to be bold.

"Why don't you come in?" she suggested.

Anthony looked at her. His eyes were red from lack of sleep. "Come in?"

"Yeah. Why bother driving to Beverly Hills? I know it's not far, but you've been driving all night. And you know what they say. Most people fall asleep at the wheel when they're just minutes from home. Besides, there's still that restraining order, right? The last thing you want to do is get arrested for going into your own house. You may as well get some sleep here, then figure out what to do next when you wake up."

Lecia took a much-needed breath after her spiel, then held it, waiting for Anthony to answer. Finally, he nodded. "Yeah, sure. That makes sense."

Her lips twitched with the urge to smile. Biting her inner cheek to suppress it, she opened her car door and got out. Anthony followed suit. She was about to search his Navigator for her belongings, but decided she was far too tired and would no doubt miss something. It was a much better idea to do it when her brain wasn't in a fog.

"I'll get my stuff later," she told Anthony. "If that's not a problem."

"No problem at all."

Was it her imagination, or did he seem . . . distant? No, maybe not distant, but at least preoccupied. But he had good reason. Besides being exhausted, he had a ton of crap on his plate. She certainly didn't need to take his silence personally.

He followed her as she made her way up the walkway. "My bungalow's pretty spacious," she said as she walked. "But nothing compared to your place."

"Doc, please. As if I care about that."

"Well . . ." *Well what?* She was rambling, and would be far better off if she stuffed a sock in her mouth.

The bowl of cat food outside her door was nearly empty. Clearly, Moaner had been by during the night. She would have to refill the bowl before she went to bed.

She opened her door, stepped into the foyer, then turned to Anthony. "Now, I do have two bedrooms, but I was sort of thinking—well, hoping—that you'd sleep with me."

"Sleep, or something else?"

Arching up on her toes, she slipped her arms around his neck. "Perhaps something else."

"I thought you were tired."

"I am." She yawned, as if on cue. "But we're back home now, and you've got stuff to deal with. And . . . and who knows when we'll see each other again."

Lecia hoped he would say, "You know we'll see each other again real soon."

Instead he said, "That's a good point."

Her heart sank.

Don't think about it, Lecia promptly told herself. *Concentrate on now. Give him a reason to come back.*

With that thought, she kissed him lightly on the mouth, but in that kiss there was hope and promise.

A slow moan rumbled in Anthony's chest. It told Lecia that he wanted her. But she sensed his resistance.

She forged ahead. "I'm wet." She took his hand and placed it beneath her skirt.

As he fondled her, the rumbling in his chest grew louder. "Aw, Doc."

Lecia stepped backward. She took his hand and led him to her bedroom.

A couple hours later Anthony was too wired to sleep. His head pounded and his shoulders were tense. He felt like he was carrying a huge burden, one he needed to unload.

He sure as hell couldn't do that here.

Here, things were complicated. Complicated because of Lecia.

Rolling from his side onto his back, Anthony moved away from Lecia's sleeping body. He told himself he should have dropped her off and headed straight home. Things were different between them now. They had to be. Their road trip had been like an escape from reality, one where they'd easily gotten caught up in the intimacy of being alone together. But now they were back home. The fantasy was over, and he was wondering what the future held for them.

If they even had a future.

It wasn't that he didn't like her. Just the opposite. He liked her a lot. But he had liked Ginger when he'd met her, which only proved that he was a lousy judge of character.

Not that the good doctor was some kind of deranged idiot. But he had a helluva lot to deal with before he even contemplated the idea of seeing someone else. He had figured that fact was obvious, but maybe it wasn't. If the way Lecia had clung to him when they'd made love was any indication, she was expecting much more. More than he could give her.

Anthony glanced at her. Her mouth slightly parted, she was in a deep, comfortable sleep. He felt an ache in his gut at the thought of moving on without her, but knew he didn't have much choice.

Carefully, he eased himself off the bed so as not to wake her. He dug his phone out of the back pocket of his jeans, then made his way out of the bedroom. He wandered to the spacious living room and took a seat on the leather sectional. The place was cozy and warm, which was more than he could say for his home.

His call display showed that he had missed three calls. He dialed his number and checked his messages.

There was one from his lawyer. Keith said he had important information about Ginger and asked Anthony to get back to him regardless of the time, which Anthony was determined to do as soon as he heard the other messages. At least, that's what he planned until he heard Ginger's voice, contrite and sincere, saying, "Tony, it's me. I'm sorry about how I behaved earlier, about what I said. I know you spoke to Sha-Shana. I know you've been to Kansas. What you don't know is why everything that's happened has happened. Look, I really need to talk to you. There's so much I need to explain, so much I need to make you understand. Call me. I'm at the house."

At last, she sounded ready to talk. Anthony immediately dialed his home number. Ginger answered right away.

"Tony?" she said expectantly.

"Yeah, it's me."

"Oh, thank God."

He paused briefly. "You're finally ready to talk."

"I am." Ginger sighed wearily. "Sha-Shana told me she talked to you."

"That she did."

"Everything's gotten way out of control," she said softly. "Will you please come home so we can talk face-to-face?"

"Why—so you can set me up for God only knows what?"

"No! Tony, I swear, I had nothing to do with all the crap that's been going on. I've been afraid of . . . of someone. If you come here, I'll tell you everything. Then you'll understand."

She sounded believable. But then, she had sounded believable when she told him about a paraplegic mother. Still, she was the only one who could give him the answers he needed, and clear his name in the process.

"I'll be there in half an hour."

Anthony ended the call and flew to his feet, only to stop mid-pivot when he saw Lecia standing outside her bedroom door.

"Who was that?" she asked while knotting the tie on her terry-cloth robe.

"Huh?"

"On the phone. Who were you talking to?"

"Right. That was, um . . ." Anthony paused. Swallowed. "Ginger."

"She called?"

He nodded. "She left me a message and I called her back."

"And . . . ?"

Lecia eyed Anthony anxiously as he made his way toward her. "She's at the house," he told her. "She wants to see me."

He stepped past her into the bedroom and snatched up his jeans from the hardwood floor.

"And you're going?"

"Uh-huh."

"Right now?"

"I have to see her sooner or later."

Anthony didn't face her, and disappointment the size of a football filled Lecia's chest. "Just hours ago you said she was still trying to extort money from you."

"She says she has an explanation for all of that."

"And you believe her?" Lecia asked incredulously.

"There's only one way I can find out."

Lecia watched Anthony slip into his pants. "I should go with you."

"Absolutely not."

"This could be a trick."

"I said no."

His words were like a slap in the face. He had dragged her halfway across the country so she could speak to his estranged wife, guide their communication in a positive direction. Yet now that he knew exactly where Ginger was, he suddenly didn't want her around.

Lecia didn't trust the woman, but she knew it would be pointless to banter back and forth about why she should accompany him.

Instead she asked, "When will you come back?"

Anthony's chest rose and fell with a deep breath. "Ginger and I have a lot to discuss."

Lecia stared at him in disbelief, but he wouldn't look at her. He was walking toward the window as he slipped into his T-shirt.

"You say that like . . . like you'd consider reconciling with her."

"She's my wife."

"As if that ever mattered to her."

"Look, I at least owe it to her to hear her out."

"My God, why?" Lecia all but shrieked. "Because your father wouldn't have done that? Are you going to base everything you do on his actions?"

Anthony's silence was all the answer she needed. She turned away from him in disgust.

"I just . . . I need to talk to her." He stood with his hands at his sides, looking at her with a blank expression.

"You need to talk to someone, all right. A bloody shrink."

"Fine. You're pissed off—"

"You're damn right I'm pissed off. You say one thing, do another. You know better, but you're about to head down the wrong path again all because you think you have to live up to some ridiculous moral ideal."

Anthony's jaw flinched. Her words had wounded him. "You have no clue what you're talking about," he said.

"Then tell me I'm wrong."

He threw his hands in the air. "What do you want me to do? Just forget about everything else and play house with you?"

"It was good enough when we were on the road."

"Yeah, well, we're back now. Back to reality."

"And what reality is that?"

Anthony started for the bedroom door. "God, I hate this. I'm not gonna stay here and argue with you. I have to do what I have to do. I'll call you later."

"Go on. Run to your precious Ginger."

Anthony halted. Turned. "That's not what this is about."

Lecia dropped herself onto her bed, fighting back angry tears. A couple hours ago they'd been making love. Now, one call from the woman who'd abandoned him and he was rushing to be by her side.

"I woke up," she said softly. "You weren't in bed beside me. It was just like those days with Allen. And now you're leaving me to go see your estranged wife."

"You know I need to resolve this."

"I know you do," Lecia said, trying a different tactic. She wasn't sure why, but it mattered that Anthony stay here with her, at least for a little while longer. "I have a ton of things to do as well. I have to go on my website, explain to patients why I was a no-show for their online counseling sessions. Then I have to deal with rescheduling my Friday patients at the clinic, not to mention talk to Dr. Merkowitz and smooth things over. But we've barely returned home. Surely we can both put off all the crap we need to take care of until after I've made us breakfast? We haven't had a decent meal in three days."

Anthony hesitated, as if considering her suggestion. He finally said, "Ginger's there now. I may as well get this over with."

Lecia's shoulders drooped with defeat.

She looked up when she heard his soft footfalls. He was walking toward her. Her heart soared with hope. He was going to stay.

Lowering his head, he gave her a chaste kiss on the cheek. "I'll call you."

Lecia wanted to scream. Instead she mumbled, "I won't hold my breath."

"What was that?"

"Nothing. Nothing at all."

Anthony regarded her with a weary expression, but he didn't try to reassure her that she would hear from him.

What did she want him to say? she wondered. "Don't worry, Doc. You'll hear from me. I'm in love with you."

How ridiculous was that!

She was a grown woman, Lecia thought. She had known what she was getting into. A fling born of the attraction they hadn't been able to suppress after all the time they'd spent together.

So what if he was the man who had helped her find her mojo? Many people had sex without forming any emotional attachment. Surely she could manage the same.

That all made sense—logically. Emotionally, however, she knew she was a wreck. And as she watched the man she loved retreat from her bedroom, she couldn't help feeling like her heart was breaking.

Thirty-eight

When Anthony entered the house, he was overcome with the scent of vanilla. It was a scent he knew well. Ginger burned vanilla candles every time she wanted to seduce him.

The curtains were closed and the blinds drawn. As Anthony rounded the corner into the living room, he saw the flickering lights of candles dancing on the walls.

And then he saw Ginger. She was stretched out on the leather sofa, one leg lying flat and the other bent at the knee. She was a vision of red lace on black leather. Physically, she looked stunning.

But he felt nothing other than a burning sense of regret.

"Hi." Her voice was deep and husky, and clearly meant to seduce.

"Ginger." Anthony spoke in an exasperated tone. "Put your clothes on."

"I know you're mad at me, and I don't blame you." She slowly rose to her feet. Her red feathery slippers clicked against the tiled floor as she strolled toward him. "But you can't believe Sha-Shana. It was her idea to play a prostitute and set you up, not mine."

Anthony went cold as Ginger's words penetrated his brain. "*What*?"

"She was hoping to extort money from me. She's an old friend I knew back in Kansas. At least, I thought she was a friend. She found out that I'd married an athlete, and she wanted to cash in on what she thought was my success. I know you must be wondering why I left Kansas City. Well, I'm not gonna lie. I got into a bit of trouble. I figured it was best to leave and start a new life for myself." Her lips curled in the slightest of grins. "Which I did—when I met you. Oh, baby. I fell for you right away. The only reason I pressed for a divorce is because of Sha-Shana. And a guy named Pavel. He's another story entirely." Ginger sighed. "I'm trying to tell you that I still love you. That I've always loved you." She closed the distance between them. "We can work this out, Tony. I'm your wife."

Anthony stepped backward, moving away from her. He knew she was lying. "And Bo? Who's he?"

There was a flicker of surprise in her eyes. But she quickly recovered. "He's . . . he's . . ."

"Your ex-husband," Anthony finished for her. "One you were seen dining with just last week. The same one who was on the news claiming to be your friend, practically telling the world that I'd done something horrible to you. Exactly how does he play into this?"

"Um . . . Well, um . . . he wants me back. I admit, I—I met with him to talk. But only to tell him that our marriage was over."

"Why didn't you tell me about him? If he was in your past?"

Ginger blinked in rapid succession. She was clearly flustered. "Because there was no point. He wasn't going to ruin what we had."

"You're lying."

Ginger drew backward as if she'd been slapped.

"I spoke to my lawyer as I was driving here. Turns out . . ." He paused for effect. ". . . you and Bo Baxter never divorced."

Her eyes widened in surprise, and Anthony fought the urge to smile. All the crap he'd endured on account of this fraud standing before him was finally over. Her bigamy was the icing on the cake, but it had freed him in grand style. His lawyer assured him that there was no mistake; Ginger had been legally married at the time she'd said "I do" to him, making his nuptials to her null and void.

"That's not true," Ginger said. "I signed the divorce papers eight months ago."

Anthony shrugged. "If you did, they weren't filed. But considering you're still hanging out with this guy, I doubt it."

Ginger's brow furrowed as she clearly tried to make sense of what Anthony had told her. Then a lightbulb must have gone off because he saw understanding in her eyes. "That son of a *bitch*. Listen, Tony. If Bo and I are not divorced, it's just a technicality. It doesn't change—"

"That technicality makes you a bigamist and nullifies our marriage."

She reached for him, placing her palms on his chest. Anthony didn't stop her. In fact, he welcomed her touch. It was the only way to know the truth, to see whether she still affected him in any way.

But he didn't feel even the least bit warm. He felt cold.

"Bo must have done this. But I swear, this can all be rectified. Sweetheart—"

"None of that matters, Ginger."

"No, you're right. We have to fix us."

She tipped up on her toes and kissed his mouth. This time,

Anthony felt something. He felt contempt stirring in his gut. Contempt over the fact that Ginger clearly believed that even after all she'd done, she could seduce her way back into his heart.

And maybe she could, if she'd held a place in it to begin with. Clearly, he had his own shortcomings, and he would deal with them once he finished dealing with her.

She sighed softly as she moved her mouth over his, though Anthony couldn't understand why. He was giving her as much encouragement as a cold fish.

"Let me make this okay," she whispered.

Anthony took her wrists in his hands and peeled her off of him. "It can't be okay, Ginger."

"No. Don't say that."

She reached for him again, but again he forced her hands off his body.

"I could blame you for everything," he said calmly. "But the truth is, it's not entirely your fault. All that's happened in the last couple months only helped prove what I've come to realize. We never should have gotten married in the first place."

It occurred to him that if you said those words to most people, there'd be a sign of some sadness in their eyes, or at least a flicker of remorse. Ginger's eyes, however, hardened.

"Spare me," she spat out.

"I didn't come here to argue. I came to see you one last time. To tell you this face-to-face."

Snarling, she turned on her heel and started back toward the sofa. He thought she was going to sit, but suddenly she was charging in his direction, wagging what it took a second for him to realize was a gun.

His blood went cold. But he didn't flinch as he said, "Put the gun down."

"We shared this house," she told him. "Half of what's in it is mine."

"Put the gun down."

Ginger started to sob. "You can't just kick me out of your life."

"You did that yourself."

"Five million dollars. That's a drop in the ocean for you."

"It's an investment in something I care about."

"Meaning?"

Anthony drew in a deep breath. "I'd give you the whole house . . ." He paused as her eyes lit up. ". . . *if* we were married. But we're not. And you know what?" Anthony stepped toward her, knowing full well she might pump him full of lead. But if he died, at least he'd die standing his ground.

He reached for the gun and wrenched it from her fingers. Ginger didn't put up any resistance, which told him she wouldn't have pulled the trigger. Instead she whimpered, acknowledging defeat.

"I don't owe you a damn thing," he continued. "You've got a lot of nerve standing here in my living room—after everything you did to try and ruin my life—acting like I owe you something."

Her voice softened. "You're going to leave me with nothing?"

"Consider yourself lucky that I'm not calling the cops. Now, I need you to leave. Tell me where you're staying and I'll send all your stuff there. You could earn a pretty penny for all that designer stuff, if you ever decide to sell any of it."

She huffed. "Thanks for the advice."

Anthony didn't respond. Instead he stood with his hands on his hips, hoping Ginger would leave without causing a scene.

She met his gaze with hard, assessing eyes, but must have realized he couldn't be sweet-talked, seduced, or coerced into changing his mind.

"I at least need to change," she quipped. "My clothes are upstairs."

"Five minutes," he told her. Then he watched her stomp out of the living room and, at last, out of his life.

Thirty-nine

Kahari tossed the basketball with an easy flick of his wrist. The ball soared in the air and went through the hoop, making a soft *whoosh*.

Anthony scooped up the bouncing ball and dribbled it with fancy footwork, but Kahari stole the ball from him and slam-dunked it in the net.

"Shit." Anthony shook his head in shame as he stared at his friend.

Kahari laughed. "Admit it. I'm the man."

Anthony scowled. "Toss the ball."

Kahari whipped the ball at him, and Anthony caught it with a wince.

"You ought to just call her."

Anthony aimed for the hoop. Took the shot. The ball hit the rim and bounced off.

"See what I'm saying? Your game is off, dawg. And I'm not just talking basketball."

"I've got nothing to say to her."

"You're wimping out."

"I don't want to talk about this with Little D here."

"He's in the bathroom."

"Shoot the ball or give it up."

Kahari shot the ball from the three-point line. Bull's-eye.

"Shit," Anthony cursed again.

"Don't tell me you're afraid."

Anthony sucked his teeth. "Afraid of what?"

"Rejection."

"I'm the one who backed off from her."

"Because you've got to prove some point. That what—you're not like your father?"

"Yo—"

"Look, you met the wrong girl and you married her for partially the right reason. It didn't work out, but you know what? Join the club. There's no reason to punish yourself for the rest of your life."

"You gonna play or what?"

"I liked her," Kahari went on as he dribbled the ball. "From what little I saw of her. And I know she liked you, too. If it's money you're worried about, isn't she making a ton with her book?"

"Yeah," Anthony conceded.

"So that's not an issue."

"Guess not."

"You know she won't try extorting money from you the way Ginger did."

"Right."

"And can you picture Dr. Love pulling a gun on you?"

Anthony actually chuckled at the absurdity of the image. "Not in this lifetime."

Kahari tossed the basketball. It flew in the air like a bird, landing in the basket.

"I still can't believe the police haven't found Ginger," he said.

"Me, neither," Anthony agreed as he snatched the dribbling ball. He jumped high and slam-dunked it. "But they will."

"All that shit she was into was bad enough. But to kill that loan shark?"

Ginger was the prime suspect in the murder of some Russian guy named Pavel. Bo Baxter had talked to cut a deal for himself while his wife had taken off. According to Bo, he and Ginger had met with Pavel under the pretense that they were going to pay him what they owed. Bo was supposed to kill him, but had chickened out. In the end, Ginger had stabbed Pavel, then grabbed the gun from Bo and shot Pavel dead.

Who knew if Bo was telling the truth or had simply been dumb enough to get caught?

"I don't want to waste any more time talking about Ginger."

Kahari took another shot, but it bounced off the rim. "Fine with me. I'd rather talk about Dr. Love, too."

"What's gotten into you?" Anthony asked. He didn't bother going for the bouncing basketball.

"Just want to see my homey back on his game."

Anthony didn't respond. He looked up at the sun, shading his eyes. How could he tell his friend that he didn't trust his own judgment? He'd married a woman who had pulled a gun on him and murdered someone else. Could he have screwed up more than that? The last thing he wanted now was to rush into another relationship. He was On for one, and the odds weren't in his favor. And given how easily he'd fallen into bed with Lecia, he was quickly following in the footsteps of his father.

Kahari walked up to him and slung an arm across his shoulder. "I've been watching a lot of Dr. Phil—"

"Dawg, living with your sister's made you soft."

"Spoken from the guy who just got his ass whooped?"

"Whatever."

"T, you're not your old man. You're nothing like him." Anthony's face must have registered shock, because Kahari said, "Yeah, you heard me. And don't look so shocked. Don't you remember how you used to be in college? A girl would ask you out, and if you didn't see a future with her, you'd stay up all night, whining about how you weren't sure you should even date her."

"I didn't whine."

"Dude, you whined. I'd tell you just to go out with the girl, then you'd tell me that's what your father would have done."

Damn, he barely remembered that.

"All I'm trying to say is, forgive yourself for what happened with Ginger. And move on. If that's with Dr. Love, it's all good."

Anthony dragged his hands over his face. He could hear Lecia's angry words to him, telling him that he needed a shrink. Maybe she was right.

"I'm trying to work it all out." Anthony pointed to his head. "In my mind."

"I know you will. Just don't expect it to be easy. Anything worth having you have to work at."

"You're a friggin' walking self-help book."

"I know." Kahari grinned. " 'Sides, LaTonya said she'd be thrilled if you and the doctor hooked up. She could have her over for that women's night thing that she does."

"I see you both have my life planned out."

"It's been two weeks, and you've been a miserable s.o.b. the entire time. Do me and everyone else who knows you a favor? Go home and call Dr. Love. *Please.*"

"I'm back!"

Anthony turned at the sound of Little D's voice. The kid wore a smile from ear to ear, and Anthony was glad to see it. His mother was out of jail, and it looked like there wouldn't be enough evidence to charge her. She had gotten a second chance, and Anthony hoped she would make use of it to better her life.

Little D retrieved the ball and hustled toward them. Anthony slung his arm around the kid's shoulders. "This is what I'm concentrating on," he told Kahari. "Little D, the center."

Kahari cut his eyes at Anthony. "You heard what I said."

"Whatever. Two on one, Little D."

Little D and Anthony dribbled the ball down the court, out of Kahari's reach. When they got near the net, Anthony lifted Little D into the air. The kid slam-dunked the ball and hung from the rim.

"Oh yeah, little man!"

For the next half an hour, they all continued to play. But try as he might to lose himself in the game, Anthony couldn't manage to keep Lecia out of his thoughts.

When Lecia learned that the huge arrangement of flowers in the office reception area was for her, her face erupted in a grin. Her immediate thought was, *Anthony.*

"You're sure this is for me?" she asked Sam.

"That's what the deliveryman said. 'Sides, my husband would never be this romantic."

"Wow." Lecia practically ran to the office with the large bouquet of white roses. She could hardly wait to open the card.

She placed the vase on her desk and tore open the small envelope.

Heard you had quite an ordeal. I've missed you at the café. Please come by soon.

Lawrence

Lawrence. A wave of disappointment sweeping over her, Lecia sank into her leather chair and closed her eyes.

Then chided herself for her stupidity.

Of course Anthony wouldn't send her flowers. What the two of them had shared had meant nothing to him.

If it had, enough time had passed that he would have sought her out. But he hadn't been lurking outside her office or her house in the past three weeks. He hadn't called to say hi or that he missed her. He hadn't even called to inform her that Ginger had been charged with murder. She'd seen that on the news.

All that night, she had tossed and turned, wondering how he was holding up, wishing she could offer him some comfort. But a night of pining over him had given her a clear head in the morning.

If Anthony wasn't giving her a second thought, she sure as hell shouldn't waste her time thinking about him.

Since then, she had resolved to move on. Before meeting Anthony, hadn't she told herself that this was the time in her life when she would concentrate on herself, on her career? A man had never been in the picture when she thought about her immediate situation, so why on earth lament the loss of one who had never given her his heart to begin with?

Work was the answer to her glum mood. Thankfully, she had more than enough on her plate. She had gone back to therapy, toyed with different ideas for a new book. Though busy, she did miss Anthony terribly, but for the most part she'd been doing okay.

Until she entered the office after lunch and saw the large bouquet of white roses.

"Oh, get over it, will you?" she said aloud. Anthony hadn't called. It was high time she accepted that he probably never would.

* * *

A little over an hour later, Lecia glanced at the clock, counting down the minutes to when the patient with her would leave and she could be alone with her thoughts. The flowers had been a horrible reminder that she would never have a future with the man who'd stolen her heart.

She tapped a palm on the desk. "Okay, Rita," she said to the attractive brunette. "I'll see you next week, same time."

Rita didn't get up. Instead she looked at Lecia and said, "Um."

"Yes?" Lecia said.

"Do we still have more time?"

"About five minutes."

"There's something else I wanted to discuss."

"Okay." Lecia settled back in her chair.

"It's . . ." Rita's voice trailed off. "I haven't mentioned this before, I guess because I'm so embarrassed. I think it's going to ruin my marriage."

"What, Rita?"

"You know how I've been telling you that I have no sex drive?"

"Yes."

"I haven't been exactly honest. I think I do know why."

"I see. You're ready to share that with me?"

Rita nodded. "During intercourse, I'm . . ." She paused. "I'm very dry."

"Oh." It wasn't what Lecia had expected her to say, but at least it was a problem that could easily be resolved. Unless the condition was something worse. "Are you experiencing any vulvar pain? Burning? Stabbing sensation? Kind of like the yeast infection from hell?"

Rita shook her head. "No. Why?"

"Just putting on my gynecologist hat. Many women suffer from something called vulvodynia, which can be extremely painful and leads many of its sufferers to forgo sex. I thought I'd ask, to see if there may be a physical cause for your lack of interest in intimacy."

"No, no pain. I just don't get very wet."

"You say this is the cause for your diminishing sex drive?"

"I kind of think so, yeah."

Odd, Lecia thought. Unless Rita was experiencing discomfort but didn't want to tell her about it. "But you're not having any pain, no problems at all with penetration?"

"I never thought so."

"What do you mean by that?"

Rita shrugged. Glanced away. "My husband thinks it's a problem."

"Meaning . . . ?"

"Meaning he's unhappy because of this problem."

"Have you tried any lubricants?" Lecia asked.

"No. I suggested it, but . . . he says he wants me natural. I feel so ashamed."

"Ashamed? Why?"

"Because if I was really excited, I would get . . . it would happen naturally."

Lecia leaned across her desk. "That's not true. Every woman is different. Some don't need additional lubricant, others do. There's no shame in that."

"But my husband says his ex got really wet. That he knew she was hot for him when she was soaking. He gets all upset with me, thinking he doesn't turn me on. He said if this continues, he may file for divorce."

Now Lecia understood why this woman was having problems being intimate with her husband. The guy sounded like a first class jerk.

"There's nothing wrong with you, believe me." For this woman's sake, Lecia hoped she believed her. Her husband, on the other hand, was a different matter.

He reminded her of Allen. Allen had always used every opportunity to put her down. She'd never told her family about it, hadn't even dwelled on it at the time. She simply internalized it. His words of condescension had chipped away at her self-esteem bit by bit.

It was no wonder she had gone into the field of therapy, and sex therapy in particular. She had never felt sexy with Allen. Never felt she could satisfy him. Why else would he have sought sexual pleasure in the arms of so many other women?

Anthony, on the other hand, had helped her feel incredibly sexy. Hell, she now wore thongs—and thought of him every time she put one on.

"Forget Anthony."

"Pardon me?"

Lecia was mortified to realize that she'd been so taken up with her thoughts that she forgot she had a patient in the room.

"Um," Lecia stumbled, "I said trust me, your husband is wrong. Using KY Jelly is not the kind of issue that pulls couples apart. If it is, there's another problem in the relationship, and I'd suggest you and your husband get couples counseling."

"Thanks, Dr. Calhoun." Rita paused, then said, "Can I ask you something else?"

"You know you can ask me anything."

"Are you and Anthony Beals dating? I know it's not my business, but since I've seen so much of you two on the news, I can't help but ask."

Lecia was too stunned to speak, and Rita went on. "I still

can't believe his wife! Murdering that loan shark? And being a bigamist? That's a crazy story, even for Hollywood."

It was, and it was the reason Lecia had taken some time off of work. The media had swarmed the office in hopes of getting an exclusive interview with her. Then they'd swarmed her home, so she had hung out at her sister's place until the story died down. She hadn't spoken to the media and didn't plan to.

"At least they caught her."

Lecia leaned forward across her desk. "What?"

"They caught her. His wife."

"Oh my God. When?"

"This morning. Would you believe the woman was in Vegas? Apparently she was wooing some high roller."

Did Anthony know? Lecia wondered. Of course he must. And yet he still hadn't called her.

But maybe he needed her support. Should she call him?

"I think it's just awful how that woman tried to railroad her husband. Feeding all those lies to the media."

"Yes, it was," Lecia replied, keeping her more detailed thoughts on the subject to herself.

Rita got to her feet. "For what it's worth, I think you two make a cute couple. And he seems so nice—I can't see him being the kind of guy to get upset over a little dryness," she added wryly.

"Rita—"

"I know. I'm here to talk about me, not about you. Next week, same time? You'll be here?"

"I'm not planning any more adventures in the near future."

"Oh well." Rita shrugged as if to say that was a shame.

Forty

"Now, Moaner. I already made an exception and let you into the house. The least you could do is sleep in this very lovely bed that I bought for you."

The orange tabby looked up at Lecia and mewled her discontent.

"What is it, hmm?" Lecia dropped to her knees and stroked the cat's head. Moaner started to purr. "Is that it? You just wanted a bit of attention? You're just like a man, aren't you? You want attention when you want it, but when you're satisfied, I don't hear from you for days. Well, this is as good as it gets, you hear? You will not share my bed." She softened as the cat rubbed itself against her leg, purring in delight. "All right. Maybe you can have the foot of the bed. Which is about as close as I'll get to any type of companionship for a long time, I'm sure." Moaner licked her hand. "No—don't get your hopes up. I'm not going to let you sleep in my bed until you've given your bed a fair chance. Got it?"

Her doorbell rang, and Lecia frowned. It was after seven in

the evening, and she wasn't expecting anyone. Still, she padded out of her bedroom and to the front door, Moaner trotting behind her.

She glanced through the peephole. Then nearly had heart failure when she saw Anthony Beals standing on her front porch.

She backed against the wall, panic swirling inside her. What should she do? She had to look ghastly with no makeup and wearing sweats.

Of course, Anthony had seen her in much worse . . . and much less.

The doorbell sounded again.

Why did she have to look good for him, anyway? Lecia inhaled a deep breath, gripped the handle, and swung the door open.

Damn if butterflies didn't start dancing for joy in her stomach at the sight of Anthony's tall, muscular frame filling her doorway.

"Hey," he said softly.

Lecia watched Moaner dash outside, not saying a word.

Anthony held up a copy of her book.

She arched an eyebrow. "What is this?"

"Your book."

"I know that's my book. I want to know why you're standing in my doorway showing it to me, as if I've never seen it before."

"It's for my mother. Seems she's a fan of yours and wants it autographed."

The mortified look on his face told Lecia he was being truthful. "So your mother's a fan. Isn't that sweet."

"I'm not too sure about that."

"Ah. I get it. You're one of those guys who'd rather believe you were delivered by a stork than accept the fact that your mother is a sexual being."

Anthony held up a hand. "Please. I don't need that visual image."

Lecia almost chuckled, but managed not to. "Shall I get a pen?"

"I was thinking I could come in."

"Oh?"

"Yeah."

She didn't move backward to invite him in. Instead, she looked him directly in the eyes and said, "There was one thing that was important to me. *One* thing. That you not get up and leave me the way Allen used to do. But Ginger called, and as soon as you heard her voice, you were off."

"Not for the reason you think."

"It doesn't matter why. It matters how it made me feel."

"I know I hurt you, and I'm sorry. But so much was going through my mind at the time, I thought my head was gonna explode. I needed to think, to figure out how I would move on with my life."

"You haven't called me in nearly a month."

"Sorting out one's feelings—you can't do it overnight."

Lecia didn't know if she should invite him in and tear his clothes off or slam the door in his face.

"If you're here because you feel guilty—"

"That's not why."

"—then you really shouldn't give what happened between us a second thought. Like you said, it just happened. We got caught up with our emotions. We were both looking for some type of comfort, and we found it in each other. We were two consenting adults. You said yourself, it was a meaningless fling."

Anthony's eyes widened. "I know I didn't say that."

"But that's what you meant."

"No, it wasn't."

"I'm a shrink, remember. Trained to read between the lines."

"Then you should have figured out that my issue had to do with how everything between us had happened so quickly, same as it happened quickly with Ginger. I didn't want to make another mistake."

"We don't need to rehash it. I understand."

"I'm not sure you do. Let me start over. Hey, Doc. I missed you. Can I come in?"

Despite Lecia's reservations, there was a part of her that wanted to swing the door open wide, throw her arms around his neck, and drag him inside. But that would get her a few hours of pleasure at best, leaving her in the same predicament when Anthony turned around and left.

"I've got Agatha," he said, then dangled a videotape before her.

"Ooh, you don't play fair."

"I'm a quarterback. I play to win."

Sighing with resignation—and a budding sense of hope—Lecia stepped back and pulled the door open wide.

Anthony moved inside, then followed her to the living room. She sank onto her soft leather sofa, dragging one of the throw pillows onto her lap as she did.

"I realized you were right," he said as he sat opposite her. "That maybe I did have more issues on my plate than I was able to deal with, and that there was no shame in talking to someone about it."

Her eyes flew to his. "You went to see a therapist?"

"Not an actual therapist, but a guy I trust."

"And?"

"And he helped me sort through what was going through my head." Anthony paused. "I think at the root of what I was feeling, guilt was the strongest emotion."

"Guilt?" Lecia asked, disbelief in her voice. But Anthony's sincere expression silenced her. She knew better. She was a therapist, for goodness sake. The last thing she ought to do was interrupt someone who was trying to get their emotions out.

But this wasn't just anyone. This was Anthony.

"Hear me out," he pleaded.

"I'm sorry. Please continue."

"All my life I told myself I would never be like my father. Yet there I was with you, spending so much time with you, and growing more and more attracted to you by the second. The next thing I knew, we were in bed together. Even though I was still legally married."

"She wasn't your wife."

"But I didn't know that then—"

"Yes, you did. From the moment she told you she wanted a divorce based on some phony story that she had concocted, you damn well knew she was no longer your wife. I mean, you knew that how she reacted to you was not the way that a woman who loves her husband reacts. Hell, once I heard you tell your story, *I* believed you and trusted you—and I barely knew you."

A feeling of warmth started to fill Anthony. Like nothing he'd quite experienced before, it spiraled out from his belly and spread through his limbs, reaching every part of his body. Reaching his heart.

Her words were only part of what touched him. It was the way she spoke them, with such passion.

"That's probably the nicest thing anyone has ever said to me."

"I'm not saying it to be nice. I'm saying it because it's true. When I think of what Ginger or Takesha or whatever she calls herself put you through, how she set you up, how you possibly could have gone to *prison* because of her—I get so angry I just want to smack the woman."

Anthony couldn't help it. He smiled.

"Why are you smiling?"

"Because. I like you."

"Gee, thanks."

"No, I take that back. I love you."

Seconds passed. Then Lecia gaped at him. "What'd you say?"

"You didn't let me finish. That's why I felt so guilty. Yeah, I knew my marriage was over. I was legally separated, on the road to divorce. But the last thing I ever wanted to do was be a serial monogamist. Or worse, a cheating bastard."

"Oh? Are you saying that's what I have to look forward to?"

"Not a chance. But it was what I needed to figure out. God, that sounds wrong. I'm trying to say that I needed to know my falling for you had nothing to do with some sort of weakness I had no control over. The kind of pathetic weakness my father succumbed to over and over. I wanted to know that if I finally met the right woman, my genetic makeup wouldn't blow it for me."

"And?"

His lips lifted in a sweet smile that touched Lecia's heart. "How could I ever blow it with a woman who loves Agatha as much as I do?"

She wouldn't make this easy for him. "So this is about Agatha?"

"You know what?" Anthony stood. "I think I should shut up, and I think you should shut up. Because you know why I'm here. And I say we leave it at that." He stopped in front of her, bracing his arms on either side of her so his face lingered before hers. "Except . . ."

Lecia's eyelids fluttered. "Yes?"

He inhaled deeply, as if breathing in her scent. "Except . . . I wouldn't mind some popcorn."

Lecia blinked. "Come again?"

Anthony put the videocassette on her lap. "You fell asleep as *Murder on the Orient Express* was playing in the car. I thought we could watch it. I've also got *Murder Most Foul, Murder, She Said,* and *Murder Ahoy* in the car. I don't have to be anywhere for a long, long time."

Lecia found it hard to breathe from excitement. Her mojo was doing the happy dance. "Planning a marathon session, are you?"

He bit his bottom lip. "Oh, yeah."

Lecia swallowed. "Lucky for you, I've got popcorn."

"I hope it's not low-fat."

"Caramel and extra butter."

"Oooh, Doc. You know how to tease."

She would never tire of his verbal foreplay. "The VCR's behind you."

"Can I get a kiss?" he asked, inching his face closer to hers.

"I thought you'd never ask."

Anthony brought his full lips down on hers, and Lecia thought she had died and gone to heaven. This was real. She wasn't dreaming.

"Aw, Doc. I've missed those lips."

She whistled lowly. "If we're gonna watch that movie, you'd better get up. *Now.*"

Anthony stood tall, grinning down at her as he did.

"Here." Lecia shoved the tape into his hands.

And as Anthony took it and headed to the VCR, Lecia smiled like a fool and hustled to the kitchen. The sound of opening cupboards mixed with the sound of the television coming to life. She had to admit, she liked the sound of a man in her living room. Finally there was someone in her life to mend the cracks in her walls, and maybe even to rebuild her deck. And of course, to give her endless nights of great sex.

"All right," Anthony called out. "Why can't I get this VCR to work?"

Okay, so perhaps she'd have to hire someone for the cracks. And the deck could wait, right? After all, she would hardly have time to hang out in the backyard when she'd be making serious use of her bedroom.

"Lecia?"

"Coming, dear," she said, then made her way to the man she loved, thinking that the great sex was a pretty good compromise.

Want More?

Turn the page to enter Avon's Little Black Book —

the dish, the scoop and the cherry on top from

KAYLA PERRIN

Lecia Calhoun's Little Black Book

Honest to God, I had *no* idea that the reaction to Chapter Thirteen of my book would be so extreme. It's been absolutely crazy! I wrote that chapter hoping it would be lighthearted—corny even—but get a point across nonetheless. Sure I wanted people to talk about it, but who knew it would be the only part they remembered?

I've heard a religious group in Tacoma wants the book banned on moral grounds. But then I also got a bagful of letters from several women in a church group in Utah, thanking me for writing Chapter Thirteen in particular. Go figure.

I've heard from teenage girls and I've heard from senior citizens. Most comment on how Chapter Thirteen has really helped their sex lives. Even some men have written to tell me that after reading the chapter, they now "get it."

I told you the reaction has been crazy.

The book is about a whole lot more than its infamous last chapter, but if that's what's making people pick up *The Big O,* I'm not gonna complain. As long as the message gets across, I'm happy.

Anyway, here's Chapter Thirteen. Read for yourself and decide if it's scandalous.

CHAPTER THIRTEEN

HOW TO DRIVE YOUR WOMAN CRAZY WITH PASSION!

TEN SURE-FIRE STEPS TO KEEP HER SATISFIED ALL NIGHT LONG

1. **Talk to her.** I thought this was a no-brainer, but apparently it's not. Men, you have to get a clue. If you want to get your woman in the mood, the first thing you have to do is talk to her. And not about sports or what's for dinner. Talk to her like you care about what she cares about. Which you should, if she means anything to you. Not only do women enjoy good conversation, talking to your woman will tune you in to what's going on in her mind. So use your tongue. It's the first step in getting to first base.

2. **Butter her up.** This goes hand in hand with the above bit of advice, but I'll take it a step further. Compliment your woman. (Really, it's not that hard!) Tell her she's beautiful. Whisper sweet nothings in her ear *and mean them*. There are many things you can say to make her feel special *and* get her hot and bothered. Imagine how turned on she'll get if you're out for dinner and you whisper in her ear, "You look stunning tonight," or "Wow, you smell good enough to eat." Simple, but I guarantee you, you will reap the rewards when you get home.

3. **Make her beg for more.** And I'm not talking about what you think I'm talking about. (I'll get to that later!) Right now, I don't want you to think about penis in vagina. I want you to think about setting the stage for an incredible night. Take your time with your woman as you get her in the mood. On your way home from dinner, dance with her under the moonlight. Picnic with her

in the park and nibble on more than the strawberries. But when your woman gets hot and wants to strip out of her clothes, don't start dropping your pants. Not yet. Think seduction. Give her even more romance so that she's ready to rip *your* clothes off.

4. **Tease her, please her.** There's more to sex than just the act of copulation. When you're making love to your woman, remember her entire body. Touch her everywhere. Tantalize her with the light touch of your fingers over every inch of her. Touch her close to but not quite where she's craving to be touched most. Master the fine art of teasing and you'll master the art of pleasing your woman. She'll remember your touch long after you've finished making love.

5. **Go wild!** Use your imagination, guys! Change it up and make it interesting. No, make it more than interesting—make it unforgettable. *You* strip for *her.* Put a blindfold on her and tease her body with the tip of a feather. Give her a massage with scented body oil that leads to much, much more. Use all of your senses, and you'll have one incredible night.

6. **Make her beg some more.** You're in the groove, both of you enjoying the sensuous ride. Bring her to the brink of orgasm, then back off. Make her beg for it before slowly starting again. Don't stop this exquisite torture until you're sure she's had enough (not even when her nails tear your skin). Make the experience last.

7. **Kiss her.** Honestly, guys, don't forget about the wonderful art of kissing! Kissing is *much* more intimate than sex. If you kiss your woman right, her entire body will be on fire. And she'll feel that making love is about more than just the sex. Which it is—or at least it should be! So use your lips to thrill her like never before. And

don't just kiss her mouth. Kiss her toes. Kiss the insides of her wrists. And behind her knees. Love every glorious inch of her.

8. **Slow down.** I wish I didn't have to point this one out, but unfortunately, I do. Guys, take your time. It's not about getting to the winner's circle first, it's about everyone getting to the winner's circle.

9. **Indulge her every fantasy.** Women have fantasies, too! And they're not just female versions of guy fantasies. So ask your woman what turns her on, and *listen* to her. A man who listens is a big turn-on.

10. **It's not the size of the boat. . . .** Trust me on this, men. Obsessing over how many inches you've got is a sure way to spoil the mood. Size doesn't matter! It's about what you do with what you've got that makes the difference. So practice your moves, and give your woman something to scream about.

KAYLA PERRIN

Ted Hollins

KAYLA PERRIN is the author of several novels, including *Tell Me You Love Me* and the *Essence* bestseller *Sisters of Theta Phi Kappa*. A certified teacher, Kayla also works in the Toronto film industry as an actress, having appeared in many TV shows, commercials, and movies, and was the 2002 recipient of the *Romantic Times* Career Achievement Award for Multicultural Romance.